Longlisted for the Leacock Medal for Humour in Literature, and winner of a Literary Titan Award, Mel Anastasiou's *Stella Ryman and the Fairmount Manor Mysteries* continues to be a reader favourite.

"Delightfully different, gently humorous exploration of sleuthing with a touch of senior citizen fogginess and intrepid zeal for the quest. Stella's life is as motivated by her passion as Sherlock Holmes's ever was and her mental health as dependent on keeping some game afoot. Author Anastasiou paints a respectfully sympathetic picture of the challenges of old folks in a seniors' home without pulling her punches or passing up a good chuckle by creating a character with enough spunk to carry the reader safely through. I'm not a lover of mysteries as a rule. But I do like to see genuinely novel looks at the human experience through the lens of established genres." – Lynda Williams, Reality-Skimming Press (5-star review on Goodreads)

"An excellent read, full of colorful characters. Stella Ryman, as a character, is quintessentially heroic—in the classic sense." – Literary Titan

"I LOVE STELLA. I met Stella Ryman a few years ago by way of a series of novellas published in PULP Literature—a fabulous quarterly journal of genre busting fiction. It's a great joy to see these stories gathered between the covers of this Fairmount Manor Mysteries collection. It's now so easy to share the love! Stella is not an outrageous genius (Sherlock Holmes) nor a well-connected socialite (Phryne Fisher) nor a caricature British spinster (Miss Marple). She's your sometimes addled and always endearing great aunt—the one you want over for tea because she's kind and curious and has great stories to tell. Mel Anastasiou has crafted a character to love, nestled in the mystery novel equivalent of comfort food. Enjoy!" – Sandra Vander Schaaf, author of *The Passionate Embrace: Faith, Flesh, and Tango*

"Stella Ryman is my new hero! I love the way the very observant author has woven dementia and lucidity and humour together." – Susan Lefeaux

"I fell in love with Stella reading her stories in *Pulp Literature* magazine. This feisty lady who changes her mind from being ready to die to being a nursing home sleuth is so human. She wants to help people, and has a passion for right and wrong. Her frail old body and mind occasionally fail her, but she uses her past experience as a teacher librarian to keep herself on track, standing up to bullies of all kinds. She is delightfully flawed and delightfully sweet, and I look forward to more of her stories." – Krista Wallace (Goodreads review)

"Mel Anastasiou's prose isn't just elegant and witty; it's also warm, compassionate, and insightful. The endearing Stella Ryman is a character who is brave, intelligent, wise, and stubborn—but also trapped. Stuck in a care home, limited by physical frailty, and at the mercy of her less-than-reliable memory, Stella is nonetheless a warrior, seeking justice for the powerless within the walls of the Fairmount Manor care home. While the context is mundane and the situations treated with gentle humour, the sharp and compassionate writing makes us care about defending the defenceless and righting the wrongs of the nursing home as much as Stella does." – JM Landels, author of *Allaigna's Song: Overture*

"Clever, oh so clever. And poignant. Did I mention well written? Literary sleuthing that only a woman could write." – Susan Pieters (Goodreads review)

Also by Mel Anastasiou from Pulp Literature Press

Fiction
Stella Ryman and the Fairmount Manor Mysteries
The Labours of Mrs Stella Ryman
Stella Ryman and the Search for Thelma Hu

Artwork and Writing Guides
The Writer's Boon Companion: Thirty Days Towards an Extraordinary Volume
The Writer's Friend and Confidante: Thirty Days of Narrative Achievement

THE EXTRA
A Monument Studios Mystery

Mel Anastasiou

Pulp Literature Press

Library and Archives Canada Cataloguing in Publication

ISBN: 978-1-988865-35-5 (paperback) ISBN: 978-1-988865-36-2 (ebook)

Material in this novel was originally published serially in *Pulp Literature*
magazine © 2019–2021 Pulp Literature Press.

Cover art and design: Kate Landels
Interior design: Amanda Bidnall
Interior illustrations: Mel Anastasiou
Printed and bound in Canada by First Choice Books, Victoria BC
International version printed by Ingram/Lightning Source

Published in Canada by Pulp Literature Press
www.pulpliterature.com

To Joan Barton Anastasiou, extraordinary editor and fan of
Newtown apples and éclair cookies;
and Dr CJ Anastasiou, who urged me to write this book and
who drove the Model A.

THE EXTRA

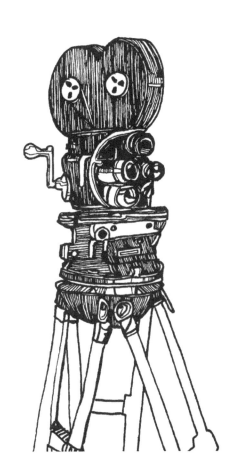

1

May 7, 1934
Paradise Gardens Villas, Sunset Boulevard
Hollywood

Sunlight through the bungalow window highlighted the needle-thin black lines criss-crossing the dead man's knuckles.

The young woman dampened a tea cloth at the sink and carried it to the sofa to clean her lover's lifeless hands and face. She took up one grimy hand and then the other, and scrubbed them with her damp cloth. There were so many tiny creases in a person's skin where soil could collect. When she was satisfied, she set his left hand across his lap and his right palm down at his side.

His hand looked empty. Forlorn.

She fumbled in her pocket and brought out an orange she'd plucked from the tree in the back garden. There were oranges everywhere in Hollywood in springtime. This one was a beauty.

She touched the fruit to her nose and smelled the bittersweet peel before bending his cool fingers around it.

Where the lapel of his jacket had slipped back, she could see the bullet hole. She made a little clicking sound and pulled the jacket straight. She would not cry. In fact, she must not cry.

She bent down beside him and kissed his mouth.

"Goodbye." It was not enough. "Good night, sweet prince."

A show-business farewell. He would have liked that.

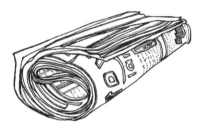

2

Nine days earlier
Vancouver, Canada
A thousand miles north of Hollywood

Francesca Ray smacked the chalk dust off the backside of
her school skirt, unhooked her stockings, and rolled them down
around her ankles. She knew she ought to peel some parsnips
and potatoes for supper, but spring weather made a person
restless somehow, as if something important were coming,
some great event that made root vegetables seem wintry and
irrelevant. She sidled past her father's bedroom and out the front
door onto the stoop. The paperboy cycled up, whistling through
his teeth, and she saw him toss the afternoon newspaper her
way just in time for her to snatch it out of the air.

Pats leaned on his handlebars and shook his head. "You shoulda
been a fellow, Frankie," he said. "You're ready for anything."

"It's Miss Ray to you, Pats." She threw the newspaper back, loose and low, the way her fiancé had shown her. "And keep the paper—Dad stopped it."

"He started it again." The paper flew back at her. "Say, Frankie, you oughta take a look at the classifieds. There's an ad in there, and if it means what I think it means, you've got trouble in your teapot."

"Cheeky," she called after him, but he'd already pedalled halfway down the block, slinging his papers in clever arcs against the neighbours' doors. Pats had never been what you'd call respectful, but he had a bean or two in his head, so Frankie opened the newspaper to the back. She looked around for somewhere ladylike to perch, but in the end plunked herself down on the top porch step to study the small-print classifieds in the light of the blinkered April sun.

Somebody had lost a dog. Somebody else had found a lady's sequinned coin purse, contents intact. A whole column of the usual hopefuls searched for work or cheap accommodation. But, at the top of the page, one black-boxed ad jumped out at her.

Talent search. Young actress …

A talent search was exciting enough for an ad in a Vancouver newspaper. But the sort of acting work proposed thoroughly electrified her.

… to work in films.

Frankie cast a glance at her father's bedroom window. She slipped the paper inside her cardigan, sprinted through the front hall, and dashed up the stairs to her room in the pointed gable above the front steps. She shut the door behind her.

With her back to her bedroom door, she snapped the paper open. Was the ad baloney, or was it not?

Talent search. Young actress to work in films.
Hollywood studio production beginning May 1934 ...

Next came the dodgy part.

She scowled and set the paper down on the windowsill atop a stack of movie magazines. Still frowning, she hung up her school skirt in her closet and buttoned herself into her blue house dress.

She pulled the orange crate that served as her hope chest up to the window that looked out over Thirty-Sixth Avenue. She spread the newspaper out on top of the *Photoplay* and *Movie Mirror* magazines and reread the ad's last bit. The dodgy bit:

... a production beginning May 1934. No experience required.
Make yourself available at the Dominion Theatre,
65 Granville Street.
11:30 p.m. to 1:00 a.m.

Trouble in your teapot. Even a newspaper boy like Pats knew a thorn patch when he saw it. *No experience required ... at 11:30 p.m.*

Trouble was putting it mildly. Still, the ad was in a reputable paper. Frankie's father had taken *The Province* off and on as far back as she could remember. She had even been a member of their Kids' Club—secret greeting, *Klahowya*. She and her friend Connie still had the tiny club totem pole pins tucked away among their treasures. Frankie was certain *The Province* would check their ads as they did their stories, otherwise what was to stop any old murderer or thief from advertising for a victim when times were lean?

Frankie became aware of a clamouring outside. She opened her window, rested her elbows on the movie magazines, and felt her scowl melt away. Her good friend Connie's progress down their street never failed to entertain. Today, Connie led a noisy parade of neighbourhood children along Thirty-Sixth Avenue. Hazel, mother to the three smallest girls on the street, brought up the rear.

"Connie Mooney, where'd you *get* that hair?" a boy in a Cub Scout shirt asked.

"For a birthday present." Connie tossed her copper head. The Scout guffawed and scampered off.

Hazel's kids gazed up at Connie adoringly. For who didn't love Connie? Who didn't smile back at her white smile, and laugh along with her easy laughter? This afternoon, Connie's excitement was such that you could almost see lights shoot out of the top of her head, the sort of conical beams that swept the indigo skies above Hollywood in magazines.

Connie, Hazel, and the kids all tumbled to a stop at Frankie's walk. At twenty-three, Hazel was two years older than Connie and Frankie, which made her the youngest wife on Thirty-Sixth Avenue. She smacked playfully at her scuttling daughters with her own copy of *The Province*, set her hands on her hips, and grinned up at Frankie. In the leaf-filtered light her freckles, and those of her children, stood out like pepper in cream. "Did you see the paper yet?"

Frankie, mindful of her father asleep in the room below, silently waved her paper back at Hazel to show that she had read it.

Connie, red hair crackling, set Hazel's youngest on her hip. She said, "Lookie here, Frankie! Clark Gable autographed our newspaper and dropped it at my door."

"Don't wake Dad." Frankie waved both hands.

But you might as well ask cats not to yowl as beg Connie for quiet. She sang out, "Hey-dee hoo-dee hoo-dee hee."

"For Pete's sake, Connie, put a lid on it!"

Hazel's kids piped out the musical reply, "Hi-dee hi-dee hi-dee hi."

A bellow burst from Frankie's father's bedroom window. From behind closed curtains, Sheridan D Ray let fly a terrible oath, one far too ripe for the tender ears of Hazel's daughters, obviously seconds away from belting out another chorus of the popular song.

Frankie leaped down the stairs, hurried out the front door, and took the stoop in one jump. She herded the lot of them away from the house and onto the grassy verge beneath the line of maple trees on the street. Connie held out the newspaper. With a glance over her shoulder at her father's darkened bedroom window, Frankie took the paper from her.

"I've seen the ad for the movie audition. And I think it's baloney. I wish I didn't, Connie, but I do."

"Thanks for your positivity, Rebecca of Sunnybrook Farm." Connie snatched back the paper. Hazel's kids chortled. Frankie pulled a ferocious face at the three of them, and they laughed louder. Hazel's youngest put her feet on top of her mother's and danced. Whenever Frankie worried about motherhood in her future — she herself had no mother for a model — she couldn't go far wrong with Hazel as a guide. Just now she caught the look Hazel sent her and was relieved to know that she wasn't alone in her suspicions about the audition advertisement. The problem was that getting Connie to listen to reason was a feat few dared attempt, for she was certain that her future shone like a diamond, like a star, like a searchlight in the skies above Hollywood. Frankie believed Connie was right. Or at least, she used to. Frankie was older now, and engaged to a man who knew his business. She was beginning to wonder whether most of the bright and shiny ambitions in this world were dime-store paste.

Hazel hugged her daughter close. "Connie, first of all, you must wonder why the ad is asking young women to show up downtown in the middle of the night."

"That's second of all," Connie said. "First of all, what will I wear?"

Frankie and Hazel exchanged a look.

Frankie said, "A midnight audition? We need to know whether the people who placed this ad are mashers."

Connie said, "I don't believe *The Province* would let a masher lay a trap in their classified advertisements."

"Well, you can't go downtown at that time of night."

"I can and I will. The streetcar is perfectly safe."

"Tell that to your mother, why don't you?"

Hazel said, "Frankie, stop arguing. Connie will go to the audition no matter what we say. You'll have to go with her. I can't go—Harry would never let me."

"Thou speakest truth, wise Hazel," Connie said.

Frankie said, "Hazel, how the dickens can you encourage her?"

Connie stamped her foot on the sidewalk. "Look, staying out of trouble in life isn't enough for me. And it shouldn't be enough for you. If you want to be safe, stay in bed."

Frankie looked again at the paper. *A young actress.* One *young actress.* Singular. If the ad was genuine, and if a scout did 'discover' an actress in the dark of night at a downtown office, it wouldn't be Frankie.

"Please, won't you come, Frankie?" Connie crushed the paper to her bosom as if all her hopes were written there.

Hazel squeezed Frankie's shoulder, and the two of them exchanged a look. Frankie's look said, *A thing that's too good to be true isn't true.*

Hazel's said, *The two of us can only envy a girl like Connie.*

Hazel's daughter wriggled free and skipped away down the sidewalk. Frankie gazed up through the spreading branches of the maple tree above them, through the young leaves to the blue spring sky. The sky looked back down at her — at the three young women in their buttoned sweaters over light flowered skirts that fluttered around their shins. Strange to think that exactly the same sky gazed down on Hollywood.

Frankie said, "I'll tell you what. When we go to the audition, we carry hatpins."

Connie gleamed with satisfaction, a trick she'd been able to do since she was a child. She hugged Frankie, and the newspaper crackled between them.

"What should we wear, do you think?" Connie asked. "Leather pumps for beauty and poise? Or galoshes in case of rain?"

"Leather pumps, though Hell should bar the way," Frankie said. "And take both papers with you, so that Dad doesn't see the ad."

3

That night it took Connie longer than usual to steal the car.

Frankie waited for the Model A in the pool of light beneath a streetlamp at Thirty-Sixth and Dunbar Street. She wondered whether she should have worn something a little fancier. Connie had gone to the trouble of pressing the dress she'd hemmed for Easter and airing out her summer-weight coat. Frankie peered down at her new school skirt and jacket and felt like Miss Plain Schoolteacher, but took comfort that at least she hadn't worn her usual squashy tam. Instead, her best hat was fastened tightly to her head with her departed mother's pearl-top hatpin. Her best leather pumps made a tapping noise as she paced the sidewalk. Frankie fished inside her jacket pockets and pulled out her right glove. She searched for the other but came up empty. She must have left it up in her bedroom. But no matter how her suit looked without gloves, there wasn't a chance against skirts and the patter of the rain. The young women stood in their line-up, quiet as angels. Frankie felt a rush of pride to be among these brave and patient Vancouverites.

"Maybe the movie people changed their minds," the black-haired girl murmured. She, Frankie, and Connie huddled themselves under the blonde's umbrella.

The girl wearing glasses pulled her collar up and grinned. "Or maybe they hope some of us will give up and go home."

"Fat chance," the blonde with the umbrella said.

"Maybe he wants to cast a part with a drowned rat," the girl in glasses said. "I could be the lucky one."

"Do you think it's a fake audition?" the black-haired girl asked.

"My mother says they're white slavers." The girl with glasses shivered.

Frankie pulled her under the umbrella.

The black-haired girl said, "Ha! I don't care. I'm a slave at home anyway."

"What chance do any of us have?" The blonde girl looked from face to face in the shadow of the umbrella. "*I'm* a dyed blonde. *You* wear glasses."

The girl with glasses said, "Don't give up hope, honey."

"Everybody dyes in Hollywood. And it's time for a star who wears glasses," Connie said.

Frankie said, "Yes, and what about Clark Gable's big ears? What about Marietta Valdes and her long upper lip? Sometimes different is better." She wondered, however, how badly the engagement ring on her own left hand would work against her in an audition. Every reader of *Movie Mirror* understood that if an actress was doing her job, she ought to fall in love with at least one or two actors for the publicity value. But she'd promised her fiancé to

Her coat trailed off one arm onto the sidewalk. The platinum-haired girl first in line at the door held out a hand to her, but she of the flowered dress burst into tears and careered down the row of girls, shaking off the hands that reached out for her like a flock of pale birds. She hurried away down the street.

In the silence that followed, Frankie touched the pearl end of her hatpin. She tugged it free, cocked her hat a little more over one eye, and slid the pin firmly back into place. If, as now seemed more likely than ever, there were mashers in the Dominion Theatre, she'd be ready.

The blonde girl leaned on her umbrella and peered up at the sky. "That poor kid. But you can't be soft if you want to be an actress."

"It's a tough business," the black-haired girl agreed.

"If you can't take the audition, how can you take direction? I hear directors can be beasts."

Next up the line, a pretty girl wearing glasses said, "You said it, sister." Her lenses caught the neon light of the appliance store. Further down the line, a good twenty more girls had joined the rest.

Rain began to fall. The blonde opened her umbrella. Somebody let out a shout of protest at the weather, and laughter travelled down the line. Not a single girl left the group, not even when the rain worsened, spattering the cigarette butts and paper bits collected against the shop walls. From under the blonde's umbrella, Frankie watched the neons blink above the shop fronts, putting a shine on raindrops and painting the wet pavement in blues and reds. Out of the dark lanes, groups of men — the jobless of Vancouver, concave in their jackets — stared as they passed on their way to search out dry places under the bridge for the night. The line of girls grew quieter, until Frankie could hear only the rustle of coats wear her ring, and after all, it might not be noticed by anybody important.

"Stick it out, girls," the girl with glasses said.

The black-haired girl nodded grimly. "Then after, let's go on a toot."

Rain poured off the points of the umbrella and inside Frankie's collar. She squirmed. Her best leather shoes would simply have to grin and bear it. No sooner had this thought passed through her mind than the rain slowed and stopped. The blonde girl tipped back her umbrella and Frankie looked up at the empty sky.

The theatre door opened again. A woman wearing a red satin dress stepped outside. She paused on the puddled sidewalk and flipped a pale fur wrap over one shoulder. Even from Frankie's position toward the end of the line, she could make out the gleam of the woman's eye. The scarlet curve of her long upper lip caught the light. Her skin glowed like a South Sea pearl. She gave no sign that she saw anything unusual about the line of gaping girls. She stood as still as if painted in the air. Once everybody had a chance to get an eyeful of her splendour, she strode to the corner of Granville Street, turned left onto Drake, and vanished from view.

The line of girls exhaled as one. Hollywood had entered their lives, lit the scene, and left them staring.

"Holy Moses," the black-haired girl grunted. "She looked exactly like Marietta Valdes."

"She *was* Marietta Valdes," Connie said.

"If she wasn't, she could earn a little money pretending to be her," Frankie said.

The girl with glasses breathed, "Look on my works, ye mighty, and despair."

Frankie said, "Anyway, seeing a real movie star is good evidence that there actually is an audition here, ladies."

"And the rain's stopped for good." The blonde girl raised her furled umbrella like the sword Excalibur. "It's blue skies and apple pie now, sisters."

Frankie could see hope rise and prickle its way down the line of girls.

"I hope they let me read my Ibsen piece," the girl with glasses said.

"I'm giving them *Mata Hari*," the black-haired girl told the others.

"I've brought my review." Connie pulled out a square of newsprint.

The blonde flicked the review with her index fingernail. "Read it."

Connie would have read it, but the theatre door banged open for the third time.

The first platinum girl stepped forward. Before she could pass through the open door, a man shouldered her out of the way. He stepped outside with the air of one who owned the city and possibly the world.

The line of girls fell silent.

He said loudly, "It's been a wretchedly difficult night, and I want to go home."

King Samson. Producer. Director.

For Frankie, this moment topped all. First Marietta Valdes, in person, and now a personage of great power in Hollywood. Frankie had seen this man's face in glossy black and white and knew his name and achievements.

Samson was owner and head of Monument Studios on Sunset Boulevard.

He looked up and down the long line. "Are you pulling

my leg? All of you came here to audition after dark, in the rain? I'll be frank. I don't want to look at any of you."

Somebody let out an angry, "Oh!"

Another girl shouted, "No fair!"

A few very young voices started up a chorus of boos.

"All right, already." King Samson flexed his hands inside gloves of butter-coloured leather. "I'll tell you ladies what I'm going to do. I'm going to save you a great deal of valuable time and look at every one of you right out here, right now. That's fair, isn't it? Nobody move."

He paced from one girl to the next down the line.

Frankie looked down at her own hands, and at her ring with the tiny diamond chip. It caught a pinprick of white light.

The producer and owner of Monument Studios moved along the line. He examined each young face, his dour expression never changing from one to the next. In another moment, he'd be level with Frankie and Connie.

Frankie slipped her left hand into her pocket. Feeling that a moment like this one would never come again, whereas marriage lasts a lifetime, she wiggled her engagement ring off her finger. It fell deep inside her pocket.

4

Granville Street at midnight had never witnessed such excitement, or at least Frankie had never heard tell of such.

She couldn't take her eyes off King Samson's butter-coloured gloves. She'd never seen a pair so rich in colour. Those gloves reminded her of all the things she knew about him—his numbered wives, his temper, his great white house atop Beverly Hills, and his film *Ambition*—two years in the making!—which, when she was much younger, she had seen twice upon its release.

Samson waved his gloved hands. The line fell silent.

He said, "Here's how it is with an open audition: even if you're chosen, you're not likely to be hired. And before you sigh and mourn, let me tell you that when I came out that door"—he gestured to the Dominion Theatre—"I intended to leave without auditioning anybody. I've had a hell of a night. And lord, how I want to go home to Hollywood."

A ripple of protest swirled through the group of girls. He scowled, squared his shoulders beneath his camel coat, and set about peering at the girls in front of him.

Frankie nudged Connie. "Move forward."

"It's not fair to the others," Connie hissed.

Now that the rain had stopped, the night grew colder. Frankie was glad after all that she'd worn her good suit of thick tweedy wool, and she felt sorry for Connie shivering in her Easter extravaganza of a cotton dress. Still, that dress might help get Connie noticed. To increase Connie's chances further still, Frankie decided that when Samson returned their way, she would push Connie out of her spot in the line, so that the producer couldn't fail to look at her twice.

Frankie was one-hundred-percent committed to the attempt. She took her hands out of her pockets, ready to shove. But when King Samson stood level with her and looked her in the eye, all Frankie could think was, *Choose me.*

With a single, hard-eyed glance, he passed her by.

King Samson reached Connie. He looked her up and down. Without a word, he moved on down the line.

"I'm so sorry, Connie," she hissed. "I meant to push you out in front—"

"Hush!" Connie said.

The blonde girl on Frankie's other side nudged her hard. "He's going to choose right now."

Frankie saw King Samson reach the end of the line. There he turned, flung out his hands and said, "I choose … none of you."

So far, even the younger, flightier girls had stood silent as angels at a graveside. But now another flutter of hostility rose in the line. A murmuring began, the words unclear but the meaning plain, drifting down the line from the platinum girl. Toward the end, Connie was trying out a few choice words of her own.

"Shh. Don't burn your bridges," Frankie warned. "You might get another chance with Samson someday."

"When pigs dance the shimmy," Connie replied.

The complaints from the girls in line escalated, and King Samson looked both ways along the empty street. Perhaps he hoped for the appearance of a car or some other mode of escape. However, none appeared, and he held up both gloved hands.

He hollered, "All right, girls. You win."

A tattered cheer rose from the line. Frankie had heard happier sounds, but it would do.

"I'll choose one among you." Several girls cried out, and he scowled. "Only one. Listen! I'm going to tell you something right now, because you're women, and I know women: as soon as I choose that one girl, the rest of you will stop listening to me. So pay attention while I tell you how lucky you are if you're not the one I choose."

The line of girls fell silent.

He said, "*I* started out where you are now. Working in a faceless city like this one"—he gestured down the night-shadowed Vancouver street toward the bridge—"standing eight hours a day behind a glass-front cabinet, selling gents' shirts and collars. Up in a two-room walk-up, I had a wife who was waiting with a hot dinner for me, and a nice kid. I was a free man. I had a happy little life. Then the Great War came, and somebody handed me a camera instead of a gun. So here I am. But would I go back? Would I?"

His heavy-lidded eyes scanned the line from one end to the other. "I don't know. And I never will know. But count yourselves lucky to stay free of Hollywood, see?"

King Samson scrubbed his hand over his forehead and walked the line again. Frankie was certain every girl there was holding her breath.

He halted in front of Frankie and Connie. His face changed, and for a moment he appeared to be a man at the end of his available powers.

She felt the breath stop in her mouth.

King Samson poked a gloved finger toward Connie. "You've got something, damn it all. You go inside. Only one. The redhead."

Connie paled. Frankie managed to stop herself from hugging the producer.

King Samson added, "And you'll have to hurry, because the cameraman's packing up. The rest of you, go home."

Without regard for the disappointed outbursts and catcalls from the other girls in line, Samson turned his back on them all. Before he had walked ten steps along Granville Street, a dark sedan pulled over beside him. Samson slammed into the back seat, and the car rocketed away south toward the Burrard Street Bridge and beyond.

It seemed to Frankie that Samson couldn't have wreaked much more upset among these girls if he'd pulled out a gun and shot out every neon light in the Dominion Theatre sign. But the unchosen girls surprised her. They ought to be drifting off in all directions, heading miserably home, but they did not. They turned as one girl toward Connie.

Connie stepped out of line. Her cloth coat bagged at the rear, and the hem of her Easter dress hung at a bit of an angle. Connie never could sew for beans. But it didn't matter that Connie couldn't sew. Frankie had always known that.

"I knew he'd choose you," she said. "Knock 'em dead, Connie."

Connie held out her hand.

"Come on," Connie said to Frankie. "We've got to rush. You heard him."

"He said for you to go." Foolish, unnecessary tears pricked at her eyes. She took a step back to stand between the blonde with the umbrella and the girl with glasses. "This is your moment. Go."

Connie took hold of Frankie's hand and pulled her out of the line. "Big patootie, I should care. Come with me, Frankie."

Frankie pulled back. "What about these other girls? It's not fair to the rest if I go. And what about the girl with the platinum hair, up at the start of the line? She was first, so she should go with you."

Connie called, "Why don't all you girls come with me? Samson's gone. He won't stop us."

Heads swivelled, and the platinum girl from the front of the line said, "No. You both go inside."

With a start, Frankie saw that the platinum blonde was addressing her as well as Connie. "I couldn't possibly go in! He didn't choose me."

"Do it." The girl with glasses sounded fierce, almost happy. "Do it for us. You represent us, the ones he didn't pick."

"You go in with your red-haired friend," The blonde with the umbrella said. "You're our revenge."

Frankie stood still, her hand in Connie's. Her eyes travelled up and down the line of Vancouver girls, all of them prettier than she was. All of them, until a few moments before, more hopeful than she had ever been.

"Thank you. He won't pick me, but I sure am happy to have the experience." It hardly seemed enough, so she added, "My name is Frankie Ray and I live on Thirty-Sixth. If any of you ever need some help, please ask me."

Together Frankie and Connie walked through the group of young women and girls toward the Dominion Theatre doors. Friendly hands smacked at their shoulders. Good luck whistles followed them as the crowd dispersed along Granville to the north and south. Frankie linked her arm through Connie's and walked her out of the dark street, into the foyer of the Dominion Theatre.

5

An old man leaning on his elbows at the Dominion Theatre desk stubbed out the remains of his cigarette. "Do you girls have any idea what time it is?"

"It's after midnight. Is the audition through here?" Frankie headed for a pair of big brass doors that looked like the kind through which Marietta Valdes would make a grand entrance, and the kind that King Samson would slam behind him when he left. "We've got the word from Mr Samson to go up."

"Nope, through there." He jerked his thumb at a smaller door that stood open to reveal a steep stairway. "You'd better hurry, girls. That fellow with the camera is packing up."

"Gosh! Thanks, mister. We'd better step on the gas. Come on, Connie."

The two girls tore for the stairway, Frankie in the lead. This was the same sort of narrow stairway she and Connie used to run up to ballet class when they were children, tutus slung over their shoulders, suede-soled slippers slapping against the steps. At the top of the stairs, the little girls' sternest critic would stand, hand on hip, a round watch pinned to her bosom. Miss McCall was no Anna Pavlova, but she held her standards high while in front of her the copper-haired girl danced with talent, and the dark-haired girl with hope. After class they'd run off together, laughing and jostling on the stairs, almost as if one were no better than the other, as if young Frankie even then were not wasting her time. They were grown up now, but they leapt up these stairs two at a time, the way they used to. And, as they still did at such moments, they pressed their palms together for luck at the top of the stairs. They stepped into a large, brightly lit audition room.

Before them a young man stood alone by his camera. His suit was well cut, Frankie observed, and almost unbelievably yellow. In one hand he held a brown fedora. Beyond him, a piano stood at an awkward angle near the wall. A heap of canvas painter's cloth lay shoved up against the wall behind it, and large mirrors, like the ones in ballet school, lined the far wall. No wonder they'd chosen the Dominion Theatre for their audition. This rehearsal room might have been made for that purpose.

The cameraman flipped a switch on the camera and spun a knob at the back.

Frankie took breath in and let it out again, the way her first amateur director had taught her. "We're here for Connie's screen test."

The cameraman said, "Testing's over."

Under her breath, Connie swore.

"Say, what kind of open-call audition closes before it even starts?" Frankie demanded.

"The kind that Marietta Valdes shows up at. Uninvited." The young man opened the film case at the top of his camera, twisted a dial, and slammed it shut again. "Case closed."

Frankie pushed Connie forward. "Look, we've got the okay from Mr Samson to audition for you. Stand in front of the camera, Connie."

"I'm ready, brother." Connie moved into place and took off her squashy tam.

Frankie took the hat from Connie and balled it up in her pocket. "Fire up your machine. What's your name?"

"Leo. Like the MGM lion." The young man at the camera opened one of the round black cases attached to the top of the machine and took something out—film, of course. He was not loading his camera, he was emptying it.

Frankie said, in her best schoolmarm tone, "Leo, please do not put that film away."

"Give me a break, girls. Put yourself in my shoes. Would you stay open when King Samson says close it down?"

"Abso-tively." Frankie strolled further into the room, from the long mirror to the piano to the window over Granville Street. A gun lay on the windowsill. She picked it up and asked, "Is this real, Leo?"

"It's a prop gun, silly. Put that back."

"I've never held a gun before. It's pretty heavy for a prop." She looked down at the gun in her hand. It looked cold—it was cast in dull grey steel—and it should have felt cold too. But it was warm. On the handle was engraved a small five-pointed crown. Frankie hefted the gun from hand to hand. It felt quite nice, hefted that way. She felt a little like Barbara Stanwyck: tough, if not actually blonde. She imagined shooting it, and aimed it first at the man and then at his camera.

"Stop fooling around with that thing," Leo said.

Frankie lowered the gun and held it out to Connie.

"Here, Connie, you can use this gun as a prop when he films you."

Connie accepted the gun and stepped closer to the camera. "Leo, audition us. Turn us down if you must, but play fair."

Leo shook his head. "Play *fair*? Don't you girls know anything about Hollywood?"

Frankie mimed firing a gun.

Connie nodded. She aimed the gun at Leo and said, "Audition us, or I'll kill you."

Leo stepped behind the camera. "Are you loony? They'll lock you up for saying things like that.

"But that was me auditioning," Connie said. "I was playing a gangster's moll. You know. *I don't want to kill you, but I will if you don't film me.*"

Leo offered Connie a pained look.

"Connie is still auditioning," Frankie explained. "You've got to admit she's got something."

"Like a hundred thousand other girls have got something. Anyway, I can't audition anybody anymore. The actor who's supposed to read with her is unavailable."

Frankie said, "Okay. Leo, you read the part with her."

Leo held out his hands. "I'm not an actor. I only run the camera."

"Point it at Connie, and *I* will run the camera."

"Not a solitary chance of that, sister."

Frankie walked past him to the camera. He couldn't do much about that, even though he was such an uncooperative Hollywood man in a yellow suit. Frankie put her eye to the lens at the side of the camera and saw nothing but shiny blackness. She steadied herself with one hand against the tripod and raised her other hand to flip the toggle to turn the thing on, but when she touched it, the top of the film case came apart in her hands like a wounded soldier.

Leo took Frankie by the shoulders and moved her away from the camera. "That machine is worth more than either of our lives in cold cash value. Go home."

"Won't," Connie said. "Anyway, where's the actor who's supposed to read with the auditioning actresses?"

"Sweetly in dreamland," Leo said. "Like you girls ought to be, safe in bed."

Frankie said, "I'll read with her, then. I'll be the man."

Frankie had acted in plays right alongside Connie, although not in primary roles. While Connie took the lead, Frankie was sometimes cast as 'Third Fairy' or 'Old Woman at the Window', but on account of her eyebrows and fairly straight build she'd enjoyed solid if unsung success in tertiary men's roles, such as 'Young Man with Tennis Racquet'. These male roles had not brought her fame, but they had given her experience. And maybe, when he saw the film, King Samson would see how talented Frankie was … *No.* Frankie was here to help Connie audition and that was all.

She said firmly, "I'm an excellent male supporting actor."

"She's quite handsome, too, in a suit and cravat," Connie added helpfully.

Leo kicked his black box shut with a bang. "You girls are hair-brains. Nobody would look twice at such an amateur film test."

"But it's Connie's talent that matters. She's got star quality." Frankie scanned the room. Perhaps it would help to change the camera's angle so as to compose a better background to the scene. There was a door at the far end of the rehearsal space. She looked hard at the drape and folds of the drop cloth in the shadows behind the piano. There was more than a simple drop cloth lying there. She walked over to the piano to see what it was.

Leo said, "Look, Hollywood's like the gold rush, girls. There are too many of you already there. Statistics are against you. And statistics prove … *Stop that.*"

Frankie did not stop that. She crouched down and steadied herself with one hand on the piano. With her free hand she lifted aside several folds of the drop cloth.

She regarded the large bony foot and lower leg thus revealed, the skin so pale it was almost blue, the black hairs on the calf as clear as ink on paper. She heaved the cloth aside to reveal the supine form of one of the world's most recognizable movie stars. Gilbert Howard was wearing long white shirt tails—and evidently nothing else.

Frankie said, "Well, what do you know? It's what they taught me in school. Statistics prove that even the most unlikely events do happen. I found your leading actor."

6

"Statistics!"

Leo said, "Dammit, Howie."

Eyes shut, the movie star stretched out behind the piano and intoned Billroth's quotation: *"Statistics are like women; mirrors of purest virtue and truth, or like whores to use as one pleases."* He shoved the drop cloth aside and sat up with his shirt tails falling around his bare legs.

Frankie knew that beautiful baritone voice well, and the way his celebrated, crooked mouth moved when he talked. She was in the presence of Hollywood, all right. Gilbert Howard had been a great star for as long as Frankie had been going to the movies. He was arguably more famous than Marietta Valdes and King Samson put together.

With a rattle of piano notes, the movie star hauled himself to his feet. He emerged from behind the piano. With his shirt cut low in front and back but high at the sides, his long white legs were almost fully exposed to the viewer. It could have been worse, Frankie thought. The tailor could have been less generous with the shirting.

He smoothed his slim moustache with a bony finger. With his other hand he held onto the top of the upright piano, off balance but at ease with the world. Even trouserless, Gilbert Howard was nothing if not a god of the silver screen.

Frankie pulled herself together. There was no point in attending midnight auditions and then standing around like a moonstruck fan. She must not miss the opportunity. Or rather, Connie must not. Hollywood royalty such as Gilbert Howard had power that no yellow-suited cameraman could hope to match. Frankie nudged Connie, who returned the nudge, digging her elbow into Frankie's ribs.

Frankie stepped up to bat. "Sorry to disturb you, Mr Howard."

Gilbert Howard revealed his famous smile. "Nothing disturbs me. I am a disturbance."

Frankie smiled back. "Mr Howard, I know it's late, but are you available to take a screen test with my friend Connie here?"

Leo said, "I've told them you're not able to audition, Howie."

Gilbert Howard rubbed his eyes. "Leo, have you ever noticed how many young women there are in the world? A never-ending supply, it seems. And all of them want to be actresses. How strange." He waved his hand vaguely in the girls' direction, and Frankie understood that Gilbert Howard was not only half-naked but entirely drunk. He was still a star, though.

"Mr Howard, won't you please test with Connie here?"

"What's that?" Howard swayed and regained his balance.

Frankie had a certain experience with men pretending to be sober when they were not. "Please, would you be so kind as to read with Connie, so that Leo can take the audition film—the screen test—back to Monument Studios?"

Gilbert Howard addressed the ceiling. "Brunettes talk too much, but redheads are beautifully responsive, don't you find?" He straightened sharply and asked the empty doorway, "What's the scene?"

Leo said, "*The Emperor of New York*, Act Three. But you really don't need to test with these girls. And I need to get back to Hollywood."

Gilbert Howard cleared his throat. "*Is this a gun which I see before me, the handle toward my hand? Come, let me clutch thee.*" He took the prop gun from Connie's unresisting grasp, looped one arm around her waist, and blinked down at her with his meat-pie eyes. Frankie had never in her life seen any man so beautiful.

The movie star swung the gun in gentle arcs with his free hand. He gazed at Connie nestled in his other arm. "I was once like you. In '22 I packed my dreams into my old kit bag and came to Hollywood, one of three hopefuls from my hometown …"

He appeared to lose himself momentarily in the tale. His grip slackened, and he came near as anything to dropping Connie to the floor. She put out a foot behind her and hung onto his shoulder.

Encouragingly, Frankie asked, "Mr Howard, what happened to those friends who came to Hollywood with you?"

Whether because of Connie's beauty, because of his professionalism, or because he was too drunk to see three feet before him, Gilbert Howard did not look at Frankie while he answered her question—if you could call it answering at all, which Frankie did not.

"The same thing happened to them that happens to most young people who come to Hollywood," Gilbert Howard said to Connie. "The same thing that will happen to you, of course, if you dare to make the journey there. Leo, roll film."

"No," Leo said. "I won't do it."

"Leo, you will do it. You were sent here to find an actress to replace Marietta Valdes. Somebody new, even newer than Marietta, to star in *The Emperor of New York*." Howard gestured with the gun toward the mirrored wall. "I was young once, not so very long ago. I got my chance and never looked back. And now, I'm here with one aim: to help a young Seattle actress find her way to Hollywood."

"We're in Vancouver, not Seattle. And that was not at all your aim, Howie." Leo leaned an elbow on the camera. "You brought Marietta Valdes to this audition because you knew that when she saw that King Samson was trying to replace her with an even younger, brand-new actress, Marietta would blow this whole open audition into a million shiny pieces. And you succeeded very nicely. But at least I can leave early to get back to my—"

"Do shut up, Leo." Howard closed his eyes. "And never forget that we are on the same side. In the end, we are all working together to make great movies. Roll film."

Leo said, "Howie, you're drunk. And I can't film you drunk."

"I am as sober as an intercontinental luxury liner," Gilbert Howard intoned. "I am as sober as Macduff."

Howard gazed down at Connie as if she were the only woman in the world. "Is this a redhead I see before me? *Come, let me clutch thee*. We've got a gun, and we've got each other. We'll make this an audition to remember. Leo, the quicker you start filming, the quicker you can pack up and drive south."

"Oh, for God's sake." But Leo took the cover off the camera lens and prepared to film.

Frankie asked, "Shouldn't Connie have a script?"

"Marietta threw the bundle of scripts down the fire stairs. Then she threw my klieg light out the window, so I can't light the scene," Leo said. Frankie remembered the crash of the light smashing down on the sidewalk.

Howard said, "A true professional never blames his tools. Anyway, the first thing an actress must learn is never to hold a script in a screen test. *Nothing* should come between a redhead and the camera."

"Except Gilbert Howard's profile," Leo interjected. "Listen, Connie, here's the line. *What do I care if they take me? What do I care if they crown me queen?*"

Connie repeated, "*What do I care if they take me? What do I care if they crown me queen?* Got it."

Frankie moved a few steps nearer to keep an eye on the camera.

Gilbert Howard, still holding the gun, took Connie by the shoulders and positioned her sideways to the camera. "*You're* a small-town waitress, and you don't know you're the long-lost heiress to an empire. *I'm* the detective sent by the evil first minister to find you and pay you off. Guess who falls in love with whom?" He wrapped his arms around Connie and bent her slightly backward so that she had to look up at him. The lights overhead caught the perfection of his profile, the sharp line of his large nose, the droop of his lovely dark eyes.

He said, "*Beauty and deception have always been allies, my princess. You are Beauty that sets the world afire, and love is the greatest of deceivers.*"

This was exactly the sort of thing Frankie always expected movie stars would say in Hollywood screen tests. She clasped her hands together. What if Connie did get a part, first time out? Such miracle castings did happen from time to time, as any serious reader of *Movie Mirror* and *Photoplay* knew. These 'discoveries' were infrequent, but by heaven, Connie and

Frankie and a hundred thousand other girls believed in them the way they believed in Clark Gable's eyebrows and Shirley Temple's curls. She'd bet the believers were the exact same 'hundred thousand other girls' that Leo had mentioned. She pictured them, dewy with hope, lined up in long chattering rows that disappeared to an unknown horizon. Like the Vancouver girls outside. The thought of all the other girls steadied her and raised her level of determination to heroic heights.

Leo waved at Connie from behind the camera. "*Say* something."

Connie gaped up at Gilbert Howard, and Howard smiled down at Connie. The moment ought to have been magical, but it was going on far too long. Was Connie's nerve failing her? She had never known fear in her life.

Connie whispered, "I can't remember my line."

Frankie prompted her: "*What do I care if they take me? What do I care if they crown me queen?*"

"What did you say?" Connie asked.

Frankie repeated the line, without result.

"Dearest, it doesn't matter." Gilbert Howard touched Connie's cheek with his free hand. "Say anything in a test. The camera will speak for you. Say something to make yourself glow. Tell us how you lost your innocence and blush for us beautifully."

"For God's sake, Howie," Leo said.

"Speak, my princess." The movie star lifted one perfect eyebrow. "Imagine you're the most appealing woman who ever set a crown on her own head, and it will be true. Speak the words that will enthral me. Captivate Leo at the camera. Enrapture every man who gazes up at your beauty on the silver screen."

It was the first time Frankie had seen Connie looking anything but beautiful. Her face was white under carrot hair, and she appeared to have stopped breathing. Leo looked at Frankie and shook his head.

Frankie imagined herself in Connie's shoes, pressed up against Gilbert Howard's famous breast, the camera buzzing away. She knew exactly what she'd say. She wouldn't stop at *What do I care if they take me? What do I care if they crown me queen?* She'd go on to give them Hector's lines to Andromache regarding royal Trojan duty. How unfair and tragic that at this particular junction of circumstances, Connie, who talked in the general way of things as if words were as cheap and plentiful as blades of grass in a clover field, had nothing to say.

However, Frankie was not about to allow Connie to fail. *Say anything in a test.* Frankie racked her brain for inspiration.

In her best radio announcer tones, Frankie began their old game. *"Hey, Connie, what do you want in a car?"*

"Quiet, brunette," Gilbert Howard said.

"My name is Frankie Ray, not brunette. Please don't interrupt, Mr Howard. Connie, *what do you want in a car?"*

Connie looked at Frankie as if she'd never seen her before and whispered, "Okay."

"Ease of control, Connie. *Trim smart lines."*

Connie's throat moved above her dress collar. *"That's what you want in a car."*

"Sturdy steel construction."

"Sweetness, balance, and security at all speeds." Connie's cheeks flushed pink.

Frankie wanted to make car noises, the way they had when very young, but decided not to.

The camera emitted a busy, efficient chatter, and Gilbert Howard gave a Falstaffian quaff of a laugh. "Got that, Leo? Let's go to the kiss."

Connie appeared to have regained some of her courage as well as her colour. "Your naked parts are touching my leg, Mr Howard. Can you please move?"

"For God's sake," Frankie muttered. "Is that why that girl ran crying out of the theatre while we were waiting in line?"

Connie wrestled her way out of his arms.

Gilbert Howard frowned. "Relax. I *am* the greatest of all actors."

Frankie ought to dislike him for boasting, but he was probably speaking a simple truth.

Howard adjusted his shirt tails and took hold of Connie again. "Be brave, redhead, for now we struggle for the gun and it goes off. Leo, roll film."

Frankie said, "Keep your good profile toward the camera, Connie."

"I will have silence, brunette," Howard said.

But Leo pulled out a cigarette and lit it. "Cut, Howie, cut. Now stop tormenting these girls and go get you some trousers."

"Not yet," Connie said.

"Don't stop now," Frankie urged the cameraman. "Give her a chance."

Gilbert Howard slashed the air with the prop gun. "Damn you, Leo, roll the film."

"Nope," Leo said. "It's over. No more of your games, Howie. We will go with what's on this film."

Howard tightened his arm around Connie, took a wobbly aim with the prop gun at the cameraman, and fired.

Leo dropped his cigarette and fell to the floor.

Gilbert Howard rubbed the gun on his shirt tails. "Nobody says no to Gilbert Howard. Leo's lucky this is a prop gun."

Frankie knelt at Leo's side. "For a cameraman, Leo is a pretty good actor. There was a bullet in that so-called prop gun, Mr Howard. You'd better hope to heaven that he's not such a good actor as to be actually dead."

Leo was bleeding through his jacket. Frankie pulled her half-slip down from underneath her skirt as Loretta Young had done as a Civil War nurse in *Wounded Heart*, folded the slip, and pressed the cloth against his chest.

"Get somebody to call a doctor, Connie," she said. "Get the police."

"He can't be dying." Connie threw herself down on Leo's far side. "Please, Leo, don't be dead."

There was so much blood on Leo's yellow sleeve that it was hard to tell where the bullet had hit him. With trembling fingers, Frankie took hold of the lapel of his jacket and peered underneath.

Frankie looked back up at Connie. "No, it's not the chest. It's the shoulder, thank goodness."

Gilbert Howard drifted over and peered down at his handiwork. "In the Great War, we'd crouch in the trenches with the wounded beside us, like this, with the Jerries twenty steps away. If any of us put our heads up for a minute, to spit or look at the stars? Odds were ten to one we'd never spit again."

Perspiration tickled the small hairs at Frankie's temples. Gilbert Howard had shot a man. Had he meant to do it? Surely not. She was all too aware that she herself had come within a hair's breadth of shooting Leo with the same gun only a few minutes before.

"*Cats.*" Connie held up the gun and studied it. "Leo himself said this was a studio prop."

Frankie said, "Somebody was lying about that gun."

Howard answered, "Everybody lies in Hollywood, don't you know that?"

Leo opened his eyes. "Thanks for that, you old bastard. Didn't you do me enough harm back home in Hollywood?"

"See, he's not angry with me," Gilbert Howard said. "And that's because there are no halfway measures — if anybody got angry with me, they'd actually have to kill me. That's how impossible I am."

Frankie stared. "You're not even sorry?"

"Not a bit. But I'm glad I didn't actually kill him. I might have been sorry then."

Frankie told Connie, "Go get a doctor. Ask at the desk downstairs." She wanted Gilbert Howard a healthy distance from Leo. "Take Mr Howard with you. And do something with that gun."

Connie slipped the gun into her pocket, took Howard by the arm, and led him to the stairs they'd come up a few million years before, or so it seemed to Frankie.

Talk about eye for an eye. Leo had lied about a gun being a prop and now was shot by that very same gun — an extreme comeuppance, even by Hammurabian standards.

Frankie said, "I'm not sure whether this helps, but I read somewhere that you don't feel the pain right after you've been shot."

Leo looked up at the ceiling and cursed it long and low. "Excuse my French, but you're wrong about that. Ah, well. Just another day in the movie biz, right? How bad does it look?"

She peered at his shoulder. "Three inches to the right, and I'd be testifying in court. Do you want me to take your jacket off?"

"No."

Sirens sang faintly through the open window.

Frankie admired Leo's calm. She cast about for something to say. "Are gunshots more common in Hollywood than here in Vancouver?"

"I've only ever been shot here in Vancouver. Tonight, I mean." Leo screwed up his face and struggled out of his jacket. He groaned as he fell backward onto the floor. She helped him replace the slip that served as a dressing.

He pressed it against his wound. "Thanks. Look, you don't want to go to Hollywood. You and Connie seem like nice girls, and dire things happen to nice girls there. I know. Oh, brother, do I know."

"I guess dire things can happen here, too." Frankie nodded at his bloodstained shoulder. "Anyway, Connie's the one who's going to Hollywood. I'm engaged."

"I'm glad somebody still believes in love," Leo muttered.

Star-crossed *and* bullet-riddled. It seemed an unhappy combination.

Frankie said, "Even though I'm getting married in the spring, I sometimes wish the future held something more exciting than a lifetime of house dresses and spring cleanings …"

She broke off, wondering why she'd tell this wounded man in a yellow suit what she didn't even want to tell herself.

"Don't underestimate wedded bliss." He leaned away from her in a dry retch. "You and Connie should get out of here. Take the other exit, the one at the far end of the room. The police will arrive any minute, and maybe the newspapers as well. You don't want to be caught up in this mess."

The sirens outside grew louder, slowed, and stopped.

Frankie looked down at Leo. "I can't leave you."

"Sure you can. Do you really think Howie shot me by accident? Maybe so. But there are issues here … Oh, it's been one hell of a night." Leo pushed at her with his good arm, but she didn't budge. "Listen, if you promise to leave before the cops come, I'll tell you the truth."

"What's the truth?"

"You are pretty. Not pretty enough. But you've got the cheekbones."

"Gosh! That's some truth." Below, on the street, car doors slammed. But all Frankie thought was, *You've got the cheekbones. You've got the cheekbones.*

She said, "I'll stay with you until the doctor gets here."

"Go." Leo's face contorted.

"Try not to think about the pain. Tell me about Hollywood."

She moved her leg to make it a better pillow.

He said, "Look, you think it's different in Hollywood, but it's not."

"It is, according to *Movie Mirror.*"

"Listen." He squeezed his eyes shut and then opened them again. "Frankie, when you get married, the man runs the house. Right?"

"So they say."

"Well, a man runs a Hollywood studio."

Frankie heard voices through the floor. Two policemen, she thought. She said, "A woman could run the studio."

Leo shook his head. "Men direct the movies. Men produce the movies."

"Women star in them—"

Gilbert Howard spoke from the doorway at the top of the stairs. "Women star in a man's movies the way women lie in a man's bed." From somewhere he had procured a pair of trousers. They were too short for a man of his stature, but they served.

Connie burst into the rehearsal room. "The doctor's coming."

Footsteps sounded on the stairs. Frankie felt her heartbeat speed up.

Leo added, "I'll be in good hands with the police and a doctor. Then I can figure out what to say to the reporters. It certainly won't be the truth."

"Damn the truth." Gilbert Howard put his arm around Connie's shoulder. "We are actors, aren't we? Let us lie, separately or together."

Was it only a few hours ago that Pats had balanced on his bicycle and tossed her the afternoon paper? *You shoulda been a fellow, Frankie. You're ready for anything.* With an intuition as sudden and piercing as that gunshot had been, Frankie understood that she was not, after all, ready to be caught up in Hollywood's perils.

Frankie and Connie exchanged a glance, and Connie stepped free of Gilbert Howard's arm. They charged to the far end of the audition room and down an unlit staircase, this one even narrower than the first.

In the darkness of her descent, Frankie slipped on a jumble of papers, no doubt the audition scripts that Marietta Valdes had earlier tossed down the stairs. She fumbled for the handrail and tottered down toward the Dominion Theatre's back exit.

Behind her, Connie let out an oath.

"I've dropped my shoes!"

"Heaven help us, Connie." Frankie bent down to feel about for Connie's best pumps, but all she found were more tumbled scripts. From upstairs in the rehearsal room, she heard the heavy tread of the boots of officialdom.

"Here's one shoe. Oh, help!" Connie fell into Frankie.

Frankie hit a half-closed door. She fell face first into the movie theatre beyond. Gaining hands and knees, she gazed upward past the plush seating to the neon ceiling overhead.

"Oh, Jiminy," Connie muttered from the bottom of the stairwell. "I've got one shoe but not the other. Help me find it."

"Sure." Frankie didn't move, only blinked up at the twisting coloured lights. Over the rows of plush seating hung the neon ceiling, tubes of blue, red, green, and orange drawing a classical scene of leaping gods and fleeing deer. "You have to see this, Connie. It's a whole ceiling picture made out of neon lights. Is that the god Orion? Or is that Diana? Chasing the deer? I can't tell which are the gods and which are the goddesses, can you?"

"Here's my other shoe!" Connie tugged Frankie toward the exit.

Frankie pulled back for a last glimpse of the neon ceiling, which vision seemed the perfect topper to the evening. This afternoon she'd been a relatively content grade school teacher and fiancée, and tomorrow morning she would no doubt be that same person again. But for this one moment — with its ephemeral, buzzing quality, like the neon ceiling that inspired it — she knew what it meant to want something larger than she had expected. To want to be an actress. Like Connie.

The door at the top of the stairs slammed open.

Frankie and Connie made their escape through the back door into the alleyway behind the Dominion Theatre. Hand in hand, they threaded their way among trash bins and crates toward the spot where they'd left the car. With all that had gone wrong, and all that had gone right, she reckoned there was a fifty-fifty chance the Model A had been stolen.

But here it was at the curb, faithful and shining under moonlight.

Frankie started up the Model A, careful not to fumble the key and more careful still not to flood the engine. She steered away from the curb in a U-turn that would take them away from the Dominion Theatre, away from the sirens, away from the prop gun that was not a prop, and onto the dark road toward home. Connie was fiddling with something in her coat pocket, but Frankie, driving at a full forty miles an hour along the right lane of the Burrard Street

Bridge, panic riding in the rumble seat, couldn't make out what it was.

"Leo will be all right. The doctor sounded sober on the telephone," Connie said. Then, beaming once again in her vast and certain beauty in the passenger seat, Connie added, "Gilbert Howard said my screen test wasn't so bad."

"Abso-tively."

"Posi-lutely."

You've got the cheekbones. That's what Leo had said, and surely he knew about photogenic faces. Frankie changed lanes for no good reason.

"Anyway, they've got you on film, Connie. Will you go to Hollywood now?"

Connie didn't answer, and Frankie looked over to see why. She felt the hair stand up on her neck. She swore under her breath and swerved to a stop beside the stone bridge rail. "Throw it. Throw it into the water."

Connie put the gun back in her pocket. "But Gilbert Howard told me to take it."

"Give that gun to the police tomorrow. Tell them you found it on the street somewhere. Promise."

"Sure."

"That's a real promise you just made, Connie."

"I already told you so, didn't I?" Connie said, one hand in the pocket with the gun.

Frankie took two breaths. She slipped her engagement ring out of her coat pocket and back where it belonged, onto her ring finger. She started up the car again and drove on.

Connie said, "I'm going to Hollywood, Frankie. You and me both are going."

I've got the cheekbones. Frankie veered off Cornwall onto Alma Street. "Champ loves me."

"Of course he does," Connie said. "And I'm never going to feel nervous in front of a camera again."

"Of course you won't." Frankie kept her eyes on the road.

The two girls, one with an engagement ring on her finger and the other with a gun in her pocket, were home before the clock struck two.

7

Guns, half-naked movie stars, and neon ceilings belonged to downtown Vancouver on Friday night. Saturday morning on Thirty-Sixth Avenue brought only the vegetable wagon. This was the same canopied vehicle that had delivered the orange crate Frankie used for a hope chest. It rattled its slow passage along the alley behind Frankie's house, heavily laden with root vegetables and bags of lettuces, its load still heavy this time of day. Frankie knew she should go out and catch the vegetable wagon before it travelled any farther. She wanted leeks, at least as much as one could want leeks. Usually she enjoyed following the wagon at a run then joining the chatter of the neighbourhood wives and mothers as they gathered around the truck bed. Today, she let it clatter off toward Dunbar Street.

She kept her orange crate hope chest at her bedroom window for a seat. It was a scratchy perch, but she liked the pictures papered around the edge. They showed radiant California fruit, so brightly coloured that she could almost smell sunshine on warm peel. The oranges were long gone, and the crate now held four place settings of silver plate cutlery, a lace tablecloth, two cotton-linen pillowcases embroidered with lighthouses, an iron frying pan, and forty-three movie magazines. And underneath it all snuggled a comfortable little nest egg of folded-over ten-dollar bills that her father did not know she had, but which she'd earned substitute teaching.

She sat on her hope chest and gazed out at the doings on Thirty-Sixth Avenue. The rhododendrons were bursting into red and purple blossom this week. Housewifely activity bloomed as well, because Hazel and the other wives on the block had begun their spring cleaning. They beat their rugs and tried to collar their offspring as they tore away from their chores and off to the river flats or the Endowment Lands bush. Frankie herself would be out there with the other wives soon enough, pounding her own rugs and collaring her own children.

But Connie would do no such thing. For Connie would by then be an actress in Hollywood.

Feeling restless beyond measure, Frankie kicked off her shoes. They thudded against the wall beneath the window. She wished Champ would hurry up and come over for his visit. He started work late on Saturday mornings, so he would often stop in to sit with her and Sheridan D. Frankie had a yen to see Champ, the picture of prosperity and good looks in his insurance salesman's suit.

Downstairs, the phone rang. It was the first of seven rings, the polite number for a caller to allow, for seven gave you plenty of time to catch the call, if you hopped it. Frankie scooted downstairs, past her father's bedroom door, and picked up.

"Champ?" She slid down the wall to crouch with her chin on her knees, her apron strings twizzling up behind her.

"No. Darn it all! Listen to reason, Frankie Ray."

Frankie rubbed her nose against her knee and felt premature nostalgia for when Connie left for Hollywood and stopped calling altogether. Long distance calls from Hollywood must be monstrously expensive.

She said, "I'm going to miss you, kid."

"Keep it down! What if your father hears? Talk in code or something."

Frankie said, "Camel cigarettes, Connie." Champ smoked Camels.

"Champ! That insurance man! How can you want to marry Champ after you've seen Gilbert Howard, right up close? And think of all the other movie stars!"

Although there was nobody to see her, Frankie shook her head. What might she say in code to answer Connie? She decided on "Nivea hand cream." This represented a wife's soft hands.

"Look, Frankie, use the brains inside your head box. We're only young once. Do you want to be Hazel with a backyard full of babies all your life? Live a little first!"

Frankie eyed her father's door. Softly she sang, "*Can she bake a cherry pie, Billy Boy, Billy Boy?*" Pastry: some called it the toughest challenge in a young married woman's kitchen. "*Can she sew a perfect seam, charming Billy?*"

"Cripes, Frankie. You are so hard-hearted." Connie rang off.

Sheridan D Ray called from his bedroom, "What are you gabbing about this time?"

Frankie leaned in his door and found her father the minister—defrocked these three years—sitting up in bed, reading his own bound book of sermons. With a jerk she understood how she'd recognized Leo's broken-hearted gaze. She had seen her father's disappointment every day of her life since her mother had left them when Frankie was a baby.

Sheridan D said, "I know everything that goes on in this house, even when you're on the telephone, talking in riddles."

"I was only talking a little modern female philosophy, Dad."

"With whom?"

"With Connie, of course."

"*That* one. Connie's a bad influence. She should listen to her mother more." He gathered the chenille counterpane around himself and screwed his head away from her to glare out the window. "The wind's changed, and it's blowing right through the window sashes."

"It's your house, so you can criticize it," Frankie said cheerfully. "Do you want some toast and tea, Dad?"

"Damn all toast."

"It's still damned from Wednesday." She closed his door and heard him chuckle on the other side.

Frankie took a glass of water out to the back porch and poured it around the roots of her red geranium. She had to admit that although sometimes she saw with happy clarity that life was long and everything was possible, at other times she did not. She leaned on the porch rail with one hand on either side of the geranium pot. The diamond chip in her engagement ring caught the morning sun. This morning, Frankie was not in a mood to believe that everything was possible. This morning, she was pretty sure that everybody everywhere wanted what they couldn't have.

She wondered whether that was the sort of feeling her mother had experienced just before she'd walked away from Frankie and her father. She had no memory of her mother's face, but was able to picture her, standing with her baby girl in the crook of her arm, on the back porch of the old manse where Frankie had been born. And every time she imagined it, the scene unsnapped Frankie's spirit like a handbag and dumped it upside down.

She wondered how Leo was getting along with his gunshot wound, what he might have told the police, and whether he'd given them her name and Connie's. She weighed the fact of Leo's yellow suit against his bravery at finding himself shot in the arm by Gilbert Howard, and decided that he probably had not given them away. However, she'd never know for sure because that had happened in another world. Hollywood had no true connection to Thirty-Sixth Avenue, or to Frankie's red geranium, or to the marmalade cat now pacing the ridge pole of a neighbour's shed.

Frankie sat on the porch steps and looked out across the alley, where a little boy was firing pebbles at an empty chicken coop with a homemade slingshot. She called to him to stop, but he kept throwing stones with a world-weary set of the shoulders as if to say, *Nobody understands a man's work but himself.* Another vegetable truck rattled past, beet greens dangling out the back. The milk van was late, as it often was on a Saturday. Nobody complained because the wives all considered the milkman terribly handsome. Frankie couldn't see it. She wondered if, after she was married, she would find the milkman handsome, too.

All marriages are not the same, she told herself. *Every single husband is different.*

And to Hades with the handsome milkman, because down the alleyway strode her fiancé, Champ McCall, in the flesh, pink of face above the collar of his business suit. Sunshine lit his hair, and in one hand he carried a bottle of milk.

Frankie snatched the bib of her apron down over her head and twisted the whole thing around behind her.

"You're handsome enough to be a milkman," she told Champ as he climbed the back steps. "Wouldn't you like to do that instead of selling insurance?"

"Sure." As he passed her, Champ bent and kissed the top of her head. "I'll be a milkman if you want. Or we might be chicken farmers, Mrs Egg." He pushed through the screen door into the kitchen and returned without the milk to sit at her side on the steps.

"Want some tea, Mr Egg?" Frankie asked.

"No, ma'am."

"I went to an audition last night."

He picked a leaf off the red geranium. "How'd it go, Mrs Egg?"

"A real audition. No joke. For Connie. For a Hollywood studio."

Champ let out a low whistle. He took her left hand and examined her ring. He picked gently at the diamond chip with his thumbnail. "How'd you do?"

"Connie did great."

"I bet you did, too." Champ let go of her hand and took a pack of cigarettes out of his pocket. Frankie disliked the taste of smoke, but she admired the way Champ tapped his unlit cigarette on the pack, and the tough rasp his lighter made when he flicked on the flame. She watched him light his cigarette. She'd been watching Champ since their schooldays, and she always appreciated the view.

Frankie smiled. "The cameraman said I had good cheekbones."

"So you do."

"I always wished ..."

"I know. Hollywood beckons. You and a thousand other girls."

Frankie glanced up at him and then away. "A *hundred* thousand other girls, somebody told me."

"But you're one in a million to me," Champ said.

"Oh, very well put. Thanks." Idly Frankie picked up Champ's cigarettes and crinkled the cellophane on the Camel package. Connie loved to greet her with the grave assertion that *more doctors smoke Camels than any other ciga-rette*. Frankie didn't smoke, but she liked these particular cigarettes because of the picture of the camel on the front. If you could somehow get inside the picture, you might ride that camel over the golden sands to the pyramid. She enjoyed thinking of Champ carrying Egypt around in his pocket. But when she flipped the packet over she found that the cigarette company had changed the picture. Changed it, just like that.

Instead of the Egyptian camel, the picture showed a man in a suit much like Champ's. The man in the picture leaned over a tray presented to him by a dark-haired waitress with a low but unimpressive décolletage. The waitress was smil-ing her approval of the suited man's choice of cigarettes, although all the cigarettes pictured in the tray were Camels. All of them the same. *It's the favourite*, the package read, front and back.

She felt her cheeks heat up at the wrongness of it. *Why* was it the favourite, when all the Camels on the tray were alike? What kind of a choice was that?

Frankie's heart rose to her throat. Her hands grew clammy, and she rubbed them together. She glanced up and down the alleyway.

Champ nudged her. "What's wrong, Mrs Egg?"

She burst out, "Champ, let's you and me and Connie go to Hollywood."

Champ laughed out loud. "It's all very well for you, Mary Pickford, but what would an insurance man like me do in Hollywood?"

"Life is long, and …" she began, but she couldn't think how to conclude her sentence.

"Life is hunky-dory." Champ settled against her and blew a puff of smoke at the sky. "We've got it sorted out right. You stay at home and be the dreamer. I'm the man who brings you the bacon."

Frankie buried her face in her hands. "Why did they go and change the picture on the Camel package? If that changes, can't everything else change?"

"Frankie, stop that." Champ balanced his cigarette on the edge of the step below. He took both of her hands in his so that the cigarette package fell onto the step between them. "No more worrying. I chose well, didn't I? I chose you. I adore you, top to toe."

She looked up into his eyes. She was the daughter of a minister — even a defrocked minister — and understood that metaphors, like sermons, could be bent to support any point of view. Frankie thought, *Here's another metaphor: love is a mystery.*

"If you'll set the date," Champ said, "I'll give you a wedding that'll be as grand as any movie-star wedding. Eight bridesmaids at Christ Church Cathedral next spring. We'll get that French organist. Picture it."

Frankie pictured it. "Connie will come home from Hollywood to be my maid of honour."

"We'll drive to Hollywood and bring her back, broke and disappointed."

"Don't sell her short. She's got something. She could make it in the movies."

"Sure." Champ bent down to pick up what was left of his cigarette as it burned down on the step below.

At a honk, Frankie looked up to see Connie drive by in the Model A, on her way to wait tables at the golf course. This time her face was set in stern lines, and her red hair flew out behind her. At Frankie's side, Champ nodded at Connie, but frowned as his gaze followed the Model A to the end of the alley and around the corner onto Dunbar Street.

Frankie took her fiancé's hands and folded them in his lap, careful of the cigarette. She asked, "Tonight, will you elope with me?"

"Reno's a four-day drive." He tapped his ash. "I bet I could do it in two."

"Sure you could. I propose that you creep across the lawn tonight and set a ladder under my window." She'd expected a pause in the conversation, and she got one. She added, "I'll leave the ladder under the purple rhododendron."

"Hot dog," he said. "But I feel sorry for those eight brides-maids standing waiting at Christ Church Cathedral next spring. Poor, ruffled creatures."

"I'm not joking." She looked into his eyes. Would he listen to her more or less often after they were married? "I'm seriously serious."

"Me, too. I'm seriously in love." He kissed her hand and twisted the ring on her finger.

She peered up at him. "Say it like you're in a movie."

He moved his cigarette to his left hand, bent her backward across his lap and put his nose close to hers. "I'd do anything for you, *chérie*."

As he let her go, Frankie felt a chill deep in her soul. She pulled her skirt straight and told herself not to be a baby, always wanting sweeter candy.

She slipped his smokes back into his pocket. "Tonight, then. I'll be ready."

He laughed. "Me, too. We'll need a couple of suitcases each. But there's one thing I want to know, Frankie. How am I going to fit the French organist from Christ Church Cathedral into the trunk of the car?"

At the end of the driveway, the marmalade cat jumped up onto Sheridan D's garden fence and eyed the pair of them. Frankie felt emptier than a holey pocket, so she leaned over and kissed Champ again on the mouth—such a warm, cushioned mouth, and just wet enough.

Champ left for work. Frankie washed the breakfast dishes. She made the juice glasses squeak and watched soap bubbles float to the kitchen ceiling, light and free until they popped, allegorically, above her head. She shone the silver and cooked up some vegetable soup her father particularly liked. While it simmered, she hopped onto the streetcar that swayed her down to the train station at Main and Terminal, its metal wheels chattering. There at the exchange wicket she changed all the money from her hope chest into American dollars: a hundred and forty of them, plus a rattle of coins in her coat pocket. And when at last night fell, Frankie sat in the front room with her father to listen to the radio while she cut his hair. Sheridan D had such a good set he got a clear *Jack Benny Show*, no matter what the weather.

Frankie parted and lifted a section of her father's hair between her index and forefinger, held it tight at an angle, and snipped. Her father's hair smelled of Macassar oil, which smelled in its turn like coconut macaroons.

"Cut it carefully," Sheridan D directed. "I paid that barber fifty dollars to teach you to cut my hair properly."

"No bowl cuts for you, Dad." She came round the side and took hold of his front hair. She lost her grip when he laughed at Jack Benny for his penny-pinching ways, then caught it again and snipped it on an angle.

"Dammit, Frankie, not too short on top."

"Sure, Dad."

"You'll still cut my hair when you're married, Frankie. Don't forget."

"What if I do forget?" she joked. "You'd have to tie your hair up in a blue ribbon."

"Funny." Sheridan D snorted. "You may be interested to know that Jack Benny divides comedy by seven basic principles." Her father held up one thick finger for each principle. "Jokes, exaggeration, mockery, stupidity, surprise, the pun, and comic situations."

"That's four more principles than a marriage service calls for," Frankie observed. "I'm going to bed, Dad. Got a mystery to solve."

"You're not amateur-sleuthing after Irene's husband again? Is our dear neighbour making his usual getaway down to the docks to find women? The old sinner." Sheridan D showed his teeth.

"Nothing so easy. But I'll figure it out."

"That's my girl. You get your brains from me."

"That's the truth, Dad." Frankie set out the tea things for her father's breakfast and climbed the stairs to her room. She gazed down at her suitcase, so neatly packed for a completely unlikely journey to Hollywood. In her coat pocket she had tucked her little roll of American dollars, which now seemed a testimony to the folly of her behaviour throughout the day. She tucked her suitcase into her closet, tossed her coat on the end of the bed, and removed her shoes. She lay down in bed, fully dressed.

Anything is possible, she reminded herself. One mustn't count on it, but anything might happen.

She pulled the blankets across her bust and straightened her clothes underneath. She'd never slept in her clothes before.

Her skirt and sweater were wool and wouldn't wrinkle, or not too badly. She tried to fall asleep, but as the night wore on she only grew colder and colder, as if she were dying.

A ladder made a clicking noise against Frankie's open bedroom window. She sat up in the darkness and said to the window, "I've been working on a new metaphor for life. What if men are the sea because they are powerful and cover most of the earth? And women are the skilled and unsung sailors of men's ocean."

"And we are always stuck with the washing up." Connie leaned her elbows on Frankie's bedroom windowsill. "What are the boats in your metaphor, then? Horses? And would the fish be mice?"

"You're a funny girl."

"I'll be a funny girl on the road to Hollywood in about two minutes. Are you coming or not?" Connie disappeared back down into the night.

Frankie shrugged on her coat, slipped on her shoes, and retrieved her suitcase from the closet. She pulled on her squashy tam and jabbed her mother's hatpin through it. Suitcase in hand, she took each step down the ladder with such caution that she didn't feel the full import of the moment until she stepped down onto the lawn outside her father's window.

Connie, leaning up against the Model A out front of the house, wore her own squashy tam, and her coat that was a little too tight.

"Are we sure about this?" Frankie asked.

"Abso-tively."

Frankie looked from her father's window to the Model A, shining under the night sky like an unbroken promise. For a short, sharp moment she thought that Champ might step out of the darkness to collect her after all, for a romantic elopement. He did not.

Connie insisted on driving, and for once she pulled away from the curb with only the quietest pop of the exhaust. Frankie leaned back and watched the black tops of the maples flicker against the blacker sky overhead.

Connie swerved around a solitary pedestrian and his dog.

"You're going to make it in the movies, of course," Frankie said. "And I always believed I wouldn't. But maybe I could."

"You've got plenty of pretty."

"Bette Davis made it. She's no beauty."

"And she doesn't have your cheekbones," Connie pointed out.

"Oh, well, what the hell." Frankie raised both hands high over her head and let the wind blow between her fingers.

"Posi-lutely. Hey, Frankie, what do you want in a car?" Connie clapped Frankie on the shoulder.

"*Sturdy steel construction*," Frankie answered.

"*Silent brake system … The Ford Model A*," Connie added. "Say, look in the glove box. I brought that gun."

Frankie opened the glove box, took in the cold glint of the gun nestled among the gas station maps, and slammed the box shut. Her hands were icy, and she pushed them deep into her coat pocket. Comb and lipstick in the right pocket, wallet in the left, with a hundred and forty American dollars wrapped round with a rubber band, plus a few loose dollars to pay for their first gallons of gasoline. And underneath it, at the very bottom, lay her engagement ring. Unlike Connie, Frankie was not a girl who burned her bridges.

She left her ring inside her pocket. Life was long, and either everything was possible, or else it was not. A fifty-fifty chance. Those weren't the worst odds in the world.

Connie tapped the Model A's horn lightly, and both girls jumped at the sound and then laughed out loud.

"*Tilting beam headlamps,*" they sang together under the starry sky. "*Reliability, economy, and long life … The Ford Model A.*"

Reliability, economy, and long life sounded like some stay-at-home's three wishes, but not Frankie's after all. Not tonight. She stood up in her seat for a block or two to feel the wind as the Model A popped and scrunched along the road toward Hollywood.

8

Frankie hunched over the wheel of the Model A. She ground her gears a little as she took the next rise. The early morning light made it much easier to see the turns in the Oregon State road ahead.

She wondered when the world would begin to look really different. Over the past two days, driving southward, the countryside had looked like the world they'd left behind in Vancouver, with clouds fanning out across the sky and conifers lining both sides of the road. She shivered, thankful she'd brought her squashy tam, pinned tight with her departed mother's hatpin. She'd hauled the scratchy brown blanket out of the rumble seat hours ago while it was still Connie Mooney's turn to drive. Now it lay bunched around Connie's slumped form beside her, the ends tucked around Frankie's lap. The gas cans strapped to the running boards were full, and so was the Thermos Connie's mother had sent—along with a paper sack of tea bags — to fill up for free with hot water whenever they stopped at a gas station.

"*Your shaving brush has had its day,*" Frankie murmured in her radio announcer's voice as the little red Burma-Shave signs by the side of the road flashed past, each one providing the reader with a line of agreeable verse. "*So why not shave the modern way?*"

"*Burma-Shave!*" Connie blinked, sat up, and put her stocking feet up on the dashboard. "Are we really on the road to California?"

"If I haven't lost track, it's Tuesday morning. We've been on the road since Saturday night. I think we should have taken Route 99 at Blaine, but it's too late to turn back now."

"Wet your whistle?"

"Sure. Let's have that Thermos."

Frankie kept her eyes on the road while Connie unscrewed the Thermos top, which served as a teacup. After drinking from her side of the cup, Connie turned it round for Frankie, who sipped at the bitter, most welcome tea. She steered with one hand and took another sip while Connie dragged out from behind her seat the box of goodies her mother had sent along with them.

Frankie geared down, thought better of it, and geared back up. The Model A bucked and soldiered on.

"Thank goodness for your mother, Connie, and for hot water at gas stations."

"And even though gas has gone up to eight cents a gallon, our money is lasting pretty well."

In fact, Frankie's one hundred and forty American dollars remained entirely intact inside her jacket pocket. They'd only used the money Connie's mother had pressed upon her daughter for essentials, like gasoline and cocoa and toast from a gas station café, with melted butter dripping out of the corners of its waxed-paper wrapping. That toast was long gone, and now they munched from the goody box as they drove along.

Connie stretched out her toes inside her stockings. "Jumping Columbus, driving to Hollywood together is such a miracle that I might as well wish for a big starring contract to appear in my pocket while I'm at it."

"You've got talent without a contract, and that's better than the other way around."

"You've got talent, too. Say, what did you tell the school board about leaving? Were they sore?"

"Lucky for me, it's Easter vacation." Frankie wasn't certain she'd have had the intestinal fortitude to walk away from a pay cheque if it had been term time.

"Did you leave a note for your dad?" It was the third time Connie had asked that question in three days' travel.

Frankie frowned and leaned into a turn. Champ had explained to her not long ago that she should speed up at the halfway point of the arc, but except for one lucky S-turn somewhere along the road, she hadn't yet picked up the knack. She'd get it, though. She breathed in the musky odour of the woods. Everywhere, pink and purple rhododendrons clustered at the roadside and shoved up against the painted board-and-batten domiciles and small towns scattered along the route. Crooked alder branches waved old man's beard at them as they rumbled by in the Model A.

At last she answered, "I didn't have time to write Dad a note, did I? I didn't know I was leaving until I left with you."

"Well, don't take a fit. My mom will explain to your dad. She promised to check on him first thing. Let's have some more of that goody box."

"I'm trying to imagine the day my father would pack me a case of apples to take to California." Frankie rolled her eyes. "Or the day he'd bless me with boxes of éclairs."

"Oh, put a sock in it. Old Sheridan D is not so bad. At least you've got a dad." Connie's father had died two years into the war, when she was only four.

Frankie took an éclair and nibbled away at the cookie on the bottom, while Connie began as always with the marshmallow on top. In the chocolate-covered silence that followed, Frankie concentrated hard on running the Model A along the side of the road, keeping out of the way of a number of cars that had passed them over and over since Bellingham. Some of these vehicles were beginning to seem like familiar faces.

Frankie and Connie raised a hand to the driver of a battered yellow fruit truck, empty but for brown sacking bouncing and sliding across the boards of the truck bed, and he honked a cheerful note as he passed. Connie leaned over and pressed the Model A's horn in return. Two coupés and a long black Cadillac were not such friendly travelling companions, and Frankie had long ago given up waving at them as they and the other cars and trucks pulled off the road for gasoline or cocoa.

Connie craned round to stare as they passed a gas station with an enormous coffee cup on its roof. "Only five cents? Turn around, let's live a little."

"Let's make those nickels last," Frankie said. "I say we have a couple more of those Newtowns."

"You're so cheap, you make Jack Benny look like Santa Claus." Connie leaned into the rumble seat and sorted through the remaining apples. Newtown Pippins were brown and yellow, and on the small side, too. They never looked like much, but they were the only apples still worth eating after Christmas.

Connie handed one apple to Frankie and bit into another. She pointed out a roadside house with lugubrious lilac clapboard siding. "Why the dickens would anybody live in a purple house like that one and never want anything more out of life?"

"Well, you can live in a purple house and want the world, can't you? Or I guess you could live out in the great world and wish you had a ticky-tacky purple house on the side of a country road."

"Did I hear you sigh? Do you want to go back?" Still chewing on her Newtown, Connie polished the windshield with one sock foot.

"I do not."

"Are you sad because of Champ? And, you know, the whole thing with me?"

At the approach of another turn, Frankie tried stepping on the brake a little so as to speed up more easily halfway through. She took the curve in satisfying style. With the inside of the cuff of her coat, she wiped a bit of juice from her apple off the steering wheel.

"Connie, you didn't do a thing to encourage him."

"I really didn't. Anyway, Champion McCall was never in love with me, only with some idea he had of me."

You know, Frankie, Champ had explained, hat in hand while snowflakes fell about them, *falling in love with Connie was like feeling the pull that marches a young man off to war. An irresistible force, that's what she is. Well, I'm back, and I'll never march off again.*

Frankie shook her head. "Whether he loved you or some idea of you isn't the question."

"What is the question?"

"If he really loved either you or the idea of you, how could he love me? He couldn't."

"Is that necessarily so?" Connie flipped her apple core onto the road. "I've never known a man to love only one thing. Anyway, he loves you now."

Frankie nodded. "Now, he does."

"And you're much more interesting than I am to talk to," Connie said. "You know all kinds of clever things from all that reading you do. Champ did beg you to marry him, didn't he?"

Frankie smiled. "On his knees in the snow." She tossed her core over Connie's head and into the shrubs at the side of the road.

Connie ducked. "That's all right, then. And now you're leaving him behind. Like … I forgot what I was going to say."

Like my mother. Frankie saw her mother in her mind's eye, a slim woman in a dark coat stepping quickly along the same sort of front path Frankie had walked down less than seventy-two hours before. Her mother hadn't looked back, either, or so Frankie had always imagined, since she'd been a baby at the time. But she was not her mother, and she reminded herself of this inarguable fact.

Frankie sped up, and the wind ruffled the crowns of their squashy tams. She fished in her pocket and dug out the ring with its diamond chip.

"I'm not burning my bridges with Champ. We're still engaged."

"Good old Champ. He knows how to make his dollar bill."

Connie opened the glove compartment where the gun was stored. She pulled the weapon out and stroked it as if it were a small grey rabbit. "What gun company carves a crown into a—what do you call it? Not a hilt …"

"It's called the handle, I think. Put it in the glove compartment." Frankie had read somewhere about hair-trigger weapons, and she saw no way to find out whether this one was hair-triggered without firing the thing.

Connie returned the gun to the glove box and clicked it closed.

Frankie nodded. "I say we leave it there and don't touch it again."

"Would you shoot somebody, do you think? I mean if you were somehow driven to it?"

"I want to say no, but I've never had the temptation and a weapon at the same time." Frankie sucked her lip and tried to imagine such a circumstance. "Maybe if we were in a dark alley with a footpad creeping up on us or something like that."

"Yes'm." Connie rolled her window up and down. Almost dreamily, she said, "Why would a big cheese like him be sitting barefoot on the roadside? Look."

Frankie looked. What she saw rated a double take and then a swerve of the Model A over to the wrong side of the road. For there sat King Samson, the producer of Monument Pictures, director of the great epic *Ambition*.

In his quality camel-hair coat, the studio head leaned against a crooked old yew. His sock feet stuck out into the road where any passing car might run them over. He looked up at the Model A as it approached and struggled to his feet.

Frankie said, "Holy Moses, I was right. Anything *is* possible. Connie, put your shoes on and straighten your hat."

She slowed down and pulled over to the side of the road in front of King Samson.

9

King Samson stood up in the gravel at the side of the road. He brushed at the broad backside of his camel-hair coat, picked up his shoes, and limped to the passenger side of the car.

Frankie kneeled up on the driver's seat. "Give you a lift this morning, sir?"

"Of course I want a lift," he growled. "Do you think I'm sitting on my hindquarters to delight passing motorists?"

"Hop in," Frankie said.

"But first I want to know something. Seeing as we're on the road to Hollywood." King Samson slapped at an insect on the side of his neck. He put one fist on the car's bonnet and glared from Connie to Frankie. "Are either of you in show business?"

Frankie and Connie exchanged looks of veiled import. How could Samson not recognize Connie and Frankie from the Dominion Theatre audition three nights before? Of course, it had been night, and they had been wearing different hats.

Samson added, "I refuse to ride with any aspiring actresses. I'd prefer to sit on the side of the road for the rest of my natural life, breathing in the smell of whatever these purple flowers are."

"These are rhododendrons," Frankie said.

"Young ladies, are you in the business, or are you not?"

Frankie balked at the direct lie, but Connie was up to the necessary. "Not us. We're a pair of rubes off to see the mansions of the movie stars," she said cheerfully.

"All right, then. You can give me a ride."

Samson leaned against the Model A to put his shoes on. Frankie nudged Connie, who nodded and tucked a few flyaway tendrils of her distinctive red hair under her hat.

Samson, now shod, gave the car the once-over. "This is a two-seater. I'll drive. Which of you is going to sit on top of your boxes in the rumble seat?"

Frankie said, "Connie, sit down."

Connie sat down. Frankie tapped a Girl Guide salute against the side of her squashy tam and revved the engine. She pulled back onto the road south.

"Is it wise?" Connie asked.

"He won't let us go."

A pebble hit the back of the Model A. Frankie hit the brakes.

"Hold on," Samson bellowed.

While Frankie pushed and pulled at the choke, Samson caught up with the Model A. Connie opened the door on the passenger side and arched herself up onto her feet so that Samson could slide himself underneath her. The head of Monument Studios grunted as she sat back down on his knee and slammed the door shut.

With exquisite care, Frankie let the clutch up and pressed the gas pedal down. The Model A pulled away like the trooper it was.

Samson said, "Look, you girls, I had to ask if you were actresses. Everywhere I go, everybody's in the business." To Connie, who was sitting on his lap, he said, "Move a little, will you? You're sitting bony."

"I've got bones," Connie said. "It's human nature."

Samson glowered at the back of her coat. "A man in my position, everywhere it's the same. I order dinner — the waitress gives me the death scene from *Camille*. I hail a taxi — the driver shoves his glossies in my face. I can't rest, and I can't get good service."

"It's a tough life when you're important." Connie covered her grin with her hand.

"You got that right." Samson adjusted Connie as if she were a large valise strapped to his lap. "Anyhow, there's nothing for girls like you in Hollywood. Nothing but trouble."

"Or a break," Frankie said. "If you were looking for a break like that in the business, I mean."

"A break in the movie business? Tell that to Cinderella when you see her, since you believe in fairy tales. Anyway, you're lucky you're not actresses. Klieg eye, that's your break: blind at forty. Or you can wait tables until you get too old to photograph. It's all the same in Hollywood."

Frankie had read all about Hollywood success stories in the movie magazines, and might have said plenty in opposing argument. Instead, she made a rather good turn and roared a little faster along the road above the ocean.

"It makes me sick." Samson lifted one arm from Connie's waist and waved it at the road leading to Hollywood. "There's a never-ending stream of golden-skinned youngsters heading south to be movie stars. All of them full of hope. It's not up to them to give themselves hope. *I'm* the one to give them hope."

Connie asked, "Do you give a lot of it?"

Samson said, "All you need to know is that I'm the best judge of who should be hopeful."

"I suppose that in a way it's true," Frankie allowed. "You've got the experience, so you can spot a winner."

Samson nodded. "Marietta Valdes, there's your example. I picked her out of a line of extras like Venus on a shelf of kewpie dolls." He glared up at Connie. "Keep still, can't you?"

He clutched at Connie and then took another, harder look.

"I know you," Samson said. He reached for her hat, but Connie held on to it with both hands.

"You do, Mr Samson. I was your waitress at the Dominion Theatre bar." Connie delivered her lie, barefaced and angel-browed. She really did have that certain something.

Samson had picked Connie once for an audition. He might choose her again.

Play those cards right, Connie, Frankie communicated, using the silent language of the eyes.

He's in my back pocket, Connie sent back. Frankie honked again, for the heck of it.

Samson turned to Frankie. "What are you? A schoolteacher?"

Frankie winced. Still, she wasn't a schoolteacher today—all the kids were on Easter break. "Cold, colder, coldest."

"Oh, she's much more interesting than that," Connie assured him. "Frankie is …"

"A bank teller?" Samson asked. "A visiting nurse?"

Frankie clattered through the middle of a pothole because she judged that he'd be improved by a bump or two.

Connie sniffed. "Frankie, a schoolteacher? That shows how much you know."

Frankie hoped to high heaven that her red-headed friend wouldn't burn any of her bridges. Not yet, anyway. Although, talking to King Samson, she understood the temptation.

"Frankie is a private dick," Connie lied snappily.

"'Zat so?" Samson looked intently at Frankie, the disbelief plain in his gaze.

Frankie stared at the road ahead. She refused to lie. But she also refused to admit to the head of Monument Studios in Hollywood, California, that she was a substitute school-teacher. She badly wanted to prove to this man how dead wrong he was in his assessment of her. If you escaped from your previous life and then brought with you the bits that you were running away from, what did that make you? A fool.

She gave him a hawk-eyed sleuth look and drove on.

"You sure don't look like any kind of private dick to me," he said.

"Wouldn't it be important to a detective to be unrecogniz-able?" Frankie asked.

"You're wasting your time. Hollywood's full of detectives. Gouging bastards."

The direct lie safely dodged, it occurred to Frankie that if she looked at it in a certain way, tracking down her neighbour Irene's wayward husband every month or so was a sort of volunteer detective work. She asked, "Is Hollywood full of girl ones?"

"Women detectives? There's a kind of knitted toe-cover for you."

"That's silly," Connie said. "I'd think that people want to get a feminine viewpoint from time to time."

"Goddamn the feminine viewpoint to the darkest pits of Hell." Samson glared at Frankie. "All right, I'll hire you. How much by the hour?"

Frankie didn't even know how much Connie had made waitressing. She herself made eighty dollars in a month teaching school, but that was no help.

She said, "First, tell me what I'm supposed to detect."

"The usual. I want to know whether somebody is unfaithful to me."

"That's so sad. An unfaithful wife," Connie said.

Samson shot her a look. "Leave my wife out of this."

Frankie blinked. "A girlfriend, then? I don't charge extra for ironic situations."

"Don't give me any of your ironic situations. I'll have you know that she's a woman of virtue, which I respect, seeing as I'm still married to the second Mrs Samson. But I want to know if she's still a woman of virtue when she's out of my sight. How long do you take to find answers?"

Frankie found it a challenge to play private detective and change gears on the Model A at the same time. And Connie seemed no closer than ever to a break in the movie business. She steered carefully, giving the cliff's edge a generous margin with the right wheels.

She said, "I'll tell you right now, free of charge, whether or not your girlfriend is faithful to you, if you'll answer me one question."

"And you call yourself a detective?" Samson smacked the glove compartment door with his open hand. "Feminine viewpoint, my illustrious behind."

"Here goes." Frankie cocked him a sideways look. "Mr Samson, tell me this: Has anything about you changed since you fell for her and she for you? Loss of money, loss of power?"

"*No.*"

"Then she's not unfaithful." The important thing was to appear certain. Frankie glanced at King Samson out of the corner of her eye to see how her acting was playing with the great producer. She wondered what it would be like to have all the power in the world, like him, but to be unsure of your woman.

"Good thing I didn't pay you," Samson said. "Listen, got a drink?"

"Some lukewarm tea in a Thermos bottle."

"I hate tea. You must have something a man could drink." Samson put his arms around Connie and opened the glove compartment. His view of the glove compartment was blocked, though, and Connie shut it quickly.

"*No.*"

"You know …" King Samson said, his eyes on Connie and his arms still around her waist, "You've got something."

There ensued an electrifying pause, but he said nothing further.

"I've been told that before," Connie said crossly. "Thanks."

They both ignored him splendidly as they drove past a doughnut-shaped café, but waved heartily at the driver of the Cadillac they'd come to recognize on the drive south. It pulled out from its spot next to a couple of north-facing trucks stacked with orange crates—one of which was the same as her hope chest back home—and tore ahead of the Model A while one of the fruit trucks rattled northward. That truck of California fruit might be headed straight up to Vancouver, on its way to rattle along Thirty-Sixth Avenue, right by her father's blue house.

"California, here we come." Frankie had never been farther from home than Seattle. She said it again: "*California.*" The word tasted exotic in her mouth, like Egypt or Siam. She looked up at the sky, and it was a clear, pale blue, different— dryer, perhaps—than an April Vancouver sky ever got, even on the brightest spring day. She sniffed the air. It smelled different, somehow. *It is a simple truth,* she thought, *that if you get in your car and drive for a day or two, eventually you really do arrive somewhere different.*

"I think I could use you," King Samson said, as Connie removed his hands from various locations about herself. "For a film, I mean. Perhaps a very small part."

"Oh, I don't know," Connie said. "I've never thought of being in the movies. I adore waitressing."

Frankie said, "You'll need to sign her to some kind of contract right away, Mr Samson. Connie's very changeable."

"I've been engaged four times," Connie said. This was true, at least if you asked her former fiancés.

"Don't you girls have a flask of gin or something in this car?" King Samson fumbled around her and opened the glove compartment again. He might have been looking for a flask, but what he found was the gun.

Frankie's eyes opened wide. She heard Connie say, "Give me that."

Connie and Samson wrestled for the gun. Frankie thought of only three ways the struggle could possibly end, and none of them were happy.

"Let him have it," Frankie cried. "I mean, let him have the gun."

"But ..."

"It's his gun, never fear," Frankie said. "Remember the king's crown on the handle? We should have known the gun was King Samson's."

Connie let Samson take the gun.

"My wife gave me this gun for a Christmas present." Samson rubbed his thumb over the crown engraved on the grip. He shoved the gun into his pocket. "Well, this raises a goddamn question, doesn't it? Why are you two *non-actresses* driving to Hollywood with a gun I last saw in the audition room at the Dominion Theatre?"

Connie looked helplessly at Frankie. Frankie gritted her

teeth, counted the cost, and did the only thing possible in the situation. She told an outright lie. "Connie found it when she was sweeping up the audition room. She's one of the concierge staff."

Connie hung onto the windshield. "I'm a hard worker."

Frankie considered it best to move the conversation onward. "Pretty soon we could stop for gas and a fresh shot of hot water for tea. And find you a cup of coffee, Mr Samson."

"Keep driving," Samson said. "No, stop."

The Model A had rounded a stand of startlingly copper arbutus. An unpaved, cliff-top lookout area stretched out before them. A long, dark car was parked there.

King Samson reached over, twisted the car key out of the ignition, and flung it out of the passenger window and onto the edge of the road. The Model A juddered to a stop inside the lookout area. Connie landed hard, first on the dashboard and then back on Samson. He swore and pushed her over, half onto the gearshift.

Frankie rested her chin on the steering wheel and breathed hard, furious with Samson's effrontery, but at the same time thanking their lucky stars that Samson's wife hadn't given her husband a cheap and unreliable gun that would go off in his pocket.

On the far side of the lookout area, toward the cliff edge, the other parked car gleamed in the sunlight. This was a long, black item, the double chrome bumper making it instantly identifiable as a Cadillac Saloon, the same one that had passed them a number of times on the journey south. Whoever had parked it had pulled up perilously close to the lookout's perimeter. Only the loose chicken-wire fencing a couple of feet away from the cliff's edge stood between the car's front bumper and a long fall to the rocks and the sounding sea.

The Cadillac's door swung open, and a woman stepped out. She closed the car door, leaned against the Cadillac in a graceful pose, and gazed at the group. The breeze played with the folds of her red satin coat and lifted her dark hair back from her lovely face. Behind her, the sea flashed and leaped under reflected halos of silver spray.

Against the rough and glorious beauty of the Oregon coastline, the movie star Marietta Valdes was still larger than life. Even at this distance, the actress's features stood out as clearly as they did on the screen, viewed from the best seats in the house.

10

The cliff-side lookout was an almost perfectly flat semicircle of pebbles and hard-packed dirt, but somehow Frankie felt as if she were looking up rather than across at Marietta Valdes. The movie star reminded her of a princess in a tower: brave, powerful, and yet in need of rescuing. Furthermore, something about the arch of Marietta's dark eyebrows reminded Frankie of the neon picture of Orion the Hunter on the ceiling of the Dominion Theatre back home.

King Samson bullied his way from underneath Connie and out the car door toward Marietta Valdes. The two Hollywood greats stood facing one another like ancient gods meeting on the sloped topography of Olympus, with the sea knocking against the cliffs below.

Connie hissed, "Holy Moses, here are Marietta Valdes and King Samson right here in front of us."

"Two giants of the screen," Frankie agreed.

"It's like we're at the heart of Hollywood already. What a kick!"

Frankie agreed. "But we must keep quiet as mice and find out what we can about these movie people. How did they get where they are? Why are they so different from you and me? That's what I want to know."

"Not me. I want to know how they're the same as us. I wish we had popcorn."

Connie leaned over the seat and rummaged in the rumble until she found the nearly empty box of éclair cookies. Frankie took one from the box, and Connie, munching, set it between them.

King Samson's voice carried well across the lookout. "Isn't it about goddamn time you called a truce with me?"

"Heavens, Sammy." Marietta Valdes smiled the sad and beautiful smile Frankie had seen a dozen times in the movies. Her actress voice carried as well, and Frankie was grateful for it. "You held a secret midnight screen test in the Canadian boondocks to replace me, and you think I'll forgive you."

"Replace you? You've got me all wrong, baby."

"Only because I'm irreplaceable."

She moved up close. He put an arm around her. With what seemed almost a tentative gesture, she touched his hair and held the pose for a long moment.

Frankie and Connie peered at them through the windshield, chewing on their cookies.

"That's so sweet," Connie said. "True love, I bet, except for his wife."

"We never asked him why he was in his sock feet at the roadside."

"Well, he's the kind of fellow you don't ask for explanations," Connie acknowledged.

They watched King Samson attempt to embrace Marietta. She pulled back.

Samson said, "No kiss? After the dirty trick with my shoes that you played back there on the road? A kiss to say *I'm sorry* is not so much to ask from the woman I love."

Marietta answered, "If you want kisses from me, you won't break your promises."

At Frankie's side in the Model A, Connie murmured, "What promises would those be? Maybe to divorce his wife?"

"And what trick did she play on him back there on the road? Oh." Frankie nodded. "How about this? Samson was in Marietta's car. She threw his shoes out the window, and when he went after them, she drove away and left him by the side of the road."

"You really should have been a detective," Connie said. "How about we each have an apple?"

They bit into their apples, and Samson managed to complete his embrace of Marietta Valdes with a hard kiss held for a long moment. Marietta laid one hand on the back of his neck and kissed him back.

Connie leaned toward Frankie. "You were right. She's not cheating. That's a sincere kiss from a virtuous woman."

"She's an actress," Frankie observed, although as the kiss continued, she found herself inclined to agree.

Then, without warning, Marietta pushed the flat of both hands against Samson's chest. Her hand slipped inside his pocket. When she pulled free of him, there was a gun in her hand. *The* gun.

Inside the Model A, the two girls blinked at each other.

"Darn you, Connie," Frankie whispered. "That gun is nothing but trouble. You should have thrown it off the bridge the first night, when I asked you to."

"Hindsight is a dirty sneaky trick," Connie muttered back.

"How did Marietta know King Samson had a gun in his pocket anyway?"

"Maybe he's always got one, like some people carry handkerchiefs."

They sank a little lower in their seats.

Marietta stepped backward, the gun held loosely in one hand. King Samson frowned and wiped at his mouth. Frankie, still playing detective, deduced, *Lipstick.*

Was there movement over by the Cadillac? It might have been the wind in the pines. She heard something that might have been the rattle of pebbles down the cliff to the sea.

"I can't believe you're holding my own goddamn gun on me." In the centre of the dusty lookout, Samson scowled at Marietta. "Have I ever steered you wrong since I pulled you out of that line of extras? You shone —"

"I shone like Venus in a line of kewpie dolls. Sammy, I'm holding you at gunpoint, with your own gun, because I'm going to make you do something you don't want to do. But first tell me, why were you searching for actresses in Vancouver? Of all the neon-soaked little backwater cities in the world?"

Connie said, "Grr," and Frankie nodded.

"Okay, here's the truth if you've gotta hear it." King Samson flung his arms wide. "Marietta, I stuck a pin in the map and said, 'Wherever this lands, I can find and create a star as bright as Marietta Valdes.' But I'll never find such a virtuous woman as you."

Frankie decided that if she were standing where Marietta stood now, holding the gun and listening to King Samson's condescending little speech, she might have been tempted to shoot him, at least in the foot. But Marietta only nodded. "As virtuous a woman? Yes. As good an actress? Maybe. But not as good a director."

A director? Marietta Valdes?

A woman director?

Frankie sat back in her seat, blinking. Could a woman be a director? She supposed there was no law against it, even in Hollywood, but such an idea had never entered her mind before. She tried to picture it—Marietta Valdes in jodhpurs and flat cap, instructing an army of extras—and found it, after all, entirely possible to imagine the scene, even if King Samson could not.

Marietta waved the gun. "Look, Sammy. You're no stranger to taking risks with a picture. Financially, you operate on the razor's edge. You're willing to take chances on a loose cannon like Gilbert Howard, and while Howie may be my dearest friend and ally, half the time he can't remember his lines as written. Furthermore, it would surprise nobody if Howie's excesses caused him to be hauled off by men in white coats before the end of filming. If you can take a chance on Howie, why won't you take a chance on me?"

Frankie peered past the actress to the Cadillac. Inside, somebody moved, and the back end of the car jounced. A pale face hove into view inside the rear window and then vanished.

"Is that Gilbert Howard in the back seat of the Cadillac?" Frankie asked Connie.

"I didn't see anything," Connie said. "I keep wondering if Marietta will shoot King Samson, so I'm keeping an eye on that gun."

"*I* want to know what she's going to use the gun to make him do."

King Samson took a step closer to Marietta Valdes. Standing as far from the gun as geometry allowed, he touched her cheek.

"I'm only trying to help you. If you tried to direct a picture, the crew wouldn't listen to you."

Marietta said, "There have been women directors before."

"Small potatoes." Samson waved a hand. "Short pieces. No big films. Nothing important."

"Like your *Ambition*? I can make an important picture. In fact, I can make a picture important."

Samson swore. "Everybody thinks they can be a director. They think you just stand there and boss people around. When I directed *Ambition*, which certain critics called the greatest epic ever made, the days were long and the cameramen were imbeciles. The actors couldn't act, and the actresses wouldn't come out of their dressing rooms. It took a towering mind and a unique grasp of cinematography and structure to create that unmatched piece of movie-making."

Marietta said, "If I'd directed *Ambition*, I would have placed the second camera above the horizon to get the oblique shot over the title. And also, you lost the tension between reality and the dream world in the third pyramid scene."

Frankie was impressed, by Marietta's vocabulary at any rate, although she couldn't remember the exact scenes in *Ambition* she referred to. However, Frankie had spent most of her life on Thirty-Sixth Avenue, staring out the window and wishing for things she could not have, and so she understood something about losing the tension between reality and the dream world.

"I want to direct." Marietta paled and tightened her grip on the gun. "Sammy, it's all I want."

"You only think you want to direct. And that's because women always want what they can't have."

"Women aren't the only ones to want what they can't have."

"Is that so?"

"It is. But Sammy, you're right about one thing. You'll never find another woman like me."

"At last we agree," he said, still scowling.

"Do we? How sweet. Now tell me something. What are you doing with those two girls in the Model A?"

"Those girls are nobody."

Marietta moved toward the Model A. Frankie and Connie slipped down further in their seats. In fact, they descended inside the car as low as they could go. Frankie noticed for the first time how relaxed Marietta appeared with a gun in her hand. She looked as if she knew what to do with one — as if she were a pretty good shot.

King Samson followed Marietta and reached for the gun. She slipped the gun into her other hand, away from him.

She neared the Model A and gazed from Frankie to Connie. "Shouldn't there be three of you girls on the road to Hollywood? Everyone comes to Hollywood in threes."

"Why threes?" Connie asked.

Right now, Frankie didn't care *why threes*. She wanted to know what Marietta was going to do with that gun.

Samson said, "Marietta, leave those girls out of it. They're not even trying to get into the movies. One of them is a waitress."

Marietta smiled. "Wasn't every actress once a waitress? Of course they're actresses, Sammy. Look at them. Look at that one with the red hair. Go home, girls. Don't you know that nothing is as it seems in Hollywood?"

"But that's the wonderful thing about Hollywood, isn't it?" Frankie scrambled to her feet and held onto the windshield for balance. Her knees trembled against the hem of her dress, but her chin was as hard as boiled candy. "I'm tired of everyone telling Connie and me to go home. You didn't go home, Miss Valdes."

Connie kneeled up on her seat. "You stuck it out, Miss Valdes."

"I did. Still, I never meant to end up an actress. For me, acting is a stepping-stone to directing. There's a lesson for you, girls: be careful when you're dreaming. You remind me of my friends and me when we came to Hollywood. What a pity you have got yourselves dragged into this mess."

Marietta looked down at the gun in her hand and moved closer still. Frankie calculated their chances of finding their key in the dirt, starting the car, and driving away before the actress reached them. The answer did not please.

Marietta said, "Even though it's not really your problem, I'm afraid this must be done."

She raised the gun and aimed it.

"Jeepers," Connie whispered.

Frankie leapt over the driver's door onto the packed dust of the lookout and tore around in front of the Model A.

She pleaded, "Don't shoot, Miss Valdes. Because if you do shoot out that tire, I'll have to buy a new one."

Marietta said, "I can't have you and Samson chasing me all the way down the coast in your pretty little car."

Frankie took advantage of the moment to pull the hatpin out of her hat.

She muttered, *"Each man kills the thing he loves."* Before the actress could shoot it flat, Frankie jabbed the hatpin into the front left tire. Nothing happened when she pulled the pin out. She met Marietta's eye, gritted her teeth and jabbed it again, turning the thick pin in the rubber to make a small hole that would result in a flat. Poor old Model A. It almost hurt her physically to do it, but a pinhole could be patched. She hoped. If not, it was a long walk along the coast.

A hissing sound from the tire advertised the imminent flat. "There. We can't follow you now," Frankie said with as little resentment in her voice as she could manage, seeing as the actress still held the gun.

Marietta laughed. "Who'd have believed there'd be two deep thinkers like you and me on the road to Hollywood?"

Gun in hand, she strolled away from Frankie, Connie, and King Samson, climbed into the front seat of her Cadillac, and engaged the motor. She leaned out the open driver's window and, with a gesture as strong and practised as a man's, pitched Samson's gun over the edge of the cliff.

Marietta called out, "I'm going on ahead to Hollywood to talk things over with our present director, and I don't want you bulling around in the room while I do, Sammy. Also, consider our engagement a bust. We're through." Marietta cocked her head. "You can always try to win me back."

Marietta swung the Cadillac into a wide, curving turn and drove away with a dusty roar, south toward Los Angeles and Hollywood. When the car neared the first curve in the road, the face reappeared in the back window of the Cadillac. It was Gilbert Howard, all right, and his hand was raised in farewell. Frankie wondered whether he was wearing trousers. Probably, but she wouldn't have bet any of her one hundred and forty American dollars on it.

Frankie, Connie, and King Samson stood beside the crippled Model A and watched the dust from the Cadillac's passage blow off the cliff edge to the ocean.

"Gilbert Howard drives off with my woman," Samson muttered. "I hate that no-good masher."

"He's a wonderful actor, though," Connie said. "He acted with me in the test."

"Connie is good," Frankie added. "You ought to see her."

"Oh, shut up," King Samson said. Frankie was accustomed to bad temper at home, and she could see past this unattractive quality and admit to herself that the last few minutes had been pretty hard on King Samson.

"Have an apple?" She found a good one for him in the box of Newtowns. He bit into it and munched furiously.

Frankie would have bet her last éclair cookie that the three of them were alone on the lookout. Of course, the last few minutes ought to have cured her of surprise at anything that happened on this journey southward, and now she saw a hand rise into view at the edge of the cliff, clutching the chicken fencing. A moment later, the climber's other hand appeared, holding the gun. The climber's head appeared, and Frankie recognized the cameraman, Leo, among the cliffside mustard flowers. He rolled under the chicken wire onto the lookout, groaned, and cradled his shoulder. He was still wearing the same yellow suit with the bloodstains on the shoulder.

King Samson said, "Leo, give me my gun."

"I don't think you should give him the gun," Frankie told Leo. "I think maybe you should fling that darned thing into the sea."

"He's had this gun for ages and hasn't killed anybody yet." Leo handed the gun, grip first, to Samson, who pocketed it and chewed deeper into his apple.

Frankie passed an apple to Leo.

He thanked her. "Say, you're the two girls who helped me out the other night at the audition. After I filmed you with Howie."

King Samson snorted. "These girls told me they weren't in the business when they picked me up. Said they never thought a moment about acting in the movies. Everybody's a liar, right, girls?"

Frankie said, "We're not really liars, Mr Samson. We're actors. Good ones, since you believed us. And that's twice now you've talent-spotted Connie, sir. In the car while we were driving just now, and back in Vancouver, in the line-up outside the Dominion Theatre. Remember?"

"No."

He'll forget you the second you're out of his sight. Marietta had spoken truly.

Frankie persisted. "But you did pick Connie out of the crowd of young women, Mr Samson. And you said yourself you had wonderful instincts about these things. So what about giving Connie that chance you offered?"

"Stuff it in your hat," King Samson said.

"Ye gods and little fishes, what a grump." Connie sat back down in the car and rested her chin on the dashboard. Frankie bent down to have a look at the tire she'd punctured.

Samson tossed his apple core over the cliff, walked to the rear of the Model A, removed the girls' suitcases from the rumble, and set them down behind the car. "I tell you what: you girls wait for a bus to Los Angeles. Then, when you get to Hollywood, I'll return your car, and maybe we'll see about a screen test for the redhead."

Connie looked up. Frankie met Leo's look. Quietly she asked him, "Connie needs something in writing right now, doesn't she?"

Leo didn't answer because he was making swift progress through his Newtown, but his raised eyebrows told the tale. Frankie opened the driver's-side door and peered under the seat of the car. All she found were a shoelace, a linty piece of toffee, and a small penknife with a broken blade.

She turned to Leo. "Listen, have you got a pen?"

"Sure, I've got a pen." Leo frowned. "In the Cadillac Marietta drove off in."

Frankie let out a long breath. There had to be a way. There was always a way. Whether it was pursuing Connie's career in the movies or fixing a flat tire, you had to think around each obstacle as it presented itself.

"No pen. Too bad," Samson said.

"I know. Write a contract in the dirt and sign it," Frankie suggested. "Then Leo could take a picture of the dirt."

"Sure, if I had my camera." Leo tried his injured arm from the shoulder and cringed. "It's in the Cadillac with Marietta."

"I've got paper." From the Model A's glove box, Connie produced a gas station map of British Columbia.

"Too bad we don't have a pen," Samson said.

Frankie took the hatpin from her hat again, screwed up her face and stabbed the tip of her finger with it. While Connie held out the map for her to write it on, Frankie peered doubtfully at the drop of blood on her finger. "People always write things in blood in murder mysteries, but I don't see how."

Samson looked from her to Leo to the pin.

"Maybe you need more blood?" Connie asked.

Leo spoke up. "What about a verbal contract for a screen test? It's binding by law."

Samson shot him a poisonous look.

Sucking at her finger where she'd pierced it, Frankie said, "What a great idea. Thanks, Leo."

"Sure, use blackmail." Samson glared. "You girls will do great in Hollywood, if somebody doesn't shoot you first."

Frankie said, "It's not blackmail, Mr Samson. You yourself said you might want to use Connie in a picture."

"My lawyers won't let me make verbal contracts. I made too many in my time, and oh, brother, did it cost me."

Samson stared at Connie from the top of her shining head to the tip of her scuffed shoes. He scowled at Frankie, and at Leo. When he'd glowered at everything in sight, including the Model A, the ocean, and the late April sky, Samson reached into his inside breast pocket and took out a fountain pen.

Then an idea appeared to strike him, and he said, "Of course, I've got to let my lawyers look at it before signing, or it's void."

He put the pen away.

"Are you kidding?" Frankie hid her fists in her coat pockets, where she felt the sharp little diamond chip on her engagement ring. She marched around the Model A and slung their two cases back into the trunk. She said, "I guess that'll teach me to count my chickens."

"They're not your chickens," Samson snapped. "They're mine."

"Anyhow, it was a pretty cheap lesson on legal contracts," Leo put in. "There are harder lessons in the world, girls. *I* know."

King Samson kicked the punctured tire. "Shut up, Leo. Nobody wants to hear about your love life. And I'm having a very bad day."

Frankie said, "Mr Samson, your bad day may be the justice of Fate. Now, which of you can fix a flat?"

"You pretended to be a detective—deduce it." Samson shrugged, looking for a moment a lot like Leo, who also shrugged, winced, and held his injured arm close to his side.

Leo said, "There's room for four in a tight squeeze, as long as one of us rides in the rumble seat with the suitcases, Dad."

Dad? Frankie started and looked at the two of them. Leo was tall and slim. Samson was wider and not as tall, but the similarity was there, once she knew to look for it, in the ears and in the profile, where the line of the nose departed from the forehead. Father and son.

Of course, Leo couldn't be Samson's son by the present Mrs Samson, a famous female fundamentalist preacher who'd married him only a few years back. Leo had to be Samson's child from an earlier marriage. Frankie shook her head. Marietta Valdes had been right about at least one thing. Nothing was as it seemed in Hollywood.

"Leo, don't call me *Dad*," King Samson was saying. "Not in front of other people. Be professional, can't you?"

"Sure," Leo Samson answered cheerfully. "As professional as you and Marietta."

King Samson made a sound of disgust. "It's what I always say: young people know nothing about love."

Frankie shook her head. If she wanted to hear the same tired old parent-and-child arguments, she could have stayed comfortably at home with Sheridan D. She bent down to examine the tire.

Connie squatted down at her side, tucking her skirt behind her knees. "The tire coming off has something to do with these big screws."

"Therefore," Frankie reasoned, "it should involve something like a screwdriver."

"Where would we get one of those?" Connie asked. "It's not something I carry in my purse."

"Some gas stations sell them," King Samson interjected. "Start walking and you might reach one by midnight."

Cradling his shoulder, Leo stood over the two girls. "There ought to be a tool kit in the car."

King Samson leaned against the hood of the Model A and grinned. "You must be joking. Do you honestly believe that these girls would have remembered to bring tools along with them on a thousand-mile drive?"

"Sure we did," Frankie said promptly, wondering whether Connie had.

"Sure, Frankie did," Connie agreed, with a sideways look at Frankie.

"The car manufacturer must have included a set of tools," Leo said. "Look under the front seat, Dad."

"Feel free to look under it yourself," Samson said. "Personally, I have fellows I pay to do jobs like that."

But as he spoke, Connie already had the passenger door open and was rattling around under the front seat. "Here are some tools and things."

Leo leaned in the driver's door to look at what she'd found. He seemed to know how to fix a tire, but his gunshot shoulder would never allow him to haul on the nuts and bolts with one of the big steel wrenches. "Those are extra nuts and bolts," he said, pointing. "And there ought to be a jack."

"What does a jack look like?" Frankie asked.

"This is going to take all goddamn year," Samson said.

Leo said kindly, "It's a larger tool than those wrenches you're holding, Connie, and you'll find that it has two angled metal pieces that fit together."

"Like this?" Connie held up two pieces of metal.

"Yes, well done."

"Heaven save us from women mechanics," King Samson said.

"You're not helping, Dad."

Frankie looked at the odd-shaped pieces warily, squared her shoulders, and picked them up. She fiddled with the jack. It was made of double-interlocking angled sections, but any way she rotated them, the bits separated in her hands and somehow ended up in three pieces instead of two.

Samson laughed.

Leo stretched out his good arm. "Let me see the jack," he said. "If I use my knees to hold the bits steady, I can put it together. You girls see if you can't loosen the bolts on the spare tire."

A few moments later, Connie looked up from her work and grinned at Frankie.

"The nuts just fly off," Frankie said with a burst of satisfaction.

Leo cried, "Take the *spare* tire off. Not the tire that's holding the car up, for goodness sake."

Frankie took the jack from Leo. He had locked the connecting sections into place, but it was still an awfully strange shape.

"The spare tire first," Leo repeated. "Don't take any more nuts off that tire until the car is jacked up."

"What do you mean, 'jacked up'?" Connie demanded.

Frankie and Connie squatted down in front of the spare tire, tucking their skirts neatly underneath them once again.

Frankie asked, "Did you find that other nut that fell off?"

"No." Connie held up something shiny between finger and thumb. "I found the car key instead."

"Won-der-ful." King Samson kicked at the mustard plants growing through the chicken wire at the edge of the lookout. He laughed satirically, and at length.

"Dad, will you please not laugh? The girls are doing their mightiest."

"Put a sock in it, Leo."

The two began to argue again. Frankie returned to the job at hand.

"Bring your intellect to it, Frankie," she muttered to herself. "You can figure this out."

There had to be some way to get the jack into place and take the wheel off without the car falling over. She breathed in the sea air and the tang of the mustard flowers nearby. The sun was warm on the top of Frankie's hat, and she didn't need King Samson to tell her it was going to be a long morning.

Once they were back on the road, it seemed a long slog before night overtook the Model A again. Frankie had a hard time keeping her eyes on the road. If only it weren't her turn at the wheel while the rest of the party slept, then she might gaze her fill at the silhouetted limbs of the Redwood forest around them. She was sure the stars between the meshing branches overhead—Californian stars—were brighter and warmer than those they'd left behind.

She gripped the steering wheel tightly. It would never do to drowse, not when she was the only soul awake in this chock-a-block automobile. She squirmed under the weight of Connie's legs across her lap. Poor Leo, with his gunshot shoulder, was jammed up against the passenger door.

But King Samson had it worst of all—folded like a clump of linens around the boxes in the rumble seat. Frankie couldn't help smiling as his snores rose, one by one, above the *pocketa-pocketa* of the Model A's engine.

They'd changed drivers in Yreka and stopped for cocoa and doughnuts in Redmond. That darned Samson had paid for the gasoline but not the doughnuts. Frankie was certain that Leo was more of a gentleman, but he'd been dozing in the rumble with the suitcases since he and Samson changed places after Yreka.

The looming lights of a car travelling northward threatened her night driving vision, and as she fastened her eyes on the right side of the road, Frankie drove straight toward the trunk of an enormous redwood tree.

"Look out, won't you?" Leo fought his way upright.

"Watch this." She drove through the tree trunk and out the other side. "I saw that last car drive through the carved-out trunk, or I would have been a little worried myself."

Leo sank back in his seat. "Sorry I can't take some of the

driving for you and Connie." He touched his injured shoulder.

"I like to drive," Frankie said. The giant shadows of the age-old trees around them made this a stirring moment to be at the wheel. "My father tried to stop me learning, but Connie's mother taught her, and Connie taught me."

"Your father was probably concerned about your safety," Leo said.

It seemed almost a criticism of her driving, and criticisms had no place in a beautiful evening like this one. She said, "My father has many good qualities, I guess, but he seems to think I'm still eight years old. Or a baby — that's when my mother left home — and — " She stopped short. What was she doing, telling a stranger all about her private life?

"You're lucky he cares. *My* father," he said, jerking a head at the sleeping figure in the rumble, "doesn't care a plug nickel about anything I do. He doesn't even care that I'm engaged. He won't even meet her. Says he's got enough wives of his own to deal with. And, of course, 'that damnable Gilbert Howard'."

"You're engaged? Congratulations."

"You wouldn't say that if you … Thank you." Leo spoke even more glumly than usual.

Frankie shivered. She pulled over to the side of the road and idled the engine while she raised the convertible top against the night air. Leo struggled with his side of the roof one-handed while Connie and Samson slept on.

"One last strap and Bob's your uncle. There." Frankie plumped herself back into the driver's seat and steered onto the empty road.

"I've got a fiancé myself," Frankie said.

"Does your father know?"

"Of course."

"Does he approve?"

"Sure." Frankie remembered the night Champ had come over to listen to Jack Benny with Sheridan D. He'd broken the news of their engagement during the advertising break. Frankie frowned, picturing the bridesmaids she'd planned to ask. Connie would be maid of honour, of course. Hazel couldn't be a bridesmaid because she was married, but Frankie thought she'd have Hazel's daughters as flower girls. "At least, I think he approves."

She drove carefully along the road between the thick black tree trunks. Presently she saw that Leo had fallen back to sleep. In the overcrowded automobile, Frankie drove a little faster, wide awake and dreaming of Hollywood.

11

This was not how Frankie had planned to arrive in Los Angeles.

Not with King Samson, head of Monument Studios, hunched over the wheel of the Model A. Not with Frankie in the rumble seat, hanging on with both hands and jouncing madly with every turn as midday wore on to afternoon.

Frankie said, "I wish we didn't have to drive so fast."

"You go ahead and wish," King Samson said. "I'm in a hurry. I gotta put myself between Marietta and my director before she drives him crazy with her woman-director opinions. *Or* he up and quits."

"I'm cold and windblown," Connie said, "and bounced halfway to old age."

"Tin-can it," Samson said. "The two of you have groused and fidgeted for three hours, ever since we pulled over for doughnuts and coffee. Cold coffee."

"Tasty doughnuts," Frankie murmured. "And my cocoa was plenty hot."

The head of Monument Studios changed gears with a roar.

With Samson doing the lion's share of the driving, they'd stopped only when the tanks showed empty. Once the tanks were filled, they'd torn past Burma-Shave ads so quickly that they missed half the punch lines. Now it was Thursday afternoon, and as California deepened around them, Samson refused to give up the wheel, ripping through grim forests of oil wells and storming seas of pastel bungalows edged with white picket fences.

Frankie wiggled her knees around on the rumble seat and thought about things. She thought, for example, that even though he'd paid for their fuel all the way south, King Samson's shoe was too heavy on the gas. Connie never learned to speed up when she was taking a corner, like Frankie did. And Leo, with his wounded shoulder, never took the wheel at all. But they'd made it almost all the way to Hollywood, and that fact alone made her smile until the wind slapped a small bit of something into her eye.

She squeezed her eyes half-shut and blinked until they were clear. Palm trees along the side of the road cast shadows that flicked over her like scenes from a stuttering movie projector. Every so often an oil derrick, smack in the middle of the road, lowed and creaked as they passed, and for a moment or two the whole world smelled like petroleum. Frankie almost lost her hat to the wind, staring goggle-eyed at ticky-tack businesses like the Coffeepot Diner — shaped, by heaven, like a coffeepot. On the left side of the road stood midnight auto supply garages, shiny with stacked hubcaps. On the right lay junkyards, prickly with scrap iron. Where, Frankie asked herself, was the grandeur? Where was the glamour?

Where was Hollywood?

She pictured her father glowering over the rim of his sherry glass. *"Fool of a girl, look to the hills, whence cometh my help."*

Even from his bed a thousand miles to the north, her father was right. Frankie looked to the hills, and there it was. She nudged Connie. Heads swivelling, they gaped at the huge, crooked letters standing chalk-white against the green and brown hills above the city.

The huge sign read *Hollywoodland.* Frankie was so overcome by the sight that she had to remind herself to breathe.

Samson leaned forward and jutted out his chin, both hands on the wheel of the Model A. They sped like an arrow straight down the street. Ahead, the road widened into a palm-lined avenue busy with traffic.

A smaller sign on the roadside read *Sunset Boulevard.*

Frankie could hardly believe they'd arrived. She could more easily believe that the four of them would sit in this car, in a tangle of mutual help and enmity, to the end of time. But they'd made it, and straight ahead of them stood a pair of gates as tall and golden as the gates of song and story. Shining letters across a great wall read *Monument Studios,* and beside the gates loomed a pair of radiant statues.

"Are they supposed to be movie stars?" Connie wondered aloud.

"They must be," Frankie answered. But when she looked again, she saw the angels' wings arching out of the shoulders.

King Samson drove straight at the Monument Studio angels. Frankie hardly had time to brace herself with both hands before he threw on the brakes at the studio gates.

"Thank all the gods I'm back," Samson growled. "I half expected Marietta had burned down my studios. I hope to heaven I've still got a director."

Connie stood up from Leo's lap and gestured to the golden angels and the *Monument Studios* sign. "Is all this really yours, Mr Samson?"

"Earned twice over." King Samson yanked the key out of the ignition and struggled to untangle his jacket from the gearshift. Something thudded to the floor of the car, but he didn't seem to notice. "All I want is control of my own movie in my own goddamn studio. Is that too much to ask?"

"You're the boss, so I guess not," Connie said. "Say, can we come in?"

King Samson turned on Connie. "Can you come in? You mean, into the *studios*?"

"*May* we come in?" Frankie asked. "Please. We'd love to see around a real studio and everything."

King Samson slumped back down into his seat. His posture was that of a man who had been handed one burden too many by an improvident and unfeeling fate.

He said, "You two groused at me for almost a thousand miles. You argued and shoved like *I* was nobody and *you* were nobody — as if we were all nobodies together. And I put up with it. I tolerated you young upstarts on the long road south. And now we're in Hollywood. And I'm a producer and studio owner. What are you?"

Frankie said, "We're somebodies who did you a favour, Mr Samson. That's who we are."

"They're within their rights there, Dad." Leo followed Connie out of the car, holding his gun-shot shoulder. "We owe these girls a thank-you."

"Thank you." Samson smacked the steering wheel with both palms, and the Model A trembled. "Thank you, impertinent and complaining girls from the undiscovered armpit of nowhere. And now I suppose you want me to make you both big movie stars as a return favour? Would that be an appropriate gesture in return for a lousy little lift in your crummy old rattletrap?"

He banged his fist on the door. Frankie leaned foward and unlatched the door handle for him. She said, "Actually, it's my father's car."

Connie added, "And we don't want anything from you, you old grouch."

"Shush, Connie. Don't burn our bridges." Frankie addressed the producer's back as he climbed out of the car. "Mr Samson, we don't want anything from you except that you honour your verbal contract with Connie to give her a screen test. Not because we gave you a ride, but because you know from your experience finding talent that she *has* something."

King Samson replied, "Somebody once said that a verbal contract isn't worth the paper it's written on, girls." He must have seen their stricken faces, because he added, "Look. If you're good enough, you'll make it."

"You ought to owe us a favour, Mr Samson," Connie said.

"Sure I *ought*," Samson said, "if life were fair. But it so happens you have to work for what you get, girls. So go to work. Learn how to act. Catch my eye, or better still, my director's eye. Get singled out for your chance. I won't hold the last two days against you. Even better—I'll forget we ever met."

"How kind." Frankie's retort was wasted on Samson.

He said, "Good gravy, would you look at that?"

Frankie shaded her eyes against the afternoon sun and followed his gaze past the guard's glassed-in kiosk, past the high walls, to a window in what must have been the office block for Monument Studios. Framed in the window, star actress Marietta Valdes looked down at them. She gestured to somebody Frankie couldn't see and stepped out of view. Star actor Gilbert Howard took her place. He touched the tip of his finger to the side of his beautifully arched Roman nose as the window blind dropped and hid him from sight.

King Samson said, "Get a gander at those two. Marietta and Gilbert, fresh as fish and cocky as hell after a meeting with my director. They're trying to steal my movie. Goddamn glamorous pirates, that's what they are." King Samson banged a fist on the hood of the Model A and stumped off in the direction of the studio gates. He flung the guard in the glass kiosk a jerk of his big dark head. A small door cut into the larger gates opened to admit him and shut again with a bang.

Frankie turned to Leo. "Is there any chance he'll repent of his temper and hire Connie?"

"Who knows? You're in Hollywood, after all. Anything is possible."

"Applesauce." Connie turned her back. "You're all full of applesauce."

Frankie was inclined to agree. The temperamental King Samson was one thing. But, as the girls had given a much-needed lift to a good fellow like Leo, she'd rather expected that he would at least offer to talk to his father on their behalf. However, she had to bear in mind that Leo was the picture of a son under his father's thumb.

Frankie almost patted Leo on the shoulder, but she remembered his gunshot wound in time. "Don't mind Connie. She's disappointed. I never really believed that she could have a second screen test handed to her in the middle of the drive south. Still, we're bound to have some good luck soon …"

She trailed off, for Leo's attention had wandered from the conversation to something on the far side of Sunset Boulevard.

Frankie checked over her shoulder, but the street was empty except for the parked cars along the sidewalk. "Leo?"

Leo started. "Sorry, what did you say?"

"You must be looking forward to seeing your fiancée."

"Sure I am."

What was the fellow staring at? There was nothing across the road but a large Spanish-style mansion, its tile roof shining a bright orange-gold in the late afternoon sun. With its streaming bougainvillea and rattling palm trees, the lot covered most of the block across the road.

Connie said, "Hey ya, Frankie, what do you say we live in a house like that?" She pointed at the mansion.

Leo looked from the mansion to Connie. "Pardon? That house over there?"

"Oh, Leo, are you with us after all?" Connie sang, waving at him with a mock cheeriness that would have sent Leo's father — or Frankie's — into a purple rage.

"Listen, I've got to go. Good luck in the movies, you two." Leo walked away toward the studio doors that had recently opened for King Samson. Did Leo's fiancée work at Monument Studios? Perhaps she was an actress. Frankie hadn't thought to ask.

Behind Leo's back, Connie stuck out her tongue at him. "Bye-bye, Leo. Don't take any wooden nickels."

Frankie said, "Darn it all, Connie. You are sticking your tongue out at the only nice person we've met on the road to Hollywood. Who knows when we'll find another one? You might try not burning every bridge we cross."

"Where's your sense of humour gone?" Connie demanded. "Did you leave it in an Oregon café as a tip for the waitress?"

"Oh, tin-can it," Frankie said, in an approximation of King Samson's cantankerous tones. The two girls leaned on the cooling Model A. The breeze was worth appreciating, even if it was only one degree cooler than her skin.

The man in the guard box outside Monument Studios leaned out his little window. His hat was so big that it rested on his ears. He cracked his gum with a sound like distant gunfire. "You there, move that car."

Frankie felt in her pockets. "King Samson took our car key."

"Holy Moses," Connie said. "King Samson is quite the old stinker. Hey, Mr Guard, can you go inside the studio and get us our key back?"

The guard said, "If you gals had any brains, you'd have an extra key."

Frankie admitted that they did not have a spare key. "Could you ask Leo Samson to get the key from his father?"

"Please," Connie added. Most often, that was all she needed to say to a man, but Frankie imagined there might be quite a few lovely girls saying *please* to the guard at the gates of Monument Studios.

"It's beyond my listed duties," the guard said. "Look, you kids better move that car fast."

Frankie asked, "Would you please give us a push onto the street at least?"

"I don't even leave this booth at gunpoint." The guard chewed away at his gum.

The girls peered into the golden west to see a uniformed police officer, ticket pad in hand, working the shining line of cars along Sunset Boulevard.

Connie said, "What if we had a flat tire? The cop couldn't make us move the car then. Go on, Frankie, stab the tire with your hatpin again."

"We have no further spare tires, Connie."

"Oh, yeah." Connie slumped against the car door. "Am I stupid?"

"No," Frankie said. "You're a complicated thinker."

The guard wiped his nose on his sleeve. "Sure. And anyway, you got the looks. But cops are as cold as ice. Lemme show you something."

Either the guard was now revealing his gentlemanly side, or else his regard for Connie's good looks outweighed his duty to his glass kiosk, for he left his post and walked over to the Model A. "You girls might as well bark at the moon as beg King Samson for your key back. But that don't matter. Watch and learn." He groped under the dashboard and pulled two wires, seemingly at random, from behind the ignition keyhole. "Wind the fair ends together. Press the starter button. Got it?"

The Model A started up beautifully.

"I think so, thanks," Frankie said. She did have it. Or she was almost sure she did.

"If you separate the wires again," he added, "she'll stop."

Frankie studied the wires. She saw how to separate them, all right, although you'd think touching them would give you a nasty old shock.

As the guard returned to his kiosk, Frankie's fatigue fell away. She felt that she could do anything and handle any circumstance. Already she was not the same girl who had left Vancouver on Saturday night. For a start, she was a far better driver. And now she had even gained the skills required to jump-start a car.

Connie snapped a salute to the guard. She hopped up behind the wheel. Frankie reluctantly took the passenger seat.

"Let's find someplace to sleep tonight," Frankie said. "It had better be cheap, though."

"Are you bananas?" Connie started up the Model A. "We

just got here. Let's drive all over Hollywood."

"I tell you what. We can do both. Let's drive around Hollywood and keep our eyes open for a place to stay."

Frankie helped Connie fiddle with the clutch. Connie leaned into one of her famous swinging U-turns, close as breathing to the fenders of a few speedy sedans. As they turned, something small and heavy slid from one side to the other underneath the seat of the car.

Ahead of them, the street was thick with cars, but on the sidewalk opposite Monument Studios there was only one pedestrian. This was a California blonde in tennis whites. The girl was so pretty she looked as if, instead of growing up here, she had simply ripened like a peach in the perfect California weather. Connie sped up.

The girl stepped out onto the road in front of the car.

Frankie was too startled to shout a warning and too late to grab the wheel. Connie slammed on the brakes, but there was no time to dodge the girl in tennis whites. The front bumper caught her hip and sent her sprawling onto the curb. Connie jammed the car out of gear while Frankie pulled up on the brake with both hands. Frankie scrambled out onto the road and almost got herself knocked down in the blast of wind generated by a panel truck. The blonde sat down on the curb next to the back wheel of the Model A.

Frankie knelt at her side. "Sit still. We'll take you to the hospital."

"Don't." The girl pulled her tennis skirt straight across her thighs and buried her face in her hands. "I'm fine."

Connie said, "Were you in dreamland or something? You might have been killed."

Frankie sent Connie a look. In their secret code she hissed, *"Anna Karenina. Juliet. Ophelia."*

Connie took a moment with the code. "Gosh. Like Cleopatra? Only a car instead of a poisonous snake?"

The girl ground the heels of her hands against her eyes. "I'm lucky, I guess. I mean, I'm lucky that you two are such good drivers."

Frankie shook her head. Something had to be said, or this pretty young woman would go and throw herself beneath the wheel of another car. She took the girl's hands gently in her own and pulled them away from her face. "Getting yourself hit by a car is a terrible way to go, don't you think? I mean for those you leave behind. And so hard on the one who mows you down in her vehicle."

The girl looked Frankie in the eye. "I wouldn't kill myself. I was singing to myself. 'Dora Heart'. You know how the chorus goes. *Hi de hi de hi ...*"

Frankie didn't believe her for a moment. Still, saying so was no way to cheer up a suicide. "Around the world," Frankie said lightly, "or down the block, the song's the same."

"'Dora Heart'? Hazel's kids love that song," Connie said.

Frankie put her arm around the girl's shoulder. Poor kid. What would drive a lovely California girl to take her own life? Beautiful women had so many opportunities. Even plain women had options. Even women somewhere in between, like Frankie, had possibilities. "What's your name?"

"Puddin' tain." The girl winced. "Sorry. It's Billie Starr."

"Pretty name." Marietta Valdes's words echoed: *Nothing is as it seems in Hollywood.* Frankie supposed there was nothing wrong with picking out your own name, especially if you'd been slapped at birth with something like Etta or Lally. Even her own name, Francesca, wasn't everybody's cup of tea. She fully understood why the girl would choose a moniker like *Starr.* She wondered, though, why *Billie?* Perhaps after Billie Dove.

Billie Starr said, "I've got everything to look forward to, you know." Her eyes strayed to the golden angels guarding the gates to Monument Studios. "I had a contract for a little while."

Connie said, "Sure. You're beautiful."

The girl shook her head. "Everybody's beautiful. I've got talent, though."

"You've got that *something*," Connie assured her. "Right, Frankie?"

"Sure. Star quality, like Connie here. Look, Billie," Frankie said, "when you've got so much going for you already, all you have to do is work hard. King Samson himself said so." It was one interpretation of the producer's words, anyway. "You'll make it someday."

"I want to make it now. While I'm at my best." Billie Starr's eyes lit up, and Frankie saw how truly lovely this girl was.

"Me, too," Connie said glumly.

They helped Billie to her feet. Frankie smelled the drink on the girl now. Maybe she wasn't a suicide, after all. Maybe she'd been walking drunk.

"Thanks. I do feel better, girls." Billie Starr stood in the shadow of a palm. She brushed at the grey streaks on her skirt. Behind her, bougainvillea blazed pink against the white walls of the Spanish-style mansion. "Come on in, and I'll make you a little drink."

"Okay," Connie said.

"Only a soda, though," Frankie said.

But at a shout from across the road, the three young women paused.

On the other side of Sunset Boulevard, Leo gestured wildly at the three of them with his good arm. He'd never before appeared so animated, not even when Gilbert Howard had shot him in the shoulder.

He shouted, "Stay out of that house."

"Why should we?" Connie called after him.

Billie Starr shot a raspberry in Leo's direction. "Don't listen to a word that fellow hands you."

"He's a friend," Frankie explained.

"That's no advertisement. See you at the movies, girls."

Billie Starr knocked on the mansion door. It opened, and she vanished inside, abandoning Frankie and Connie outside on the walk.

"Hot patootie, what a dame," Connie said.

"She's not herself, that's all."

"You mean she's tippled."

"And in a spin regarding life in general, I'd say. I'm sure she didn't mean to be unfriendly." Frankie waved at Leo, who was moving in their direction on the other side of the noisy, busy street.

He called, "Come back, please, girls. Listen, I've got the key to your car."

Frankie called back, "Can you bring it over to us?"

"I'm not going near that house," Leo said. "Come get the key."

Connie said, "What do we need the key for anyway? We could jump-start it again, like the guard showed us."

Frankie reviewed the guard's instructions. *First find some of the wires, then press the starter button. Or the clutch. Not the brake, that's for certain.* "The key is a good backup anyway. And we'd better watch our step crossing." She eyed the traffic, fierce and smoky like Tolstoy's trains. "No *Anna Karenina* tragedy and mayhem for us."

"Mayhem, shmayhem."

"Abso-tively."

"Posi-lutely."

Frankie waved a hand to Leo to show him that they intended to cross, but traffic was so wild that Frankie feared night would fall before they found a break in the flow of cars. It was as if every vehicle ever assembled in America, every rattling trailer and chugging truck, had been lined up around the corner waiting for two Canadian girls to try to cross to the other side. Just when she thought the flow must let up, half a dozen battered, luggage-heavy vehicles turned the corner by Monument Studios. Old men sat at the wheel, women at their sides, young men and children perched on running boards and bumpers, hanging on by the ropes that secured their luggage. There was a rocking chair strapped to a couple of old mattresses on top of the first car. Was that a hip bath tied up on a car roof?

"Okies," Frankie told Connie. *Poor as gruel,* her father said of them. "Looking for work, I guess. I wonder if they'll get jobs in the orange groves."

"The Okies should try to get work in the movies, like us," Connie said.

One of the drivers, shirtsleeves rolled up, let loose a wolf whistle.

Connie whistled back. "We're really in California, aren't we?"

"Bet your bottom dollar." *This is Sunset Boulevard. That up there is a clear blue Hollywood sky. The air is velvet, and the flowers blaze in the sunlight. But a beautiful girl just now maybe tried to kill herself, and chances are that the Okie kid with the friendly grin and the whistle won't eat his fill tonight.*

In a week or two, a month or two, would this new world drag down Connie and her as well? There were a million hard-luck stories everywhere. But she didn't believe anything bad could happen to her or to Connie—didn't believe it deep inside, where a person keeps her luck.

As if to prove Frankie right, heaven sent down a break in the traffic. She seized Connie by the hand. The two of them dashed for dear life from one side of the road to the other.

12

"You girls have got to be more careful crossing Sunset
Boulevard. You could get yourselves killed." Leo Samson
stood at the curb, still in his yellow suit with its bloody
shoulder and grimy cuffs. Above him towered the angel
statues and office buildings of Monument Studios. The
sky had turned a deeper blue as the afternoon wore toward
evening, and the air was as warm as bathwater.

Leo held out the car key to Frankie. "I took it back from Dad."

"Oh, Leo, we don't need a key," Connie said. "Any mutt
knows how to jump-start a car."

"And then do you know how to put the wires back together
so that you can use this key?"

"The guard showed us how to do everything." Frankie
took the car key from him. And, even dog-tired in a strange
city without a place to lay her head, it was easy to recognize
this as one of those moments when she should count her

blessings. Frankie thanked him for the car key and slipped it into her pocket.

Checking his watch, Leo nodded. Although he was nothing like Champ in appearance, Frankie recognized the look in Leo's eye. He was the picture of a polite man with somewhere else he wants to be.

"Look here," he said. "Where are you girls staying for the night? You got somewhere safe to go?"

Frankie wondered whether they shouldn't park the Model A by the side of the road and sleep in it for free. She thought of the Okies, without homes or money, and made a fist around the little wad of dollars in her pocket. She began, "We'll buy a newspaper and check the advertisements—"

Connie interrupted. "That's the old-fogey way. Instead, let's drive around town looking for signs. *Room to Rent.*"

"Sure," Frankie said, although she didn't feel sure.

"Or how about this?" Connie jerked her thumb at the far side of the road where the mansion stood, framed by palm trees. "Maybe us two Vancouver girls will spend our first night in a fancy place like that. Maybe we'll ask Billie Starr whether we could stay overnight with her."

"She closed the door in our faces," Frankie pointed out.

"Then she can just open it again," Connie said.

Leo shook his head vehemently, but Frankie thought that sleeping overnight with Billie Starr was a brilliant solution, if she'd let them in the mansion. It was the sort of place that had dozens of rooms. "We'll trot across and ask her."

Leo said, "You shouldn't. It's …"

"It's what?" Frankie asked. When Leo hesitated, she added, "I really think everyone should finish their sentences."

"Or go to prison," Connie agreed. "It's very annoying in a man."

"I can't think how to tell nice girls like you. I guess I'll just say it. That's not a Hollywood mansion." Leo looked about ready to melt into the sidewalk. "That's a brothel."

Traffic tore past, lifting the hem of Leo's jacket and stirring the girls' skirts while the three of them stared at the house. Frankie had seen a brothel before—the time she fetched home her neighbour Irene's husband from a raddled old building in Vancouver's dock area.

But this was not a dock area. "A brothel, right across the street from Monument Studios? And you mean to tell us Billie Starr is not an actress after all? She's a …" *Prostitute* seemed a harsh word for such a pretty girl as Billie.

"A streetwalker?" Connie finished for Frankie. "And that's a house full of them? I can't believe it."

Leo nodded, and in his eyes Frankie saw all the sorrow a young man in a yellow suit could contain.

She said, "Gosh. It's the danger of Hollywood, isn't it?"

"It's one of 'em." Leo dug into his pocket and once again held out his hand. Another key lay in the flat of his palm. "Take this, Frankie. It's for a bungalow at Paradise Gardens, Villa 7B, a little further down Sunset Boulevard."

Frankie stared at the key as he held it out to her.

"We mustn't," she said.

"Mustn't we?" Connie asked.

Frankie said, "We both know that we mustn't. Thanks anyway."

Connie huffed at Frankie and took the house key from Leo. Frankie took it and gave it back to him.

Leo frowned. "Listen, Frankie, you gave me and Dad a lift when we needed one." He touched his injured shoulder. "You helped me out when Gilbert Howard shot me."

"Be that as it may—" Frankie began.

Leo flung his arms wide open then hunched up his wounded shoulder. "Damn it all, I'm not offering to pay the rent. All you women jump to the wrong conclusions."

Connie glared at Frankie. "*I* don't. Kindness is human nature."

Frankie scowled back. While keeping within the borders of his fatherly duties, Sheridan D had done what he could to substitute for her absent mother. Meanwhile, Connie's mother had taught Frankie the facts of life and general mores at the same time as she'd taught them to Connie, with varying results. And both parents had made one thing very clear: a young woman did not accept a gift from a man who was not family or fiancé. There was no way around the rule. Not so much as a box of candied peel was allowed. Certainly not a bed for the night. Because although Connie's mother and Frankie's dad never specified what a woman would owe — it would, one reasoned, depend on the sort of man in the case — she would owe the man something.

Frankie said, "Human nature is exactly why we can't accept that key."

A woman dressed in very smart trousers banged through the door from Monument Studios and pointed her finger at the guard in his glass kiosk. "I can break all those bastards, Dickie."

"Yes, Miss Carver." The guard leaned out of the kiosk window and touched two fingers to the brim of his cap. "Not me, though."

The woman patted the guard's cheek. "No, Dickie, you'll be happy forever here in your little glass coffin outside the studio gates."

Miss Carver. Frankie stopped worrying about a place to sleep. *Blanche Carver.* Blanche Carver was the star columnist for the *Los Angeles Morning Gazette.* The other two famous gossip columnists, Hedda Hopper and Louella Parsons, might have slightly larger readerships, but they couldn't compete with Blanche Carver's looks or her excellent grammar. Frankie shuffled her feet in wonder at seeing, in person, this former Ziegfeld chorus girl who wrote the Hollywood gossip column *Tell the Truth*. Connie stood, open-mouthed, and Frankie swallowed hard to steady herself. Back home, the only people she ever recognized on the street were ordinary folks—fellow teachers, neighbourhood children, and members of her father's former congregation. But it seemed that in Hollywood, there were giants everywhere.

The guard said, "I heard that under your suit jacket there's a heart of gold, Miss Carver."

Blanche Carver sniffed. "I've got no heart at all, Dickie. Don't need one to write a good story for the *Gazette*, especially when it's an interview with a liar like King ruddy Samson." The columnist put her arm around Leo. In softer tones, she said, "My darling child. You look terrible. Who's been bleeding on your jacket?"

"Nobody, Mom. Just me." Leo put his cheek against hers.

Frankie could have kicked herself for forgetting this bit of Hollywood dynastic history. Anybody who read *Movie Mirror* or *Screenplay* knew that Blanche Carver had been King Samson's first wife. Leo's mother would be a valuable ally to have in Hollywood, almost as important as King Samson. If only Connie could make an impression on the columnist. Frankie wondered how best to begin. But before she could set her mind to answer this delicate question, the columnist gave Leo a peck on the cheek and turned her attention on Connie and Frankie.

"What are these, Leo? More aspiring actresses for the movie mill?" Blanche Carver walked around Connie as if she were a statue in a park. "Well, this one's got something."

Leo nodded. "Reminds you of Janet Gaynor, doesn't she?"

"I don't look even an inch like Janet Gaynor," Connie protested.

"She's a Gaynor, all right, Leo. Like the last three or four you brought in." Blanche patted Connie's bright hair. "Actress types come in weather patterns, like hurricanes. We get a storm of redheads and then a calm of blondes."

Boldly, Frankie spoke up. "Where does that leave us brunettes, Miss Carver?"

"Lowering your necklines." Blanche Carver's golden hair gleamed as bright as the angels on the gates overhead.

Frankie shook her head. Another unhelpful giant in the business. Considering how much these people knew about getting ahead in Hollywood, they certainly offered little assistance to a newcomer.

Leo said, "Look, Mother, will you vouch for me with these girls? They seem to think I'm on the make. I'm trying to get them a place at Paradise Gardens."

"Good for you, girls. Wear purity like a raincoat, and it'll keep you dry. Mind you, Paradise Gardens is one hell of a nice place, and my son Leo's an honourable fellow. But I'm sure you're right to refuse him."

"He's a man, and we can't accept—" Frankie began.

"These are the rules of life, I know," Blanche Carver interrupted. "I don't live by them, myself. I live by the truth in a town full of lies. And a lot of liars made up the rules of life, as far as I can see."

Connie took a step forward. "Miss Carver, I want some advice about making it here in Hollywood. And please don't tell us to get on the road and go home."

The columnist said, "Advice? Here's some advice for you: all that young girls like you have to offer to Hollywood is a saleable pulchritude. Therefore, keep it on display and locked up tight."

Frankie and Connie exchanged looks. Their parents had taught them much the same.

"And listen," Blanche Carver added. "Forget your damned small-town rules. If you can't change your habits and attitudes for Hollywood, lord knows Hollywood won't change for you. That's my advice, free of charge. You won't get anything else for free in this town."

"Those two pieces of advice don't match up," Connie pointed out.

Frankie said, "Be quiet, Connie. At least she didn't tell us to hie ourselves home to Vancouver. Thanks, Miss Carver."

But the columnist was no longer listening. She said, "Darling Leo, take me out to dinner soon, someplace swank. After you see my doctor about your shoulder. And throw that yellow suit in the trash."

Without a farewell, she walked five steps away along the sidewalk and then stopped. With all the statuesque dignity of the Ziegfeld chorus dancer she had once been, she inclined her golden head toward Frankie and Connie.

"You kids will fit in well at Paradise Gardens. You remind me of myself when I first arrived in Hollywood. I remember stumbling into this town, my two friends and me, with a battered case bumping the backs of my legs, looking for a place to lay my curly head. And I remember how life took its own turns no matter how hard I hauled on the wheel." Hands in her pockets, Blanche Carver rocked on her heels. "Roads run both ways. Right, Leo?"

She didn't wait for an answer. Raising a hand to the guard as he leaned out of his kiosk, the columnist snapped her way along the sidewalk, smart and boyish in her trouser suit. She slid into the driver's side of a tan-and-red roadster with whitewalls. The roadster pulled out into the Sunset Boulevard traffic. Once it was gone, Frankie experienced a burst of unreality, as if the whole trip south were one of her youthful imaginings and she were really back home, sitting on her back porch, dreaming about Hollywood. Soon she would return to real life. She would water her red geraniums and warm up her father's radio in expectation of a happy evening with Jack Benny and his studio orchestra. She would sit on the porch and lean against her fiancé Champ while he smoked Camel cigarettes.

But when she took a deep breath, the memory of her life in Vancouver gave way again to the reality of California. The air here was nothing like the air back home. It was warm and dry with no scent of moist soil. Here on famous Sunset Boulevard, palm trees waved in jagged symmetry.

She said, "Okay, let's find a place to sleep tonight."

"No." Connie took the key to the place in Paradise Gardens back from Leo and pocketed it. "It's time to join the modern world and face the facts of life, Frankie. Miss Carver is right. This is 1934. We're in Hollywood, and I'm done with the old rules."

Frankie countered, "If we were in a Hollywood movie script, and if we took an inappropriate gift, round about two-thirds of the way through the show, payment would be exacted from us in some unexpectedly dire way."

Connie said, "But in the movies, your father would not keep sherry under the bed and your mother would never have walked away when you were a baby."

In the second's pause that followed this statement, Connie appeared to regret her outburst. But Connie never apologized. She only added, "Anyway, you're a respectable girl. An engaged young woman. You're old enough to think for yourself."

The trouble was that everything Connie had said was true.

Frankie said to Leo, "It's 1934. We accept the key. With thanks."

Connie breathed, "Huzzah."

Frankie slipped the key into her pocket. She looked up and down Sunset Boulevard. It was only one street among many in Hollywood. "Where do we find Paradise Gardens?"

Leo gestured with his good arm. "Follow Sunset Boulevard a few minutes west, thataway. Paradise Gardens is one gate past the Garden of Allah. Good luck to you both."

Here at last was another break in the traffic. Frankie and Connie thanked Leo and darted back across the road to where the Model A hummed to itself at the curb. Frankie climbed into the driver's seat, and for once Connie didn't argue. Frankie fiddled with the choke and contemplated the brothel where Billie Starr had so recently slammed the door on them.

Connie asked, "For cat's sake, who would work in a brothel? Not me. At least a girl could sling bacon and eggs somewhere."

Frankie said, "Such a thing will never happen to Vancouver girls like you and me." But she remembered searching downtown Vancouver for her neighbour Irene's husband and following a lead into a lobby that smelled like rum and Coca-Cola. There she had met a madam with heavy eyebrows and a cash box in her lap, listening to Jack Benny on the radio. The 'lady of the evening' Irene's husband had visited looked about seventeen years old, with her hair combed straight back and tied as if by a mother's hand, a grubby brassiere strap showing in the armhole of her blouse. The girl had asked

Frankie if she swooned for Bing Crosby. At some point in her life, that young girl must have decided, *I'll do that. I'll work in a brothel.*

Frankie leaned over the steering wheel and, with hardly a whisper of complaint from the gears, pulled away from the curb.

She determined not to look back at the brothel, but she did glance into her rear-view mirror at the angels at the gates of Monument Studios. She had always known Hollywood could make a beautiful girl into a movie star, but not that the same city could turn an equally lovely girl into a streetwalker.

"Billie had a contract." Connie sucked on her upper lip.

"Everybody's story is different."

Frankie slowed down as a huge black truck tore past. Her teeth rattled, and behind them a car horn sounded.

Connie put her foot over Frankie's on the gas, and the Model A sped up. She said, "I know that back home you thought I was special."

"Everybody did and still does," Frankie assured her. "You're so special that you almost hit it big on the road to Hollywood. But you know what you need to do now, Connie."

"What? Search for another sock-foot movie producer on the side of the road?"

Frankie shook her head. "Do what King Samson told us. Work. For once in your life, you're going to have to go to work like a hopeful girl does when there are hundreds and thousands of other girls trying to get the same thing she wants."

"But if I've got the star quality they're looking for … ?"

"Star quality gets you to Hollywood, but no further."

"I want to succeed or break my heart trying. Because I'd rather break my heart and try than get married to some fellow or other and live a stupid ordinary old life like … I forget what I was going to say."

"Sure." Frankie slid her finger into the ring in her pocket, rubbed the diamond chip with her thumb, and slipped it off again.

She looked back along the palm-lined boulevard in time to see Leo, in his yellow suit, step out into the busy traffic and lope across the road toward the brothel door. She said nothing to Connie. They had faced enough dark mysteries of life for one day.

The angels guarding the gates of Monument Studios cast their long shadows down Sunset Drive, and Frankie looked over her shoulder again to see whether, in perspective, they appeared protective or even welcoming. She thought they did not; the gilded eyes were too scornful and heavy-lidded, and the palms of their hands turned inward. They were aloof—but glorious.

Her heart did a quick triple beat, like the slide step Ginger Rogers took while dancing the carioca with Fred Astaire. It occurred to her that the movies were very like life in that everybody truly did have her own story. You wrote your own movie, and you starred in it. One way or another, you made decisions and stood by them.

With a warm wind tossing her hair, Frankie was at this particular sundown content with her choices.

13

In the few minutes it took to drive along Sunset Boulevard, dusk overtook the Model A. Frankie pulled off to the side of the road to park between an old flatbed truck and a battered motorcycle. The swinging green-and-white sign above a gate in a stucco wall read *Paradise Gardens Villas — No Vacancy*. It was lucky Leo had gotten them a place here already, and a good thing Connie had insisted upon their accepting it. Frankie patted the pocket of her coat, where the key lay next to her diamond-chip engagement ring. She smiled to think she'd soon discover what Blanche Carver had meant when she'd said, *You kids will fit in well at Paradise Gardens.*

"Can you smell them? Oranges." Connie leaned out the passenger window.

"You've got a good nose — all I smell are cars. But those are orange trees, all right." A grey-and-white dove flew low over the Model A and landed atop the stucco wall beside them. She never would have heard its call had there not been a break in the traffic, but there it was: a soft dove coo that sounded like, "*Who cooks for you? Who cooks for you?*"

They'd been sitting outside Paradise Gardens for less than a minute, but already Frankie was halfway in love with the place. It was so very unlike Vancouver, as different as Marietta Valdes's movie star–red dress was from Frankie's schoolteacher suit. Along this section of Sunset Boulevard, palms and orange trees shadowed the fence, the latter bearing fruit so round and perfect that Frankie thought it prettier than any fruit of the gods could be.

"*Who cooks for you?*" the dove called again. It seemed that even the birds spoke on cue in Hollywood, for she and Connie had nothing to eat since cocoa and doughnuts on the road into Los Angeles. The warm evening wind filled Frankie with an electrical excitement that had nothing to do with the painted oranges on her hope chest back in the blue house on Thirty-Sixth Avenue. Or maybe her excitement had everything to do with her hope chest, because that orange crate was a thousand miles distant, and her hopes for today were right here in Hollywood, California.

She said, "I feel like some big hand in the sky has just castled us at chess."

"We castled ourselves," Connie said. "Do you think we're winning?"

"I think we must be. But maybe it's like Blanche Carver said: everybody feels this way when they first arrive in Hollywood." Her stomach growled. Thank goodness there was at least one Newtown apple left to be shared between them. She'd heard it sliding around on the floor of the car as they drove. But when she wiggled herself around the steering wheel to look, there was no apple underneath. The object that had been moving around was King Samson's gun.

She picked up the weapon. She held it in both hands. The two girls stared down at it.

"That gun must like us," Connie said. "It follows us everywhere. Want me to hold on to it?"

"I'll keep it." Frankie slid the gun into her pocket — not the pocket with the key and her engagement ring, but the other, with her one hundred and forty dollars. "One of us can give it back to Samson. Again. If we decide it's advisable."

"It would be kind of an *in* with King Samson, wouldn't it? Giving his gun back to him?"

"If only he weren't such an ungrateful old so-and-so." Frankie pocketed the car key as well. Objects crowded her pockets: keys to the car and the place at Paradise Gardens, lipstick, money, engagement ring. Gun.

"You know what's strange? I was happy a second ago." Connie sucked her upper lip. "Now I feel a little shy."

"Connie, you weren't even shy on the first day of school. You're probably not even shy right now." Frankie pushed in the clutch. "You're tired and hungry, that's all. And we're out of apples."

"Think our place will have a kitchen?"

"*Who cooks for us?* We do. At least, we'll soon find out." Frankie climbed down from the driver's seat. "Let's leave our cases stashed in the rumble. I'm sticking to this gun, though. There's nowhere safe to hide it."

"I almost want to stay with the car while you go and come back and tell me how it is in Paradise Gardens."

"You'll be sorry if there's any fun and you miss out on it."

Connie exited the Model A, slammed the passenger door behind her, and slipped ahead of Frankie through the gate in the stucco wall.

Frankie reached up as she passed beneath the *No Vacancy* sign and tapped it so that it juddered from side to side. She nipped at Connie's heels along a brick pathway that led between clusters of pink stucco bungalows. How short and friendly were the palms, how pleasing to the eye the dusk-dimmed purples and pinks of the bougainvillea hanging at the windows of the little cottages. She leaned over a low brick edging and ran her hands over tangled blossoms so that they tickled her palms. Ahead of her, Connie jogged up the path to the door of one of the villas and moved a fan of green leaves aside to reveal the villa's number — 12A. The door flung open, and Connie jumped back out of the way of a bare-chested, laughing young man.

He pulled a blue sweater over his head and loped down the path, followed by a green glass bottle thrown by an unseen hand in the doorway. It smashed against the path, and they all three jumped out of the way.

A woman shouted, "That's the last time you leave me this way, Tom."

Tom tucked his sweater into his slacks and winked at Connie. "I've got to stop dating bearcats and blondes. Or blondes who are bearcats. What are you gals doing, coming or going?"

"Moving in," Frankie said. The broken bottle was followed out of the door by a blue-and-white plate that flew much better than the bottle had. She ducked. She supposed she ought to be put off by this first meeting at Paradise Gardens, but instead she felt rather at home. Her father threw things, too — books of sermons mostly, and with no better aim than the unseen blonde, toward whom the youth in the blue sweater was now blowing a kiss. Usually it was because Sheridan D felt he was not receiving adequate respect and consideration from those around him, and she supposed that blondes must sometimes feel the same way. Somewhere nearby, a saxophone wailed. She pulled out the key Leo had given them and read the number etched at the top. "We're taking number 7B."

"Villa 7B?" Tom frowned. "Sorry to be the bearer of bad news, dolls, but there are no vacancies at Paradise Gardens. Didn't you see the sign?"

"But we've got the key to 7B," Frankie protested.

In the face of these trim bungalows with their brilliant bougainvillea, sleeping rough in the Model A seemed to Frankie now as intolerable a way to spend their first night in Hollywood as it had earlier seemed to Connie.

"Sorry, kids. If it were up to me, you know?" Tom said. "It cracks a fellow's heart in half to break bad news to a pair of lookers like you."

Frankie shivered. Connie swore. The air had grown cooler as the sunlight became watered with shadow. Frankie slipped her hands into her pockets. She had a sudden wish to pull out King Samson's gun and wave it about, calling, *Sanctuary! I demand sanctuary for two maidens in distress.*

She asked, "If there were an empty place, what kind of rent would they charge?"

"Money's not enough. To live here, you have to be able to ..." Tom looked over his shoulder, brows knitting. "Maybe ... Like I said, it's not up to me. But do you ... ? No."

"*Sure* we do," Connie said. "Whatever it is you're stammering about, I guarantee we do it."

"Anything!" Frankie agreed. But, thinking of Billie Starr and the Spanish-style brothel, she added, "Well, almost anything."

"And we're pretty smart," Connie said. "Frankie here got an A in Classical Studies."

"And History," Frankie added, for what it was worth.

"I'm not talking about Greek myths," Tom said. "This isn't about Hercules or Ponce de León. What we know about at Paradise Gardens is movie stars."

"We know lots about movie stars—" Connie began.

Tom interrupted her. "Not what you read in some monthly movie magazine. We want up-to-date items for the news. Blanche Carver owns Paradise Gardens, and gossip is how we pay her our rent."

"No wonder Leo had a key," Connie said.

Frankie added, "So that's what Blanche Carver was talking about when she said we'd really fit in here. She wants gossip, right?"

"You're smoking now, kid. Gossip about movie stars is a business, and we don't reveal our sources to anybody outside Paradise Gardens, even under torture."

"Ha, ha," Connie said.

"I'm as serious as can be. And getting the secrets of the stars is hard labour." Tom raised an eyebrow. "We work days, in the hotels and restaurants where the great ones sleep and eat. And we're extras in their movies. How could new girls like you keep up, straight off the farm?"

"What farm?" Frankie bridled. "Do we look like farm girls to you? We're from Vancouver, Canada." She cast about for an appropriate reference. "Our Dominion Theatre has the biggest neon ceiling in the world, you might like to know."

"Don't take offence. I'm from cow country myself." Tom held out his hands. "But do you sophisticated ladies know any movie stars?"

Connie said, "We certainly do. We know Gilbert Howard, and—"

Tom interrupted her. "*Gilbert Howard?* Cripes, I'm supposed to be over there right now." He hesitated, and then added.

"Look, are you on the level about knowing Gilbert Howard?"

Frankie began, "And we know King—"

Connie nudged her, and Frankie stopped mid-sentence. There was no sense spending all they had by way of acquaintance when their mention of Gilbert Howard was still hot in the pot.

Connie said, "We know Gilbert Howard. We've met him twice."

Which they had, if you counted the face in the back window of Marietta Valdes's long Cadillac on the ocean road in Oregon. Frankie added, "He's quite an interesting character."

"Interesting? Gilbert Howard?" Tom laughed. "Maybe you do know him. Come on, then. Follow me. There are still no vacancies at Paradise Gardens, but at least I can give you a taste of Hollywood."

Tom loped along the path, which crooked around a corner between two bungalows. From behind them, the blonde in Villa 12A shouted out her window, "Good riddance, dames!"

"Want my autograph, blondie?" Connie called back. She slapped palms with Frankie, and they tore off down the path after the blue sweater.

Tom led the way around the back of a small villa into an overgrown backyard thick with bent grass and the scent of mustard seed. It was bounded by a gardenia hedge not much taller than Frankie. With a grunt, he pushed the laurel branches aside and gestured the girls through. The three crawled inside the greenery and peered through at the bungalows next door. The place on the far side of the hedge had something of the air of Paradise Gardens, but there was a more expensive feel to it.

Tom said, "Those are the Garden of Allah villas. Some big names in the movies live here, and there's not even a fence between us and them."

Frankie leaned forward to get a better look through the branches. She made out a swimming pool and cottages grouped around it.

"They have bungalows, like ours, but bigger and pricier."

Hollywood architects, Frankie thought, must all admire the Spanish style. Like Paradise Gardens — and the brothel by the gates to Monument Studios — the Garden of Allah bungalows were roofed in red and stuccoed off-white.

She sat in the dry dirt, among the laurel roots and stems, and gazed through the screening leaves at the Garden of Allah. Its swimming pool was lit underwater and glowed like a turquoise jewel. She experienced a moment of envy that vanished when she remembered that her suitcase in the rumble of the Model A didn't contain a bathing suit. The door to one of the white cottages on the far side of the pool opened, and Frankie caught her breath as she recognized Gilbert Howard: tall, lean, and — once again — bare of leg. His hair was perfectly tousled, and his shirt was mis-buttoned down the front.

Gilbert Howard covered a yawn with one hand while the other clasped the shoulder of a blond young man.

The young man stood on Howard's far side, so Frankie couldn't see his face clearly. However, even at that distance, there was no mistaking the look in Gilbert Howard's eyes. Good heavens, Frankie thought. She would never have guessed that Gilbert Howard, the great screen lover, liked men instead of women. But Marietta had spoken truly. Nothing was as it seemed in Hollywood.

Tom pulled a folded blank paper out of his back pocket. He scribbled something, peered out through the bushes, and scribbled again.

Frankie found that her coat was caught on a sharp twig and she shook it free. Something thumped to the ground, and she felt around for it. The gun had fallen from her pocket. She'd have to look for it.

But not now. To improve her view, she pushed leaves and branches to one side. She was rewarded by the sight of Gilbert Howard, that notorious lover of women — on screen and off — leaning down to kiss the blond young man on the lips.

As she watched, the young man unbuttoned his shirt and trousers and dropped both to the ground, revealing not only a complete lack of underwear, but a body unmistakably female, tanned, and lovely. This golden girl turned her back on Howard, sped naked to the lip of the pool, and leapt in.

"Good heavens," Frankie muttered.

At her side, Connie smoothed her skirt across her knees and grinned. "Jumping Jehoshaphat. We certainly are a long way from Vancouver."

"Not so loud," Tom warned. "We're spying, remember. It's no secret that Gilbert Howard likes his females to wear men's clothes."

Connie joked, "When we met Gilbert Howard, he wasn't wearing his trousers then, either. I just thought he was thrifty."

"Somebody ought to tell him men's suits come with a jacket and two pairs of pants," Tom kidded back.

But how funny was it really? Frankie remembered the first girl from the audition, crying her way along Granville Street. She remembered the movie star's boast: *Nobody says no to Gilbert Howard.* For a handsome man, and with all his charm of manner, Gilbert Howard certainly had an unattractive side. Frankie saw it — even if other girls, like this golden swimmer, did not.

Pencil at the ready, Tom shook his head. "No story here yet, unless some rube somewhere finds skinny-dipping an eye-opener. Still, it's always worth sticking around when Gilbert

Howard is living large. You'll see." He wrote something else on the paper, scratched it out, and wrote again. Frankie couldn't make out what he was writing.

Frankie heard the blonde girl call Gilbert Howard's name. The movie star didn't look round. He raised both arms and looked up at the sky. The only word to describe this particular moment, Frankie felt, was *impending*.

"Here we go. See how Howie is standing? He looks like he's on stage or in front of a camera." Tom readied his pencil. "When Gilbert Howard gets ready to spout Shakespeare …"

"Wait a second." Frankie leaned way back and scrabbled among the leaves and stalks. Where in the world had that gun got to?

"Lost something?" Connie asked Frankie.

"Clam up, honey. Watch," Tom said. "If we're lucky, Howie will give us his Hamlet."

Frankie sat back up. *Hamlet*, acted out in front of them by Gilbert Howard? This was no longer spying. This was spectatorship. And spectatorship had a corollary: its audience. She was Gilbert Howard's hidden audience. Frankie moved a laurel bough aside to get a better view.

Teetering a bit drunkenly at the lip of the pool, Gilbert Howard watched the naked girl swim the Australian crawl back and forth across the swimming pool. Her golden arms formed arcs above the water, like shining bows lifted again and again in the hunt. Frankie surprised herself by wishing she were as free a young person as this golden girl, willing to dress in a man's clothing and then take said clothing off right in front of everybody.

Gilbert Howard walked the length of the hedge that hid Frankie, Connie, and Tom. In a voice that seemed to rise up in a wave and spread out across the palms, the roofs, and the hedges around the Garden of Allah, Howard looked up at the sky and asked, *"What would it pleasure me to have my throat cut with diamonds?"*

"Oh," Frankie breathed.

"Is that Shakespeare?" Tom asked.

Frankie whispered, "No, it's Webster. *The Duchess of Malfi. Or to be smothered ..."*

Almost as if he'd heard her, Gilbert Howard called out across the roofs of the Garden of Allah, *"... or to be smothered with cassia?"*

Frankie held one hand tight in the other. She thought, *This is what it feels like when you fall in love.*

"He's the best ham in the business," Tom said. "Premium-quality, smoke-cured bacon."

"Be quiet, will you?" Frankie shook Tom's arm. "This is something. This is ..."

Gilbert Howard swung his body in a circle, his right heel the fulcrum, and came down hard on his left. His shirt tails swung out like a Scotsman's kilt. He touched his own neck, and in that particular moment she believed in his vulnerability as much as his strength. She believed that somebody would be pleased to cut his throat with diamonds or to smother him with cassia.

She felt privileged to watch him—free of charge. Gilbert Howard might be every woman's downfall, but he was also larger than life. Now that he was acting, he seemed in every way greater than the common man. He was somebody who ...

He was *Somebody.* There in the bushes on her first day in Hollywood, Frankie decided that she wanted to be Somebody, too. How did you get to be larger than everyday life, though? How did you get to be Somebody?

Was Gilbert Howard born that way? Perhaps a regular person like Frankie, a substitute schoolteacher who only dreamed of acting in the movies, could never be what Gilbert Howard was. Perhaps you needed to be born under a special star, or sired by Zeus, or constructed from very special family attributes that show up early and destine you for greatness.

So much did she desire to be like Gilbert Howard that she nearly howled with frustration. She put both hands over her mouth to keep herself quiet. At the side of the pool, Gilbert Howard avoided a splash from the naked girl in the water by taking two steps closer to the hedge that hid Tom, Connie, and Frankie.

Frankie pulled back deeper into the bushes.

Gilbert Howard raised his fists and shook them at the heavens. *"What would it pleasure me to be shot with pearls?"*

Tom muttered, "I'd pay money to see this. Luckily, it's a free show, like his skinny-dipping girlfriend there." Tom took a flask out of his pocket, uncapped it, and offered it to Frankie. She was thinking of accepting when the branches over their heads rattled and parted. A diamond of sky framed Gilbert Howard's face. He gazed down at the three of them.

Swift movement at her side told Frankie that Tom was tucking his pencil and paper out of sight. "Now we're in for it," he muttered. "He hates it when we spy."

But Gilbert Howard only said, "Young women in the bushes, coo-ee!" He held out his hand to Tom. Tom handed over his flask.

Gilbert Howard took a swig. He eyed Frankie. "I know you, don't I?"

Frankie took a deep breath. "Sure, Mr Howard. I'm —"

"Don't tell me." Howard took another swig from Tom's flask. "I don't want to know your name. You'll be the brunette in the hedgerow, and that's special, isn't it? Thanks for the refreshment, Tom."

Connie began to struggle to her feet. "Hi, Howie. Do you remember me?"

"Sit down, honey," Howard said. He hardly glanced at her. "Sit down before my swimming sweetheart over in the pool sees what you do to me. Say, what the hell is cassia? Does anybody know?"

"Cassia is a kind of yellow flower," Frankie told the actor.

Gilbert Howard guffawed. "If you're going to say something so wantonly intelligent, at least have the decency to wear glasses." The movie star leaned down and patted the crown of Frankie's head. "You know, you've got something, and I think it's a creeping cleverness. But brains are no use in the movies. *I* know, because I used to teach school long ago, in my first youth. Talent's the thing. Talent and hard work, damn it all. But if brains don't help, they won't hold you back, either, so take heart."

Gilbert Howard had been a schoolteacher. Like Frankie.

With a journalist's aplomb, Tom asked, "Say, what's it like to be at the top, Mr Howard?"

"It's like the top of anything, isn't it?" Gilbert Howard's smile deserted him for a moment. "There's only one way from here."

He took another slug from Tom's flask, tucked the flask into his shirt pocket, and walked away.

"Gilbert Howard doesn't remember me," Connie whispered. "It was only a few days ago, but he doesn't remember."

Frankie hardly heard her. She was too engaged in watching the movie star turn his back and walk, barelegged, barefooted, and a little stooped about the shoulders, across the pool toward one of the villas. He might be Somebody now, but Gilbert Howard had once been a regular fellow. And so must all the so-called gods and goddesses of Hollywood have started out as everyday people. They had talent, looks, and luck, but they were all human—Greta Garbo, Clark Gable, even Marietta Valdes—like Frankie.

"I could be a movie star," Frankie told Tom. "I've said it before, but I didn't believe it. I thought you had to shine, to have *something*—like you, Connie—in order to be more than just a bit actress. But now I see that if I'm good enough, and if I'm lucky, then I can shine, too. Like Gilbert Howard. And like Marietta Valdes."

"How come he didn't remember me?" Connie asked. "Men always remember me."

Tom said, "Maybe he'll remember you next time. Say, when you're big stars, girls, do me a favour. Get my flask back from Gilbert Howard, will you?"

Frankie felt the joy of unlimited possibility travel through her like cold water on a hot day. She looped her arms around Connie's neck and Tom's. "I've got a hundred and forty dollars," she said, which was more than she meant to tell a stranger, but this was one of those moments where anything went. "I'll buy you a new flask."

"You're the gnat's elbow, kiddo. And that was the best quote I've ever collected from Gilbert Howard, thanks to you two: 'There's only one way from the top'." Tom fought his way out of the hedge, and Frankie followed. "I'm going to tell the Queen about you."

"What queen?" On hands and knees, Frankie followed Tom the last few feet out of the laurels. It felt good to stand up, and she stretched her arms over her head.

"The Queen of the Extras."

Connie said, "You know, between Gilbert Howard and King Samson, I'm starting to feel like a broken blossom."

"Come on, petal. You've still got that something, and we've only been in Hollywood a couple of hours. It's too soon to give in to despair." Frankie dusted leaves and bits of grass out of every fold and corner on her person. She held out her hand and pulled her friend to her feet. Behind them, the Garden of Allah held its collection of big shots. Before them stood the back doors of several Paradise Gardens bungalows, cheap and cheerful but a part of the real silver-screen Hollywood.

"Where's the music coming from?"

In the distance, she heard the opening notes of 'Dora Heart'.

Tom sang, *"Hey de ho de hee …"*

Connie answered, *"Hi de hee de hi …"*

Frankie ducked around a little orange tree behind the nearest villa, thinking that 'Dora Heart' was like the moon. No matter how many miles she travelled, there it was. Then again, maybe all great songs were like the moon.

Frankie dodged a string of Christmas lights hung a little too low from a villa window, noting as she passed that the lights were made in the shape of parrots: red and green, yellow and blue, the connections loose and sparking. She remembered the gun she'd left in the bushes between Paradise Gardens and the Garden of Allah and turned back the way they'd come.

Tom caught her by the arm. "You girls like to dance a conga?"

Frankie knew she ought to turn back and make a proper search for that gun, but she told herself it was too dark to find anything in those bushes. Anyway, nobody else had seen it. It was perfectly safe to leave it there until morning.

With a feeling between her shoulder blades that should have been caution but instead felt like excitement, Frankie followed Connie into a crowded, open courtyard. They arrived at the centre of Paradise Gardens in time to see the sun set with a final flash of light through the slatted branches of a palm tree.

14

Frankie decided that she had never seen anything as lovely as Paradise Gardens Villas. Here warm air and a soft starry sky set the scene for a convivial group of young men and women who danced together in the tiled courtyard amid cottages and palms. Somebody had set up a gramophone, and conga music sounded large drumbeats like soft fists against her chest. In the middle of the courtyard, a small fountain bloomed and reflected coloured lights in its spray. Dancers snaked in a conga line around the fountain. *One-and-two-and-three. Kick!* She felt Connie grip her arm and hold it for a few syncopated bars, and then some fellow dragged her off to dance. Frankie was left alone on the sidelines. She moved a little to the music, wanting more than anything in the world at that moment to be dancing too, but nobody asked her. She supposed she must have a bit of the schoolmarm look about her. Not like Connie, who had already vanished from view on the far side of the fountain.

And then, without quite understanding how, Frankie found herself in the arms of a man she'd never seen before. She was smoothly integrated into the snaking line of dancers. *One-and-two-and-three. Kick!* She lost sight of the first man almost immediately, but it didn't seem to matter as she danced across the courtyard and around the fountain, her arms on somebody's shoulders and another pair of hands clasped around her waist. She looked over her shoulder, but all she could see of Connie — if it was Connie at all — was a flash of copper hair. Around the fountain — *one-and-two-and-three. Kick!* — the drumbeats pushed at Frankie, and she pushed back. The line ducked under a swinging row of Chinese lanterns.

And now they were all circling the fountain in the centre of the courtyard, where music nearly drowned out the splash of water. She looked about for the gramophone and spotted it on a table beside an older woman dressed in black and seated in a wicker chair. Her hands lay clasped across the bosom of her black dress, and her eyes were shut. Electrical cords snaked from the phonograph around a stack of records at her feet.

A young man's voice shouted in her ear from behind. "Tell me, sister, what brings you to Paradise Gardens?

"We want to live here. We're actresses," she shouted back. He called out, "The new girls are actresses."

The line returned a ragged shout, and Tom called, "Who ain't, darling?"

Tom danced across the line, took her hands, and put them around his slender middle. He broke her free from the fellow behind her then spiralled her in and out, around and through the conga line, so that she hunched as she danced under the hands that made the chain. Once — twice! — a kick landed on her rear end, so she learned very quickly how to duck and dodge among the dancers. Somebody turned up the sound.

Clarinets blared, and Frankie could almost see the music, as if it were written by hand across the roofs of the little villas, the notes shining as they rose to join the stars in the deepening sky. She stumbled and hung on tighter to the shoulders of the fellow in front of her. The sky spun overhead, and the bricks tripped her from underneath. Never in her life had Frankie been quite so happy—or so homesick. This place, with its laughter and unreasoning welcome, its heaving dancers under starry skies, its flowers and firecrackers and Chinese lanterns, made her feel sorry for her old home in Vancouver the way she'd feel sorry for a poor cousin wearing brown at a wedding.

The music switched to a jazz ballad, and the line broke up into smaller, chattering groups.

"There she is." Tom cocked his head at the old woman next to the gramophone. "The landlady. I told her you helped me get a great quote from Gilbert Howard."

Meeting the landlady of Paradise Gardens seemed to Frankie to be another of those moments that resembled dancing the carioca: you didn't want to get off on the wrong foot. Nevertheless, she tripped over the snarled extension cords and knocked the stack of records sideways so they splayed across the old woman's feet. Frankie bent and shoved them back under the gramophone, conscious of the landlady's stare.

Frankie straightened up and introduced herself. "Ma'am, I'm sorry to begin so badly, but my friend Connie and I would like to move into Villa 7B if that's all right with you. We already have the key and the previous occupant's permission. But I understand you're the one who makes the final decisions."

"Is that so?" The old woman bent, picked up a record, and set it on the gramophone. Bing Crosby crooned out 'June in January'.

"Yes, ma'am," Frankie answered smartly. "I used to be a

substitute teacher, but now I hope to act in the movies. How much is the rent, please?"

"How long is a piece of string?" The old woman looked up at Frankie from under a black fringe of hair. Her mouth was too small for the current fashion, and her chin appeared to have been drawn by an uneven hand, but her eyes were pools of beauty, dark and heavily lined with kohl. "Don't talk business to the Queen, girl. Make a wish."

The landlady called herself a queen? Something deep inside Frankie whispered, *Oh dear.*

"May I ask, queen of what? I can't tell from your accent ..."

"The Voodoo Queen, the Robber Queen." The old woman had a pleasant voice, firm of timbre and clear of consonant. "You haven't told me your wish."

"I ..." Frankie frowned. She'd hoped to have a fair and honest conversation with the landlady about moving into Villa 7B. And now a wish? When she and Connie had been little, they had scorned anybody who found a magic ring or a fairy but couldn't think what they wanted. They'd always had three wishes picked out just in case. She couldn't remember what her first two had been, but the third was a bottomless pocket of candy.

"I wish to move into Paradise Gardens," Frankie said. "And I wish you'd tell me what I have to do to get in here. Tom said something about writing reports on the movements of movie stars ..."

"Got any secrets?" the Queen asked.

Frankie answered that one with confidence. "In the last thirty-six hours, I've met two movie stars, both of them armed with a gun. I've seen an actor shoot a cameraman. Also, driving south to Hollywood, I picked up a studio head barefoot on the side of the road, and sat in his gunshot son's lap for the better part of the day. I saw a married man kiss his movie-star fiancée and saw that same movie star hold him up at gunpoint for a chance to be the first woman director in Hollywood."

Once Frankie had finished, she felt a little grimy of character. She had revealed other people's secrets. She wished Connie were beside her, but Connie was over on the far side of the courtyard, making friends with everybody in sight. As usual, not a man within range could stay away from her. Flames burst from the open top of an oil drum in the middle of the courtyward as Tom, lit up as if by the belly of Hell, leaped back from the fire he'd started. He held aloft an emptied gas can to general applause from the young people. Frankie longed to join the group.

The Queen murmured, "What a lot of good secrets you know. How soon can you get more?"

Frankie took a deep breath. "Might I simply pay the rent, please, and not worry about all these secrets?"

The Queen frowned. "No."

Frankie felt a pinch above her right elbow and Connie stepped up beside her. "Frankie, do you know, one of those girls over there is actually a fellow?" She gleamed in the firelight. "He says he's disguised as a waitress to spy on Clark Gable at Camillo's Fine Bar and Grille. What fun!" She looked past Frankie to the Queen and grinned. "You did his makeup, ma'am. The Queen of the Extras! Tom says your screen name is Loretta Desirée. Gosh, what a moniker."

"I give wishes, you know." Loretta Desirée, Queen of the Extras, inclined her head. "What do you wish for, pretty red-haired girl? Riches, fame, or love?"

"Fame?" Connie frowned. "Do you think it's right to offer me wishes you can't grant?"

With a warning look, Frankie kicked Connie in the ankle. Connie kicked back.

The old woman held out both hands to them. "Me? What

has it to do with me? This is how it is—you say a wish, and it comes true."

Connie said, "Okay, I'm hungry. I wish for something to eat."

Over by the oil drum, Tom put two fingers in his mouth and whistled. Connie stretched out a hand to catch something small he threw to her. A bit of sausage. She popped it in her mouth.

"That's exactly what I asked for. You grant a good wish, my queen. Go on, Frankie, you make a wish, too."

"I already did. My wish is to live here." Frankie shook her head. "She didn't grant that one, though."

Connie said, "Holy crow, that's not fair. Frankie gets another wish, doesn't she?"

The Queen said, "One more wish."

Was it any more foolish to make a wish to the Voodoo Queen of the Extras than to wish on the evening star? Frankie breathed in the smell of spiced meat. She screwed her eyes shut. What should she wish for—riches, fame, or love? She wanted all three. And a bottomless pocket of candy, too. But at that moment, as Crosby crooned and sausages popped and sizzled on the fire, what Frankie desired more than anything else was far more magical.

Frankie said, "I wish to act in the movies."

"Granted, provisionally." The Queen of the Extras tapped her nose. "You do know what happens with wishes. You lose your soul."

Frankie laughed out loud. "My dad's in charge of mine, and you couldn't pry anything away from him with a crowbar."

The fire in the oil drum crackled. The Queen stood up and yawned. Twenty years dropped away from her. "Not bad. Not bad at all for a first day. You and your pretty friend will fit right in with my lovely band of young monkeys. You have the key to Villa 7B? Use it."

"Thank you," Frankie said.

"You're welcome. And since you've got it, and nobody else here has a dime, it will cost you a hundred dollars for three months' rent, in advance."

It was far more than she'd anticipated. It was, in fact, the sort of rent you might expect to pay at a high-end hotel back home. Even in Hollywood, there had to be cheaper accommodation. Was it worth the investment? Frankie knew what Champ would say: *Frankie, keep your dollars close to your chest and deal yourself out of any bet that might lose them.* There wasn't much Champ didn't know about money.

But she'd made this money herself by substitute teaching. She fiddled a hundred dollars out of the wad in her pocket, leaving four tens behind, and handed the money to the Queen.

The Queen slid the bills up one voluminous sleeve. "You'll be glad when I remember these hundred dollars, down the road when *you* don't have a dime for the rent. In the meantime, learn how to keep an eye open for gossip. As for the movies, you start tomorrow."

"Sure thing." The woman was making fun of Frankie's dreams and ambitions. But she found she didn't much care—she had Villa 7B and all her future ahead of her. Or maybe she was too overwhelmed to mind. Anyway, queens did as they wished.

The record came to its scratchy end, the needle bumping against the centre of the disc. And in the sudden silence, a cracking sound rang out, like somebody had shot off a gun.

A gunshot. Somewhere near Paradise Gardens. Frankie almost laughed—everything about Hollywood was so far over the top. Even night noises sounded like something in the movies. Back home, she'd have known it was a car backfiring or a door slamming shut. Here in Hollywood, she'd have sworn it was a gunshot.

She laughed at herself as Tom dashed over, bearing oily newspaper spread with bits of sausage.

"We made it. We're here. We're in Villa 7B," Frankie told him. He slapped her shoulder and kissed the top of the Queen's head. Frankie bent and picked up a record that had slipped out of the fallen stack. She read the title and asked Tom, "Do you dance the carioca?"

"Never on a first date, darling. Put on 'Moonglow'." Tom flipped through the stack of records. Frankie removed 'The Heebie-Jeebie Blues' and handed Tom 'The Carioca'.

"Go to bed," the Queen advised her. "If you want to be in the movies tomorrow, go to bed."

"I don't want to go to bed. Not ever again," Frankie told her. "Even though you're probably right. But it's my first night in Hollywood, and I don't want to miss anything."

The Queen nodded. "Most young people don't take advice. I certainly didn't. Listen. Here's some more. Don't fall in love in Paradise Gardens."

"All right." Frankie swayed, eyes closed, as the first notes of 'The Carioca' rang out. *Don't fall in love in Paradise Gardens* was one bit of advice that the diamond ring in her pocket guaranteed she'd follow.

At a touch to her sleeve, she turned to face a young man she'd not seen before. "I don't know you," she said. "But I'm Frankie Ray."

"I know who you are," he said. "Frankie Ray, do you dance the carioca?"

"I do."

He was about her height, so she looked him straight in the eye. The fact that he was fair in his colouring from top to toe — suit, face, and hair — made his person a neutral palette for the coloured lights to play upon.

"But I should say that I've only practised the carioca with other girls," she told him. "And usually I lead."

"Do what you need to do," he said.

As the strings rose, the grey man took her in his arms, and she danced the carioca around the fountain, sometimes leading, sometimes following, her coat billowing out around her as if it were made of feathers. Finally, as he dipped her and swung her back onto her feet, she got around to asking his name.

The grey man hesitated, probably due to the switch in lead. "Eugene Ellery. That's what they call me."

Eugene Ellery! It sounded as phony as *Billie Starr*. Frankie slid backward and missed the fire by an inch. She joked, "Does everybody choose their own name in Hollywood?"

"Doesn't it sound like a natural name?" He smiled into her eyes. "Doesn't it sound like a name a couple would give to their little boy?"

"Nothing unnatural in alliteration," she said. "You know, they say a man will tell you everything you need to know about him the first time you meet."

"I'm a faithful fellow," Eugene told her.

"An attractive quality. I'm an engaged woman, myself."

She'd bet her bottom dollar he was a writer — a screenwriter. She took three quick steps backward and dipped him for a change. He smelled of Burma-Shave, like Champ. "I want to be an actress."

"I see. Quite a lot of nonsense, the movies, don't you find?"

She didn't mind a difference of opinion while dancing the carioca. "Then you're not a writer? Or an actor?"

"Aren't we all acting, all the time?" He laughed and dipped her in turn. "Great Harry, that sounded condescending. Let's change the subject."

Eugene Ellery's timing was perfect, because the music soared into a bit that Frankie had practised to perfection, and so she took the lead back and spun them round the fountain. When the carioca stopped at last, Eugene squeezed Frankie's arm and melted into the group around the fire.

"Has he gone home?" She took a swig from the bottle Tom proffered.

"Who? Our Eugene?" Tom looked at her sideways.

Frankie nodded. There was still a group gathered round the fire, but their numbers were dwindling. The Queen was nowhere to be seen. A couple of girls closed up the gramophone and packed records into a small leather trunk with handles. On the far side of the fire, a few of the fellows had produced musical instruments: a banjo and a couple of harmonicas.

Tom said, "Eugene Ellery lives in Villa 7A right there, doll. He's the boy next door to you two. Look, there's your 7B."

Frankie looked. Villa 7B was the bungalow on the far side of the patio, the one closest to the Garden of Allah on the next lot, not far from the bushes in which she'd so recently hidden to watch Gilbert Howard recite Webster's beautiful, chilling words. Villa 7B was hers. Hers and Connie's. The windows were all dark, of course, and because it was a place she'd taken without looking first, the unlit cottage should have had an empty look. Its windows should have looked like eyes, blank and strange and a little scary. Instead, 7B looked like a sweet, loyal dog lying in the shadows at the edge of the brick patio, waiting for her to come home.

Frankie took a deep breath of smoky night air and released it. Then, feeling herself fading as surely as the final titles of a movie, she stumbled in the darkness along the walk to the Model A. Connie found her before she'd hauled the suitcases halfway back along the path. Frankie gladly handed over half the load. Between them, suitcases in hand, they managed the door to their bungalow.

She paused in the doorway of Villa 7B, taking in with enormous pleasure the sight of the green plaid sofa framed by matching plaid curtains. To her right there was a dainty kitchenette with a kettle on the stovetop and a toaster trailing its cord down to the linoleum floor. Beside that was the tiny bathroom, then the door to the bedroom and a back door next to the sofa. With a whoop of delight, Frankie dropped her case in the middle of the floor and toppled onto the sofa. Outside, the harmonicas hummed a sorrowful tune, but nothing could make Frankie feel blue at that moment.

Already she felt quite the mistress of the house. She stuck out her legs and slouched low with her head on the back of the sofa and her hands in her pockets, where her fingers played for a moment with her forty dollars. She was tired, but she wasn't foolish, so she tucked her money safely under the sofa cushions. The gun was safe where it was, in the bushes behind their villa.

Connie swung open one of two doors to the right of the sitting room by the kitchenette. "The bedroom's cute, and there are twin beds and bedding. The bathroom's cuter. Don't know if it's clean."

"It's perfect. It's ours. And there's a toaster." Frankie kicked off her shoes and pulled her feet up beside her on the sofa, resting her head on the arm. It smelled a little of somebody else's hair. She was deeply tired, but at the same time she was keen to sit and listen to a few of the fellows crooning melodies outside in the square. She drifted and was vaguely aware of a blanket sliding over her as Connie lifted Frankie's feet and tucked them inside.

Connie whispered, "Are we in Hollywood or in Heaven?"

"Both," Frankie murmured. "We're sailing a sea of stars."

Moonlight through the living-room window woke her. It must have been very late, because the music had stopped and the moon had moved across the sky. She found her way to the little bathroom and used it. She washed her hands and face in the dark. She considered joining Connie in the room they were to share but decided she was enjoying her sleepy solitude too much. The darkness and silence felt as cosy as the blanket around her, and she sat up for a moment or two, her chin and arms on the back of the sofa, admiring the gleam of the oranges on the little tree in the backyard they shared with Villa 7A.

It was the tree they shared with Eugene Ellery. Frankie yawned. Eugene Ellery, she repeated to herself. And, as if by magic — again by magic! — there he was. Eugene Ellery was standing in their shared yard in the middle of the night like the answer to a Vancouver maiden's prayer — if such a maiden were not engaged to somebody else. His back was to 7B, and surely he didn't know she was watching him standing below 7A's rear window with a shepherd's crook in his hand.

Yes, with crook held upright, he might have been keeping watch over his flock, although there was nothing in front of him but the short expanse of their shared lawn and the hedge that separated Paradise Gardens from the Garden of Allah.

But it couldn't have been a shepherd's crook. That was silly. That was the sort of thing that came into your head when you were half-asleep in a new place. Eugene Ellery was holding a tall stick upright in his right hand, that was all. It was probably a walking stick. Or a shovel. She blinked heavy lids. Of course, he was holding a shovel.

The weight of her head dragged her back into sleep, and she dreamed of riches and fame, love and candy.

15

Frankie woke up in a little bedroom so thick with green light filtered through the curtains that she might have been in a deep forest. It was impossible to say what time she'd abandoned the sofa and crawled into her own bed here in Villa 7B, nor could she guess the hour now. At some point during the night she must have thrown off her skirt and blouse, because there they were, tangled in her blanket. She rolled over and bunched up the pillow under her cheek. Here she was—in Hollywood. Settled in Paradise Gardens!

Never was there a girl as lucky as she. Everyone should be so lucky. Why not? She understood, of course, that the world was in a tough situation. She hadn't forgotten the lines of cars hung about with earthly goods and thin-faced children, nor the open doors of soup kitchens near the waterfront back home where men lined up, holding their hats against their chests.

But if money was scarce, good fortune was free. *There's plenty of luck to go around,* she wanted to tell those thin-faced kids hanging on the running boards of the Okie's cars. *Leave home and pursue it. Break the rules like a piñata, and the luck will come a-tumbling down.* You didn't need money, though she was glad of her forty dollars under the sofa cushions in the living room. It wasn't money that had gotten her this far. It was persistence.

A bird called outside the open window. She sat up in bed and remembered how, when she was little, her father used to wake her with the old rhyme about the birdie with a yellow bill, the one that ended, *Ain't you 'shamed, you sleepyhead?* As she blinked sleep away, the green plaid curtains lifted a little to let in the morning light then fell back again. Connie's bed, the second one, was empty, and Frankie got the sense that she might be missing out on things on her first morning in Hollywood. The door to the bedroom stood ajar, and she smelled that Connie was burning toast for breakfast …

An unwelcome thought interrupted these observations: *I'm not supposed to be here.*

Sure I am, she countered silently. She stretched both arms and legs out wide, feeling larger than life in the little green bedroom. She gathered the bedclothes into her arms, chenille coverlet and all, ready to make her bed. Instead, with a bubble of happiness growing inside her, she lumped them on the floor and left the bed unmade.

Snatching up her coat from where it lay crumpled at one end of the sofa, she buttoned it over her petticoat. She called out as she left the bedroom, "Hey, Connie, what does it mean if you dream about a handsome man holding a shovel?"

"It means you ate burnt sausages before bedtime. Hey, Frankie" — and here Connie put on her radio announcer's voice — "*how do you know you've got a really great cup of coffee?*"

Frankie intoned, *"It's good to the la-a-ast drop."*

A short stack of burnt toast at her elbow, Connie leaned over the little table by the front window and set two places with bright blue dishes. In the middle of the table, a bowl full of oranges glowed like a good idea. The little kettle bubbled on the stovetop.

I should be back home in Vancouver. The unwelcome thought elbowed back in. *I should be sitting in a ladylike way on the porch step beside my red geranium. I should be waiting for Champ to come around.*

No, darn it, I should not.

Frankie shut the bathroom door on the smell of singed crusts and strong tea. She gave herself a quick wash in the little pink tub — hardly more than a sponge bath, but, after almost four days on the road, Wordsworth had it right: *Oh, the difference to me!*

On a hook by the little window, somebody had left a threadbare towel embroidered with a red strawberry and two green leaves. She dried what she could of herself with it and put her coat back on. Then she took a good look at her face in the mirror over the sink. Seashells glued around its circumference made her reflection look like a mermaid peering out to see how the folks in Hollywood lived. Hollywood folks: that's what Frankie and Connie had become overnight. Now *there* was magic for you.

Still wearing her coat, Frankie pulled two of the three copper-wire chairs up to the table. She took a big bite of dry burnt toast. It stuck to the inside of her teeth and had to be washed down with black tea. Connie made the worst toast of anybody she knew. Her method was to hold one finger on each knob of the flop-down toaster until the first lick of smoke signalled it was ready. Even so, for atmosphere, Frankie decided it was about the best breakfast she'd ever eaten.

It's about eight o'clock in the morning. I should be running out to the vegetable truck to buy parsnips and potatoes to peel for my father's supper. But she was here in Hollywood, and that was that.

Connie poured herself and Frankie a second cup of tea. "To us."

"Yes, ma'am." Frankie clinked a blue cup against Connie's. She was pleased to find the sturdy blue crockery in Villa 7B's little kitchen. A kitchen in a furnished suite ought to come fully equipped. And Connie's mom had packed them that paper sack of tea bags from Vancouver.

"Where did you get the bread?" Frankie asked.

For an answer, the door to Villa 7B snapped open and Tom strolled inside.

"I've fixed those wires in your car so the key will work again. And this is for you, the new birds."

He set a little glass pot on the table, bent over between the two girls to lift the glass lid, and, with a little tin spoon, scooped a bit of gem-red jam onto Connie's piece of toast. Frankie pulled her coat tighter around her and decided that privacy was a reasonable exchange for strawberry jam on your first morning in town.

Tom pulled the third chair up to the table. "Doris keeps us in jam. She works in the Beverly Hills Hotel on odd weekends, disguised as a bellboy with a waxed moustache since she got herself fired from room service for eating a pound of steak tartare. She saw Clark Gable last week with a fish as long as your arm. The chef cooks the fish Gable catches, but the lady who dined with him wasn't his wife. No, sir."

"Gosh." Frankie passed Tom a cup of tea while Connie peered into the jam pot.

He went on, "Mickey in Villa 5B gets the day-old bread. While we're still in dreamland, he delivers for a bakery to all the biggest houses . One time he saw Katherine Hepburn in men's pyjamas. She was all alone, though, so there was no story that he could sell."

"I think men's pyjamas would be comfy if they weren't too big for a girl," Frankie said. "Maybe I'll get me some."

"Me, too," Connie said. "When we're in the money. Yellow pyjamas with a green stripe. Say, where do these oranges come from?"

"From you," Tom said. "You've got the best tree in Paradise Gardens, right out back."

Tom took three oranges from the bowl and began to juggle them (the ceiling was a little low for the trick, Frankie thought), but one careened off, bounced on the plaid sofa under the window, and rolled into a corner. He ran to retrieve it.

A girl with honey-coloured hair appeared in the window over the table and introduced herself as Doris. She leaned in and accepted a piece of toast.

"Hey, chums, pleased to meet you. Nine-o'clock call on the Monument lot, Tom." Doris talked around a mouthful of toast, her elbows resting on the windowsill. "Powder your nose and meet us on Sunset Boulevard in an hour. Where are you two girls from?"

"Vancouver, Canada. You?" Frankie spread jam on more toast and handed a piece to Doris. She gave a second to Tom to take with him as he ducked out the door.

Doris took the toast with thanks. "Wichita, Kansas. I came west with a couple of friends."

Frankie started. Three of them, then. Marietta Valdes had said almost the same words on the cliff above the ocean before she'd driven off with Gilbert Howard in that long Cadillac. And Blanche Carver had said much the same about her own arrival in Hollywood, a number of years before

Marietta's advent. Frankie murmured, "Everybody comes to Hollywood in threes."

Doris said, "Sure. *Or* in pairs, like you gals, *or* quadruples, *or* on their own. My two friends went back home to Wichita a week later, but here I am like a bump on a log. I'll never go home now."

"Me neither," Connie said. "How soon can we sign up to be extras?"

Tom popped back in, snatched another piece of toast and jam, and said, "Girls, you're in. You start as extras *today*, courtesy of the Queen."

"We're extras? In the movies?" Frankie sat back hard against the wire chair. They'd been in Hollywood less than twenty-four hours. Frankie thought, a little wildly, that she could have used a little time to get used to the idea. "The Queen granted my wish after all."

"We're in the movies today? Jiminy." Connie stood up, her hand at her throat.

"You girls are mighty lucky." With a smacking noise, Tom kissed the crown of Frankie's head. "We leave in half an hour."

"Half an hour." Doris swore. "I'd better rinse out my snood." She grinned and ducked away from the window.

Connie swept the dishes off the table and into the sink. "I love you, Tommy boy. Now beat it while Frankie puts some clothes on under that coat. We've got half an hour to get ready!"

"Got an iron?" Frankie crammed the last bit of toast down her throat. Tom galloped off for the iron.

Frankie was half-dressed by the time it warmed up. She located a wall-mounted, pull-down ironing board in the kitchenette and did a slapdash job on their two clean dresses, pounding out the worst of the wrinkles with the flat of the iron. The familiar housekeeping task calmed her down and sped up her movements. With fifteen minutes to spare while Connie made herself up, Frankie checked that her forty dollars were still snug and safe under the sofa cushions in the living room. Then she rushed off the back stoop onto the sunny lawn and flung her stockings back and forth to dry them. Under her bare feet the lawn felt coarse and already dry, though perhaps they didn't have dew in California. Or in Heaven, either. She gazed at the orange-laden branches of the small but enterprising tree in their little backyard.

Opportunities grow like oranges on a tree, she thought, *and all you have to do is pick them.* Still swinging her stockings, Frankie caught sight of a glitter of turquoise through the hedge that divided their yard from the Garden of Allah, its swimming pool, and the rich and famous who lived there. Maybe she'd live there too, someday, right next door to Gilbert Howard. This morning she was happy to stand exactly where she was in easygoing Paradise Gardens, drying her wet stockings. The sky was blue, and the leaves were green. The air shone as bright as the neon ceiling in the Dominion Theatre.

Then, for the first time that morning, Frankie remembered the gun she'd dropped in the bushes between The Garden of Allah and Paradise Gardens. There would be time to find it soon — all the time in the world. She might look for it that night, if they got back from the studio before sunset. And if not, there would be the next day to search for it, and the next.

With nobody to hear her, her stockings waving madly round her head, she sang 'Dora Heart' out loud. *"Hi de ho de hee —"*

Behind her, somebody cleared his throat.

Frankie jumped. There between their two villas stood the fellow next door, Eugene Ellery. His skin appeared paler in daylight than when they'd danced the night before. Today, with his slender shoulders under a well-cut jacket, he appeared almost delicate, and Frankie hoped he wasn't ill. But although TB made you delicate, it also gave you a high colour, and Eugene certainly didn't have that. Frankie thought him very handsome, but nobody in the world was handsome enough to distract her from the happiness of the moment.

Still, he was very handsome.

Eugene cleared his throat while the cuffs of his grey summer-weight suit flapped in the morning breeze around his shiny brogues. "Could you spare a few minutes, Frankie?"

Frankie screwed up her eyes. "Sure thing, but it'll have to wait," she said.

He looked down at his well-polished shoes. "It won't take long."

In about twelve minutes, she would have to meet the rest of the extras on Sunset Boulevard. "I've got a nine o'clock call," she explained.

"There's something buried out back," he said.

She frowned. "In your garden?"

"Our shared garden, yes. And it can't wait for later." He met her eyes. "I need a witness while I find out what it is. I need your help, neighbour."

She was about to ask him to find somebody else in Paradise Gardens to help when she realized that he had called her *neighbour*. And now that she looked more closely at him, she saw the last thing she would have expected. In Eugene Ellery's eyes she saw not only his entreaty, but that of her neighbour Hazel back home as she begged for help finding a photograph of her dead brother, whose face she could no longer remember. He reminded her of the way Irene had looked when she came to Frankie, at the end of her rope with her wandering husband. And her neighbour Mattie, the bank teller, asking her why the hell he'd been fired, not knowing that the whole world believed his fingers danced in the till. Even on her first morning in Hollywood, Frankie couldn't let a neighbour down. On Thirty-Sixth Avenue or on Sunset Boulevard, to dishonour a neighbour's plea was unthinkable.

So, obligingly and with a certain curiosity—but keeping count of the time—Frankie slung her stockings over her shoulder. She followed Eugene across the grass to 7A, where he stopped. A little breeze ruffled the leaves of the orange tree behind 7B and lifted the white silk ascot Eugene wore at his neck. Looking down at the grass, he said, "There's something buried there."

Frankie took a step to one side. Sure enough, she made out the shape of a low mound where the grass had been cut away, perhaps with the edge of a shovel, and then relaid. The mound extended about six feet from the centre of the lawn toward the hedge that divided Paradise Gardens from the Garden of Allah. The buried shape was about a foot and a half wide, she guessed, and not quite straight.

She had to leave for the studio in ten minutes.

"It might be a dog," Frankie suggested.

He sent her an oblique glance.

She added, "It would of course need to be a very large dog."

"It might be a water tank," he said. "The kind they collect rainwater in, buried by former tenants."

"You're quite observant," Frankie said.

"A water tank of that sort is about the size of a human torso."

The sun was growing warmer by the minute, but Frankie felt cold.

"I'd better dig," Eugene said.

"With what?" Frankie followed his glance to the shovel leaning up against the side of Villa 7A. If the set-ups were the same in both cottages, the handle touched his bedroom window. So either she had dreamed a prophetic, Joseph-like dream or—

She heard Connie shout her name, and called back, "In a minute!" She looked Eugene dead in the eye. "I'm just wondering why you were standing out here in the middle of the night, holding a shovel."

He inclined his head. "I suppose not mentioning that I'd done so was—"

"A lie. Of omission. Why?" Frankie watched him carefully, but Eugene's calm eyes and smooth brow gave no hint of his feelings.

"People lie from greed, revenge, or love," he said. "Or from fear. So I've always understood. But, in my case, I didn't want to give you the wrong idea. Last night, I was going to dig up the mound, but on reflection I thought I ought to have—"

"A witness." She nodded her understanding.

Eugene crouched down by the middle of the mound in the grass. Barehanded, he tugged up a roundish divot of turf. It came up neatly and fell in a lump at his side.

From inside Villa 7B Connie called out, "Six minutes."

Frankie watched Eugene dig. It seemed that everything in the sunlit world of Paradise Gardens was still except the gentle, mouse-like sound of his fingers brushing at the dirt. He let out a long breath.

"I thought so," he said, hunkered over his bit of the mound.

"Is it a water tank?" But she knew it wouldn't be.

"No, it's not so much a water tank." Eugene brushed a little soil off of something flat and pale he'd uncovered.

Frankie looked hard at it, at the three little bumps next to a three inch-square plane planted with sparse, dark hair.

Eugene Ellery dusted the thing he'd uncovered, but he couldn't remove the dirt from the creases in the knuckles.

Feeling ill, Frankie sat back on her heels. Eugene was touching the body. His hands lay across the corpse's fingers as if trying to warm them.

With heartache, she remembered the time she and Connie had found a robin under one of the great elms outside Frankie's house. She had never forgotten the soft prick of the ruffled pinfeathers as she picked it up. The two little girls had knelt in the dirt, and first one, and then the other, attempted to stroke it back to life. In the end, they named the dead bird *Tige* and buried it with kindness, as Connie said, in a Buster Brown shoebox in the dirt under the back steps of the Rays' house. Frankie had been hard-pressed to stop Connie from kicking the next cat she met. And to stop herself from doing so as well.

Eugene rose to his feet. He looked down at his palms and then shoved his hands deep into his pockets. "Let us not give in to emotion."

"I'll do what I want," Frankie answered. She closed her eyes. She hardly knew what she was saying. "My father says that if emotions made sense, we wouldn't need them. Logic would see us through every circumstance."

"Four minutes!" Connie's voice sounded more urgent than ever, but this time Frankie couldn't find the words to respond.

She felt a warm breath against her cheek. Frankie opened her eyes to see Eugene Ellery's face up very close to her own. His grey eyes showed pink at the inside corners.

"Go," he said. "Join the others at your nine-o'clock call. I'm sorry I've upset you. Still, you've been my witness. My insurance, now that I can call the local police. You may have to give them a statement."

"Yes. Although I hardly know what I'd say. Aren't you going to ... ?" She gestured to the patch of uncovered flesh: the corpse's white hand, its dirty knuckles. "Aren't you going to uncover him?"

"Him?"

She nodded. "The hairs on a woman's fingers would be softer."

"Him, then." Eugene Ellery helped Frankie to her feet. "There's no sense in uncovering him. We'll let the local police handle it. Poor fellow."

"But if he's buried in your backyard ..." She couldn't finish without asking whether he was the one who had buried that body. But then, why dig a dead man up again? You'd have to be insane to do such a thing, and there was one thing she knew: Eugene Ellery was not crazy.

"Our shared backyard," he reminded her. He untied his white silk ascot from around his neck and wiped their hands clean, first hers and then his.

She asked, "Who do you think this was?"

He crushed the silk into his jacket pocket. "It's bound to be somebody's old aunt."

"Uncle," she corrected him.

"Somebody's old uncle, then, who died, and there was no money set aside for a funeral. It happens a lot in common spaces these days. Although usually they bury them deeper ..."

"So he's buried in the yard like a dog?" Frankie said.

"People love their dogs," Eugene pointed out. "Look, I don't need to give you any more nightmares about shovels. We'll leave him covered. Go. Do what you were going to do."

"I don't know if I can." Frankie took a deep breath. "I don't know if I can drive at all right now. I'll wait with you for the police."

The Extra

"Well, didn't they tell you? I am the police." Eugene Ellery made the sort of gesture that accompanied, in Frankie's experience, a person's reluctance to explain things she wanted to know. "I'm a policeman. Not from around here, though. This is not my jurisdiction. Still, now I've seen the body, I can call out the local coppers."

Connie called out through the back door, "Frankie, if you're not ready, the extras will leave without us!"

Was it wrong to leave the body here? To go off like a snap of busy fingers to be a Hollywood extra, caring about nothing but herself? Frankie would have liked to ask the dead man what he thought. She would say, *Excuse me, sir. This is an important day for me, but I guess I could say the same for you. Would you like me to stay? I'll give up my first day as an extra in the movies if you need me to.*

She tried to imagine how it would be to lie dead in the grass and dirt while a young woman, with all her life ahead of her, asked that question. She could not. All she knew was that she owed the dead man something.

Frankie bent down and touched the three pale fingers. They were cool, but not cold. They were much the same temperature as the cool morning air. Shivering, she forced herself to leave her fingers on his for another moment. "I'm sorry you had to die, sir," she said. "I don't know what to do right now to show my respect. Should I wait here with you and Eugene?"

It was hard to put oneself into a dead man's shoes. She closed her eyes and waited for an answer.

When a moment later the answer came, she didn't feel any sort of ghostly spookiness. Nor any sort of warning. The words simply came to her from inside herself: *You owe me nothing. One person waiting at my side is company enough on a sunny morning.*

Frankie stood up. She took a deep breath and headed back toward Villa 7B.

Eugene Ellery called after her, "Frankie Ray, you are a very unusual young woman. You've earned my ..." He stumbled over the words. "My loyalty."

Conscious of Eugene's stare, she stumbled up the back stoop into Villa 7B, where she found Connie in a frenzy of impatience lest they be left behind when the other extras left for the studios. Frankie snatched up her shoes and car key. *Hurry, Frankie, hurry.* She dug her lipstick out of her coat pocket, but her hands were too unsteady to apply it. She hung her coat on the hook inside the bathroom door. It fell to the floor, and she hooked it up again. At the last moment, she remembered her engagement ring. There was no time to hide it in the sofa with her forty dollars, so she slipped her ring into the pocket of her green-and-blue dress.

"Come on, pokey," Connie urged. "They're going to leave without us."

"Put my lipstick on for me, will you? My hands are shaking."

"We're just extras, you know. But I'm aflutter, too." Connie obliged and then peered at her handiwork. "My big chance might come anytime. Blot your lipstick on your wrist."

With Connie at her side, Frankie hustled out through the villas toward Sunset Boulevard. She couldn't stop thinking about the pale, grubby hand she'd watched Eugene uncover. And she couldn't stop picturing Eugene as she'd seen him the night before, leaning on his shovel under a starry sky.

Eugene is a policeman. He wouldn't bury a body in his own backyard. She was right about that, anyway, and she was also certain that Eugene had been wrong about something besides the sex of the corpse. The person buried — presumably with kindness — in the backyard had not been old. Those were not the knobby knuckles of an old man.

She caught sight of Tom's blue sweater vanishing around the corner of Villa 12A, where the blonde woman who played jazz records and threw dishes lived. She and Connie caught up with him under the swinging sign for Paradise Gardens. Out on the road, a pickup truck loaded with young people huffed and sagged as Tom leapt in. "Follow us," he said.

"Why don't we go along in the truck?" Connie stood on the running board of the Model A. "It looks like fun."

"We have to meet the Queen to sign up at Central Casting." Frankie slumped behind the steering wheel and fumbled with the key. "I'm kind of tired. Would you mind driving?"

"Sure thing." Connie scrambled over her into the driver's seat. "Off we go." Connie squeezed Frankie's shoulder and started up the Model A. Frankie was grateful for its loyal ignition and companionable chuddering. Before the truck and the Model A had covered fifty yards, the crowd of young extras in the truck bed ahead of them had begun to sing: *"Come away with me, Lucille, in my merry Oldsmobile ..."*

Connie sang along. Frankie sat and brooded.

"Down the road of life we'll fly ..."

The body in the backyard was not an obstacle. It was a sad fact of life. In these hard times, a man had died. For lack of money to pay for a funeral, somebody had buried him in a beautiful spot beside an orange tree. Worse things than that could happen in these times of want and need. She remembered the Okies in their dusty rattletraps the day before, and the sharp bones and thin face of the smiling boy who'd waved at her.

"Automo-bubbling, you and I ..."

She must pull herself together. She felt she owed it to Connie — and, strangely, to the dead man — to keep her chin up. She must not tremble. She would not cry. Neither action was professional except under directorial guidance for the sake of a scene. If she was an actress as she claimed, she ought to be able to wear the face of a girl who hadn't seen a dead body.

"Come on, gloomy," Connie urged her. "Sing out so that the others can hear us. *You can go as far as you like with me, in my merry Oldsmobile!*"

Frankie watched out for a place for Connie to park. Once she entered the studios, she would have to act a part. She would have to look and behave like a girl who still believed, as she had that morning under the little orange tree behind Villa 7B, that everybody in the world could be lucky.

16

To Frankie's eye, the Monument Studios sound stages looked like squares of white store-bought cake. Beyond them rose the fabulous tiled roofs and gilded pinnacles of the ancient city set of King Samson's 1928 opus, *Ambition*. Any serious reader of movie magazines knew the glittering buildings were constructed out of plywood and wooden poles. It was a convincing glamour, and Frankie knew she ought to be tremendously excited to see a famous Hollywood landmark. More, she should feel over the moon that Central Casting had taken her photo and stamped her paper: official acceptance of the Queen of the Extra's endorsement of Frankie and Connie to work as general extras in the films. But even here, watching the big gate between the two golden Monument Studios angels open to let them inside, Frankie couldn't stop thinking about the poor dead man in Villa 7A's backyard.

The two brand-new extras followed their Queen inside the gates of the studio. Connie touched Frankie's sleeve.

"You're awfully quiet, kiddo. Are you craving lunch?"

"I'm okay. You?"

"Ask my stomach, sister. It's got something to say." Connie stopped dead. "What in the world is that?"

Above the wall that separated one set from another, the black ears and snout of a dog-faced Egyptian god pointed straight at them.

Loretta Desirée, the Queen of the Extras, wrapped her arms around the girls' shoulders. "That is a genuine imitation of a statue of Anubis for King Samson's greatest film to date, *Ambition*. And I was an extra the day they burned the virgins alive. Girls, I was the first to fling myself into the flaming sacrificial pit."

Connie said, "How exciting! Did you land on a mattress?"

"Two!" The Queen's eyes lit up, and then dimmed. "It breaks my heart to think that tonight's the night they're going to burn the *Ambition* set to film the big fire scene in *The Emperor of New York*."

"Burning down the set of *Ambition*! What a travesty!" Connie scowled. "They should keep those Egyptian statues forever. They ought to charge visitors money to see them, like a museum."

At the thought of burning down *Ambition*'s beautiful set, Frankie tried to feel angry. She could not. All she could think of was that poor dead man in the back garden.

"Are you all right, Frankie?" The Queen frowned. "Your colour isn't good. And you look awfully sad."

"Frankie always comes through," Connie said. "Gold-plated and guaranteed."

"Sure." Frankie pulled herself together as best she could.

"First-day jitters! Without 'em, you'd hardly be human." The Queen gave both her new extras an encouraging squeeze and hurried them on toward the marshalling area.

Connie hissed, "Frankie, will you cheer up and start enjoying yourself?"

"I'll try." She *must*. Because they were *here*. In *Monument Studios*, ready to report for their *first day* as *extras* in the *movie business*. With these italicized thoughts she tried to drum up the proper excitement into the moment, but the memory of that dead white hand weighed on her like lead-lined luggage. Frankie pinched the webbing below each of her thumbs, an old trick of hers when she wanted to concentrate.

They rounded the corner of a sound stage to a gravelled area where a crowd of extras milled noisily about a coffee and sandwich trolley. Among the extras, Frankie identified Doris by her honey-coloured hair. She scanned the buzzing, cigarette-puffing crowd for Tom's blue sweater. She had looked right past him twice before she saw that although he was still wearing his usual sweater, he was also sporting a white skirt patterned with red cherries. He wore a flowered scarf around his head, with a few curls teased out.

Tom met her startled look with a mischievous, lipsticked grin. He adjusted the tie of his headscarf. "What are you dolls staring at?"

Connie laughed. "Look who's calling who a *doll*."

"You bet your bottom dollar." Tom swished his skirt. "This picture's set in wartime Paris. The young men are off fighting, so casting wants old men and young girls for the scene. Either I'm a girl, or I don't work."

"It's all par for the course around here. I don't even have to apply his mascara for him anymore," the Queen said. "How late are we, kiddo? Have these girls missed a shot?"

"You haven't missed a thing. We're waiting on the assistant director. And he's going to keep us waiting, bet your socks. As per usual."

"I'm due at Paramount for the voodoo scene. Look after these girls, will you?"

"I'll defend them with my very life," Tom said. "I'll lay me doon and *dee*."

The Queen kissed his closely shaved cheek. "And listen hard for what's new in studio gossip, all of you. Ask questions. We need seven new items of interest for Blanche's Tuesday column by this Sunday night." The Queen looked closely at Frankie's face. "Frankie, are you sure nothing's the matter?"

Frankie bit her lip. "I'm fine."

The Queen laid her palm against Frankie's forehead, as if checking for fever. "You look like you've seen a ghost."

"Do I?" Frankie tried her eyebrows up and then down. She quirked the corners of her mouth. "Better?"

"No." The Queen patted Frankie's cheek. "That's not acting, dear, that's mugging. I never guessed you for the nervous type."

"She's doing her best," Connie said.

"Look, if I miss the voodoo night scene at Paramount, I'll be snookered." The Queen slapped Tom across the shoulder. "Cheer this Frankie girl up."

Tom said, "I'll tickle her toes."

Frankie couldn't help feeling how unfair it was that she should have to deal with seeing a dead man on her first day of work. But how much more unfair to be dead oneself.

"Will you for crow's sake tell us what's wrong with you?" Connie demanded.

Frankie gave in and told them about the body in the back-yard. It was difficult to get the words out, for they wanted to stick in her mouth like dry biscuits.

"And you *touched* the dead man's fingers? I wouldn't do it if you paid me." Connie exchanged a look with Tom. "Would *you* bury your old uncle in a stranger's backyard?"

"Maybe, if there was nowhere else to put him." Tom shook his head. "It's a lean year. A funeral might set you back a couple hundred bucks. I'm sorry, Frankie, but you have got to rise above it. It's only the assistant director who's likely to notice, but it's better to go home sick than foul out. He already thinks we're a herd of untalented cattle."

"Frankie can do it. She's ready for anything," Connie said. Frankie nodded.

Connie whispered, "You're still pale as paper, kid. Do you want to go home?"

"Don't keep talking about it," Frankie begged.

"Thank heavens it's only the assistant director working with the extras today," Tom said. "The only way she could be luckier would be if it were the assistant to the assistant director."

Tom pointed out the extras' toilet block. Across from it, a line of extras waited near a storage shed for a cup of coffee. Most wore ordinary women's day clothes, like Frankie, Connie, and Tom, but a small boy in short pants with a cigar hanging out of the corner of his mouth held a cup of coffee in one hand and a sandwich in the other. Smoke drifted to the brim of his school cap, divided, and drifted upward. The smell of it made Frankie want to throw up.

Frankie asked, "Why is that child smoking?"

"Hey, Bruno, why are you smoking?" Tom called to the boy.

"It's a free country," the boy growled. But of course he wasn't a boy at all, Frankie saw, but a very small man in his twenties, close-shaven, wearing a schoolboy's cap and short pants and smoking a well-used cigar. Tom said, "Do you recognize him? Bruno used to be a child star in the single reels."

"The big time." Bruno grinned. "Now look at me, just an extra."

"Gosh." To Tom, who was dressed as a woman, Frankie murmured, "Nothing is as it seems in Hollywood."

Above them, palm trees lined the studio wall. Around and about, a series of sheds and crates provided shadowed seats for at least fifty extras. They appeared a happy-go-lucky brigade of men and women, chatting over cups of coffee and smokes.

"How about a sandwich?" Connie asked. "I'll get you one."

"I'm not hungry, thanks," Frankie answered, but Connie returned with a sandwich and insisted Frankie take it. Cheese. That was good. If it had been tomato, she wouldn't be able to slip it into her pocket for later, as she did now.

Through a wide gap between the buildings, she spotted a camera — no, two — like the one Leo had brought to the Vancouver audition. In the centre of an open space stood a weather-darkened bronze statue of a soldier astride a horse. Even from this distance, she observed that the horse had three feet on the ground and one raised, as if to advance across the square. All in all, the square looked to Frankie's eye quite believably Parisian. In the shadows of a pillared façade that looked like a bank, two men in fedoras stood head to head, jutting their chins at an argumentative tilt. It reminded her of Leo and Gilbert Howard, which in turn reminded her of the way Connie had frozen in front of the camera. She mustn't allow that to happen again.

"Say," Frankie asked Tom, "do any of these professionals know how to deal with a case of camera shyness?"

She caught the pointy end of Connie's look and added quickly, "It happens to me sometimes." She whispered in

Connie's ear, "For Pete's sake, I'm not about to tell anybody it happened to *you*."

"It won't happen again, you'll see," Connie hissed back.

"Girls, there's one thing you can get for free in this town, and that's advice." Tom waved a crowd of other extras over and spread their names around until Frankie was thoroughly confused.

"Camera shyness?" Doris chewed on the rim of her paper cup. "I know a girl who beat it through breathing. Count to ten, and then puff into a paper bag." She put her hand to her belly and sucked in the air loudly.

"Okay. Like this?" Frankie sucked in her breath and Connie followed suit.

A grey-haired fellow in a pinstriped jacket piped up. "Freezing up in front of the camera is simply a result of lack of preparation. As professionals, you must learn your lines."

"We don't have any lines," Tom pointed out. "We're *extras*."

"Gilbert Howard forgets his lines all the time these days," a young woman in blue said. "And nobody kicks him off the lot when he starts spouting Shakespeare instead of his real lines in the middle of a speakeasy scene."

A professional argument developed between Doris and the man in the pinstriped jacket.

"You people have missed the mark," an elderly man in rusty black interrupted. "The trick is to communicate with the audience, to imagine their support, as if you were on stage and could feel their presence in the dark."

"Really?" Connie asked. "That sounds so complicated."

"*Booze.* There's your mother courage." Bruno shifted his cigar from one side of his mouth to the other, reached into the back pocket of his schoolboy trousers, and pulled out a leather-covered flask.

"*What* were they all again?" Connie looked from one extra to another, blinked, and counted on her fingers.

The sun moved across the sky and the extras waited patiently, if not quietly, scoffing cup after cup of coffee. The sandwiches had long been demolished, and Frankie judged it to be nearing three o'clock by the time one of the two chin-jutting arguers in fedoras and long raincoats stepped into the waiting area. He barked, "All right, girls and boys, we're ready for the take."

"The assistant director," Doris explained.

"From his crooked toes to his pointed head," Bruno added.

Frankie's legs felt heavy. Her throat was dry. On the positive side, though, her knees were steady. Around her, she sensed a rustle of professional reluctance, as if the extras were soldiers rallied to the front. The crowd crushed cigarette butts into paper coffee cups, set them down in the gravel around the storage shacks, and made their way onto the set. They stood in a bunch in the middle of the square, between the statue and the bank building.

The assistant director took off his fedora and scratched a bald spot. "Listen, you lugs. You're meant to gather in this here square, in groupings of two or threes, and walk where we showed you this morning. No mugging for attention. Do what you're paid for. And you—yeah, *you*, Bruno the Kid—try to look like you didn't slit your mother's throat."

At Frankie's side, Bruno muttered, "The only way I'd get less respect is if I were a woman." A snicker rippled through the extras nearest him.

"Shut up. And by the way," the director's assistant added, "anybody looks at the camera, I'll personally remove both your eyes."

"Charming," a pretty girl in purple laughed. Her hair was damp but combed, and her dress stuck to her in several places.

"You—put some underwear on next time," the assistant director retorted. "And walk behind somebody today. Only stars have nipples, kid."

The girl in purple pulled a moue. The extras moved onto the set.

"Here, take the car keys," Connie whispered. "I don't want anything spoiling the line of my dress. And give me that sandwich, will you? I want to make a wish. Like on a turkey wishbone."

Frankie dropped the keys to the car and the bungalow into her left pocket and pulled her uneaten cheese sandwich out of her right. Connie took hold of one side of it and pulled it in two. Frankie stared at the smaller portion that was left in her hand.

"I'm making a wish." Connie closed her eyes for a second and then opened them wide while she ate the bit of sandwich. "Frankie, the wish came true. We're in the movies."

"Don't bet on it," Bruno said from behind them. "Like as not, we'll all end up on the cutting-room floor."

"Either way, we're on film." Frankie put what was left of the sandwich back into her pocket. She held out her unsteady left hand and Connie pressed her palm against it. "For luck."

Connie held tight to Frankie's arm. They followed Tom, Bruno, and the other extras across the square. The assistant director jerked his thumb up. Did that mean the cameras were rolling, or was this a rehearsal? She supposed it didn't matter. She'd do her best either way. She and Connie walked around the statue of the soldier on his horse. Frankie felt more like an awkward automaton than an actress, so to add a little realism and to keep from looking at the camera, she gazed up at the mighty horse. At close quarters, Frankie could see that it was not cast in bronze but in painted plaster. She wondered what her father would say if he could see her right now on this movie sound stage. Probably he'd say, *Frankie, when a statue horse has four feet on the ground, it means the rider died in bed. Three legs on the ground means wounded in combat.* Like he hadn't told her a thousand times. *When the horse has two legs off the ground, it means the rider died in battle.*

"Act like I'm talking to you, Connie," she suggested. They walked arm in arm like the schoolgirls they had recently been, across to the edge of the square. There, Connie stumbled a little on a flowerbed made of brown burlap.

"Cut," the assistant director called. For a terrible moment, Frankie feared he had cut the take because of Connie's error. But no voices were raised, and Connie was not picked out of the crowd, so he must not have noticed. Around the square, cameramen chewed gum and leaned on their cameras.

"Anyway, I didn't freeze," Connie hissed. "Was the camera on me when I tripped?"

"I don't know. After the assistant director's threat, I was looking everywhere except at the camera. Anyway, people trip in real life. I think it's a good bit of business." Frankie squeezed Connie's shoulder. "There! We're on film. *Klahowya.*"

"*Klahowya.*" They grinned at each other.

Frankie would later remember this as the last carefree moment of her young life before everything changed.

From the left, somebody shouted, "*You.*"

An extra on the other side of the lot asked, "Who?"

"*That* one." Across the lot, a woman in a bright-red dress shaded her face with one hand. Marietta Valdes carried her shoes by their slender straps. She walked barefoot past the assistant director toward the extras. She was joined by a man in black Frankie had never seen before. On Marietta's other side strode King Samson.

177

The Extra

Frankie had a craven impulse to run and hide. She braced herself with the thought that she was an extra, one of a group of extras. And this group appeared to have no keen interest in Marietta Valdes the movie star, or even in King Samson the producer. No, it was the man in black who drew all eyes. The extras turned to him like sunflowers to the light.

Frankie had seen the man in black's picture in the movie magazines. He was a well-known director. Her heart filled with a sensation that was not exactly new, but one she had never before identified. It was the feeling that an important moment loomed, and that a turning point approached. Simply by participating in her small way in the making of a film, she was poised atop the fulcrum around which the world rotated. She might be nobody, but she was in the movies. She couldn't wish for anything more, she thought, wishing all the while for a real live part. She wondered whether the others — Connie, Tom, Doris, Bruno, and all the other extras — felt the same.

"You," the director said. He nodded to Connie as she stood at Frankie's side. "Come here. I want to use you in a shot."

Connie caught one hand with the other and held them tight to her middle. She stepped forward.

Frankie whispered, "I *knew* they'd pick you."

An angel out of a row of kewpie dolls. That's what they said about Marietta Valdes. And now they'd say it about Connie.

The director shook his head. "Not you. *You.* You, with the sorrowful phiz."

Connie stepped back uncertainly. Frankie pushed Connie forward again.

"Are you deaf? Not the redhead." The director was waving both hands. "*You,* the sad sack. The pale and mournful brunette. You're the one I want."

Connie stepped back. Director, star, extras, and cameramen—everybody stared at Frankie. To her horror, she found herself shifting uncomfortably from one foot to the other. Shifting weight was the certain identifying mark of the amateur actor.

She held herself still.

It was the strangest thing: standing barefaced and alone in front of the director caused her peripheral vision to blur and her concentration to narrow to the point where she could hold only one thought at a time. The rest of her mind, the unused bits, felt as if she'd wrapped them up in greyish batting and put them in a bottom bureau drawer. She did her best to concentrate on the director's scowling face.

Frankie blurted out, "What would you like me to do?" There was something wrong with that sentence. She added, "Sir?"

The director looked at the assistant director.

The assistant director barked, "Do what you're told."

"Do what we chose you to do." The director grinned around the cigar in his mouth. "Look sad, kid."

One of the extras laughed. There was a shifting sound, as if from a crowd of grass-skirted kewpie dolls. Behind the extras, the back of King Samson's camel-coloured coat flew out behind him as he stormed off the set.

17

Frankie faced the director. She was distantly aware of Marietta's red dress, the movie set of a square in Paris, the enormous gleaming cameras, and the crowd of staring extras. If she didn't grasp this chance at a part, even one without words, one of the other extras surely would.

Look sad, kid.

Frankie checked her physical position. It wouldn't do to put her hands in her pockets, so she cupped one hand inside the other to stop her fingers shaking. She guessed that amateur actors, if asked to look sad, would screw up their eyebrows and cry. Instead, Frankie did nothing but think about the body behind Villa 7A. It wasn't difficult — she hadn't stopped thinking about that poor man all morning.

The director grunted and tapped the ash from his cigar.

"I told you," Marietta Valdes said. "She is right for this scene."

"There's no screen credit in it," the assistant director told Frankie. "And same pay—as a general extra."

This was rather unfair, but she said, "Yes, sir."

"Don't talk. You have no lines." The assistant director jerked a thumb at the pedestal underneath the statue of the soldier on the horse. "Where's that damned pigeon handler?"

A cooing, bird-filled box on legs stumbled out of the crowd of extras, and the pigeon handler set the box down at the edge of the square. He opened the wire net door and shooed a small but talkative flock of pigeons toward her. She managed not to take a step back as the flock approached.

The assistant director pointed his chin at Frankie. "Sit on the pedestal, in front of the statue, pigeon girl. Feed the pigeons. And don't make it look like you're enjoying yourself."

Frankie nodded. Would they give her something with which to feed the pigeons? Birds could not be expected to act.

The director himself spoke again. "And don't make it look too easy. Don't throw it away, you know what I'm saying?"

"Yes, sir." She knew exactly what he was saying. Not everyone would, she supposed, but she did. The director wanted focus and sorrow.

She sat down among the pigeons on the grey-painted wooden pedestal by the statue's hoofs. She expected the birds to take off in a purring chaos and settle atop the soldier's hat like they did at the war memorial back home, but not a bird among the lot took wing. Although pigeons couldn't act, they apparently were trainable, because against all her experience of pigeon behaviour, they tottered around on the pavement at her feet like so many feathered wind-up toys.

A movie camera almost as big as its operator rolled on rubber wheels toward her. Frankie kept her eyes on the birds.

The Extra

The pigeons must have had their wings clipped. It was a sensible way to control birds, although hard on the creatures themselves. She held out her empty hand—she was, after all, acting—and wished she really had some feed to give the poor flightless creatures. All at once she remembered the cheese sandwich Connie had given her before filming. Had she eaten it? She touched the pocket of her green and blue dress and pulled out a bit of bread. She scattered the crumbs to the pigeons. Ought she feed them dry bread instead of this fresh stuff? Well, there was nothing to do about that. And she dared not give them bits of cheese—it might make them sick.

She couldn't hear the camera. She tried not to imagine its hum as it recorded the work she was doing. She'd bet her forty remaining dollars—housed under the sofa cushions at Paradise Gardens—that thinking about the camera was almost as unprofessional as looking into its lens. Instead she focussed on the pigeons as they bustled around her, pecking at the crumbs. She felt that the scene was going quite well until a seagull swooped over the wall that separated this movie's set from the top of the gilded towers of the old *Ambition* set.

Without meaning to, she jerked her head up to watch the seagull dive at the pigeons. The director made a cutting motion to the assistant director, who called to the cameraman to stop the shot. The cameraman waved to the pigeon handler. The latter dealt with the situation by shooing the seagull away. It flew off, shrieking.

Marietta Valdes stepped up beside the director. The actress's red dress gleamed as she gestured with one pale hand. "Freddy, I know I don't have to tell *you* that with a non-speaking part, the shape and movement of the actor's body is translated into sound."

"Teach your grandmother." The director screwed his face into shapes that would terrify a dog.

Marietta leaned toward Frankie. "Movement produces sound you cannot hear, the way a person produces a shadow even on a cloudy day." She turned back to the director. "Give her another chance, will you?"

Another chance. Frankie stared. Horror gripped her. She had been certain she was acting well. To discover that she was failing was like believing she could fly, only to plummet to the ground like a dying bird.

Marietta told the director, "Shoot the scene again, Freddie."

The director glowered. "You are a damned back-seat-driving female actress, and I ought to walk right off this set. Whereupon the insurance company will take everything Monument Studios has got, right down to Samson's silk underdrawers."

Marietta Valdes smiled her goddess's smile. "Freddie, what did Gilbert Howard say to you the last time you raised the question of his insurability?"

"That damned no-show Gilbert Howard. Where the hell is he, anyway?" The director raised his arms to the sky. "But hellfire, Marietta, you're right. We'll shoot the scene again. Did you hear what she said, pigeon girl?"

"Yes, sir," Frankie said.

"All acting is changing from the light to the dark, or from the dark to the light," Marietta added, looking directly at her.

"You've said enough, Marietta. Put a sock in your pretty mouth." The director pointed his cigar at Frankie. "You understand what she means? Even though you're a pigeon girl with no lines, transformation is what I'm looking for. Understand?"

Frankie was so far from understanding him that she nearly burst into tears. With a blast of certainty, she knew the role would go to Connie, as it was always meant to go. Or even to an extra she didn't know. Nature would take its course, and Frankie would return to the anonymous crowd where she belonged. How foolish she had been, how optimistic, how blind, to think that, because Gilbert Howard had started out a schoolteacher like her, she could act like him. She was not an actress. She was an engaged woman, here for the short term and properly one of a large group of extras. Being an extra in the movies had been enough for her an hour ago. It would have to suffice again. *Darn* it all to the deepest pit of Hades.

Then, as one holds one's nose and leaps from the highest board into a swimming pool far below, she clasped both hands before her and said, "I understand completely."

"All right. Jesus H Christ! Shoot it again." The director pointed his cigar stub at her. "Feed the blasted pigeons, you sad little pigeon girl."

There was a sudden silence on the lot.

How lucky that she had been too sad to eat. She crumbled up more of the bread from her pocket and scattered it in front of the pigeons. She ignored the cry of the seagull, shrieking somewhere behind the dog-faced god over the wall that separated the Parisian square from the set of *Ambition*, soon to be burned. It circled back overhead, still racketing, and landed among the pigeons to peck at the crumbs in the gravel at Frankie's feet. The seagull didn't look even slightly Parisian. Its grey and white lines were a graceful reminder of the seagulls that were so much a part of her home near the coastal waters up north. Like Frankie, this bird was a west coaster and was bound to spoil the shot.

The director threw his hat on the ground. "Dammit, do something about that bird."

The seagull took wing again. The pigeon handler fumbled in his box. Frankie supposed he must be after a net, whatever good that would do him with a high-flying seagull. She fished in her pockets for another bit of sandwich and thus she didn't see what he did. She heard it, though, a sound like a firework, or like a car backfiring—a sound similar to the echoing *crack* she'd heard the night before, under the starry sky at Paradise Gardens. But this was closer, of course, and it scattered the pigeons around the statue's base. She looked up to see the pigeon handler lower a gun to his side. The grey and white body of the seagull thudded onto the gravel at his feet. Its breast was torn into a jagged red mess.

Frankie stood up, crumbs falling from her lap. She stared at the dead bird, then sat down again, tears coursing down her face. With trembling hands, she found in her pocket a few more crumbs for the pigeons. The pigeons gobbled at them without the least regard for their dead avian colleague.

The director swore. "Luigi, get the goddamn close-up."

"*Fottiti, bastardo.*" Luigi pulled the camera closer. To Frankie he said, "Little extra, the show must go on."

Frankie nodded. She knew it was true, but it didn't help. Still sobbing, she tucked her legs under her and spread her blue-and-green flowered skirt a little for the shot as the camera rolled closer. She tried not to think about the camera, the dead seagull, or the dead man at Paradise Gardens. Instead, tears streaming, she focussed on the pigeons. She gave them names. *Cleo, Henry, Farthingale, Martha …* Somehow she retained enough sense not to say the names out loud. *Isabella, Chip …*

Marietta Valdes called out, "*Cut.* Look about you, pigeon girl. There's more in this world than pigeons."

"Shut up, Marietta," the director bellowed. "Luigi, you don't cut unless I tell you to. Marietta's right, though, pigeon girl. Look around so we can see your sorrowful face."

Luigi remounted his camera and rose slowly to an overhead vantage.

Frankie tossed the birds her last bit of sandwich, and then pretended — *acted* — as if she had more. She held her character. She fed the pigeons, and Luigi filmed her feeding them.

"Bury your face in your hands, now, pigeon girl," the director said. "Weep but don't move. Don't move a muscle."

Go slow, kid. In Vancouver, her first stage director had told her so again and again. Now, Frankie went slow. She lowered her face into her hands. She wept for the dead seagull and for the poor soul buried in Eugene Ellery's backyard. She wept, but she didn't move her shoulders. She wept until she ran out of tears.

"Cut and print," the director said. "Money shot, that one. Not so dusty, Luigi."

"*Che cazzo,*" Luigi muttered.

"Burn it, AD. Send the pigeons and the extra crew on break."

There was a groan of pleasure from the extras, and Frankie rejoined the crowd as it headed for the refreshment trolley. She wanted to shout, "*Klahowya!*" She wanted to tell her long-gone mother everything and compose boastful missives to her father and Champ. Above all, she wanted to talk the whole scene over with Connie.

Tom, with a hoot of pleasure for her victory on the set, took Frankie by the arm. He grabbed a cup of coffee somebody handed back to them and passed it to Frankie. She tipped the cup back, thanking her stars the liquid was lukewarm and could slide straight down to her firmament.

"Where's Connie?" Frankie asked. "Did she see the take?"

"She's your best friend, isn't she? How could she miss it? Maybe afterward she ran to the bathroom." Tom shrugged. "You want more coffee?" He walked off toward the trolley.

"Not bad for a pigeon girl," a voice said from behind her.

She turned. The director nodded his head at her. Before she could think what to say, he had joined the assistant director, who was locked in what appeared to be some kind of power struggle with the cameraman.

The director stabbed at his assistant director with his cigar. "I want you to find that dilettante Gilbert Howard and tell him the next time he doesn't show up for a scene with me, I'll have him roasted and served up for supper."

He stalked away in the direction of the farther sound stages.

"Thank you, sir," Frankie told the director's receding back, although she knew he'd never hear. She'd had her moment on film. The director had searched her out personally and approved her in her first role—and perhaps her last, depending on her luck and the twisting winds of fate. Now she was an extra again. For good.

Or maybe not.

She cursed herself for a coward and raced after the director, without the slightest idea how on earth to stop him. But he stopped on his own. He dropped the stub of his cigar into the gravel path at his feet. He fished in his pocket, pulled out a fresh cigar, bit down on one end, but didn't light it.

A massive soundstage stood open and workmen hustled by, smoking and carrying paint cans and pails full of tools.

Frankie said, "Sir? May I please ask you something?"

"Who's that?" The director frowned and produced a wet sound from behind the cigar. "Oh, the pigeon girl. Again. Listen, are you one of those pushy, overtalented English?"

"No, sir. I'm Canadian. From Vancouver." She stopped before she told him her street number.

The director walked on, but he didn't swear at her, so she walked alongside him, ducking around the workmen, who hardly seemed to see her.

"Sir, in your next picture, are there any parts uncast? That I might be cast in? Since I was your excellent choice for pigeon girl?"

She held her breath. This man reminded her so much of her cantankerous father.

"I didn't say *excellent*." The director strode toward the building that the Queen of the Extras had pointed out to Frankie and Connie as the commissary. Frankie hesitated no more than a second before rejoining him, trotting along at his side. When he stopped without warning, Frankie did a little dance step to keep from thudding up against him.

"But, sir, you did mention I was good as the pigeon girl."

He said, "Sure I did. You were right for the pigeon girl role, but I gotta tell you: you don't have the looks to make it in this business."

"Yes, sir." As she tried to keep her chin up, Frankie had to duck around three men and a ladder. She was really going to have to develop a thick skin about all these negative comments regarding her looks — the way writers needed to develop a thick skin about having their manuscripts returned marked *boring and redundant*. Her father's collected sermons had several times been marked thus by unappreciative publishers of religious prose.

She said to the director, "But can't you see me as a not-so-pretty secretary or the friend who never finds love?"

"You're too pretty for that. But in twenty years you might make a decent character actress." The director chewed his cigar wetly.

"I see, sir." Too late, Frankie understood that she'd gotten the director's type wrong. He wasn't like her father after all. He was like the principal at the school where she used to teach. They both had that particular square-shaped back and low, shiny neck. If it was no skin off his nose, a man like that didn't mind a question, respectfully phrased and appropriately punctuated. But he wouldn't give a dog he liked a bone it wanted.

So she thanked him again for the pigeon role. Then she turned and walked away.

And to be truthful, Frankie would have been an ungrateful beast not to feel pretty darned good about the morning. She was sorry nature hadn't given her the correct combination of gumption and beauty—like Connie's—with which to convince the director to cast her in a speaking part. But for now it was enough to know that she had excelled at what she'd always known in her heart would be her first step on the path to stardom in the movies: being an extra. The director had pulled her from the ranks. He had tested her without warning. And she had not been found wanting.

Furthermore, this same director, a man whose every behaviour proved that he was not given to polite white lies, had hunted her down among the other extras to tell her she'd done well. *And* he'd told her she was too pretty to play plain. She watched him as he rumbled toward a building that appeared more administrative than theatrical, ducking to avoid three men hefting a flower-embellished coffin. Frankie knew it for a phony, movie-set coffin—as a defrocked minister's daughter, she knew it would take six men to carry a real one—but her heart thudded and her eyes welled. She wondered what they did with the coffins after the movie. Might there not be one for the dead man buried in the backyard at Paradise Gardens? She felt an odd pivotal sensation in the area of her stomach. Without further thought, she scurried after the director and caught up with him again. "Sir—" she began.

"Listen, pigeon girl, you're becoming a pest. You're lucky I never remember an extra's face." The director glared.

"It's a blessing, I guess." Frankie swallowed. "Haven't you got *any* small role I could play?"

"When I say *no*, I mean *go to hell*." He stomped two paces off, spun on his heel, and stomped the two paces back. "Yes. I do have a part for a sad little manicurist. The actress that was to play her ran off, the devil knows where. Like Gilbert Howard, damn his eyes. The part's not much, a few lines for a very sad little girl with a very sad little life."

Frankie hardly understood what he was saying at first. She had to run the words back through the channels of her mind, weed them of her negative expectations, and listen to them again. She said, "Yes, please," then added, "sir. Thank you, sir."

She felt her face lighting up with joy and wonder. She'd never feel sad again.

The director scowled. "I said be *sad*. I need a *sorrowful* girl. Don't get happy on me before Monday. That's when I'll test you. Two days later, we start shooting. What's your name?"

"Francesca Ray, sir." She stood up tall, schooling her features into sorrowful lines — but not too sorrowful. She was not a ham. She was an actress. An actress who, this coming Monday, would win a role in a moving picture. An actress who in two days would have lines.

An actress.

The director said, "I'll never remember your face or your name. It's the way I am, and I like it. If you tell me you're the pigeon girl, then you can test. Get it?"

"Got it." It took all her acting talent and discipline not to burst into joyous song right in front of the director. As an actress with lines, Frankie would have her name at the end of the movie. She would roll with the credits: *Sad Little Manicurist … Francesca Ray*. Frankie was so happy, she could have hugged the director all the way around his long canvas coat, and what a mistake that would be. Her eyes widened, and she wished above all things that the director would go away before she simply … popped.

He called over his shoulder, "Show up at 5 am two days from now and see casting. And, pigeon girl …"

"Yes, sir?"

"You're a manicurist. A sad one. So you're going to have to dye your hair blonde."

Her heart raced. "Yes, sir."

"*Platinum.*"

"I will, sir," she called to the director's square back as he slammed through the door into the commissary.

Frankie walked back along the path to the extras' gravel yard, taking in the smell of cigarette ends and paper cups of coffee like heaven's aroma. The dead body in the backyard at Paradise Gardens still haunted her, but for now those white fingers couldn't touch her.

Alone among the smoking, sipping, milling extras, she held her great new chance close to her. In that moment, she understood how it would be to be Loretta Desirée, the Queen of the Extras, and to want to give her boys and girls all the good luck a day could possibly bring them. She wanted to hug every single extra to her breast, individually and in a group, and offer them all roles with their coffee. She'd love to lead them all in a chorus of "*Hi de hi de ho.*" And then she would take the whole lot for a ride in the Model A, straight down the middle of Sunset Boulevard with all the kids hanging out the windows. She wanted to call out to the sellers of Maps of the Stars, "Print up a new map, and write our names around the edges in gold type." But most of all, she was dying to tell Connie.

She looked toward the crowd at the coffee trolley, and over into the shadows by the toilet block, but Connie was nowhere in sight.

"Hey, Pigeon Frankie." Tom, leaning against the wall with his skirt bunched up behind him, raised his coffee to her.

She asked him where she might find Connie, but he shook his head. "She might have gone to the beach with Doris in the truck. There's a loose board in the fence. Some of the less motivated extras use it to get out of the studio, go swimming, and creep back in without losing their day's pay."

"Connie would never sneak away to the beach. Even if the others did." Frankie frowned and took one of the remaining tomato sandwiches from the trolley. "Connie's too much of a professional to skip out on the day. I'll try the WC again."

But there was no sign of Connie at sink or in stall. Frankie, chewing on her soggy sandwich, got directions to the loose board in the studio wall and slipped through it onto the street. A limousine drove past at high speed toward Sunset Boulevard, its driver in an outside seat, hanging onto his cap by its brim. Two policemen in white and blue paid no attention to the speeding car, but looked her up and down before rounding the corner. Her afternoon shadow moved blackly against the high, grey studio walls. She saw no sign of Connie.

Frankie stood on the sidewalk in the sunshine. She swallowed her last bit of sandwich. If she were Connie, where would she be? When they were children, if Connie wanted to escape, she would hide under the weeping willow down by the reserve land. But that was when she was in a fury because she hadn't gotten her way. Whenever Connie got into a temper, Frankie was always the one to end up in some kind of trouble.

And now, Frankie had left the movie set on her first day on the job. Without permission. She must make her way back to the set before anybody in authority noticed she was gone. She must not spoil her chances. Not for anything.

A big sedan drove by. Long and sleek, it was at a guess twice the size of the Model A, and probably four times the price. It purred past her, and for a moment, Frankie envied the passenger sitting in what must be a luxurious back seat. As the sedan sped up, the passenger turned to look out. Connie stared back at Frankie through the rear window.

Frankie ran after the sedan, but it rounded the corner and passed out of sight.

18

The black sedan's license plate read *3T 59 90*. Frankie had no way to write it down, but she did her best to commit the numbers to memory. Feeling every second as a yard or more that Connie was travelling in who-knew-what perilous situation, Frankie broke into a run along the sidewalk that bordered the high studio walls. *3T 59 90*.

She saw with a start that the Model A was not empty. A blonde woman sat in the passenger seat. Frankie yanked open the driver's door and flung herself behind the wheel.

"Either get out, or you're going for a ride."

"Okay, honey." The blonde blinked at her sleepily, and in the seconds that it took Frankie to push the key into the Model A's starter and turn it, she recognized Billie Starr, the girl from the Spanish-style mansion. Billie Starr, from the brothel. The girl who had tried to walk under the wheels of the Model A the day before.

This afternoon, Billie was dressed in a pair of men's heliotrope-striped pyjamas. She said, "I knew I remembered your car from yesterday, when you almost hit me."

"We didn't. You walked into us."

"Well, no hard feelings," Billie said. "I found you anyhow. I was about to invite you to our house tonight. The other girls and I are going to sit upstairs and watch them burn the set of *Ambition*. But a ride is always nice. Where are we going?"

"Oh, for heaven's sake. Hang on." Frankie put the car into gear.

"Hurrah," Billie said.

"Look here, Billie. You're my eyes. Watch for a black sedan, license plate *3T 59 90*. When you see it, stand up and holler out, *Stop*."

"Okay." Billie folded her hands in her heliotrope-striped lap. "I'm a smidgen drunk, though."

"Wonderful. Just look for *3T 59 90*, will you?" Frankie signalled with her left hand, and a van with a cockroach painted on the side almost clipped the front left bumper of the Model A.

"You have to check the traffic before you pull out," Billie explained.

Frankie gritted her teeth and entered traffic, narrowly missing a brightly painted truck full of handsome young Mexicans sitting on crates of oranges in the truck bed. One of the young men grinned and lobbed a couple of oranges at them. Billie stretched out both hands like a lifelong outfielder and missed them both. The fruit splatted down onto the road behind the Model A.

Frankie leaned over the wheel and steered east along Sunset Boulevard. "Is that a black sedan up ahead?"

"Nope. Brown. Say! I know this road. This is how you drive to Mexico."

"Lord, I'll never find Connie in Mexico." Frankie drove faster along Sunset Boulevard. Without thinking, she said, "Today, I won an audition for a role in Samson's new film, *The Emperor of New York.*"

"I knew it! Congratulations." Billie clapped her hands together like a little kid. Then she bent down and pulled up from the floor a bottle of something brownish. She unscrewed the top and raised the bottle in salute.

"Thanks," Frankie said. "I don't really know how to behave like a movie actress, but I guess I'll learn. And …" She felt her excitement mount and had to remind herself to watch for black vehicles. "And I have to become a platinum blonde."

"Blonde is best. Yikes!" One hand on the windshield, Billie half stood in the passenger seat. "Stop!"

"Do you see the sedan? Where is it, Billie? Hang on." Frankie pulled over with a juddering groan to the wrong side of the street. With a cough, the Model A rolled in beside a drugstore, one wheel up on the sidewalk, which saved her having to switch it off. She shielded her eyes with one hand and peered out from the shadow of the drugstore's green-striped awning, up and down the road of shops. It was difficult to see straight with so many stripes — on the awnings, Billie's pyjamas, and in the shadows of the swaying palms that cut diagonally across cars, people, and even the road itself. "Where's that black car?"

"I didn't see your black car." Billie opened the car door. "I stopped you because I need to go into this drugstore for a minute."

Frankie reached out too late to stop Billie as she stepped out of the car into the path of an oncoming laundry truck.

The driver sounded his horn and Billie blew him a raspberry. Her pajama top lifted slightly with the wind as she crossed in front of the Model A and entered the shadows under the green-striped drugstore awning.

Frankie opened the car door to follow Billie into the drugstore, but before she could step down, Billie emerged, a pair of men's dark glasses on her pretty nose and another pair in her hand, along with a small green bottle. Given the lack of any sort of money-carrying pocket in those pyjamas, or indeed anything else except Billie herself, Frankie had to ask, "Did you pay for those things?"

"Think I'm a chump?" Billie climbed back into the Model A. "Better drive fast, Frankie. Here, put these on. They're all the rage now."

Billie settled the second pair of men's sunglasses on Frankie's nose as an angry-looking woman bustled through the drugstore door into the shade of the awning. Would the woman listen and understand, or would she call the police and have both Billie and Frankie arrested? With a squeal of conscience, Frankie pulled back out onto the road and tried not to remember Sunday school lessons regarding honesty with tradesmen.

She snatched the dark glasses from her nose and hid them in her skirt pocket.

Billie tucked the little bottle into Frankie's other pocket. "That's peroxide, is what that is. We'll have you dyed as platinum as Jean Harlow in no time. Maybe I'll go from blonde to platinum, too."

Billie opened the glove box and pulled out a pack of Lucky Strike cigarettes that she must have stashed there. With a start, Frankie remembered King Samson's gun, and thanked her stars that it was no longer in the glove box for Billie to fool around with. She reminded herself to look for the gun in the bushes between Paradise Gardens and the Garden of Allah. That's where she had dropped it while she, Tom, and Connie had watched Gilbert Howard with his lover, the golden swimmer.

Billie was uncorking her bottle. "Say, chum, want a drink?"

"Not now, thank you, Billie." Frankie steered straight ahead.

Billie held out the pack of cigarettes. "Here you go, Frankie."

"I don't smoke, thanks."

"No, sweetie. Your friend Connie left the pack for you."

Frankie started. *"Connie* did?" She took the pack from Billie. It was empty.

"You know — Connie. That red-headed girl you were with yesterday."

"Yes. I do know Connie." Frankie breathed into her diaphragm to calm down, the way they taught you in acting class. *"When* did she give you this cigarette pack?"

"Couple minutes before you ran up to the car." Billie took another swig from the bottle. "She tossed it to me before she got into a black car. She said you'd understand."

These cigarettes must be a message from Connie, in their secret code. Frankie could almost hear Connie sing out, *Hey, Frankie, what do you want in a cigarette?*

Frankie tried the question aloud as she drove along Sunset Boulevard. *"What do I want in a cigarette?"*

"If you don't know, sister, I can't tell you." Billie took another swig. In her blonde glory, in her pyjamas, she looked like a movie star on the lam.

"This cigarette pack is a coded message," Frankie said. "Connie and I always talk in code." However, their excellent private code was much easier to understand when Frankie was able to ask Connie face-to-face exactly what it meant.

Billie peered at the pack. She read out loud, *"Lucky Strike* cigarettes. Maybe Connie struck it lucky?"

"Yes." Frankie nodded sharply. "Or cigarettes might mean a *smokescreen*—but hiding what? And why drive away like that, right after I was chosen to be pigeon girl and had wangled an audition …" She trailed off.

"Maybe she feels funny about your good fortune?" Billie shot Frankie a sideways glance. "A teeny bit green about the gills with envy?"

Possibly. But Frankie answered, "Never."

"Well, then." Billie took another drink. "It stands to reason that if Connie was handing me cigarette packages, she certainly wasn't being strong-armed into that shiny sedan."

Frankie gripped the steering wheel and logicked furiously in and out of a dozen different dead-end directions. At last she said, "I think you are right. I think Connie had some good luck. But what?"

"Maybe she got a ride home," Billie said.

Frankie took her eyes off the road to stare at Billie. *Out of the mouths of babes and drunkards.* "You're a genius, Billie. While I was talking to the director, Connie would have looked for me, and when she couldn't find me, I'll bet she accepted a ride."

Billie sucked her lip and nodded. "A ride home, like the one I wish somebody would give me. I'm sick of that mansion full of prostitutes."

"Sure as shooting. You're coming home with me, Billie Starr," Frankie said. Grinding the car into gear, she made a great bleating U-turn back through the traffic. Then she headed down Sunset Boulevard toward Monument Studios. "Connie and I can crowd together to make room for three at Villa 7B."

"I'll dye your hair platinum," Billie said happily.

"You'll have to stop drinking," Frankie told her.

"I drink because I'm so unhappy." Billie's smile was sunny. "I'll stop when I'm a star in the movies. I knew you'd be good luck for me the minute you picked me up from the sidewalk yesterday. And I'm going to be good luck for you, too. Because I've got a friend who can help us all."

"Who?" Frankie drove past two straw-hatted movie-star map sellers touting their wares in front of the golden angels of Monument Studios. On the other side of the road, the Spanish-style mansion Billie had so recently left stretched out amid its flowered gardens. A tan-and-red roadster rumbled out from the studio drive. Frankie wavered at the wheel, and, coming up behind, the roadster honked like a goose.

"Who can help us?"

"What?" Billie asked. "Who do you mean?"

"You said you have a friend who can help you, me, and Connie in the movies."

"Yes."

"Who?"

"Guess," Billie answered.

Bearing up behind them, the blonde at the wheel of the tan-and-red roadster honked at them again.

"Ye gods!" Frankie peered into the rear-view. Blanche Carver, the Hollywood columnist, sat at the wheel, and beside her in the passenger seat sat Leo. "Would you look at who's behind us?"

"Who?"

"Guess."

Billie made a squeaking noise and stood up backward in her seat, leaning on the passenger backrest. "I don't need you anymore," she shouted at the roadster.

"Sit down, Billie." Frankie pulled at Billie's pajama hem, but Billie paid no attention. While Leo half-rose to his feet in his mother's sports car, Billie shouted, "I've got somebody who can really help me now!"

"If you fall out of the car, you'll be bashed to bits," Frankie said.

Billie called out to Leo, "I'm friends with Gilbert Howard. A great big famous movie star! So there!" She threw herself back down into the seat and then pushed her own foot upon Frankie's foot over the gas pedal. Frankie felt the Model A lurch forward. She held on hard to the steering wheel, all the while pushing at Billie's foot to regain control of the accelerator. In this unsatisfactory manner, they pulled up to Paradise Gardens, where Frankie hauled up on the hand brake and landed them on the gravel verge.

Billie stared up through the orange branches at the wooden sign that read *Paradise Gardens.* "Didn't I used to live here?"

"Did you?" Frankie couldn't imagine anybody leaving this place if they didn't have to. Certainly not for a brothel. She asked, "Billie, were you the girl who broke Leo's heart?"

"Leo doesn't have a heart."

"He seems like a nice enough fellow to me."

Billie made a scornful face, and Frankie gave up the sales job.

The extras ought to be back soon, but in the meantime Paradise Gardens seemed to be abandoned by all except for the birds and, as it turned out, the blonde in Villa 12A.

Billie called out to 12A's open window, "Hey in there, do you wanna buy a duck?"

"Get a robe, pajama dame." All they saw of the blonde in 12A was one white arm reaching out from the shadowy interior to slam the window shut.

"You know, you and Connie are going to get along fine." Frankie smiled at the thought. Almost home now.

The Extra

Frankie glanced at Billie, who — even in men's sunglasses — looked very young, balancing in her bare feet along a row of rocks that edged the yard of Villa 11B, and hitching up her pajama bottoms with one hand. Billie was a waif and a guttersnipe. She was Oliver Twist, and Frankie and Connie would be the wise and kindly grandfather who saved her. Connie was probably home in Villa 7B by now. She might even have had time to stop by the market for milk and butter and other necessary supplies. Even now Connie was likely to be cooking her patented creamed tuna on toast, the recipe for which she'd received an *A* in high school home economics because she'd added a pinch of pickle relish in the final five minutes of cooking. Frankie imagined Tom leaning in at their window, all of them laughing, eating creamed tuna, and learning to juggle oranges off their own tree out in the backyard.

The backyard. Frankie recalled almost for the first time in an hour the unknown body that was buried there.

She said, "Listen, Billie. We'll choose you a new screen name, and you'll begin your career at the movies all over again."

"Start all over again?" Billie asked. "That sounds terrible."

"You can start at the bottom, as an extra like I did, and —" She heard Billie's snort of disbelief. She stopped the girl in the pathway and looked her straight in her dark glasses. "And then you can learn as you go. Maybe you are the world's best actress, Billie, and maybe so am I. But if I'm honest with myself, I know I'm not yet ready for a *starring* role. Today, I got a chance at a small part, and that might lead to a bigger part. It'll happen to you too. I know it. You got off to a bad beginning, you maybe listened to the wrong person." She wondered who had been the one to suggest working in the brothel across from Monument Studios.

"Hi de hi de hi de hi, I've got Gilbert Howard to help me," Billie sang as she walked down the little path to Villa 7B. "Maybe Howie will help you, too. *Ho de ho de ho de ho ...*"

Frankie nipped past her. With a dramatic gesture of welcome, she opened the door to Villa 7B.

Billie walked by her, still singing. Once inside the living room, however, she stopped mid-stanza. She made a strange little sound and stood still.

Frankie joined her. She left the door open at their backs to let in the warm evening air. The bathroom and bedroom doors stood open as well. She saw no sign of Connie. Disappointment struck her, followed closely by the realization that she and Billie were not alone.

Before them on the sofa, propped up, sat Gilbert Howard. He looked as if he'd been waiting for them for quite a while, in patient solitude.

As she looked at him more closely, Frankie noted that, for once, the movie star was fully clothed below the waist.

She saw that the fingers of one hand were curved around an orange.

And she saw that Gilbert Howard, star of the silver screen, was dead.

19

The young woman buttoned her shirt up to her neck. She checked the clock beside her bed again. The long afternoon was at last wearing on toward evening.

What would they think when they saw the orange clasped in Gilbert's dead hand? When she'd placed it there, it had seemed an almost random addition to the scene she had set, but now she saw that it might also be interpreted as a symbol of the bounty of Gilbert Howard's spirit.

And at a second, secret level, the orange was a reference to the way his hand would touch her cheek when they were together.

How lucky she was that they'd had those few hours the night before. She'd had him almost to herself, curled up warmly in his arms before her swim. She sighed as she remembered diving into the pool, and how the water skimmed along the surface of her body. It was a sensation at once intimate and impersonal.

Swimming naked was nothing a decent woman in her hometown

would contemplate, even for a moment. But Gilbert had taught her not to care who saw her. He said, "The best way to keep your secrets, my darling, is to reveal them to an uncaring world."

She would never have him to herself again.

But then, except for a few sweet hours now and again, she never had.

20

Frankie put out a hand to the bungalow wall to steady herself. She felt as if she were two people: one who trusted her own eyes, and a second Frankie who, even with the movie star's corpse seated here in front of her on her own rented sofa, couldn't believe Gilbert Howard was really dead. How was her brain supposed to reconcile this cold, pale figure with the vibrant man he'd been the night before, reciting Webster to the blue California sky as dusk fell and a naked, golden girl leapt from his arms into the water beside him? She remembered how the spray from the girl's dive had caught the light like diamonds suspended by invisible threads, like movie magic.

Right now, around the country — no, around the world — there were hundreds of marquees with Gilbert Howard's name written on them. And only she and Billie knew that his movies and this empty body were all that remained of him. No matter that she'd only met him twice, it was plain to Frankie that the world couldn't go on without him. At least it wouldn't carry on in the same way, any more than if all the peacocks in existence spread their tails and died.

"Billie, we have to tell somebody right now."

"Not yet." Billie's tears slipped out from under her dark glasses and crept down her cheeks to the neck of her men's pyjamas. She knelt at the actor's side. She touched the orange he was holding and then the hand that held it. Gently she stroked the straight black line of his right eyebrow, and his left. "Say something."

"He can't." But of course, Billie wasn't speaking to Gilbert Howard. She was asking Frankie to say something. Something appropriate.

But Frankie could think of nothing to say. She remembered the churchyard taunts: *Shoemakers' children go barefoot, ministers' children go bad*. She knew so many quotations—from the Bible, from Shakespeare, from Shelley. But all she remembered now were Webster's words as Gilbert Howard had recited them beside a shining pool wherein an unnamed blonde girl splashed naked the night before: *"What would it pleasure me to have my throat cut with diamonds ... to be shot with pearls?"* It was almost as if, by declaiming Webster, Gilbert Howard had presaged his own death.

Billie cocked her pretty head to one side, apparently thinking hard. At last she said, *"Now cracks a noble heart."*

Frankie remembered the next bit: *"Good night, sweet prince."*

"Yes! *Good night. And flights of angels sing thee to thy rest*. What will I do without you, Howie? How can I manage without your help?" Billie bent and kissed the corpse's pale cheek.

Frankie spoke past the lump in her throat. "I didn't realize you knew him so well. Did he have heart trouble?"

"Heart trouble? Howie?" Billie put her hand over her mouth, as if to stifle an ill-timed laugh. "Of course, we know who killed him."

Killed him? How could Billie say such a thing? And at such a moment? With sudden comprehension, Frankie remembered that Billie must still be drunk.

"Nobody killed him, Billie." The breeze at her back reminded her of the greater world outside Villa 7B, where this news had not yet travelled. "Even though he was a movie star, he … died. The way everybody dies, in the end. Do you see?"

Billie looked over her shoulder. Without another word, she got to her feet and slipped out of Frankie's living room by the back door. Her shadow flitted away into the darkness in the direction of the Garden of Allah bungalows.

The sound of an indrawn breath was all the warning Frankie got before Blanche Carver stepped into the room.

The columnist said, "A woman called my office. She didn't leave her name. Said Gilbert Howard had missed today's shoot at the studios and was up to something … *gossip-worthy* in Paradise Gardens …"

Frankie could think of nothing to say. She clasped her hands together and waited for the columnist to digest the truth of the scene laid out in front of her.

Blanche took two steps past Frankie toward the sofa where Gilbert Howard's body sat.

"Oh, God," Blanche said. "Howie, you *can't* be dead."

"Howie? Dead? What's happened?" Leo appeared out of the shadows outside the door. He moved toward his mother and wrapped his good arm around her. Over Blanche's shoulder, he said to Frankie, "I can't believe the old fellow's dead. He and my mother went back a long way. And on your sofa?"

Blanche lifted her head. Tears had coloured her pale cheeks pink. "This is impossible. We are old friends. We came to Hollywood together — Howie, Loretta, and me. Have you called the studio?"

Frankie managed a tiny, negative movement of her head. Then, without warning, and without reason, her silence ended. Involuntarily, as if she had become a puppet through whom somebody else was speaking, words began to flow out of her mouth, quietly at first, and then more loudly.

"You mean, have I called the police? No, I don't have a phone, and I should have run to find one, it would have been the right thing, but we've just — *I've* just — found him, and I'm so sad and so *stupid* to do nothing to help, but the thing is that I've never — " Frankie clapped her hands across her own mouth to halt the flow.

She had been about to say that she'd never seen a dead body before in her life, but that would not be true. Her father had presided at funerals. And she'd seen that other corpse this very morning, buried out in the backyard between Eugene Ellery's bungalow and her own, hers and Connie's. That made two dead bodies in the course of one long, blue, Californian day.

Blanche stood up straight and wiped at the tears on her cheeks. "Leo, Loretta has a telephone. Call the studio."

"I'll go and tell the Queen, then, and telephone from there." Leo's voice sounded rough. Holding a hand to his shoulder where Gilbert Howard had shot him a few days before, he hurried away.

His mother sat down at the kitchen table where, that morning, Frankie and Connie had shared a lighthearted breakfast of burned toast and tea. Blanche picked up her pen and opened the notebook to a clean page. "Gilbert Howard is dead, rest his lovely soul. The rest of the world will make up lies and fairy tales around him. But I want to get this story right. In Howie's honour. Is this your home?"

"Mine and …" Frankie stopped as the woman began to write. "Yes. Mine and Connie's."

"That young redhead I met with Leo outside Monument Studios?" The columnist's eyes darted around the place to the plaid curtains, the little kitchen. She looked hardest at the orange, which had fallen from Howard's hand when Billie had touched him.

Frankie burst out, "It's terrible enough that he's dead. But he shouldn't have died *here*. Not in this little place, on that old plaid sofa. He was too grand for that."

The columnist looked narrowly at her. "What an odd thing for you to say."

Frankie wanted to ask, *What is so odd about speaking an obvious truth*? But outside, doors to other bungalows began to bang open and slam shut. Voices — young voices — were raised, calling out to one another, rising and falling in urgent interrogative tones. The news of Howard's death must have travelled through Paradise Gardens, via Leo and Loretta Desirée, Queen of the Extras.

The Queen's kids began to pour into the small room, overflowing in their numbers out the front door and onto the path leading to the patio where, the evening before, they had danced around the fountain. A buzz of distressed voices swelled in Villa 7B's little living room. The press of bodies crushed Frankie against the wall nearest the bedroom. She felt invisible. She was glad to be so.

The crowd of kids craned and stared at Gilbert Howard's body on the sofa. Tom shouldered through the crowd, his voice rising above the agitated buzz in the room, asking what had happened, and then falling silent as he saw Howard's corpse. Eugene Ellery was among the last to make his way through the crush of young people, and when she caught sight of him, Frankie felt a relief so strong that it was almost like having her father there.

The volume and pitch of the chatter rose. Leo returned, supporting a very pale Queen at his side. Blanche Carver laid a protective hand across the Queen's shoulder and helped her to her seat. She said, "Loretta here needs something hard to drink."

"There's no drink in the world hard enough to help with this." Tom headed for the door. "But I'll get some of the Queen's own store for her."

"What happened to Howie?" This from the girl nearest Gilbert Howard's body. Frankie didn't know her name, but she remembered her as one of today's extras. "How can he be dead?"

Doris made a stricken noise. "Howie looks like he's sitting waiting for somebody."

"Where's that girl who lives here? The one I was talking to before?" Blanche asked. "Francesca. She found Gilbert's body."

There was a stirring in the crowd, and Frankie felt the mass of the Queen's kids turn to look at her.

She gazed from one questioning face to another. "I found him dead. But last night I saw him alive." It was hard, but these were her neighbours, and they had a right to know everything. She swallowed once, twice, thrice, and continued. "Larger than life! He was reciting Webster. *To have my throat cut by diamonds*, he said. *To be smothered by cassia* ... But he wasn't cut. He wasn't smothered. He's just dead."

"'Just dead'? I'm sure you can think of something better than that. Let's get this right for tomorrow's edition, all you mugs." Blanche addressed the group of young people standing about Villa 7B's living room. "It's clear to me, as it must be to all of you, that Howie was waiting for his girlfriend, Francesca, here—"

At this outrageous inaccuracy, Frankie found her tongue. "I'm not his girlfriend. I hardly knew him."

Frankie felt an arm slip around her shoulder. Tom had given the Queen a glass of something that looked like gin, and now he returned to stand at Frankie's side. She shot him a grateful look and focussed her attention back on the columnist.

Blanche said, "Or was he waiting for that red-headed friend of yours? Maybe so. Maybe it was even love at last for poor old Howie. Heaven knows enough of us girls tried to make him happy."

There was a moment of feminine agreement in the room. Doris asked, "You, too, Miss Carver?"

"Didn't everybody, at one time or another?" Blanche looked blank for a moment. Then she appeared to pull herself together. "Never mind. While he was waiting for Frankie here, Gilbert Howard slipped away. Dreaming of his new love, perhaps?"

Frankie cleared her throat and tried again. "Look, Miss Carver, even if I had been involved with Gilbert Howard, which I was not, I'm telling you that you've got the *wrong story.*"

"I agree." Eugene joined Tom at Frankie's side.

Blanche Carver said, "Let me get the facts right, Francesca. Step forward and clear this matter up: Was it you, or your friend Connie, who was Gilbert Howard's final lover?"

"Neither one of us," Frankie said, hanging back. "And you should be writing your story about how he was such a great *actor.* That's the important part."

"Yes," Eugene said, as the Queen's kids made noises of agreement. "He must be honoured—"

"Quiet! He was my friend. So don't worry your sad little hearts," the columnist said. "I'm determined to get the story right. Everybody who reads about his death will be comforted to know that Gilbert Howard, adored by millions, fell in love at last. I think that's wonderful. I think it's *beautiful.* Tell us how you met him, before the cops get here. We're all behind you. Aren't we, kids?"

Frankie had to struggle to keep from shouting at the woman. "Miss Carver, you should be writing about Gilbert Howard's talent, not about who his last girlfriend was. Write about how the planet may still turn, but the world won't be the same now that he's gone."

Eugene squeezed Frankie's hand, and on her other side Tom tightened his arm around Frankie's shoulder. The rest of the kids made it clear by word and posture that they were behind Frankie one hundred percent.

On the far side of the room, Doris looked out the window by the front door. She called out, "Jiggers, here come the cops!"

The crowd nearest the door parted to let a pair of policemen through. One was tall and the other handsome. The two of them approached Gilbert Howard with difficulty through the crush.

"Is it really Gilbert Howard? It is, and no mistake." The tall policeman pouched his lower lip.

The handsome policeman addressed Blanche Carver. "We've called the precinct captain. He'll send the detectives."

"But we will begin without them." The tall policeman gazed down upon the crowd in the little room. He asked, "Who here knows how Gilbert Howard died?"

The Queen of the Extras had not spoken for some time, but now she set her glass down on the table and rose to her feet. "Everybody knows. You only have to look at poor Howie, sitting up on the sofa as if he were alive. Anybody can see he … slipped away from life."

Blanche Carver put an arm around the Queen. "Loretta has hit it on the button there. A natural death. You can see that this dear man died happy, and free of pain."

The second policeman bent over the body. He pulled Howard's jacket aside, revealing a blossom of red so dark it was almost black.

Frankie stared at the bullet wound.

She tottered and felt Eugene's supporting hand at her side. Gilbert Howard had not simply fallen dead of natural causes. Somebody had shot him.

"Murder." Blanche Carver stood up.

In Villa 7B's little living room, a sort of electricity arose and travelled through the crowd, like a wordless rumour that grew in strength and conviction as it spread.

21

In memory, Frankie heard Gilbert Howard's voice again: *What would it pleasure me … to be shot with pearls?* Gilbert Howard had not died a natural death at all. It may not have been with pearls, but he certainly was shot.

Despite the draft from the open back door behind her, the crowd in the little living room of Villa 7B was so dense Frankie found it difficult to breathe.

We all know who killed him, don't we?

Frankie had no idea whom Billie might have meant. How could anybody, no matter how black of heart and murderous, kill such a talented man? That person had to be punished. She would very much like to be a part of the machinery of the law. She wanted to see Gilbert Howard's murderer tried and sentenced. And one early morning, to the sound of convicts tapping their metal cups against the bars of their cells, she would happily witness the killer's long walk to the electric chair.

With a gaze fully as judgmental as Frankie's thoughts, the second policeman stared from face to face in the crowded living room. He asked, "Which of you found the body?"

Frankie felt Eugene's nudge. She freed herself of Tom and Eugene's support and stepped forward. "I did."

"Your name, miss?"

Frankie gave it, along with the details of finding the body. It was all perfectly true but for a lie of omission: she couldn't give Billie's address without getting her in trouble with the law for prostitution. So, she decided not to mention Billie at all. It would not, in any case, make a difference to the investigation.

"How long ago did you find the body?" The tall policeman asked.

Frankie swallowed hard at the memory. "About twenty minutes ago."

"Were the lights on in the room when you found Mr Howard?"

"No."

"Was Mr Howard's body as we see him now?"

"Yes."

"Exactly as he is now?"

"Yes."

"You didn't touch him or move him in any way?"

Frankie mumbled, "I didn't touch him. It wouldn't be respectful."

Eugene squeezed her arm. She looked gratefully at him, and then back at the policemen.

"Did you find a gun in the room?"

"No."

"No weapon at all, in the house or around it?"

"Nowhere." Frankie was glad beyond all reason that she had dropped King Samson's gun out in the bushes the night

216

before and didn't have to explain why she had it. "No gun at all."

He licked his pencil and jotted down a note.

"Do you own a gun, Miss Ray?"

"No," Frankie stated truly. "I have never owned a gun."

"Did you know the victim, Mr Gilbert Howard, well?" the tall policeman asked. The handsome one, now apparently busy catching up on his notes, looked up as his colleague asked the question.

Blanche Carver set her notebook down. "Frankie was his lover. You don't need to wait for plainclothesmen to tell you the implications, do I?"

"I was *not* his lover," Frankie said. The sounds came out in mumbles, most unlike her usual clear tones. It was like trying to speak in a dream—every word cost her an enormous amount of energy. "He was barely an acquaintance."

The tall policeman walked over to the body. "So you say. But others say you were known to be romantically connected to the victim, and he was found in your home."

"Yes." Frankie wasn't sure she said it aloud, so she said yes again. "But only to the first part. The only times he talked to me—"

"Save the finer points for the detectives, sister. Gilbert Howard's been dead awhile, from the look of him. Our job is to ask for your movements throughout the day."

"My movements?" Frankie stared.

Tom took her elbow again. "Frankie was at the studio today. We all saw her."

"I was," Frankie said. With difficulty, she drew in a breath of thick air. "But I'd never—"

"Yes indeed. Why would she kill him?" Blanche Carver's tone was icy. She took up her pen and thumbed a new page over in her notebook. "Motive's the thing, wouldn't you say, gentlemen?"

As the columnist spoke, Frankie experienced a sensation of ... slowness, in addition to her growing breathlessness. Everything in the room seemed to have slowed to half speed while she attempted to follow the turn the conversation had taken. A murmur animated the Paradise Gardens residents around her, a susurrus that sounded almost wary—possibly even unfriendly.

"Love. Jealousy." The tall policeman sucked his lower lip. "Did you love him, er, Frankie?"

"*No.*" She clasped her hands together. "Yes. But the way everyone loved him. As a great actor."

"I begin to see the truth of it now," Blanche Carver said, and crossed something out in her journalist's notebook.

Frankie's fingers went cold at the tips. She had never felt such a sensation before in her life.

"Was it you who phoned my office to say that something had happened to Gilbert?" Blanche Carver touched the point of her pen to the tip of her index finger. She studied the small dot it made on her skin. She asked, "Did you kill him, Frankie?"

For a moment, Frankie felt nothing at all, and then in the centre of her field of vision she saw lights swirl against a background of darkness, as if every star in the firmament had extinguished itself between her last breath and this one.

The crowded bungalow living room came back into focus. She looked from the columnist to the police, and from the extras to their Queen. Connie was gone, and Billie had run away. Her neighbours—Tom and Doris and Eugene, as well as the rest of the extras—had fallen silent. In the middle of this crowded room, Frankie was stranded as surely as if she stood on the shore of a desert isle crowded with savage beasts and encircled by sharks, with no help in sight.

Frankie glanced behind her at the open door that led out to the backyard, through the bushes, and into the Garden of Allah. But only fools tried to outwit the law. You stood your ground and let justice take its course. She didn't even need the hundred radio dramas and cinematic lessons every listener and moviegoer heard and saw every week of their life. Simple common sense, as well as her fairly good education in citizenship and history, told her that an innocent person need never fear the arm of the law. Guilty persons ran away.

Then, close to her ear: *"Don't answer."*

Frankie met Eugene Ellery's calm grey gaze.

A murmur rose in the little room. Somebody called out, "There are more coppers on the way."

Another voice added, "No more of you Keystone fellows. Plain clothes!"

"Tie a tin can to the comments, you people. It's about time we cleared the room." The two policemen conferred quietly. The handsome one jangled something in the hip pocket of his uniform.

The tall policeman faced Blanche. "Our colleagues will think it's interesting that the suspect says she loved him, and yet she isn't crying."

"You saw that, did you? She seems more disturbed than sad." Blanche touched her pen to her lower lip. "About time you fellows noticed. I'd almost given up on the perspicacity of lawmen."

So fogged was Frankie by the unreality of the proceedings that at first she hardly noticed that her neighbours at Paradise Gardens were moving to stand close to her. Casually, still chatting, the young people shifted to form a protective wall around her in the little room. In that moment the community of extras at Paradise Gardens stopped being acquaintances and became friends. She read in their expressions belief in her innocence and fear for her safety. They quietly edged her toward the back door.

Eugene Ellery touched her shoulder and made a small gesture with his head. He whispered, "Out the back door with you. Quick as a wink."

Frankie hesitated. It was so difficult to think, to reason things through. Guilty persons ran away. However, despite everything she'd always believed, there was at this moment more comfort in the extras' concern, and in Eugene's calm and trustworthy gaze, than in the faceless, long-armed law represented by those two policemen.

The Queen's extras had entirely encircled her. Knees weak, dangerously near falling, Frankie found herself manoeuvred out the back door of Villa 7B.

Eugene followed her out, took hold of her arm, pulled her inside the back door of his own Villa 7A, and shut the door. In the unlit living room, Frankie noticed again that Eugene smelled of Burma-Shave, like Champ. The irrelevant thought startled her back to her senses. She shook herself free of Eugene's grip and faced him.

"I didn't kill Gilbert Howard. Why didn't you let me stay in Villa 7B and tell the police so?"

Eugene shook his head. "Frankie, I know cops. I *am* one. Even the best policemen want a quick arrest. Many more would be happy to create a scapegoat in a high-profile case like this one. Unless the real murderer shows up and hands himself over with a bow on his nose, they've got you with *motive* and *opportunity*. All they need are *means*—a gun. With your fingerprints on it."

The only gun she'd ever had in her possession was King Samson's gun, and it remained safely somewhere out in the bushes behind Villa 7B where she'd lost it the night before. How lucky she didn't have it now. Frankie held her cold hands tight together and stared into Eugene's face, a pale moon in his darkened living room.

Such a misunderstanding as this couldn't happen. Not to the daughter of a minister, not a good neighbour who helped people where she could.

Eugene said, "The police and the papers would like nothing more than to show the world that Gilbert Howard's murderess has been brought to quick and certain justice."

"I shouldn't have run," she said. The words tasted tinny in her mouth. "I'm innocent."

"Yes, of course." Eugene peered out his front window. "But I think — and all your friends here would probably agree — that you should hide for now. If the police arrest you tonight, they won't look for the real murderer. You'll be on every front page in Los Angeles and around the world. Tried in the papers and sentenced over breakfast tables." Eugene shifted suddenly. He let go of her. "But maybe you're right, Frankie. Look, if you want to go back, I'll take you. You're a smart girl, and you may be able to talk your way out of arrest. I'll stand by you if you do, through booking and trial. I'll assure them that I believe you are innocent. All the way, Frankie."

Blankly she said, "I have to go to a screen test on Monday morning." She wrapped her arms around her own waist and held herself tight. "I'm up for the role of a sad manicurist."

She had never for a moment believed that jails would have any place in her life, but now she saw that the law could take you like a wolf in the woods when you strayed too far from home.

22

Eugene turned away from the window and led Frankie into his unlit bedroom. He switched on a bedside lamp with an iron base and a ruffled shade, a twin to the lamp next to her bed in Villa 7B. Like her own and Connie's bedroom next door, Eugene's bedroom was equipped with a built-in closet and twin beds. His bedroom felt a bit roomier than theirs, for he had apparently taken the second bed to bits. The mattress and frame stood against the wall, covering the window that opened onto the back lawn he shared with 7A.

"You're a policeman, Eugene." Frankie clenched her fists and moderated her tone. She felt as if she were back in front of the camera, acting brave and calm. "As this is a murder case, what will happen now?"

"There will be a door-to-door search. Despite the Queen's kids' best efforts to cover your absence, the police will have noticed by now that you are missing. And since we're the first door the police will knock on, we'll have to move quickly."

Move where? Did you think of that before you convinced me to run away? Frankie scowled. She was tired of acting brave when really she was angry. She couldn't say another word lest she raise her voice in fury to Eugene and give herself away to the police outside. She had never realized that being accused of murder would make her so angry she'd want to kill somebody.

Or was this burning emotion really anger? Very hot and very cold materials were said to feel the same. Perhaps *in extremis,* anger and fear were also indistinguishable. With an effort she kept her peace and scanned Eugene's bedroom for a hiding place.

She saw only two alternatives: under a bed or in the clothes closet built into the wall. There was nothing else in the room large enough to conceal her. She shook her head and headed for the bedroom door.

Eugene took her by the arm. "You must not leave. You'll be arrested."

Frankie could keep quiet no longer, and she found her tongue, or her tongue found her. "You're a policeman. Why don't *you* arrest me?"

Eugene released her arm. They stared at one another. Eugene lowered his eyes.

"Frankie, I watched how you treated Gilbert Howard — with honour. I know you didn't kill him. I'll stand by you as long as you need me."

Frankie swallowed. Something tied up tight inside her loosened a little. She thanked him, but she still felt like a mouse attempting to conceal itself inside an open orange crate.

Eugene said, "Hide in my closet."

Frankie followed his gaze from the tidy row of clothing on hangers to several pairs of shoes lined up on the floor. The police would enter his bedroom and find her in seconds. She imagined the satisfaction in their voices: *Now we've got you.*

She said, "That closet is the second place they'll look, right after they check underneath your bed. I'm going to have to run out the back and keep to the shadows. I've got my car out on Sunset, and I'll take my chances that the city cops don't have my description yet."

"You won't get ten feet from my door." With a clatter he shoved the clothing in his closet to either end of the rod, leaving an open space in the middle. There followed a businesslike click of wood on wood as he removed a secret door at the back of the closet. This door was cut along the bevels of the original construction, and could be replaced without any obvious seam. Inside, the space was dark.

Eugene said, "Amazing, isn't it? It might have been made expressly for hiding innocent women suspected of murder."

You won't get ten feet from my door, Eugene had said. It almost sounded like a threat. The choice was clear: stick with Eugene and his closet, or take a chance on a dash for the Model A. Which meant the choice was between a hiding place that looked like a trap but probably wasn't, or a race for what seemed like it might be freedom but would very likely result in capture. Neither of these alternatives appealed. What Frankie most wanted was to throw herself down on Eugene's chenille-covered bed and sob with fatigue and distress.

Instead she climbed in among Eugene's suit jackets, trousers and shirts, all smelling, like their owner, of Burma-Shave. Once inside his closet, she peered through the opening in the false back. As she had suspected, there was just about enough space inside to hide her.

"I left my money under the sofa where Gilbert Howard is sitting—"

"I'll search for it tomorrow morning. I'll bring it to you. I promise."

"Thank you, Eugene. You are a faithful fellow."

"That I am," he replied. "Faithful until death. And past it, I might add."

Somebody knocked at the front door.

Frankie crouched down in the closet. With a wiggling motion, she made her way through the hole to land in the little cubby at the back. She'd expected the floor to be gritty and hard, and she was not disappointed.

She heard the click of wood on wood, and then she was alone in the small unlit space.

At a second click, she started, but it was Eugene again. "You'd better take this with you." An object clattered onto the floor near her feet. "And be quiet—the wall you're leaning against adjoins the living room in 7B. Blanche Carver is still in there with any policemen who aren't searching Paradise Gardens."

"All right," she breathed. He slipped the false back of the closet into place.

In the dark, Frankie wrapped her arms around her legs and rested her chin on her knees. Her back was to her own Villa 7B's living room, where Gilbert Howard's body sat upright on her couch. The wall in front of her was shared with Eugene's living room. She got to her knees, leaned forward, and pressed her ear to the wall. Among the buzz of voices, two sounded deeper than Eugene's—the police, of course—but she couldn't make out any words.

She remembered that Eugene had thrown something that clattered—something made of metal, perhaps—into the little space with her. She felt around the floor with both hands and discovered a small heap of cloth—no, of clothing. She could feel seams and buttons, which she tucked out of the way to bunch the clothing beneath her. The fabric made a welcome bit of cushion for her backside.

Were the police gone?

No. Men exchanged mumbled words on the other side of the wall. Nearby, a door cracked open.

Eugene said, "In here, fellows. Please, look where you like. I wouldn't want to harbour a murderess under my bed."

In her hiding place, Frankie scowled at the epithet.

A male voice called Eugene *mister* and thanked him. A second added, "Please step out of our way."

That wiped her scowl away. She had never before been hunted by the police, but she was astounded to recognize the feeling all the same. It was very much like playing sardines at parties, this tension of waiting to be found. Was this how an animal felt when it was prey? This lit-up, rapid-pulse sense of expectation? In her mind's eye she saw the neon ceiling in the Dominion Theatre: the shining robes of the Goddess, the sharp eye of the Hunter, and the stags leaping away from the arc of his bow. How could the Hunter miss?

The Hunter wouldn't miss. And neither would the police, she thought, as one of them let out a throaty noise. She guessed that this was not a policeman who got down on hands and knees to look under beds too often. Gilbert Howard had been an important movie star, and the station would have sent their top men to look into his murder. Top men got soft from working at their desks. But top men were smart—smart enough, perhaps, to spot a false back in a cupboard.

Frankie strained to hear the click of the cupboard door opening, holding her breath as if it were a mouthful of water she mustn't swallow or spill. When the sound didn't come, she realized that Eugene was clever enough to have left the closet door open on purpose, to lend an air of innocence to the room—but she heard his clothes being moved aside, the hangers clicking on the rod.

She wrapped her hands around her middle. If Eugene Ellery had killed Gilbert Howard, now would be the moment for him to lean forward with a keen eye and tap the back wall of the cupboard. *What's in here, fellows? Shall we have a look?* And they'd find her in the dark.

Her heart beat faster and she felt dizzy. When they found her, what would they say? Something like, *The jig is up, sister.*

What would she answer? She would need to be hard like Barbara Stanwyck and sharp like Marietta Valdes. She mouthed the words, *Let go of me, copper. I can walk by myself.*

It was warm in the cupboard, but the shivers took her, and she fumbled in the cloth around her to see whether there might be a sweater. Her fingertips brushed a hard object on the floor. This must be the object that Eugene had tossed inside with her before shutting the door to her hiding place.

She had found the gun.

Silently she picked up the weapon and cradled it in her hands. It might be Eugene Ellery's gun—he was a police-man, and he would have a gun, wouldn't he? But she knew it wasn't Eugene's, even before she rubbed along the grip of the gun and caught the tip of her thumbnail on the lines of the crown etched there. This was the gun that had first appeared at the audition—the gun with which Gilbert Howard had shot Leo Samson in the shoulder.

It was the gun that Connie had taken from the audition in Vancouver and stowed in the Model A's glove box. King Samson had taken it back, and Marietta Valdes had taken it from him in turn before she flung it over the side of the cliff. Leo had retrieved this gun and given it to his father, who had forgotten it in Frankie's car. Frankie had lost it again in the bushes behind Paradise Gardens. There she'd believed it safely concealed.

Now, in this little room, she was learning that there was no such thing as safe concealment. Somebody had found the gun in the bushes. Somebody had shot Gilbert Howard with it. Now, Eugene had tossed it in with her. Had Eugene fired it? Had he killed Gilbert Howard? But Eugene appeared sincerely respectful of the dead actor. And furthermore, if Eugene was the killer, then why would he help her?

Outside her hiding place, Eugene's bedroom grew quiet. Perhaps the police had already left. Was the room too quiet? Maybe they were waiting for her. She pictured policemen poised on each side of Eugene's bedroom door, ready to spring upon her.

She hefted the gun from one hand to the other. She might have to fire it. Not *at* somebody, though. She'd fire it down into the floor. Better still, she'd shoot bullets up through the ceiling and make her escape in a snow of falling plaster.

She rolled onto her side and, at the sound of a tiny click from inside her pocket, only just saved herself from crushing the men's sunglasses and breaking the bottle of peroxide Billie had stolen for her from the drugstore.

She mouthed, *I'm no murderer, your honour. I'm a victim of society.* Indeed, she was as much a victim of society as Billie Starr.

Footsteps tapped the bedroom floor. She heard the snick of wood against wood. She shrank back against the cupboard wall and held up the gun.

Eugene hissed, "All right?"

She lowered the gun and managed to open her dry mouth. "Abso-tively."

"Don't move, Frankie. There are police all over Paradise Gardens. Let's keep the status quo, shall we?"

"Posi-lutely. Eugene, where did you get this gun?"

"Now, that was a lucky thing," Eugene said.

"Was it?" she asked.

"I spotted it in the grass outside your back door at Villa 7B. I'm certainly glad I found it before the local cops did. Sleep as well as you can." The door to the opening clicked shut.

In the darkness, Frankie touched the soft articles of clothing she'd found. A woman must have left them behind in this space at some time in the past. What woman? An actress, of course, like Frankie. A former resident of Villa 7A. Had she left the clothes hidden here when she gave up her dreams and went home a failure? Or was it for a joyful reason? Had the woman who lived here discarded these, her old clothes, when she became a success in the movies? At the very least, Frankie hoped it was not a story like Billie's.

Nor a story like Frankie's own.

How had she come to this point? In films, a series of violent energies united to make murder. But these last hours seemed thick with blind, random events that flashed like lightning, snapped themselves whip-like around her, and dragged her into the centre of the storm that had killed Gilbert Howard. Worse, her involvement might so easily have been avoided if she'd stayed home in Vancouver. But if she hadn't accompanied Connie to Hollywood, perhaps it would have been Connie hiding in Eugene's closet, accused of murder.

What if Frankie herself had somehow *set off* the concatenation of circumstances that resulted in poor Gilbert Howard sitting up dead on her sofa next door? Had her arrival in

Hollywood somehow set events in motion, strained tempers, and exacerbated great-minded jealousies and ambitions so that somebody killed him? She shook her head. Impossible. A substitute schoolteacher from Vancouver was a distant outsider in Hollywood's power circles. Frankie couldn't affect the fate of a fly.

The air in the cubby was heavy but not stifling, so there had to be an opening somewhere. Moving noiselessly, she plumped up the clothing—there was a slip, judging from the lace and satin, and a blouse with inconveniently large buttons. She pulled a coat's arms tighter around her to feel a little less alone. She wished Connie were here. She recognized this as an ungenerous thought—the hiding place was too small for two, and she didn't want her friend to be hunted by the law—but still she wished Connie were here. She tried to worry about her, but the cold truth was that Connie wasn't in a dark nook with the police searching for her as a murderess. She was certainly somewhere better than this. In imagination, Frankie heard Connie ask in radio announcer tones, *What do you want in a hiding place, Frankie?*

I want a pillow that smells as fresh as summer rain …

… and a gun.

Frankie wondered whether a police photographer had already come, and if Gilbert Howard's body was gone by now. She remembered his white hand and the way his fingers had curled around the orange. The hairs on his fingers, black against his skin. She sat up straight. His white hand looked the same as the hand of the body buried under the lawn outside Villas 7A and B. Not as dirty, perhaps, but certainly the same hand.

That meant there was only one dead man in Paradise Gardens, and that man was Gilbert Howard. Somebody had first of all buried him out back of Villa A where she had watched Eugene uncover his dead hand. Then somebody had finished digging up Gilbert Howard and moved his body into Villa 7B's living room. She didn't know why deducing that progression of actions made her feel even worse.

She pillowed her head in the clothing and took a deep breath. She knew one thing about the woman whose clothes these had been—she used Ivory soap, like Frankie and Connie did. This brought her a little comfort.

Holding the gun in both hands so as to be ready for any contingency, Frankie prepared herself to stay awake and alert, all through the night.

The first time she woke, her hip was giving her a hard time, and she considered leaving her hiding spot to creep into Eugene's bedroom. She knew what her father and Mrs Mooney would say if an engaged girl were to sleep in another man's bedroom, but she wondered whether they might make allowances for such behaviour in the case of a true emergency. Perhaps it might even be all right if the man put his arms around her, this once. Perhaps not. She fell back asleep before she could decide.

The second time she woke inside the closet hidey-hole, she heard a sound she was certain came from Eugene's bedroom.

A woman's sigh.

The third time Frankie woke, it was morning. She knew because birdsong travelled through the walls into her hiding place. She slipped the gun into the pocket of her green-and-blue dress. The tips of her fingers touched the dried crumbs of the sandwich she'd fed to the pigeons the day before. Otherwise, her pocket held only her engagement ring and her car key.

Frankie sat up straight in the darkness. Then she knelt on the gritty floor. How grubby her dress must be by now.

With delicacy she eased the boards out of the back of the closet. She climbed out across Eugene's shoes, disarranged after the police search the night before. Remembering the female sigh she'd heard in the middle of the night, she wasn't sure what she'd find in Eugene's dawn-lit bedroom, but he was alone now, humped up among his covers. Perhaps she'd dreamed the sigh. She stood at the foot of Eugene's bed, studying his face. Above the neck of the white cotton undershirt he slept in, his cheek looked as soft as an innocent boy's.

Her intuition over the last few hours told her that Eugene was on her side, but Frankie had never been much for trusting her feelings. Logic and common sense were her preferred guides, and both instructed her not to linger in Eugene's bedroom a moment longer, at the mercy of a man who seemed to care about Gilbert Howard's death as much as she did but who'd had in his possession the gun that had most likely killed him.

What day was this? Yesterday had been Friday, her first day as an extra in the movies. Now it was Saturday morning. She wished that Friday had turned out differently, and that Gilbert Howard were still alive. Right now she would be climbing out of her own little bed in Villa 7B with hope in her heart, anticipating her hard-earned audition for the part of a sad manicurist on Monday.

Frankie crept into the living room and peered out Eugene's front door. Dawn lit the quiet cottages and bricked pathways around Paradise Gardens. For a miracle, there was not a single policeman posted outside Eugene's Villa 7A. Frankie sidled out Eugene's door and up to her own. The plaid curtains were drawn across the living-room window. Had they taken Gilbert Howard's body away?

Of course they had. But why was there no policeman guarding the scene of the murder? Could her luck have changed as night had changed to day? Frankie remembered her little hoard of forty dollars left over after paying the Queen her rent money. She needed it now, for she had not a cent in her pocket for an escape north to Vancouver. And she knew exactly where to find it: under the sofa cushions on which Gilbert Howard's body had been sitting.

She tested Villa 7B's front doorknob. It turned. It creaked open.

At her back, so close that she felt her skirts move, somebody whispered, "Just where do you think you're going?"

23

Two hours later, in the middle of a sunny Saturday morning
in the Queen of the Extras' Paradise Gardens, Frankie stood
at the mirror in the movie royal's bathroom and gazed at her
brand-new, peroxide-blonde hair colour. It was the Queen's
idea of a disguise.

It might so easily have been a policeman that found her
outside Villa 7B. If so, she would be in a police station now,
pleading in a harshly lit room for the law to believe her
story. Instead, the Queen had found Frankie and hustled
her into nearby Villa 1. Without drawing breath, the Queen
had bleached Frankie's dark hair white with the help of the
peroxide Billie had stolen the day before.

Frankie leaned a little closer to the mirror. The light in
the Queen's bathroom was not good, but she believed that
this new platinum-blonde appearance suited her. Frankie
murmured, *"Hey Connie, what do you want in a hair colour?"*

If Connie had been there in the Queen's bungalow instead of off who-knows-where, she might well have replied, *"A powerful peroxide for a perfect blonde."*

Frankie pulled, hard enough to hurt, at her newly pale hair. She said aloud to her reflection, "A blonde accused of murder, pursued … but not cornered."

"A blonde who's going to make it out of town safely." The Queen of the Extras appeared in the mirror behind her. Loretta Desirée studied Frankie's new hair colour with an intensity equal to Frankie's own. "If I go with you as far as the road, we ought to make it past the police to your car on Sunset Boulevard. Remember that you're pretending to be that noisy cheap blonde in 12A, the one who throws dishes. I heard they searched her place already. So if the cops stop us, talk tough, and give your delivery a bit of the Jean Harlow."

"It will be hard not to, with this hair." Frankie grinned.

"Platinum always gives a girl a certain *je ne sais quoi.*" The Queen took her sharp little golden scissors and snipped at a couple of silvery-white locks so that they curled around Frankie's ears. The rest waved down around her shoulders.

Frankie said, "The important thing is for me to be *je ne sais* who."

"I guess you'll have to change your name. Can you think of a good one?"

Frankie blinked. "I was going to change my name anyway. I'm getting married."

"My goodness, how lovely," the Queen said. "What will he say when he sees your hair?"

"I can't imagine what Champ will say. Nor my dad." Frankie's hair felt light on her head. Her eyebrows stood out as clean dark lines below the silver-white locks. How many times back home had she been cast as a man because of those eyebrows? And because of her figure as well, it must be said. "I should have dyed my hair platinum years ago," she said.

"If you had, it wouldn't be much of a disguise now."

Frankie gave her new hair her fairest evaluation. She frowned. She looked good as a platinum blonde, but she also looked a lot like Frankie as a platinum blonde. "I don't know, my Queen. I'm afraid that I'd still look pretty recognizable to somebody who knows me."

"The police don't know you." The Queen inclined her head. "Maybe if we pouffed it up a little more, or bobbed it to your ears?"

She lifted Frankie's hair experimentally and raised her golden scissors to make another pass. Frankie, a little awe-struck by her new platinum glamour, felt a certain resistance to cutting any of it, on the grounds that *more* beautiful hair was always preferable to *less* beautiful hair.

The Queen added, "What if we curled you up like little Shirley Temple?"

"Oh, dear! She's sweet. But please and thank you, no." Frankie felt in her dress pocket for the men's sunglasses Billie Starr had stolen for her. Were they still in one piece? She pulled out the sunglasses and put them on.

"That's better," the Queen murmured.

"The dark glasses do help. Thank goodness I'm so new in Hollywood. I wouldn't get two steps out the door if there were a photograph of me to show around."

"A photograph of you?" The Queen fell silent.

Frankie remembered the flash and pop of the camera at Central Casting. They'd taken a picture for her application form. How long did it take to develop a photograph from a glass slide? If the police were doing their job, and the Central Casting offices opened at nine, her paperwork would be in their hands already. It would be a slim little folder—she was only a first-day extra—and her photograph would be lying right on the top when the police opened it.

From Central Casting, it wasn't a long hike to Monument Studios. There, Luigi had pictures of Frankie the pigeon girl from yesterday's filming.

She experienced a fizzing, weakening sensation that began in her fingertips and spread through the rest of her. "There are at least *two* pictures of me."

"Poor Frankie." The Queen gave Frankie's shoulder a squeeze. "But they won't recognize you now. You're a young blonde woman in sunglasses, and there are thousands like you around Hollywood."

Reluctantly, Frankie disagreed. "Platinum hair is not a good enough disguise. What if you make me look older?"

"How much older?"

"Yonks. I mean decades."

"Aging makeup is the most difficult to get right." The Queen looked Frankie up and down. "With your young-gal figure, we'd have to pad you too, and even then you'd only pass at night, if the cop who talked to you was nearsighted or stewed to the gills."

And of course, she'd have to walk a little differently, remove the spring from her step and that ingénue hope from her expression. But she was an actress, wasn't she?

"I need a fairy godmother to turn me into a mouse. Or a pumpkin. Or a prince."

The Queen looked up sharply. "That's more like it," she said.

"That's an acting secret, isn't it? I need a disguise that focusses the observer on the whole rather than the changing bits of me. What if I became a nun? Then people would see the habit I wear instead of the person inside it."

"A nun?" The Queen looked doubtful. "I was going to suggest something easier. But if you really think a nun is best …" The Queen tugged a towel off the rail and wrapped it tightly around Frankie's face to make a wimple. "You can use my black robes, and we'll pin the towel into the right shape."

Frankie straightened her phony wimple and stared at herself in the mirror. Although she had grown up in a religious household, she was a most unconvincing nun. It was something about her ironic jawline, where it cut against the wimple. As well, her gaze was so secular that she'd need a lot of acting experience under her belt before she was offered a part as a *réligieuse*. For fun, she donned Billie's sunglasses again, and they both laughed. Frankie wondered if doomed people—like the French aristocrats waiting in their clammy cells to be called to the guillotine—sometimes shared a joke.

She said, "I wish Jack Benny were here to tell a funny story right now. Jack Benny wouldn't turn me in, I bet. Maybe he would change clothes with me, like Sidney Carton did in *A Tale of Two Cities*. Then I would walk away freely."

Frankie pictured herself making her way out to the Model A, her arms swinging, her manly step firm on the sun-dappled pavement.

"Now you're talking," the Queen said. "I was going to suggest just that. You're the type, with those eyebrows—"

"And my figure." She didn't want to be a man. But she reminded herself that there were many things one didn't want to do in this world.

She closed her eyes. If she had to do it, she wouldn't waste another moment. It was her fervent hope that the Queen wouldn't have a better idea once the deed was done.

She picked up the Queen's golden scissors and hooked a section of her silvery hair between her forefinger and middle finger. She'd cut her father's hair often enough. Her fingers were less steady than they'd ever been, but she could probably cut a man's hair on a ship in a gale out at sea, or perched high among the tossing branches of a tree, or under water. But cutting her father's hair underwater, she considered, would be easy compared to cutting her own. She'd have to get the Queen to help with the sides and back. Taking a deep breath, she snipped.

The little fan of platinum hair fell to the floor. She must remember to sweep up in case the police returned to search the Paradise Gardens bungalows again.

Arms folded, the Queen watched her snip. "I'm going to find you a man's suit, Frankie." The golden scissors snipped at the ends of Frankie's hair: short, shorter, shortest.

Frankie met her gaze in the mirror. "We'd better make sure it's a pretty loose fit, my Queen. I'm going to have to carry a gun."

"Walk like a man, Francesca Ray." The Queen of the Extras took another stitch in Eugene's trouser bottoms.

Eugene was, after all, only a little taller than Frankie, and the Queen was taking them up just that half-inch because, she said, the way a man's trousers cut across the instep of his shoes was more vital than money.

"I *am* walking like a man." *Exactly* like a man. There had been a dearth of boys in high school who wanted to be in plays like *Joanie Gets a Boyfriend*. Frankie's drama teacher had been very clear in her praise: when the part called for it, Frankie walked like a man. She did it now by mentally broadening her shoulders and slouching with her hands in the pockets of Eugene's jacket, which she was wearing over her dress while she waited for the trousers to be done. The Queen had agreed that the male voice was Frankie's best trick, though; she could produce a sort of gentlemanly tenor without half trying.

"Is Eugene back with my forty dollars yet? I left it right under the sofa cushion in the living room." She would be much happier when she had that money safely in hand. Frankie threw herself down at the kitchen table. "Are the trousers nearly done?"

"Invisible stitches take as long as they take, sweetie. Not much difference in height between you and Eugene, but that makes no difference to hemming time." The Queen turned a bit of trouser hem over her index finger, holding the cloth taut with her thumb and middle finger as she made her tiny stitches. "I started out as a dresser for Marie Tempest on her American tour, but I enjoyed taking understudy roles far more, and I left Miss Tempest's dressing room for the stage. I 'discovered' Gilbert Howard, you know."

In a sad sort of way, Frankie had discovered him, too: dead on the couch. She said, "Poor Gilbert Howard."

"You'd never believe it, but dear Howie was in love with me when he started out."

"Certainly I would believe it," Frankie said politely.

"We were good friends, as well, which not every one of his lady loves could claim. I met him when he was straight out of the army. He was captured, you know, by the Germans."

Connie's father had been killed in the war. However, Frankie's father, Sheridan D, had been too old to be called up by the time it started, and when he tried to sign up they showed him the door. Frankie tried to imagine Gilbert Howard as a soldier in the war. "I'll bet he was brave."

"Yes. And Howie looked wonderful in uniform." The Queen stretched out the unfinished cuff of Eugene's trousers and picked up her little golden scissors. "The Germans found

Howie in a foxhole, declaiming Shakespeare. He didn't stay captive long, though. He escaped in the middle of the prisoners' Christmas show, dressed as the pantomime Dame, and he made his way back in skirts to England."

"Good heavens." Frankie had almost forgotten the trousers, as well as the murder accusation, so wrapped up was she in the story. "That would have made a wonderful movie, if only he could have starred in it."

Footsteps sounded lightly on the path outside Villa 1. The Queen's face lit up. "Hello, Eugene."

"What's all this?" Eugene stared from Loretta Desirée to Frankie.

"The Queen is disguising me as a man," Frankie said.

"Good heavens, Loretta."

The Queen said, "Eugene, you mustn't fuss."

"Yesterday she dressed Tom like a woman for the movies," Frankie pointed out.

Eugene said, "She's always dressing somebody as something. May I ask, are those my best trousers you're cutting up, Loretta?"

"Yes, indeed. How is the situation regarding the police?"

"It's quiet just now. The force seems to pass through in flocks, like pigeons."

Frankie asked, "Did you find my forty dollars?"

"Here, hold out your hands."

Frankie did. He took hold of her hands and studied them, much the way Frankie used to check her student's hands before letting them eat lunch.

"My Queen, you've clipped Frankie's nails short and straight. Perfectly like a man." Eugene held out his own smartly-trimmed nails and grinned at the Queen, who smiled back. A mother's smile, as if for a favourite child.

Eugene turned Frankie's hands palm up again. His own fingers were as cool and gentle as his voice. He folded her fingers around four one-dollar bills. "This is all the money I have. I couldn't find the forty dollars that you hid in the sofa cushions. Somebody must have taken your money—maybe the police, though I hate to say it. But these four dollars will get you enough gas to get you out of town. After that, you'll have to work your way back home to Vancouver."

The Queen said, "It's a sin and a shame somebody took your money, Frankie. I'm afraid that I've none to give you, for Blanche, although sorrowful over Howie's death, somehow remembered to collect every dime of the Paradise Gardens rent money."

At the loss of her forty dollars Frankie felt her disappointment like a blow between her shoulder blades. Of course the police would have taken her money—as evidence, possibly, although in the movies you learned lots about graft and corruption.

The Queen picked up the grey trousers and draped them over her shoulders. "I must press these pants before you wear them, Frankie. Doris has a working iron, and Betty's got the big ironing board." The Queen hurried out of the house.

Frankie became conscious of her half-and-half state under Eugene's steady gaze. With her man's haircut and jacket, but wearing her dress, she must have looked a sight. "What do you think? Will I pass for a man?"

"It's not bad for a disguise," Eugene said. "I think the right word for you is *grotesque*."

"Thanks," Frankie said dryly. "I was hoping I looked like an ordinary fellow from the waist up."

"*Grotesque* is a term in Italian Renaissance studies," he elaborated. "It was used in paintings or sculpture for people or animals caught at the moment of changing from one aspect to another."

"Okay," Frankie said. "I don't mind being Italian. And a half a man. Anyway, I think the Queen has done a good job."

"She's a master of disguising other people, isn't she?"

"She seems to change one gender to the other whenever the extras need different work."

"And she also disguises the extras to help them sneak into hotels and restaurants to collect gossip for Blanche's column." He smiled. "You've seen Bruno. From the back he can pass for a child, but face-on, he looks like a small man in his thirties. But a couple of years back, when the Queen was disguising him as a little boy, he was making a hundred a week in the kiddie reels. He lasted a year."

Frankie tried to think how it would be for Bruno to live as a child for a year. "But if Bruno was making such good money, and getting steady parts in films, why did he go back to working as an extra?"

"There are problems with being somebody you're not for any length of time. Day after day, you know. It eats the soul. That's what Bruno told me, anyway."

Frankie shook her head. "Maybe it's true for Bruno. It does seem disrespectful to pay a boy well for his work, but not a man. But staying disguised wouldn't eat my soul," she said positively. "I would look on it as acting—as sustaining a part. For a successful year's run, like they do on the stage."

"But you're lucky, Frankie, because you'll never know." Eugene said. "You're going home to Vancouver. Keep a low profile, and they'll never find you on your way out of Hollywood."

"They will if the Canadian Mounties are called in. The Mounties always get their man." She raised her eyes to meet Eugene's. She held his gaze for a long moment. Then she stated the truth that revealed itself to her at the same moment she spoke the words. "I want to stay in Hollywood."

"You must not." Eugene looked away. "Who knows how long even the best disguise will stand up?"

"The Queen is an expert."

"Yes. But a burst of sunlight might illuminate the curve of your beardless jaw. Or somebody with an eye to earning a fat reward might find himself blessed with an unprecedented, superhuman instinct. Leave town, Frankie. Do it early. Do it quick."

Eugene's urgency was such that if she hadn't had such a tip-top disguise, she might have followed his advice. She said, "I'm going out into Hollywood, dressed as a man, to investigate this murder. I'll find out who killed Gilbert Howard and clear my name. Will you help?"

He took a step away from her. "If you fail, you know what it might mean."

Frankie nodded. The night before, in Eugene's closet, she had faced that particular terror dead-on. But who could fear the electric chair when the sun was shining and you were young and full of ideas? She said, "Listen. I have two clues."

Eugene, grey eyes graver than ever before, sat down at the Queen's kitchen table. He steepled his hands and then studied them. Frankie imagined the impatience that this professional police officer would feel when confronted with an amateur's ideas.

"Eugene, you must listen to what I have to say. I'm not police, but I know things about the murder that the police don't. The first clue is Billie Starr. She was there with me when I found Gilbert Howard's body on my sofa."

Eugene looked up, a spark of interest in his eyes. "I didn't know she was there."

"When she saw him dead, Billie said, 'We all know who killed him.' She knew Gilbert Howard had been murdered, even though nobody else could tell until the police showed us the bullet wound. One of us needs to question her."

Eugene shook his head. "I know Billie, Frankie. She used to live here. She always had a bottle somewhere, and—"

"Yes, she was drunk last night, too. But she seems to operate quite efficiently in that state." Frankie remembered her own panic and shock upon confronting Gilbert Howard dead on her sofa. "She reacted far more quickly than I did. Drunk as she was, she said a lovely and respectful farewell and then left before Blanche Carver or the police knew she'd been there. Maybe they would have suspected her too, although I wouldn't wish it."

"Billie wouldn't murder Gilbert." Eugene's tone was firm, as if speaking to a police subordinate who was wasting his superior officer's time on red herrings. But he had missed her point completely.

"I didn't say Billie shot him. I said she said she knows who did. That's the first clue that must be followed up." She decided to ignore his look of doubt. "Here is the second clue," she continued. "Gilbert Howard had a secret girlfriend. Among his many public girlfriends."

"Hold on, now—" Eugene began.

Frankie interrupted. "I don't suggest we interview everybody Gilbert Howard ever kissed. But this girl, who was swimming naked in the pool next door in the Garden of Allah two nights ago, was with him in the hours before he died."

"I really don't think—"

"And she may know who killed him. Or she may have killed him." Frankie saw that he was about to interrupt again and surprised herself by holding up her hand for silence.

"But listen to this, Eugene. It looked to me as if she were not simply one more star-struck girl to Gilbert Howard." She pictured the scene she, Connie, and Tom had witnessed at the swimming pool. *The kiss.* Of course Howard was an actor, and a great one, but … "*I* think he was really in love with this girl, and that she knew things about his life that others didn't."

She hoped her guess was right. At any rate, she had him now, for Eugene nodded, and she was certain of the sincere sorrow in his grey eyes. "Frankie, you may be right."

"Good." She felt almost faint with relief. "I'll search out the golden swimmer — the girlfriend — and you go talk to Billie. I'd bet any money she's back at the brothel across the street from Monument Studios."

"No," Eugene said firmly. "I have the resources for a search, and may safely ask door-to-door as well. You may have the dubious pleasure of interviewing Billie Starr."

Even quiet men always wanted things their way. Frankie said, "Will you call in your colleagues?"

"My colleagues?"

"The police."

"No." He hesitated. "I may have inadvertently misled you, Frankie. I'm more of a private detective."

Somehow, Frankie was not surprised. She wished with all her heart that Eugene hadn't been lying to her about practically everything from the start. But she remained nearly certain that, though a liar, he was innocent of the murder. If he'd been guilty, he would not have protected her. He would have seen to it that the police found her last night and put her in jail. Eugene was not transparent, and he lied at will, but he was at least sincere. Frankie was almost sure of that, too — especially since he was not a professional actor. She refused to think more deeply about her feelings on the matter than that.

She said, "I'll meet you back here tonight. And one more thing, Eugene …"

"What?"

Frankie burst out, "*Why* didn't you call the police to dig up that body in the backyard when you said you would? If they'd taken him away, then nobody would have been able to dig him up and put him on my sofa—and I wouldn't be in this mess."

Eugene inclined his head. "Exactly who do you think knew it was Gilbert Howard buried in the backyard? Not me. Not you. All we saw was one hand uncovered in the grass and soil. We decided he was a poor anonymous fellow whose relatives had buried him there out of poverty. So I left him buried—out of kindness. Respect for an unknown dead man. I thought it would hurt nobody if he rested in peace. I did not foresee the consequences."

He looked directly at her. Frankie tried to read anything but truth in his eyes. She could not.

The door opened. The Queen returned. Across her arm hung a beautifully pressed pair of grey men's trousers. In her other hand she held a pair of men's brogues.

"Those are my shoes," Eugene said.

"Yes. And this is your suit," Frankie retorted.

"Have I any belongings left at all?" But his manner as he slipped out the door was exactly that of a man who could be relied upon to track down a movie star's nameless blonde girlfriend.

"Don't look at him like that," the Queen admonished Frankie. "Frankie, you must never fall in love in Paradise Gardens. It leads to heartbreak and discord."

"It was not that kind of look." Frankie wriggled out of her dress and into the shirt and trousers. "It was a look of hope and professional respect."

The Queen's face softened, and Frankie added, "Eugene is like your favourite child, isn't he?"

"I never had any children of my own," the Queen said. "But if Eugene were my child, he would be the apple of my eye. Poor darling!"

"Why poor Eugene?" She tugged on a pair of argyle socks that the Queen had ironed for her, and then stood while the Queen tied the brogues onto Frankie's feet. They were a little big, so she took them off again and they stuffed a bit of tissue into the toes. She tried to feel like a fellow with the weight of the world on his shoulders. The word for that, she knew from her father's sermons, was *gravitas*. "Eugene seems all right to me."

"He's lonely. Now breathe in," the Queen directed her. She lifted up the hem of Frankie's shirt and proceeded to fasten about her middle and chest a terrible elasticated bit of business that she referred to as the Xeno-Flex Combination. "Every girl was flat as Nevada for fashion a few years back," the Queen said. "If you wore a Xeno-Flex Combination, you were confident that your beads would hang straight down the front of your dress."

The Xeno-Flex Combination cut Frankie's breathing room in half and pinched her around the middle. It seemed a lot to suffer, but Frankie reminded herself of the stakes.

Standing poised for an instant on the stoop of the Queen's bungalow, Frankie felt upon her brow the Queen's parting kiss. That kiss was a sort of mother's blessing. The sensation was new to Frankie. It made her feel like the youngest brother in a fairy tale, leaving home to pursue a fate.

Gravitas. Masculine gravitas. Frankie took several solid, manly steps along the Queen's garden path, keeping an Eagle Scout eye out for the police. Through Billie's dark glasses, Paradise Gardens took on a brilliantly coloured glow and an almost Maxfield Parrish intensity. She remembered her male roles in amateur theatre back home: 'Young Blade with Tennis Racquet', 'Joanie's Boyfriend', 'Hal, the Handsome Butler in the Lady's Confidence'. She reviewed her first and most basic acting lessons, taught her by a gifted elderly director who had spent a year in New York City before washing up in Vancouver. He had insisted that it was artistic suicide to trust to inspiration to interpret a character. You had to focus on the work. She squared her shoulders, buttoned her coat around her *gravitas*, and rested her hand on the gun in her pocket.

What a hopeful young woman she had been two nights before, dancing the carioca with Eugene and trying not to lead like a man. Now she *was* a man and a lead in a criminal investigation, albeit an amateur. Hands in her pockets, her brogues loping toward Paradise Garden's central patio, she tried not to feel self-conscious of her short hair. There was a breeze around her ears, and the novelty of the sensation threatened to put her off her stride. But at the same time, she felt taller than usual, as if she were growing upward from the top of her head.

Frankie stopped at the path to her own front door.

An idea presented itself. Disguised as a man, she could slip inside Villa 7B and have a quick look for her forty dollars. Eugene might well have missed the little wad of bills, but she knew exactly where in the sofa cushions she had hidden it. How swift could she be? *As swift as thought.* Frankie tensed to make her move. Then, in the moment preceding action, she caught sight of several policemen searching the hedges that bordered Paradise Gardens and the Garden of Allah. As the men peered about, their caps reminded Frankie of blackbirds hopping along the branches and searching for berries. But these were not birds, and they were not searching for berries. They were searching for her. She counted three policemen within view.

Once again, she had nearly been rash. Would she *ever* learn? Like that darned old Icarus. When Sheridan D had first told her the story, she had been disgusted with Icarus. He had wasted those beautiful wings! Now she saw how such an error might occur, all in a second's rash decision.

Striding more cautiously now, she approached Eugene's pathway.

A young woman stumbled around from behind the bungalow, then tripped and fell in a swirl of red skirts. Weeping, she sat down on the grass not six feet from Frankie.

Frankie hesitated. Red of dress and high of heel, the sorrowful woman was Marietta Valdes. Marietta had met Frankie twice before now. Would she recognize Frankie in her man's disguise? Frankie nearly turned tail and ran.

But far better to test her disguise here, where she had Eugene and the Queen to back her up or hide her again, than out in greater Hollywood and entirely on her own.

It was emphatically better to test her disguise on Marietta than on a policeman. Frankie braced herself for the test of creditable manliness, and came as close as nothing to failing it by asking Marietta, *What's wrong?* Just in time she stopped herself. A man would not ask clarifying questions. A man would act. So Frankie felt in her breast pocket for the handkerchief she knew must be there, knelt, and offered it to Marietta Valdes. Marietta accepted it, buried her beautiful face in it, and then looked up again at Frankie.

Marietta said, "The world has too few gentlemen in it." Even with her mascara smudged beneath her eyes, her superior bone structure shone in the early afternoon light. With the handkerchief she wiped at the smudges under her eyes and said, "I'm sorry. No, I'm not. I was overcome by sorrow at the death of a friend."

Gilbert Howard. Marietta's face buckled into tears again. Frankie tried and failed to figure out how anybody could wear a twisted, weeping face and still look beautiful. "I'm sorry for your loss. I was so sad to hear the news as well."

"Thank you. Howie was the only person in the whole world on my side. He tried and tried to help me in my struggles to direct films. I suppose that seems crazy to you." Marietta blew her nose gracefully. "You look like an actor. Are you?"

Frankie shook her head. If only she were. And she would have been this coming Monday, if only the world had revealed itself a friendlier, fairer place.

She cursed herself for breaking character and swore not to do so again.

"No, I'm not an actor."

"It's hard to believe."

She held out a hand to help Marietta to her feet. Marietta rose like a flag on a pole and then tottered in her heels on the grass. She slipped one shoe off and then the other. She looked deep into Frankie's eyes and added, "You should be an actor. Any professional can see that you've got that something."

You've got that something. How Frankie had always yearned for somebody to say exactly that to her, and not only to Connie. She wanted to laugh, or possibly cry — yes, sit down on the grass, bury her hands in her face, and weep for her lost chance at her audition for a role as a sad little manicurist in Samson's new epic *The Emperor of New York.*

Instead, she said, "Thank you, Miss Valdes."

Marietta stepped barefoot onto the pathway, a shoe in each hand. Her gaze was searching. "You know me, but I don't know you."

"Everybody knows you, Miss Valdes," Frankie said. "My name is Franklin. Call me Frank."

"But Frank who?"

Criminy. She couldn't give her own surname, *Ray.* She might as well tear off her disguise and step out into the world as her murder-suspect self. At a moment like this, she certainly missed Connie. *Hey, Connie, what do you want in a man's name?* But instead of Connie, Frankie's father Sheridan D whispered in her ear: *Here's a good name for you, Frankie. Solid, and built on classical lines.*

"I'm Frank Achilles."

"A good name for a knight in shining armour."

"Thanks," Frankie said. Too late she recognized the unsuitability of Homer's *Achilles* for a name. Achilles was a hero, of course, but he had sulked in his tent. And he was certainly not a gentleman. But it was too late to switch to *Frank Ulysses,* and anyway Ulysses, with all his clever tricks, was no gentleman either. "Keep the handkerchief, won't you?"

Marietta said, "A fellow like you, with those cheekbones, your moonlight head of hair, and your slender build?" She touched red-tipped fingers to the lapel of Frankie's coat, and Frankie was grateful for the flattening security of the Xeno-Flex Combination. "Frank, any director worth his salt would see the possibilities in you. If you're not an actor, what are you?"

"I'm …" What was Frank Achilles? Frankie pondered the question. What were men, anyway? Ministers, roaring and hiding their sherry. Insurance men like Champ, pink-faced and close to the money. Haberdashers. Shoe salesmen. *Detectives.* She grinned. "Well, maybe I'm an actor of a sort after all."

"Of course you are." Marietta smiled, although her eyes were still a little pink about the edges. "I saw it immediately. It's a director's instinct. If only I had a movie to direct."

"I believe," Frankie said politely — no, *with chivalry* — "I believe you would make a fine motion picture director, Miss Valdes."

"Do you?" Marietta took a step closer. "That's encouraging to hear. Very encouraging indeed. I hope we meet again, Frank Achilles. With Gilbert Howard dead, I need all the discerning actors in this godforsaken town that I can get on my side." Without a goodbye, Marietta Valdes strolled away, swaying like an expensive ship crossing the swell of the sea.

Frankie watched the actress walk away in the direction of Sunset Boulevard. She had two successive thoughts. The first was that she had passed the test of believability. Her disguise had held up: even at close quarters, Marietta had believed that Frankie was Frank Achilles.

Her second thought was that as soon as she got out of these men's clothes, she really had to learn to walk like Marietta Valdes.

As the distance between them grew, Frankie put her hands deep into her pockets and rocked, manlike, on the heels of her brogues. Thus, she was completely in character to receive Marietta's backward look, a glance pulled straight out of Cupid's quiver and fletched in gold. In return, Frankie touched her forehead in a male salute to Beauty.

Graceful in bare feet, Marietta swung her red shoes by their straps and sailed away through Paradise Gardens. Once the actress had disappeared from view, Frankie did not hesitate. She headed off in pursuit of the truth — to be exacted from Billie Starr.

24

"Brother, do you know a gal with a heart of gold?" Frankie sang in her best tenor imitation as she drove up sunny Sunset Boulevard in her father's reliable Ford Model A. The solid brogues she wore made a difference: they rode heavy on the gas and light on the brake. It was not that Frankie had become a better driver because she looked like a man. She might have been sitting with a man's confidence, and she might have had her elbow hooked out the driver's window in the manner of a man, but these were part of the professional actress's toolbox. The real difference was that she sported trousers rather than the usual skirt. The first time Frankie had seen Katherine Hepburn wearing trousers in *Movie Mirror* the previous year, she'd been startled. But now she understood what Blanche Carver, in her white trouser suits, must already know: trousers aided competence and freedom. As well, there was more freedom in the knee and thigh area

than Frankie would ever have expected from a simple pair of grey twill trousers.

"She'd turn a king's head, that's what I've been told … Hey de hoo de hee …" She trailed off in the middle of the chorus of 'Dora Heart'.

"We all know who killed him." Frankie echoed Billie's words, spoken out of the blue not long after the two of them had found the body on Villa 7A's living-room sofa.

Billie was a drunk and lived in a brothel.

Still, she had seemed so sure.

Frankie hoped it would not be difficult to negotiate a meeting with Billie Starr. She only needed to ask the girl that one question: *Who killed Gilbert Howard?* Frankie pushed the Model A a little harder, made a U-turn, and pulled up in front of the brothel. She drove up onto the curb and then down, with a hearty slap and a scrape of tire that told her she'd landed accurately. She hauled on the brake and considered swinging lightly out of the window of the Model A without opening the door, but decided it would be too conspicuous and exited the car in the usual manner. She strode beneath the palm trees, up the walk toward the Spanish-style mansion that was really a brothel, her trousers flapping, her short platinum hair riffling in the afternoon breeze, and one hand in her pocket to cradle the gun.

She knocked on the brothel's door. The boy who opened it reminded her of Pats, her cheeky paperboy back home. Behind him, a tidy entry hall glowed with natural light. At the far end of the hall, a stairway curved up to a landing.

"I'm here to see one Billie Starr," Frankie said.

"Best of luck to you, young man," the boy responded cheekily.

Frankie hid her smile. "Go polish an apple, kid," she said.

Still barring her way, the boy looked her up and down.

"You're an actor, aren't you? Jeepers, you look like one. That hair!"

"Sure I am, kid." She grinned back. "May I step inside, then?"

He salaamed. "You can do handstands for all I care, mister. But you'll have to get by the manager to go upstairs."

A woman in a brown suit entered the lobby. Anywhere else, Frankie would have pegged her as a manager of a high-priced dress shop, or maybe a legal secretary.

The madam shooed the boy away. "Scamp. Go make yourself a sandwich." She smiled after him. "He's the apple of my eye, but he's no angel."

"Those are the best kind. They're independent thinkers," Frankie said courteously.

She followed the madam into the lobby. What with the large electric candelabra and clerestory lighting over the stairs, the place was so bright and modern that you had to wonder whether it made a difference doing what must be very unpleasant work in a building designed on such pleasant lines. She said, "My name is Frank Achilles. I'd like to see one of your girls for a moment, if I may."

"Of course, Mr Achilles. I'll need your reference." The madam looked over her shoulder at the door through which the boy had left. "I sure hope that kid doesn't mess up my kitchen. He makes more of a disaster putting together one sandwich than a raccoon in a trash can."

"My reference?" Frankie touched the gun in her pocket.

"A written reference." The madam's smile was patient— Frankie guessed she'd explained these procedures before. "It protects the girls, *you* understand. And cash on the barrelhead, of course, unless the studio is covering your tab."

The studio! Paying for prostitute services. Good heavens. Frankie felt out of her depth. "I want to talk to her, that's all. She's a friend of mine and I need to ask her a question."

"What sort of question?" The madam asked evenly. "And which girl do you mean?"

Frankie shifted her shoulders under her jacket. With no reference and almost no money, she saw two choices ahead and approaching quickly, like Burma-Shave ads on the side of the road. First, she could leave and wait outside until Billie emerged on her own. Or she could pull out her gun and threaten the woman with it until she produced Billie. Frankie doubted that a madam would call the police to a brothel, but a person who operated outside the law might herself be armed. In such a case, there might ensue complications involving gunplay for which Frankie was not prepared.

Frankie knew from her reading of *The Odyssey* that the best, most intelligently concocted lie was the one the woman would want to believe. A lie that wouldn't get the madam into trouble.

Remembering the young boy's conviction that she looked like a movie actor, Frankie said, "Ma'am, I'm the new lead actor in King Samson's movie *The Emperor of New York*. I won't need a letter for your file because pretty soon my face will be on every billboard in town. I'm going up those stairs to see Billie Starr for a minute, but I guarantee it's not a paying trip. All right?"

"Oh." The woman rolled her eyes. "Billie Starr. *That* one. I truly have no objection. Go on up and do your worst."

"Which door is Billie's?"

"Room 11. I don't think it'll help you any, though."

"Thank you kindly."

Frankie took the curved stairs two at a time to the floor above, the gun in her pocket bumping against her leg. At the top of the stairs Frankie came face to face with Mae West's clever leer gazing out from a line of framed posters that brightened the shadowy hall: Moira Shearer, Clark Gable, Leslie Howard, and, of all people, Greta Garbo — dressed in men's clothes as the star of *Queen Christina*. Frankie gave Queen Christina an Eagle Scout salute. She ventured along the corridor and counted up the numbers. A window at the end of the hallway looked out across the Spanish tiled roof. Room 12 was to the left of the window, and 11 to the right. She knocked and tried the knob, but the door to Room 11 was locked tight against her — or rather, against somebody. How odd it was that a prostitute should lock her door. She knocked again and then hammered on the door, but there was no answer.

Would nothing ever be easy? Frankie gave the knocking a rest and leaned against the windowsill at the end of the hallway to rub her sore knuckles. She craned her neck out the corridor window and made out the side view of Room 11's open window sash. She cast her gaze further, over the angled, red-tiled roof and across Sunset Boulevard. There stood the angels on each side of the Monument Studios gates. It seemed insulting and unfair that yesterday she'd been inside that studio, in front of the cameras, and now she was bruising her knuckles on a brothel bedroom door.

She hammered a little louder, and then louder still. A voice from a nearby room shouted, "Stop your racket, noisy!"

"Sorry!" Frankie had hoped to keep the discussion one-on-one with Billie, but as the door to Room 12 opened at her back, she saw that even the smallest actions in a place like this would have consequences. A girl stood in the doorway, fresh in a blue gingham housedress, as if she'd just come from hanging up the wash. The line from the old poem chanted inside Frankie's head nonsensically: *The gingham dog and the calico cat, side by side on the table sat.*

She glanced from Frankie to the door. "Brother, have you got your wires crossed. *That* one never answers."

"She's inside, then?" Frankie looked from the girl in gingham to Billie's door. "Why doesn't she answer?"

The gingham girl inclined her head. "She's got some kind of a deal with the management. A friend in high places, if you ask me." She looked over her shoulder into her room. "Gotta go. See you, handsome. Ask for Maggie next time."

The door to Room 12 closed, and Frankie heard shouts from inside. The argument worried Frankie, because when you're wearing the colours and shape of a man, you have to be ready to do a man's work. How likely was it, she wondered, that at some point she would be called on to use her fists to defend a woman? Frankie knew enough to keep her wrist straight when she released a punch. Champ had taught her to do so in a playful sparring match one evening while they listened to the radio, but she was certain there was no good substitute for the fisticuffs boys learned in the rough-and-tumble schoolyard.

The shouts grew fiercer in volume inside Room 12. Maggie the gingham girl seemed to give as good as she got — so far. Frankie took a deep breath preparatory to breaking into Room 12, but all at once the racket stopped, and somebody — the gingham girl, she was certain — laughed once, as if she had won a point in a long tennis set.

Frankie returned to the problem at hand: Billie didn't answer her knock. And Frankie was not capable of breaking down a door. Again, she remembered the tears, like pearls, on Billie's cheek when they'd found Gilbert Howard's body. *We all know who killed him.* Billie had been drunk, of course, but not too drunk for sense. And she might have been sobered, perhaps, by the shock of the great actor's death.

The Extra

At any rate, drunk or sober, she was Frankie's best clue. If Frankie couldn't get through to Billie, all she had was the nameless golden swimmer who had kissed Gilbert Howard a few hours before he was shot. She wondered how Eugene Ellery was coming along in his search for Gilbert Howard's mysterious girlfriend.

Frankie craned out of the window next to Billie's closed door. She scanned about the building and down through the palm trees to the ground two stories below. If she climbed outside the building to reach Billie's window, she'd have to rely on her sense of balance and good luck. If luck deserted her—as it had been doing off and on with devastating consequences for the last twenty-four hours—she was plenty high enough to fall and break her neck. She pictured herself falling two stories down to lie crumpled in the brothel's garden beneath the rattling palms. She imagined Marietta Valdes, of all people, bending over her, a sad and final farewell in her eyes. Frankie produced some good final words: "'Twill serve, 'twill serve."

But when she imagined the headline—*Murderess Francesca Ray Falls to Her Death: The Justice of Fate*—the unfairness so infuriated her that she was ready to give up on the whole project rather than give Blanche Carver the satisfaction of writing such a phony obituary. But maybe she could make the climb without disaster. After all, she had taught as a substitute for Millicent Biggs in girls' Phys Ed class. During that time, she had climbed the ropes to the roof of the school gymnasium and lived to descend them again. Her balance was good. She only lacked rooftop experience.

Frankie got her hip up on the sill and swung herself out of the corridor window onto a narrow tiled ledge on the outside of the Spanish-style mansion. She found a foothold on the sloping tiles—not only sloping, but loose as well. All at once the enterprise seemed a foolish, daring deed, and she found herself grinning like a pirate. Like the great star Douglas Fairbanks in all his swashbuckling glory.

She spared a glance across the road for the angels at the gates to Monument Studios. *Look, girls, I'm as tall as you are.* Between the studios and the mansions, cars rambled and raced along Sunset Boulevard, which made her dizzier than altitude alone could achieve. But she would never have slipped had it not been for Marietta Valdes.

On the far side of Sunset Boulevard, unmistakable in red even from that distance, the actress stood on the sidewalk outside the studio, looking up at the roof of the Spanish-style brothel. She shaded her eyes with her hands. Frankie supposed that Marietta might be looking at something else in Frankie's general direction, but there was nothing more likely to catch the eye than a man in a grey suit sidling along the rooftop toward an open window.

It was a dicey moment, and she lost her balance. She recovered herself and sent Millie Biggs and the Phys Ed students at Magee Junior Secondary School a prayer of thanks. She slid a few more unsteady steps along the roof tiles, hanging onto the eaves with both hands and cursing her stiff and slippery men's brogues, as well as the darned constricting Xeno-Flex Combination around her chest.

Down in the street, Marietta was making her way through the door into the studio. Was she going to call the police?

Frankie took hold of the window frame and peered inside. She crouched down, got one leg over the windowsill, lost her balance completely, and fell through Billie's window.

25

Frankie landed flat out on Billy's bedroom floor. Overhead a flock of brilliantly-coloured Chinese kites dangled from strings tacked to the ceiling. Embroidered cushions lay about the bed and the floor as if Billie were expecting a lot of visitors from the Far East.

Billie, cross-legged atop the neatly made bed in the middle of the room, shut her book with a snap. It was one of Frankie's favourites: *Anne of Green Gables*. Billie pulled a quart bottle of something golden up from the floor beside the bed and took a drink, despite the early afternoon hour. That was Billie, all the way.

Frankie hauled herself to her feet and buttoned up her men's jacket. "Don't be afraid, Billie. My name is Frank Achilles. I'm a friend."

"I'm not afraid. And you're not my friend. I've never seen you before in all my born life. And what do you mean by coming in through the window? Why didn't you knock like a normal fellow? You must be cuckoo."

"I did knock."

"You didn't."

And meanwhile the manhunt was on. Frankie let out a hissing breath. She said, "You're right. I shouldn't have gotten carried away climbing on rooftops and risking my neck. But I'm trying to help a mutual friend of ours, and I need you to answer a question about Gilbert Howard's death."

"Poor old Howie." Billie drooped over her bottle. "What mutual friend are you talking about?"

"Our mutual friend, Frankie Ray." Frankie held her shoulders wide and her chin straight and manly. "Frankie stands accused of killing Gilbert Howard."

"Frankie!" Billie exclaimed, and for a terrible moment Frankie was certain the girl had recognized her and was calling her by name. And if Billie, in her cups, could pierce her disguise, a policeman ought to know her a block away. But to Frankie's relief, Billie went on, "*Frankie* didn't kill him. What empty noggin came up with that idea?"

"Then who killed Gilbert Howard, Billie? When you first saw his body, you said — according to *Frankie*, you said — you knew who had killed him."

Billie blew an empty, hollow note across the top of her bottle. "Anybody would know *who*."

"Then for heaven's sake, *who?*"

Unfairly, frustratingly — but somehow inevitably — the door to Billie's room opened and the Chinese kites overhead swung and rattled. The house madam removed her key from the lock and vanished with an air of studied tact.

What now? Billie's mysterious *friend in high places*? The cops?

But Marietta Valdes, still barefoot and carrying her shoes, sauntered into Billie's room. King Samson strode in close behind her.

Samson said, "Be quick, Marietta. I've got no goddamn time to spare."

Marietta said, "*There* you are, Billie."

Billie threw herself at the actress the way a child rushes to its mother's arms. "I thought you'd never come. Will you get me out of here?"

"And about time, too." Marietta told King Samson, "Billie and I are going across the way. To the studios."

Billie darted a look at King Samson. "Can we really go to Monument Studios? Without asking anybody?"

"Marietta gets everything she wants. Didn't you know that?" King Samson's sarcasm was as thick and dark as his well-trimmed eyebrows.

"If only that were true," Marietta retorted. "Incidentally, Billie here is my kid sister, so say hello and make it nice."

"Pleased," Samson said. He didn't sound pleased.

Frankie stared from Marietta to Billie and back again. How could sisters lose track of each other so completely? Billie hiding in a brothel, Marietta in full view of the world in the movies. But then, Frankie herself had lost track of Connie in no time at all.

Samson said, "Marietta, I'll be damned if I'll screen-test your every relative and acquaintance, no matter what you say."

"I'll get Billie cleaned up, Sammy, and you'll talk out of the other side of your face."

Up to now, Frankie might not have been in the room. But with a jerk of her head, the actress said to Samson, "This here is Frank Achilles. I told you he'd be big. I'm going to leave you here to work things out with him the way we discussed. Come on, Billie. I'm going to get you a screen test or bust."

Marietta led her sister out of the room.

The door slammed behind her, setting the kites spinning. Samson batted at the tail of a dragon kite. He pulled down the kite and tore it across the wings. "All I want is control over my own goddamn films in my own bloody studio," he said. "Is that too much to ask?"

"Not at all."

"Worse, I've got to manage this rotten cast." Samson moved about Billie's room, yanking more kites down from the ceiling by their strings and tossing them on the floor. "I hired two of the biggest stars in the world to head up *The Emperor of New York*. One of them Gilbert Howard! A manipulative bastard, completely uninsurable, who now gets himself murdered. And as co-star I sign Marietta Valdes, who always has to know best about my movie and won't even take an engagement ring from me."

Frankie said, "Life is a bed of rocks, I guess."

"You got that right. Now Marietta says, *Frank Achilles has got something. And he's a new face. And, with his colouring, he'll look wonderful up close next to me.* Hell! She's right, though."

Frankie started. Right about what? About *Frank Achilles*? Could it be that the producer was interested in her as a leading man? Ye gods and little fishes! She'd always daydreamed about being 'discovered' by a producer or a director as she was riding a bicycle or perching on a stool at a drugstore counter, sipping a milkshake. Never once had she imagined being offered a screen test while wearing a man's disguise. In a brothel.

If it weren't so funny she didn't know how she would have stopped herself screaming her frustration out Billie's window. She decided that even though she had to turn him down, of course, at least she would do her utmost to enjoy every minute of this farcical dream come true.

Samson said, "You've got something new about you, I guess."

Frankie replied breezily, "Well, then, I'm like a hundred thousand other new faces. *I'm* nothing special."

"No, you're not," Samson said. "Because no actor is anything special until somebody like me gets his hands on him."

"That so? Well, I have no great desire to be a movie star anyway. All that glamour could get on a fellow's nerves."

Samson glared. "Can you act?"

Frankie proved that she could act by drawling, "Are you really going to let *me* decide how to answer that question?"

"You've got that right. I got a more important question: Can you handle Marietta Valdes for me?"

Manlike, Frankie shrugged.

Samson nodded. "Then I'll test you. You seem to be a fellow who can take no for an answer if it turns out that you're lousy on film."

"I can *give* no for an answer, too." Frankie wished for a hat to tilt over one eye. "So here goes: nope. Don't want a screen test. Thanks, though."

"Don't argue with me." King Samson shook his head. "I hate men who argue all the time. Look at that damned Gilbert Howard, God rest his soul."

"I like a good argument, myself." It occurred to her that her current plight — being sought for murder — was a sort of life-and-death argument as well, some of it with the newspapers and some of it with the police. She added, "I lived with an arguer all my life — my dad. Anyway, isn't everything you see on the silver screen an argument — all those actors and actresses suffering and kissing and battling and rescuing? With the hero carrying the day during the ninety-minute black-and-white debate?"

"A smart guy." King Samson snorted. "Like I need one when I've got Marietta Valdes. You'll test. Come on." Samson opened the door. "And less of the backchat when I'm trying to do you a favour."

Like a bolt, Frankie saw that Samson was offering her a vital opportunity to follow Billie inside the studios and question her again about who really killed Gilbert Howard. But she kept up her cool attitude.

"A screen test offer is not much of a favour," Frankie replied. "I'm a busy man."

"You know what, Achilles? I guess I don't need you after all." Samson spun round and left the room.

Frankie stared after him, feeling sick. She was an actor, all right. She'd just acted herself right out of grilling Billie about Gilbert Howard's murder. Now she would have to rely on Eugene to find the golden swimmer that Frankie, Connie, and Tom had seen with Gilbert Howard in the hours before he was killed. Without a name, address, or even a better physical description than *slender, blonde, and naked*, that other girl witness was definitely a shakier prospect.

Frankie followed Samson out Billie's door and trotted after him past the numbered doors in the upstairs corridor.

To the producer's back she said, "You're right. I'd probably photograph poorly. Sure as shooting, a screen test won't come to anything."

"Like *you'd* know since you're such an expert." Samson faced Frankie at the top of the curved staircase. "Shut it, fella, and get your grey-suited caboose over to my studio. Tell Marietta I said to go ahead and do the test."

And now the big thing was not to allow Samson to guess how relief sent the blood rushing around her head, arms, and legs. She paused for a count of three. "I guess I can give you an hour or two if it means that much to you."

"Thanks so very much," Samson said, ironic as Alexander Pope.

"It's your nickel." As she followed him to the stairs, Frankie schooled her features into an expression of calm disinterest.

She trailed King Samson down the staircase to the brightly lit foyer, covering her smile but also aware of a nasty sinking feeling inside. She was still trailing after Billie Starr, looking for answers. Billie Starr! Who was perhaps — after Gilbert Howard himself — one of the least dependable people on the face of the earth.

26

A Publicity fellow in a pinstriped suit led Frankie along winding corridors to Make-Up's station, a little room that smelled like no room Frankie had ever been in before. Perfumery would be below Frank Achilles's notice, of course, but as a woman Frankie wanted to bury her face in all the blowsy, bosomy scents, as thick and un-French as porridge. Instead, she hurried to smear on her pancake foundation before the make-up artist, Leda, could snatch the tin from her. Frankie's jawline was square enough to pass as male, but her chin was far too smooth for a man of her purported age, even one who had Burma-Shaved his face before setting himself down in Make-Up's shiny, mint-green chair.

Leda placed one hand on top of Frankie's platinum hair. "Publicity says you've got the last screen test of the afternoon. I can work hard on handsome you for at least an hour, what do you say? Want to be a star, darling?"

Frankie chuckled. "It's like this, Leda. I do my own shaving and make-up, like all the other men do."

"They most certainly do not. You have your job, Mr Achilles, which you got by being born photogenic. I have mine, which I got by training as a professional."

Leda's logic was inarguable. What was worse, Frankie was achingly aware of the irony of her present situation. For years she had dreamed that a professional make-up artist would improve her face. Now Monument Studios was doing for Frank Achilles exactly what Frankie Ray had despaired of. She couldn't decide which was worse: to dream of being 'discovered' by a movie producer and never have the dream come true; or to be discovered as somebody else, *viz.* her alter ego, the non-existent Frank Achilles.

What made the whole experience truly unbearable was that as Frank Achilles, she didn't have time to prepare for a screen test. She'd already been sitting here at Leda's mercy for ten minutes. How long until she might make her escape? She must find Billie. She eyed the door. Marietta might have taken Billie anywhere inside Monument Studios, but here in the central building was as good a place as any to begin looking for her.

Leda crossed her arms over the bosom of her mint-green smock, which was the same colour as the mint-green walls. The colour-matching between employee and décor should have been charming, but the effect was to make Leda's head appear from certain angles to be floating freely above the ground. "Young man, we're in a Depression, if you hadn't noticed. Are you trying to rob me of my job?"

"Certainly not. But I have my ways. And, I won't tell if you don't, but I already shaved, er, an hour ago." In case Leda's sharp eye had noticed how superhumanly smooth her chin was, Frankie chanted softly as she smoothed peach-coloured paste makeup along her cheek, "*Does your husband misbehave? Grunt and grumble, rant and rave? Shoot the brute some Burma-Shave.* Maybe you saw the ads on the drive south, flicking by, little red signs on the road?"

"No."

"Burma-Shave works like a dream," Frankie added. She gave her own cheek a slap. "Smooth as Shakespeare. Listen, Leda, how about a glass of water for a fellow? Please."

But instead of leaving Frankie alone in the room to make her escape, Leda opened a cupboard and took out a glass. She slid aside a panel on one of the counters and revealed a hidden sink. She turned on one of the taps.

Darn it all. Frankie would have to send Leda farther afield. "How about a sandwich, too?" She herself liked a cucumber sandwich with butter, salt, and pepper, but that was strictly female fare. However, she well knew Champ's collation of choice and swiftly added, "Roast beef, please. With horseradish." It was becoming easier and easier to act like a man.

"Anything else you want? Champagne from a golden fountain?"

Frankie laughed appreciatively. "You oughta be in pictures, Leda. You're a pretty funny gal."

Leda huffed through her nose. "With your attitude, you'd better be famous soon, kid. Sure, I'll get you a sandwich. But you'll have to wait. The cafeteria isn't open for another hour."

Frankie pictured every man she'd ever been acquainted with, at school and in church back in Vancouver. She tried to recollect how each left a room. As far as she could see, only one believable pretext remained for a fellow to take his leave of a lady. Frankie rose from her chair. "Leda, I love you dearly"—what was Champ's phrase for *spend a penny?*—"but I gotta see a man about a dog."

"Get along with you, cheeky," Leda said, but she showed the first signs of a smile.

Frankie snatched up her jacket, tipped Leda a Boy Scout salute, and slipped past her into the empty corridor. As an afterthought she tugged off her make-up bib and dropped it behind one of the tall steel ashtrays dotted at intervals between doors along the hallway. Which way to find Billie? Frankie shrugged and turned right. The weight of the gun in her pocket set it swinging with each brisk step she took as she made her way, trying doors at random and finding them locked. She took side trips up a short corridor opening off the main way and found herself cornered in a cul-de-sac by a small stand of mops upright in buckets. Wrong turn.

Back in the main hallway, Frankie found a door that opened when she tried it. The room was packed with chrome racks and hung about entrancingly with clothing. This was Wardrobe, magical Wardrobe, and she had no time to explore. She swore one of her father's irrevocable ministerial oaths to return one day, and shut the door firmly on all that silken and spangled glory.

Seven or eight locked doors later, at the end of what seemed an interminable corridor, Frankie came upon a door marked *Make-Up 3*. Without much hope, she tried the knob. When it turned, she peered in at a sky-blue room where Billie Starr sat at a sky-blue vanity table, finger combing her honey-coloured hair. To Frankie's relief, the room contained no sky-blue attendant.

"Now look here, Billie—" Frankie began, but she was brought up short by the calibre of the swear word Billie let off.

"Frank Achilles! It's always the same, isn't it?" Billie said. "Hurry up and wait forever. Why, oh why, didn't I at least bring a flask? Have *you* got one?"

"Certainly not. Darn it all, Billie, I figured you drank so much because you were sad not to get into the movies. I thought you'd be glad as a dog with two tails once you got past the studio doors."

"I *am* pleased to be inside the studio." With Billie, you never had to wait long for her to change gear. Now her smile was so sweet that Frankie couldn't understand how this perfect girl had failed to be signed to a studio in the first place. "I want my flask, that's all."

Frankie thanked her stars that she had spent her entire life around Sheridan B Ray and Connie Mooney, and so was capable of keeping her temper.

"Billie, you must listen to me. Your unlucky friend Frankie Ray—remember her? Frankie? She's in trouble. The cops and the papers think she murdered Gilbert Howard. If you want to help her, answer me a couple of questions. And this time, no funny business."

"Okay." Billie gazed up at Frankie. "And you answer me this: how do you think I'd look as a brunette?"

Frankie answered, "You'd look like what you are— Marietta's younger sister."

"Who told you she's my sister?" Billie demanded. "How would you possibly know that?"

Billie had already forgotten the scene in the brothel. She was certainly an awful witness, but she was still Frankie's best clue.

Frankie said, "I'm a detective. I know things. Now stop talking about hair colour and tell me about the night you and Frankie, she ..." All these nouns and pronouns were confusing, especially in a room that was all one colour—this one had a sky-blue floor, walls and ceiling, which made you wonder which way was really up. "When you and Frankie discovered Gilbert Howard's body on the sofa—"

"Oh, Howie! I'll be heartsick for him, even in Heaven." A tear shone in Billie's eye and she blinked it away. "I *won't* cry. He'd be the first to say not to. I haven't had a single still photo taken for my test yet."

"Please hurry up and answer my question," Frankie begged. Out in the corridor, rapid steps neared and stopped outside the sky-blue make-up room door. Frankie held her breath. The footsteps moved on. "Who killed Gilbert Howard? You said it was obvious."

"How do I know that you're really on Frankie's side? You could be a cop, out to arrest her."

Frankie flung out her arms. "Do I look like a policeman?"

"You look like a dreamboat, and that's so unfair to me." Billie twisted in her chair. "You're such a dreamboat of a man that Marietta is determined to get you a big starring offer. *I* am a dreamboat woman, but nobody helps me. Even Marietta, my own sister, says she can't do much for me. A few stills, and then it's out the door with a *hey de hoo de hee.* Everything everywhere is easier for men."

Frankie had been a man for several hours now, and she was beginning to doubt this truism. "Billie, let's forget about stardom for a minute and think about poor old Frankie, accused of murder. You told her you knew who killed Gilbert Howard."

Billie screwed her pretty features into an incredulous expression. "Who *doesn't* know who killed him? Everybody knows."

"Tell me, then," Frankie said sternly.

"I will say it. And then you'll know. And our friend Frankie will be all right, because of course Frankie didn't kill him."

"Well?"

Billie paused and nodded cooperatively, but replied, "I'll tell you when you help me."

"That's rich. You're in the studio because Marietta already

helped you. We need to help *Frankie*. I thought she was your friend."

"Gilbert Howard was my friend, too, and we can't help him because he is dead," Billie said.

"We help Gilbert Howard by finding out who killed him." Frankie asked, "Don't you want that, if you were such a close friend of his?"

"Keep your mind out of the gutter, please, Mr Frank Achilles. Howie was a gentleman who stood by me when Leo wouldn't go to his famous parents to help me star in the movies. If not for Howie, I would never have had the brilliant idea of hiding out in a brothel."

"That's one heck of a good idea, I don't think! Why in heaven's name did Gilbert Howard tell you to go to a brothel?"

"Well, Howie used his influence to get me a private room with the madam — no visitors. Except Leo. Howie said that Leo would do anything to rescue the woman he loves from the brothel. Howie said that Leo would finally stand up to his father, King Samson, and get me a movie contract, and stand up to his mother, Blanche Carver, and get me some newspaper coverage — "

"Howie said!" Frankie shook her head. "Did you do everything that fellow told you to do?"

Billie laughed. "Don't you know? Everybody did what Howie said."

In fact, Frankie had as well, for Gilbert Howard had changed her life when he told her that he had been a schoolteacher like her. He urged her onward to an acting career. And he had changed her life again by turning up dead on her sofa.

"Billie, who killed Gilbert Howard?"

"I said, I'll tell you when you help me. You may look like a matinee idol, but you don't hear so well, do you, Frank Achilles?"

"Darn you, Billie!" Frankie took a deep breath. "Help you how?"

The make-up chairs were of the expensive swivelling sort, and Billie swivelled in hers now. She held up her slender index finger to make a number one. "After the screen test, the studio is supposed to send me out to somewhere like a nightclub or a fancy restaurant on a date with a fellow like you, to put me in the public eye. First, lots of photographers take my picture. Then a columnist from one of the papers will speculate on my future and my past. Also, everybody there will see me dine with a man who is a bright new face in the movies. And then the next morning, my name is in the papers." Billie was counting off the steps on her fingers. "After that, King Samson or somebody like him offers me a contract and a speaking role. It's a series of logical steps, do you see?"

"And where do I fit into all this?"

"The bright new face at the studio — that's you." Billie nodded at the door. "Go see Publicity. Get me a dinner date with you tonight. Get it at Camillo's, so reporters will be watching us eat the best food in town. And that will put me on the road to a very good part."

It was not so much the transaction itself that worried Frankie as her suspicion that Billie would not keep her promise.

She said, "All right. I'll keep my word, Billie. But don't forget yours. At dinner, on our date, tell me who killed Gilbert Howard."

Billie smiled, bright and golden as a Monument Studios angel. "Frank, you're a decent fellow. And I know you'll keep your word. So I'm not going to wait until dinner. I'm going to tell you right now who killed Howie."

Halfway out the door, Frankie turned back and stared. A free gift of an answer? From Billie Starr?

Frankie said, "I'm listening."

"It's perfectly simple."

Frankie's heart hammered.

"Listen good," Billie said. "King Samson killed Howie."

The bully. King Samson. The producer's name chattered in Frankie's head, and she spoke through it with difficulty. "Billie, that can't be. Why would King Samson kill Gilbert Howard? He would never in a million years risk his kingdom to kill a star who made him money and brought him good reviews."

"I guess you don't know a thing about the movie business, Frank Achilles. King Samson killed Howie for the insurance."

"But Gilbert Howard was uninsurable," Frankie said. "He was too drunk and unreliable to be insured. Killing him wouldn't bring Samson a dime. In fact it would lose him money by setting movie production back."

Billie frowned. "Well, then, King Samson killed Howie because he hated him." She returned Frankie's gaze with an expression of sincere compassion. In those blue eyes Frankie read the message clearly: Billie Starr believed Frank Achilles was a gullible sap.

"You don't suspect Samson at all, do you?" Frankie asked. She could only think of two people Billie would want to protect, and one of them—Billie's sister Marietta Valdes—had no motive. But the other person had lost Billie to the brothel, under Gilbert Howard's encouragement.

Frankie said, "It was Leo you thought of when you saw that Gilbert Howard was dead, wasn't it?"

Billie shook her head.

Frankie pressed harder. "You believe that Leo shot Gilbert Howard, don't you? Not because Howard shot Leo at the audition in Vancouver. You think Leo murdered him because he sent you into the brothel to be a professional prostitute, as far as Leo knew."

Before Billie could answer, Marietta Valdes entered the make-up room. She was decked out in the most outrageous silver dress Frankie had ever seen, on screen or off. There were more bits cut out of the fabric than were left in. The Hays Office would never sign off on such a costume, but Frankie read enough movie magazines to know that some bargaining chips must be offered up to godly Hays, and she would bet her forty dollars, wherever it might be, that this dress was a bargaining chip for censorship.

Marietta tugged her makeup bib from her neck and hurled it to the floor. "Leo most certainly did not kill Gilbert Howard. I admit freely that I was listening at the door. Frank Achilles, you need to understand that what looks like a complex sin in the little towns we all grew up in, is simply acting here in Hollywood. The camera observes but does not judge, so that the viewer can bring her own ethics to the case. Don't you think?"

"I'll have to think about that one." Frankie covered the befuddlement she always felt when Marietta started talking by fishing her sunglasses out of her pocket. She put them on and felt better. Smarter.

Marietta turned to her sister. "Billie, only an idiot would accuse King Samson of murdering his own star."

"Sez you." Billie scowled into the mirror.

Frankie asked, "Miss Valdes, you knew Gilbert Howard, but did you know him well?"

"And I liked him! Better than most."

"Then if not King Samson, or Leo, or Frankie Ray, then who do you think killed him?"

Marietta said, "Every woman he ever met killed him."

Frankie's investigative energy faltered. A sinking feeling came upon her. The motive for Howard's murder—the revenge of women seduced, scorned, and betrayed—was strong, and the cast of suspects was long. However, that was no help. As far as the papers, the public, and the law were concerned, whose name would be written at the top of that particular list? Frankie Ray's, even though Gilbert Howard had neither broken her heart nor smashed her virtue. All he had done was recite soaring prose by the side of a pool and urge Frankie to follow her dreams.

Frankie took a step back. "Miss Valdes, are you telling me that every woman Howard ever met wanted to shoot him, except you? In the whole wide world of his romantic adventures, you're the only woman who never wanted to kill him?"

"I was never one of his conquests." Marietta smoothed the silver leathery bits that made up her dress. "Howie saw me as his equal in the professional field. He was my best chance at directing. Now go away, Frank Achilles. I'll see you again soon enough." Marietta sailed out the door.

Billie said, "So will you keep your promise, Frank Achilles? Like I kept mine?"

"No, not like you kept yours. I'm really going to help you." Frankie said. "Do tell me: which way is Publicity?"

"Thataway." Billie jerked her head to the right and swivelled her chair around to face the make-up mirror.

Frankie strode manfully along the hallway in the direction Billie had indicated, trying to appear self-confident while feeling completely let down. Still, she had never, at any time in her life, seriously contemplated giving up on anything or anybody. She had never even lost hope that her mother might one day return to the blue house to see how her daughter Francesca was getting along. She would not give up now. She reached the door labelled *Publicity*. It opened to reveal the same sharp-looking fellow she'd met earlier. Behind him on a small desk stood two large telephones.

Frankie told Publicity what she wanted.

Publicity chewed his lip. "You telling me my job?"

"Only this once."

"Okay, sport. I'll do what you ask today. After that, you're in my pocket on a permanent basis. You'll go where I send you. Deal?"

Frankie nodded. "My word on it."

"Okay. After your test, you'll meet Miss Billie Starr outside Camillo's Fine Bar and Grille on Sunset Boulevard at eight pip emma. Your first acting job is to look romantic."

"How?"

Publicity rolled his eyes. "You're an actor, aren't you? Now show me your profiles."

Frankie showed Publicity both her profiles. "Is one better than the other?"

"How I love a greenhorn. Your right profile is a bit on the feminine side. Always have the photogs snap your left. Any questions?"

Frankie did, but they weren't the kind she could ask Publicity. *Who killed Gilbert Howard? Was it the golden girl, as she'd always suspected? A jealous Leo Samson? A wronged woman, as Marietta insisted?*

The pot of suspects was too large. Gilbert Howard must have left a trail of envy and broken hearts clear across the city. His murderer might be a heartbroken actress, a resentful character actor, a disappointed fan, a passing maniac … or a girl he'd talked into living in a brothel. Or the sweethearts or spouses of any of those.

Frankie herself did have plenty of motive, precisely as the police and Blanche Carver believed. And so did the one person Frankie least wanted to suspect of the crime. Her best friend, Connie Mooney, had disappeared the very day that Gilbert Howard's body was found in Villa 7B. But Frankie knew Connie as well as she knew herself. Connie wouldn't kill anybody. And if she did kill somebody, she wouldn't let Frankie take the blame. So that gave her two people to rule out—Connie and herself—among the many suspects.

Frankie traced her path along the snaking halls of Monument Studios' central building and reflected on Sherlock Holmes, who, with daring, logic, and disguise, could accomplish more than Scotland Yard and its numbered investigators. Like Dr Watson, Frankie had always admired Holmes above other detectives. But she decided that logic, intuition, and experience were useless when you had a city full of suspects. You needed a great army of policemen.

She experienced a sudden dizziness, along with a strange and terrible sense that something was about to fall on her from a great height. She looked up, but there was nothing above her but the spackled white ceiling of the studio corridor. Still, something washed over her from her platinum head to her brogue-shod feet. It was wet and chilly, and its name was Common Sense.

Frankie shivered. The soles of her manly brogues tapped against the seemingly endless corridor flooring. She passed doors on each side with little plates reading *Writer, Editor, Assistant Writer, Casting.* She wondered how she had ever believed she could solve a murder by dressing up in a man's clothes. She put her right hand in her pocket and wrapped it around the gun, hoping for a little cold, hard comfort.

27

Frankie drove the Model A under a starry evening sky toward Camillo's Fine Bar and Grille. She frowned through the windshield at the busy road ahead. Lord, how she hoped Billie was wrong and the killer wasn't King Samson. Frankie had no wish to bring down Samson and his great Monument Studios. Think of all the people Samson employed — actors, extras, and all the others lucky enough to have jobs in this place. Tom and the kids from Paradise Gardens — and Bruno! — and Luigi the cameraman, who'd helped her succeed as the sad pigeon girl. Frankie would never do anything to take away anybody's chance to get ahead in life. King Samson must not fall. Still, of all the people Frankie had met, who had the worst temper? Who was most likely to explode out of control? And who owned the cursed gun in her pocket that had killed the movie star in the first place? King Samson. But such reasoning was instinctual, the way Billie herself would reason. Frankie was determined to be sensible. King Samson was a terrible bully, and he was impossible to like, but he couldn't be Gilbert Howard's killer. Samson's film project depended on the uninsurable Howard showing up on set. Samson needed Howard alive.

She changed gears from first to third and fiddled with the choke. One good thing about her time in Hollywood—she was a better driver every day. But with every yard the Model A travelled toward Camillo's, she grew more certain that Billie's reveal was not worth the price Frankie had agreed to pay—a dinner date at Camillo's under the sharp eye of Hollywood's press. What if Blanche Carver were there, nosing about? Disaster might strike, and although Frankie felt confident in her role as Frank Achilles, she was weary after her long night in Eugene's cupboard, the excitement of tracking Billie, and the sitting and walking for a lightning-fast screen test. Further, she felt distracted by her hopes that Eugene had tracked down Gilbert Howard's golden swimming girlfriend and made her tell him something useful to the case. But Frankie was here to keep her word, risking the exposure of her disguise with every moment she spent in this very public setting. All in order to give Billie Starr her opportunity to be seen and photographed on a warm Hollywood evening at Camillo's Fine Bar and Grille.

She pulled up to the curb around the corner from Camillo's, satisfied at least that she was doing the honourable thing in helping Billie. However, the fates offered no reward for honour tonight, for when she stepped down from the Model A, a policeman stopped her.

Her heartbeat stuttered and nearly stopped. She'd known this moment would come. Still, she was an actress. So she would act.

Frankie put one hand casually into her suit pocket and touched the gun she carried there. She said the words an innocent man would say: "Yes, Officer?"

"Have you seen this girl, pal?" The policeman, a heavyset fellow, held out a glossy photograph. "Take a look, wouldja?"

The first thing was not to answer too eagerly. Frankie breathed in and out, as one did at the beginning of acting class. *Sunglasses off or on?* Twilight was past, but a good percentage of the glamorous motorists driving by were still wearing sunglasses. And anyway, she was playing an actor in the films, arriving for a date with an actress. She took out her sunglasses and put them on.

"Sure thing."

"Look close, mind you." The policeman held out the picture of a dark-haired girl with good cheekbones, straight brows, and bright eyes. Frankie had to look twice over the top of her sunglasses before she was certain it was her own photograph. Yes. It was the still shot the woman at the Central Casting wicket had taken of Frankie when she'd signed up to be an extra two short days before.

"No, can't say that I have. What did she do?"

"Killed a movie star."

"Not Gilbert Howard."

"Yep. And neither you nor the rest of the world has seen her." The policeman took back the photo, tucked it into his uniform pocket, and rolled in his policeman's boots the way Frankie rolled in her brogues, back and forth from heel to toe. "Well, it's the end of my shift, and I've got sore feet."

Emboldened by success, Frankie nodded at the picture in his hand. "I bet she'd rather have sore feet than this manhunt."

The policeman chuckled. "Ain't that the truth, pal. But we'll catch her."

Frankie hid her anger. "What sort of evidence have you of her guilt, anyway? What if this woman didn't kill Gilbert Howard at all?"

"She killed him. Sure as shootin'. It was a lover's quarrel gone bad, bet your socks on it. Well, that's it — I'm done for the day. Gilbert Howard will go unavenged on my shift." He patted the pocket with her photograph in it as he ambled away. "Dirty bastard Howard was, too — I shouldn't say, but we almost got him on indecency charges a few times. And that's the polite word."

Frankie said to the policeman's back, "So Gilbert Howard gets a pass for crimes he did commit, but Francesca Ray gets the chair for a murder she didn't commit?"

But the policeman's sore feet had already taken him too far along Sunset Boulevard to hear.

Frankie made her way to the restaurant's entrance. She paused under the striped awning over its double Deco doors, as Publicity had instructed her to do, to stand near the doorman and await the starlet Billie Starr and Publicity's photographer.

The doorman held open the glass doors for a young couple. The man wore dinner whites, and the woman wore satin and a melting look, which she bestowed upon Frankie. She slung her spotted fur over her shoulder, the long end trailing after her like a faithful, boneless pet. The doorman shut the door after the couple, but not before the heavy aromas of cherry pie and creamed chicken had slipped out the doorway and up inside Frankie's nose. Her stomach growled.

The doorman must have heard the rumble. "Are you going inside, sir?"

"My dinner companion is late arriving."

"The prettier they are, the later they arrive. Cigarette?" The doorman looked over his braided shoulder at the door and held out a pack to Frankie, adding, "I wouldn't ask, but you seem a bit jittery. And it's nighttime."

She frowned. "What about it?"

"It's nighttime, and you're wearing dark glasses."

"I'm a movie actor, aren't I?" But Frankie removed the glasses, and the doorman held out the cigarettes again. They were Camels, Frankie noted, refusing them with thanks. As if Connie were at her side, she heard the confident whisper: *What do you like in a smoke, Frankie?* Frankie always used to answer, *"Good health and long life, because doctors recommend Camels over any other cigarette."* She thought of Champ smoking his Camels on her father's back porch, wondering where his fiancée might be.

Well, here she was. Frankie stepped out from under the restaurant awning and looked up at the sky. Stars came out no matter how far you were from home, or how many policemen were showing your picture around town. Even if the cops caught her, convicted her, and took her the short mile to the electric chair, the stars would keep coming out, one by one, each night.

Frankie said to the doorman, "I feel like a lemon drop Hollywood picked up, rolled around on its tongue a couple of times, and then spat out into an ashtray."

"Sure you do." The doorman grinned around his cigarette. "I was like you, pal, not so long ago. I *was* you, hoping I'd made it right out of the wrapping paper and into the movies. Never panned out. Now I open and close the door here at Camillo's Fine Bar and Grille."

"Bad luck, I guess," Frankie said politely.

"Well, there are worse things than failure."

It occurred to Frankie that everybody who was anybody came to dine at Camillo's, and a doorman was a darned good source to ask about the night of the murder. "You got that right. Look at Gilbert Howard."

"Now there's a case in point. Howard was always here, dancing in patent leather shoes, dipping the girls over the bend in his arm. Now he's boxed up, nothing left but his movies, poor old chap." The doorman tapped the ash from his cigarette into the low box hedge by the door.

"I guess you've seen it all," Frankie said. Several more people passed by, and she recognized two of them from the movie magazines. She knew their names, and she knew their movie roles, but she found that she didn't much care. The time was right to ask the question.

She asked, "Was Gilbert Howard here two nights ago?"

"Sure he was. Poor old fellow. He was always kind to me."

"Who was he with?"

"Who wasn't he with? He was one of the fortunate few, all right. Listen, here's what happens to most fellows in Hollywood. What happens is, at the start a young man like you who's new in town gets invited everywhere. Like I did. We're like the male ballet dancers, you know? To hold up the ladies to view. You get the invite to Cukor's or Thalberg's mansions, you play a couple dozen sets of tennis at Chaplin's, and then *voilà*! You're old hat. Some new face comes to take your place at the parties, with the ladies. Soon enough you realize they're moving you along a conveyor belt of minor fame and out the flap at the back. Us fellows got to face facts." Gloved hand held out for his tip, the doorman let a slick fellow in perfect black tie pass on through. "Say, see that woman over the other side of the road, her in the leopard skin? I spooned with her once at a party beside a champagne fountain. Think she remembers? Nix. But I do. I remember everything. Say, cast your eyeballs at the Packard, chum."

Frankie nodded appreciatively at a large car as it slowly approached the awning. She tried again. "Last night, before he was murdered, was Howard here with a blonde girl? Slender, bobbed?"

But the doorman had lost interest in Frankie. The Packard pulled up to the curb. Under the streetlights it had appeared grey, but on closer inspection it proved to be a lustrous lavender shade. The Packard attracted a small crowd from up and down the sidewalk, to rubberneck at whatever famous person was inside it.

The doorman pushed through the gogglers. Frankie moved after him. "Please tell me, can you remember whether Gilbert Howard at least danced with a blonde woman last night?"

"What? Sorry, I got to do the job." The doorman bent to open the Packard's door. Frankie and the crowd were treated to the sight of a silver lamé shoe, a perfect silken ankle, and a swath of pleated chiffon skirt the same platinum colour as Frankie's new froth of hair.

Billie Starr. A pale hand tipped in rose-red nails extended itself to the doorman, who bent to help Frankie's date out of the Packard's shadowy interior.

"Watch the merchandise," the starlet called out to the driver. Startled, Frankie fumbled her dark glasses off to see better. The starlet's voice was all too familiar, and it wasn't Billie Starr's.

Connie Mooney, dressed to the nines and beyond, climbed out of the Packard.

Frankie wished for a chair to sit down on. But she'd spent the day in character as Frank Achilles, and she was not about to abandon the role now. She set her dark glasses firmly on her nose, shot her cuffs, and said, "Evening, Miss Mooney."

"Mr Frank Achilles. Publicity told me you'd be waiting for me." Connie lowered her eyelids and exuded a peculiar well-rounded dignity that she'd employed to poleaxe males since her twelfth birthday. "Pleased to meet you. Look out, they're going to take the first shots."

A man in a pinch-waist suit hurried around the back end of the Cadillac, hefting a flash camera in one hand while he gestured with the other. "Right, children, stand together, suck in what stomach you can and gimme some enthusiastic teeth."

Connie straightened up. "Like this?"

"Publicity said to shoot my left profile," Frankie told him.

The photographer said one of several words Frankie's father didn't know she knew. "Let a professional do the work, fella. And don't waste time." The photographer jerked his chin at the restaurant door. "I heard Garbo's on her way. First sighting since February."

"Greta Garbo is a quiet woman." The doorman moved to stand outside camera range. "Sensitive about her long feet. I myself think they are perfectly in proportion."

Frankie and Connie stood side by side. The camera flashed. Frankie mumbled out of the side of her mouth, "Hey, where's Billie Starr? I promised to take her to dinner."

"You'll have to ask Publicity, Mr Achilles. I'm doing what he told me." Connie was checking the hem of her dress and didn't look up. The bulb flashed again, and again.

The photographer eyed the doorman, who had edged into the last shot. "Say, what's your game, buddy?"

"No game. I open the doors. You folks have a happy evening," the doorman said. To Frankie, he added, "In answer to your question, by the way, I guess Gilbert Howard was mostly with Marietta Valdes. Or was that the night before?"

"Please try to remember." Frankie held out her elbow to Connie.

"With fellows like Gilbert Howard, anything's possible,"

the doorman said. "There's an available blonde on every corner when you're that big in the films. But I thought he was dancing with Miss Valdes the night he died. Or maybe it was Blanche Carver. Or both of them."

Frankie was more disappointed in this answer than she would have believed possible.

"Mr Achilles, you're a bit shaky," Connie muttered. "Don't tell me you're as nervous as I am."

"I haven't eaten all day," Frankie told her. She lifted her sunglasses so Connie could get a good look. "Look, don't react. It's me, Frankie."

Connie made a little noise and looked Frankie in the eye for the first time. "Frankie! For the love of Michelangelo. Is dressing you up like a man Publicity's joke? Tonight wasn't supposed to be funny."

"Keep your voice down. I'm playing a role."

"Oh, sure, the bigshot movie star," Connie said, but she said it quietly.

Frankie asked, "Where have you been? You should have left me a note to explain why you weren't coming home at least. All kinds of things have happened. Haven't you read the news?"

"Not today." Connie said. "And there's no bigger news than this: I was with King Samson. Being groomed for tonight. I left you a message—the Lucky Strike cigarette pack. Cats, Frankie! If you didn't understand the message *Lucky Strike*, I despair of you."

"What's so important about tonight?" Frankie asked. "What's such a big deal that you couldn't at least telephone the Queen?"

"Frankie, stop it. You are acting like my *mother*. I thought the whole idea was that we were going to try and be movie stars." Connie peered in through a side window into the restaurant through the bank of gardenias inside the anteroom door. "It's all set up for tonight. I'm supposed to have my picture taken at Camillo's having dinner with a handsome actor. And then later on, something big is going to happen — that photographer has no idea how big."

Something big? Gilbert Howard was dead. What was bigger than that? And how was it possible that Connie had spent the last twelve hours in Hollywood and did not know that one of its greatest stars was dead?

A fellow in a dinner jacket stepped forward and flashed another camera at them. "Don't mind me, I'm the house photog, folks."

"Swell," Connie said to him. To Frankie she hissed, "We don't tip these photographers, do we?"

"I think that if you tried to tip that first fellow he'd black your eye for insolence. Listen, so much has happened that I don't even know where to begin." With the murder? Her escape? Billie Starr's accusation? Or with Eugene Ellery, whose every move invited further questions?

But at the far end of the foyer the head waiter was holding the door open for them. So commanding was he that it seemed best after all to begin by taking Connie's elbow.

Tall mirrors on both sides showed the two of them stepping toward the dining room, into an eternity of reflected and diminishing distances. Ahead of them she made out a room panelled in dark wood, from which flowed curlicues of piano music and a hum of conversation. Frankie snatched a glance at Connie's expertly painted face, recalling the time when they were six and wore Connie's mother's rouge to school and had their cheeks scrubbed nearly raw by the vice-principal.

Under her breath, she asked Connie, "Then haven't you heard about Gilbert Howard? He's dead."

"Oh! Not poor Howie?" Connie paled beneath her makeup. "That's terrible. Heart attack?"

"Somebody shot Gilbert Howard." Frankie stood up straight and took a step forward into the room. A waiter stood to each side a little way behind, holding the doors wide as one would hold back a stage curtain for the star to take a bow. Ahead of them at the bottom of the steps, glorious in black tails, stood the head waiter, waiting. And beyond him Frankie was aware, in a confused and distant sort of way, of mermaids and palm trees and an unexpectedly white piano.

She put her sunglasses back on. "The police think I murdered him. Smile."

28

To enter Camillo's dining room, you had to travel down a couple of steps. Frankie remembered Publicity's directive to pause a moment here at the top. Publicity had predicted that all eyes would turn their way, and he was right. Frankie surprised herself with a sudden desire to turn and run, but curiosity steadied her. She had never expected to see in a high-class eatery a half dozen living mermaids, dressed in silken fishtails and beaded clamshells and posed about the room on raised boxes. More traditionally, round tables glittered with glassware and candles. Waiters crisscrossed the restaurant, balancing trays and dishes with chrome covers. A well-dressed clientele at the tables contributed a warm buzz of voices to the carelessly perfect vowels of a talented alto leaning against the gleaming white piano. Frnkie did her best not to rubberneck as she and Connie followed the maitre d' across the room.

Connie hissed, "The police believe you killed Gilbert Howard? Listen, Frankie, this is no time to joke. And take off those sunglasses."

Frankie obliged. "No joke. Abso-tively true."

"Applesauce," Connie said, although there was a note of doubt in her voice.

"No ma'am. No apples anywhere, Newtown or Gravenstein."

They settled at a central table for two. A busboy wove his way toward them through the mermaids and diners, set a bucket of ice beside them on a chrome-plated stand, and moved off again. One of the mermaids near the white piano began combing her hair, which Frankie had always heard mermaids did, although she herself had been raised not to comb her hair in the dining room. "We're a long way from cantaloupe and ice cream at the Aristocrat Café."

"We're puttin' on the ritz. Now, Frankie, be serious. Any fool would know that you didn't murder Howie."

"Of course not. But the foolish world thinks I did."

"No baloney?" Connie asked doubtfully.

"I'd be happy if it *were* baloney, but it's not. Check the papers. You'll see my picture reprinted from the shot they took of me at Central Casting."

"Phooey. Well, your disguise is good. We'll have to wait for the silly world to catch on that you're innocent."

"The only problem with that—" Frankie began.

Connie waved all Frankie's problems away with her menu. "I can't get over your disguise. You look like a very handsome man."

"It's acting more than anything," Frankie pointed out. "You know my tenor voice I use in men's roles? But I must admit that the Queen of the Extras showed me how to walk like a man."

"She's an artist. By the way, the dinner tab's on the studio. We can order what we like." Connie peered around the side of her menu at Frankie. "Do you think we should order the Lobster Newburg or the New York Steak?"

A waiter advanced upon them, soft footed. He suggested the Chicken Halibut.

"How can you have Chicken Halibut?" Connie demanded. "Mother Nature says it's got to be one or the other. Make up your mind, buddy."

Frankie smothered a smile as the waiter explained that Chicken Halibut was simply young halibut. "Like a chick is young, miss. And by good fortune, we have two servings left."

"You've got to be kidding. Halibut? You can stick that in your hat," Connie said. "Tell him what we want, Frankie. I mean *Frank*."

Frankie took a deep breath and ordered champagne. Connie ordered lobster for both of them.

Once the waiter had left, his disappointment in their choice nearly hidden behind a professional exterior—which was a sort of acting, too—Connie let out a huff of breath. She rested her elbow on the table, chin on hand.

"You did *tell* them you didn't kill Gilbert Howard?"

"It's a long tale of bad luck and sorrow," Frankie said. "Let me tell you what happened."

"Wait a minute, somebody's taking our picture over there. I should take up smoking. It shows off a girl's manicure." A bulb flashed across the room, and Connie craned her neck around. "Now the photographers are taking pictures of the mermaids, though it won't help their acting careers much. Who looks at your bone structure when you're wearing a shell brassiere?"

The waiter reappeared and poured them two long-stemmed glasses of champagne.

Frankie said, "Blanche Carver accused me of killing Gilbert Howard. Wait! That house photog is snapping our pictures again. Raise your glass."

"Link arms," Connie suggested. Another flash went off. She added, "Oh, shoot! I wish you'd been a real movie star. It's hard to keep a straight face and act lovey-dovey when it's you."

Frankie laughed out loud. Everything was different now that she was no longer alone. Connie was stubborn, and she didn't always notice what words came out of her mouth, but when the chips were down, she was true-blue. Frankie's mood improved still further when she saw the waiter coming their way with a large platter balanced on his shoulder. He set before them two steaming dishes of lobster, with sauce thick with cream and as rich as seven bankers.

"Frankie, tell me everything while we eat."

Frankie began with her great moment as a pigeon girl, which it turned out Connie had missed since King Samson had pulled her aside to talk to her about a screen test while Luigi was filming Frankie. Connie listened, satisfyingly wide-eyed, as Frankie related the finding of Gilbert Howard's body, her night in Eugene Ellery's cupboard, her transformation into Frank Achilles, and her subsequent pursuit of Billie Starr in her so-far failed attempt to find out who killed Gilbert Howard.

"Has the world gone crazy? There's not the slightest case against you," Connie said firmly. "*I* think the murderer was Marietta Valdes. She came by the studio in the afternoon, but she was off again by dinnertime."

"But Marietta is the last person in the world to wish Howard dead. He was *helping* her become a director, and about the only person willing to help a woman, too."

"Bushwah," Connie said. "Nobody could seriously suspect you, Frankie. You're safe as houses."

"Don't underestimate the police. There's a circumstantial case against me," Frankie pointed out. "And don't forget the power of the law to railroad a swift trial—"

"Don't worry about any of that nonsense," Connie interrupted. "You're innocent. Stay disguised until the thing all blows over. I bet they'll find the real killer by tomorrow. And listen, I was kidding—I don't *really* mind that you're my escort for the evening."

"Thanks." Frankie frowned. Perhaps it was as well that Connie appeared not to have a complete understanding of the danger of Frankie's circumstances. It might very well be that her nonchalance would serve them well. A panicky Connie at a roadblock or border would help neither of them when they made their escape.

Frankie held a sip of champagne in her mouth so that the bubbles pricked her tongue. She remembered the song they used to sing at Girl Guide camp when she and Connie were eleven. They sat side by side with arms folded on knees before the campfire, faces hot where the heat caught them, backs chilly where the warmth didn't reach, singing in the night. *Make new friends but keep the old, one is silver and the other is gold.* The sparks had sounded like firecrackers dancing up against a black sky. Next day, she and Connie had been sent home for sneaking out of camp for a midnight swim, but what stuck with her were their voices, uncertain in key, piping the roundelay.

You could accomplish anything with the help of a friend. You might even find a way out of town when the police were on your tail.

"Connie, I'm going to need your help."

"And I'm going to need yours." Connie set her fork down on the plate.

Frankie said, "Tonight, the most important thing is to get back to Paradise Gardens and see whether Eugene managed to find the girl who was kissing Gilbert Howard beside the swimming pool."

"They're snapping our picture again. Lean in."

Champagne corks and flashbulbs popped around the dining room.

Connie said, "Look, we've talked about your situation. Now it's my turn."

"But—"

"No buts. I've got a big opportunity ahead of me tonight, with the burning of the huge *Ambition* set—"

"You don't understand the severity of my situation." Frankie took a deep breath. Connie hadn't seen Gilbert Howard's body. She hadn't lived through the long dark hours hidden in Eugene Ellery's closet. No wonder the peril didn't seem real to her. "Just now, a policeman was showing around my picture. They have my name. Blanche Carver will show up at this restaurant any moment. It's a matter of time before my disguise—"

"No, *you* don't understand." Connie made the puffing sound she always made when her mother offered a suggestion she considered too misguided for human consideration. "Look, Frankie, I'm not going to let anything happen to you. We'll work through this together. We always have. A smart policeman will take over from the stupid ones and find Howie's killer—I still can't believe he's gone—and you'll be fine."

Frankie shook her head.

Connie ploughed onward. "Publicity's got a terrific photography shoot for us in a few minutes. And I've got an even better plan, one I thought up when King Samson mentioned that an army of engineers and firemen will burn down the big *Ambition* set at the studios tonight. Keep your nerve, Frankie, stay disguised as Frank Achilles, and everything will be all right."

Frankie said, "Connie Mooney, this is a matter of life and death. I didn't want to say so before, but if I don't solve Gilbert Howard's murder soon, somebody's going to recognize me. When they do, they'll call the police. Then the police will either throw me in jail, or they will shoot me trying to escape capture. Do you want that to happen?"

"Of course not." Connie leaned close. "But tonight is the night they'll film the *Ambition* set burning. It's the only night I can make my plan happen. After that, you can hide out in Paradise Gardens. You're one of the Queen's family, like me. The kids won't turn you in."

"The police will search Paradise Gardens again. Do you want Tom and the Queen and the other kids charged with hiding an accused murderess? That's not like you, Connie."

But possibly, Frankie thought, it was. She remembered the many times she'd shut her ears to her father's diatribes against Connie, and the even more frequent occasions when she'd stood up to him on the subject.

"Connie, listen—"

"*You* listen. I'm trying to tell you my plan for being noticed in the movies, and you keep changing the subject. Darn! Here comes another photographer. Get ready."

The photographer raised his camera. "Let's have a smile for the folks in Peoria." The camera flashed. The smell of the burned-out bulb hung in the air as the cameraman popped the bulb out of his camera and replaced it with another from a bulging pocket. "Thanks on behalf of *Movie Mirror*, Miss Mooney and Mr Achilles."

When the photographer was at a safe distance, Frankie said, "You are threatening our lifelong friendship, Connie."

"I don't believe that for a minute. You're the one that's acting selfish. This opportunity I thought up for the fire at Monument Studios isn't only for me, you know. The further I get in films, the more I can help you. That's how we planned it, and that's how it's going to be."

Frankie shook her head, chewing away. "Right now this creamed lobster is the only thing I like about this conversation."

"Frankie, the big fire later on tonight is really a complicated set-up. And as for what is going to happen right now and right here at Camillo's, it's that photo opportunity that Publicity thought up for us. I don't have time to explain, so follow my lead. *Act*. Here she comes."

Frankie turned — every head in the room turned — as the doors opened. She expected Blanche Carver to stride through them, hot on gossip's trail, but instead a vision in red entered. Marietta Valdes posed at the top of the steps, overlooking the dining room of Camillo's.

Expectation ruled the moment. The room grew almost quiet as Marietta, gleaming, descended the steps to the floor. All eyes followed her.

With a swish of red taffeta, Marietta sauntered past diners and photographers as if they were so many shell-bedecked mermaids. A little kerfuffle arose as the photographers picked up their cameras. Frankie noted that there was quite a bit of business necessary to work the flashes.

An elderly couple gaped across their champagne glasses as Marietta stopped at their table. She said, "A lot of people don't know this, but a director is not a craftsman. He is a magician, and story is transformation. May I?"

She took the elderly woman's upraised glass of champagne, drained it, and handed it back. "The Monument Studios publicity head doesn't understand dramatic tension. I would have set up tonight's scene in the front lobby, I think, where one passes through a narrow casement. And I would film the shot from the right into the mirrors, bearing in mind the golden ratio, that rectangle beloved of the ancient Greeks." She turned to a solitary female diner nearby. "Don't you think, dear?"

The woman fingered her beads and said, "I never thought anything like that in my life, Miss Valdes."

Across from Frankie, Connie was slowly turning pink. She muttered, "Marietta ought to be over here, having her picture taken with me, looking jealous. With you and me. I should have known she would ruin things. She's corned to the eyeballs."

Frankie felt this was a fairly safe interpretation of the scene, but Marietta Valdes drunk was still more interesting than most people sober. In that way, Marietta was rather like Gilbert Howard.

Marietta asked the room at large, "Does anybody here believe that a woman can direct a major motion picture?"

The room fell silent. Frankie waited. Marietta's face paled as the silence lingered. When one of the mermaids let out a stifled giggle, Frankie could bear it no more. She rose to her feet.

Connie snatched at her sleeve, but Frankie pulled free. "*I* do. I believe you'd craft an excellent motion picture, were you to direct it, Miss Valdes."

Marietta Valdes sashayed over to their table. "Mr Frank Achilles, don't say *craft*. A director is not a craftsman. A director is a god."

Connie muttered, "For Pete's sake, this is all wrong. I'm going to have to get this whole scene back on track. Help me out, Frankie." She stood up at Frankie's side. "Are you looking for me, Miss Valdes?"

Marietta said tiredly, "Ah. The redhead."

"Jiminy, about time," Connie hissed to Frankie. "Marietta and I worked through this yesterday afternoon. I should have known she'd forget her lines and ruin everything."

But Frankie knew that Marietta Valdes was a star because she didn't ruin anything. She improved it.

"You're supposed to say 'young talent'," Connie hissed to Marietta. "I'm much younger than you."

"Marietta's all of twenty-two," Frankie hissed at Connie.

"I'll say the lines. *Youth!*" Marietta snatched up Connie's glass of champagne and drained it. "*Nobody* takes my co-star."

She placed one strong hand at the base of Frankie's back, the other behind her puffball hair, and kissed Frankie on the lips. Flashbulbs flared. Once she'd gotten over her natural surprise, Frankie decided that being kissed by a woman was almost like being kissed by a man you were not actually involved with, like when you played Spin the Bottle. However, there was a subtle difference, lying perhaps in the element of surprise and the transfer of lipstick.

Marietta let Frankie go.

One of the mermaids called out from beneath a potted palm, "Hey, photog, how about that new fella, Frank Achilles, kisses some of us mermaids? And you take the shot for free."

There was a scattering of applause, but the scene felt as if it were over and the tension resolved. Frankie sensed that the audience was losing interest. Certainly most of the diners at Camillo's would, like Frankie, be regular readers of *Movie Mirror* and other Hollywood publications. They would know that some little star-studded drama was often to be found on the menu.

Connie's face had changed colour again, to a deeper rose. "Sit down, *Frank Achilles*. You're making fools of us."

"Redhead, don't you know why you're here?" Marietta sat herself down on the edge of Frankie and Connie's table. She took Frankie's glass and poured a slug of champagne into it. "No matter what lie Publicity told you, this newsworthy scene is not about raising you to my level. It's about King Samson making me look down into the abyss where you dwell."

Connie hissed, "What do you mean, *abyss*?"

Frankie answered, "Marietta means that King Samson set you, a nobody, up as a scare tactic to stop the real movie star, Marietta, from asking for more power than Samson wants to give. It's exactly like the audition in Vancouver."

"Is that so? Well, you don't know anything about anything, Frankie. *Frank.*"

Raising her glass, Marietta said, "Here's to you, Frank Achilles. You're going to make a very good movie star if I have anything to say about it."

Connie said, "Miss Valdes, Frank Achilles is never going to be a movie star."

"Is he still acting hard to get?" Marietta nodded. "That's the way to play the game."

There would never be a better time to question Marietta Valdes about Gilbert Howard's murder.

Frankie said, "I need to ask you something, Miss Valdes. When Gilbert Howard left you here at Camillo's two nights ago, where was he going?"

"I don't know." Marietta poured champagne into Frankie's glass, raised it in a toast, and drank. "Bless Howie for a free spirit."

"Didn't he say anything at all? It's really important."

"If it's so important, you should ask the right question. He didn't say *where*, but he did say *whom* he was going to.

Into his true love's arms. Some unlucky woman. Howie was a great actor, and he believed I could direct, but he never saw the point in being faithful to one woman."

"And that's all he said? That he was going to see his own true love?"

"That's all." Marietta glanced at Connie. "I suppose I *should* apologize to the redhead here for veering off the script. Sorry, dearie. It was your big moment, and I spoiled it, didn't I? Aren't stars *terrible*?"

Connie said, "This dinner was supposed to be a big dramatic scene for me. I was going to be in the papers."

Marietta beamed. "Serves you right, redhead. This was supposed to be my sister Billie's evening. Publicity promised to send Billie to dinner with Frank Achilles tonight. But Sammy must have told him to change the schedule."

"No wonder King Samson doesn't love you anymore," Connie said fiercely. "You'd better watch out, Marietta Valdes. You might already be a has-been."

And there in the middle of Camillo's dining room, Frankie learned something about herself that she would rather not have known. She had always imagined that she was like her mother, optimistic and longing for an independent life. But now she felt the unhappy spirit of her father, the once Reverend Sheridan D Ray, rise to its feet. Her anger expanded under its black surplice. She felt the colour rise in her cheeks and the bile in her belly. She stormed up to some imagined pulpit inside herself, growing larger with each step. She placed a hand on each side of the lectern, leaned out, and passed a roaring internal judgment on Hollywood, its heartless and unintelligent police force, its malicious columnists and cruel producers, and on Connie herself, who she saw at last through her father's eyes.

She said, "You keep your mouth shut unless it's to apologize to Miss Valdes, Connie Mooney."

Rarely did Connie turn a true camellia white. There had been the long-ago instance when she'd punched a fellow who'd put his hand somewhere he ought not have. And the last time she'd turned so pale had been during her screen test at the Dominion Theatre. But she'd never in her life looked at Frankie that way. A whole lifetime's friendship appeared to have boiled down to this one moment.

Connie said, "I hate you, *Frank Achilles.*"

Frankie shot her cuffs. "I don't even like you that much."

Without pause or regret, Frankie exited Camillo's dining room through the door the waiters used. It led through the kitchen, where dark eyes and Spanish voices cut through the steam. Now the tears fought their way into her eyes, so that she bumped into a fellow in whites. He swore as a platter of cutlets fell to the floor.

Frankie strode past him, past the ranges and the ovens, through a vast pantry and out into the alleyway smelling of cats and greens past their prime. Careful of her brogues, she stepped around a slick of black oil. Once out of the alleyway, she found herself on a much quieter Sunset Boulevard—the evening Sunset. She hurried east toward the movie theatre near where she'd left the Model A.

A young man, dark as night, walked out from under the movie-theatre marquee into the centre of Sunset Boulevard, plunked a bag down on the blacktop, and pulled out a trumpet. Frankie stopped in her tracks and stared.

Without a glance at the cars that blew past on either side, he raised the trumpet to his mouth, puffed his cheeks like a bullfrog, and blew the first long, brassy note up at the sky, so that the note swept the heavens like one of the searchlights over Hollywood. On the far side of the street the marquee lit him from behind and cast a long black shadow across the road. And still the note went on and on as his bullfrog neck puffed out and sweat beaded the hills and planes of his face. Frankie stood astonished by the glory of it while he pulled that silken sound out of his yellow trumpet.

He stopped eventually, of course. He had to snatch his bag up in time to step out of the way of an oversized produce van. He saluted it cheerfully with his instrument, and Frankie fell in love with the young trumpet player, the same way she'd fallen in love with Gilbert Howard and his irresistible talent.

She raised a hand to the musician and called out, "What's the name of that song?"

He crossed to Frankie's side of the street. "'The Jailhouse Blues'."

How appropriate. She closed her eyes for a moment and pictured herself in jail, all in grey, with her tin cup and tray. And that was better than imagining herself in the so-called hot seat at the moment when the warden's hand took hold of the big U-shaped power switch.

Startled by the silence, she opened her eyes to see the musician watching her, polishing the mouthpiece with the cuff of his suit jacket.

"Do you know 'Dora Heart'?" she asked him.

"I know everything. But I'm sick and tired of blowin' 'Dora Heart'."

She nodded. "I'm alone and a complete failure. Do you think I should go home to Vancouver?"

"Who'd have thought it? A white fellow in a good suit, giving up." The trumpet player laughed. "And I got picked to play a scene in the movies today, me and my trumpet. Ain't it funny?"

"I'm glad for you." She wished she were not so bone-deep tired.

And, if wishes came true, she'd stand there and listen to this fellow play forever. But the police were still after her.

She urged him, "Blow, brother, blow!"

"That's all I do, buddy." He grinned around his mouthpiece, threw back his head, and blew.

Frankie tore off to the car.

29

Frankie had trouble getting the Model A started. She fiddled with the mix, got the choke and the ignition backward, and prayed that the engine wouldn't flood. When at last it started, she hit a curb pulling out onto Sunset Boulevard, so that the back wheel slammed up and then down again with a shrill complaint of springs. The rumble seat popped open with a *thunk*. Adrenalin pumping, she rode the clutch the way Connie had taught her in the back alley at home in Vancouver, where chickens shrieked and fluttered out of the Model A's way and not a garbage can in the neighbourhood was spared.

Both hands on the wheel, she steered straight along Sunset Boulevard. Monument Studios, with its formidable angels, appeared and then vanished on her left. She passed the brothel with its glowing yellow windows and safe, friendly air. More of Hollywood's illusions.

She kept a heavy foot on the gas and sped through the shadows. She nearly missed the sign for Paradise Gardens, so that at the last second she skewed between two parked cars at a shockingly bad angle. Frankie decided that neither she nor Frank Achilles gave a cool nickel. She switched off the ignition, walked around the rear of the Model A, and slammed the rumble seat shut.

"All I have to do," she muttered, "is find out whether Eugene tracked down the golden swimmer who loved Gilbert Howard. Then Eugene can tell the police. And I can go home to Vancouver."

She would say thanks and farewell to Eugene and the Queen. Then she would find something she'd always heard of but never been inside — an all-night hockshop. She had something valuable that she might sell for gas money to get home. The diamond in her engagement ring was just a chip. "But the ring itself is gold. Fourteen-carat!" Champ had so informed her the first time he'd slid it onto her finger and asked her never to take it off.

She'd broken that vow, all right, for she hadn't worn her ring since she and Connie left Vancouver. Hocking it was worse still. But Frankie couldn't make it home without money. She felt in her right pocket for her engagement ring. When she didn't find it right away, she told herself not to panic, but her heart beat faster as she fumbled her way past the gun into the deepest area of her pocket. It was empty. Hastily, she felt the inside of her left-hand pocket, but found only a pinch of lint.

She growled, "Men have such a lot of pockets. It is entirely ridiculous over-tailoring!"

She fumbled her way through each pocket with no result at all. The ring was gone. The disappointment was too much to bear. And that was when somebody shone a bright light into her eyes.

She held up a hand against the glare. "Watch where you're pointing that thing, buddy."

A male voice invited her to step away from the car.

She reminded herself to keep her temper and her head about her. This was a free country, darn it all, and a citizen had a right to park on any public thoroughfare.

She said, "What's it all about, Officer? Can a man about town help in any way?"

"We've got an investigation rolling, and I'm looking for witnesses. Do you live at Paradise Gardens?"

Frankie coughed. "Nope. What's the case, Officer?"

"Can't say, sir." The policeman added, "We're looking for a young, dark-haired, out-of-town girl. Seen any girls like that?"

"Can't say as I have." Inspired in equal measures by fury at the intransigent single-bloody-mindedness of the police and a wish to appear urbane and witty, she asked, "Out-of-town girl, is she? Have you searched out of town?"

"Look, you. No nonsense, please," the policeman said. "I've got a report to write up in about ten minutes or the captain will hang my ears from his belt buckle. What's your name and address?"

Frankie's knees within the grey suiting were none too sure of themselves. As the man about town, she said, "Well, here's how it is, Officer. I've come to Paradise Gardens to see a friend of the gentler sex. And I'd rather not give my name or my address, as there's a different little woman at my home address who might require a full and lengthy explanation. You understand, Officer."

The policeman sighed as if his pockets were full of second-hand woes. Frankie would like to have informed him that no matter how depressing the policeman's circumstances might be, they were honey compared to being hunted day and night for a crime one hadn't committed.

The policeman asked, "Are you drunk, young fellow?"

Did she dare to attempt the portrayal of a drunken man about town? "Yessir. I'm drunk as Methuselah's doctor."

"Away you go, then, mister, and sleep it off."

Blinking, Frankie looked from the car to the Paradise Gardens sign. "Where do you suggest I go to sleep?"

The policeman said, "If it was me, buddy, I'd go where judgment and imprecation were thinnest on the ground."

Frankie bowed unsteadily. "Thank you, Officer. Carry on with your hallowed task, protecting us from out-of-town girls."

As she walked away, Frankie wished she were wearing a hat—a man's hat, not her squashy one—so that she could raise it a little too high. Her stage training told her that the best way to look drunk was to try not to look drunk, which was complicated in this case by also having to try not to look afraid. She stumbled a little under the swinging sign and passed through, along the path among the bungalows, past Villa 12B where the noisy blonde threw things at people. At the spot where the main pathway through the bungalows branched into the paths for Villas 7A and 7B, she paused. Here she was, on her own again under the deep, dark California sky. *Alone, alone, all, all alone.* The Ancient Mariner had gotten that right. Above her a bird fluttered—no, a bat. With a weighted flick it slipped past her ear and up over Villa 7A so quickly that she had no time to shiver as its passing lifted the ends of her puffball hair.

The little brick path ran from the toes of her shoes toward the central brickwork patio. It split to lead straight to Eugene Ellery's front door. She shoved her hands into her pockets and polished the toes of her brogues on the back of her trouser legs. All her earlier distrust of Eugene seemed now the nerves of a foolish young girl. Pretending to be a man all day had somehow made her feel more of a grown woman, one who could think for herself.

She took the path to Villa 7A and Eugene Ellery's front door. A part of her, the weary part, wondered whether Eugene Ellery might not take charge of everything and save her bacon for her. She pictured herself in the passenger seat of the Model A, with Eugene at the wheel, motoring up the long sunny highway to Vancouver.

But Eugene's front window was dark. Disappointment nearly overcame her, but she realized that he might still be home, in another room in the little bungalow. She took a couple of steps around the corner and sure enough, his bathroom light was on. She gazed at the window with its glowing curtain, yellow against the dark exterior wall. A symbol, perhaps, of hope — of Eugene finding the witness to clear her name. A golden light, a golden swimmer. All things seemed possible when a window glowed against the darkness.

Then the click from Eugene's front door brought her running back around to the front of the villa.

"Frankie, I'm sorry." Eugene stood in his darkened doorway. "I didn't find that blonde woman you're looking for. The one who was swimming with Gilbert Howard the night he died. The police will find her, sometime soon. I'll make sure that you know when they do. Leave Hollywood. Go home."

A light breeze lifted the leaves of a nearby palm and let them fall again with a gentle pattering that reminded her of Vancouver rain. Inside her pockets, she made two fists. She would not cry.

"Leave Hollywood?" she asked. *Without you?*

"Yes. Be careful, and drive like the wind. The police will never find you in Vancouver, because nobody at Paradise Gardens will ever tell them they saw you." He lifted a hand in farewell, and the door snicked shut.

And at that moment, as if written upon the closed door of Villa 7A, the solution to the problem of the blonde swimmer came to her.

No, it didn't *come to her.* Like Cinderella, it struck her for twelve. Frankie had a sudden, crazy desire to laugh, but she couldn't quite manage it. She and Eugene had been looking for the wrong blonde. They'd been searching for Gilbert Howard's true love, the faceless golden swimmer.

Perhaps not so faceless! How had she overlooked the obvious? There was a blonde woman nearby, in Villa 12A in Paradise Gardens. The blonde in 12A — the shouter, the thrower of plates, the passionate one — must be the woman Gilbert Howard came to Paradise Gardens to see. *She* was the one who visited him when she wanted to swim in the turquoise pool next door. Although Frankie had caught only glimpses of the blonde in 12A, she knew she would have no difficulty recognizing the young woman's slim figure and cropped, boyish haircut.

Frankie turned on her heel and strode back along the walk toward Villa 12A. A jazzy piano piece spiralled out a side window. The best way to approach the blonde would be a swift attack. Frankie would accuse her straight out and leave the woman no choice but to stammer out her story, and possibly even her guilt. As for clearing Frankie's name, she would have to force the blonde to come with her to the police to tell them her story. Then down at the station among the boys in blue, Frankie would have two choices: reveal her true identity and trust the coils of justice to release her on the blonde's testimony, or continue in the guise of Frank

Achilles while the golden swimmer testified and Frankie's name was cleared. The first option was as dicey as anything she'd ever dared in her life. The second option—remaining disguised—was safer, but as Frank Achilles, she would have no opportunity to argue her own innocence.

If there was a third way, she'd think of it. In the meantime, if she had to use force to get the girl to talk to the police, she still had the gun in her pocket. Frankie knocked at the door of 12A.

A voice from inside called out, "Keep your trousers on." Frankie, increasingly impatient, heard the sound of kitchen pots crashing to the floor and a steady string of words she'd last heard from Billie, and before that from her father, Sheridan D. At last the door opened, and a blonde woman in a green dress leaned against the jamb and asked, "What's cooking, brother?"

Frankie stared. It was not out of the question that those long curls were false and that underneath them lay the short pale locks she'd seen on the girl in the pool. But the green dress this blonde in 12A wore would have fit Connie's mother equally well. Without Frankie ever having had a good look at the golden girl's face that night by the pool, she knew this blowsy blonde could not possibly be the slender young woman who had kissed Gilbert Howard so passionately the night he died.

"I'm sorry," Frankie managed to say. She heard the female tones of her voice, and added in her tenor, "You're not the one."

The blonde said, "Don't be sorry, fella. You're not the one for me, either." She threw back her head and laughed, her bosom bouncing heavily under the green bodice. She slammed the door shut, and Frankie found herself alone again in the night.

On shaky legs, she walked through Paradise Gardens toward Villas 7A and B. Eugene's house was dark again except for his bathroom window. Inside, light bloomed and vanished as the bathroom curtains moved in the breeze. She stopped to watch, thinking one clear thought over and over, like the stroke of the bell that ends the day: *With all my hard work and positive attitude, how can I still be in such a fix?*

The breeze picked up slightly, and Frankie took a deep breath of the gardenia-scented air. The perfumes from the white-flowered shrubs smelled stronger at night, she decided, and then the breeze lifted the curtain of Eugene Ellery's bathroom and showed her a brief view of its occupant.

Frankie took a step back, stricken to her centre by the image of the young woman, slender and golden, in Eugene's bathroom. The young, blonde woman stood with her back to the window, drying herself with a towel.

This was the girl she was after—the golden girl who'd kissed Gilbert Howard and then dived into the water while he declaimed murder down upon himself. The girl she'd been looking for was standing naked in Eugene Ellery's bungalow bathroom. And not only that—she must have been in the bathroom a few minutes before, when Eugene answered the door in his shirtsleeves. The blonde must have been inside the house when Eugene had told Frankie that he had not found her.

Another bat flew past her, and another memory overtook her: on the night she spent hiding in Eugene's closet, she had heard a woman sigh. *The blonde swimmer. In Eugene's bed, but gone by morning. That girl had been no truer to Gilbert Howard than he had been to her. No truer than Eugene's word to me.*

She walked back along the path again, this time toward the front door of her own Villa 7B. She knew the police might still be there, although she would surely have noticed lights and movement inside. But they might be waiting for her. It was, she supposed, one of those moments when a criminal, after planning everything perfectly, makes a blunder that breaks the case wide open. She was not a criminal, but she could blunder with the best of them. She had to, now that she had lost her ring. There was nothing for it but to see for herself whether her forty dollars were really missing from the sofa cushions, for it was entirely possible that Eugene had lied about looking for the money, too.

Villa 7B appeared to be perfectly empty. Once inside the front room, Frankie didn't turn on the light—she was not so foolish as that. In darkness she made her way to the sofa. She set the cushions on the floor, thrust her fingers deeply into the crease at the back and into the corners, and sat back on her heels, empty-handed. Her money was not there. What to search next—kitchen, bedroom, or bath?

She entered the unlit bedroom and stopped still. On Connie's bed she made out a black shape stretched out asleep. Connie was back. Frankie stepped up to shake her awake and ask her where the money was. Her brogue found something slippery on the floor by the bed and she barely managed to catch her balance.

She put out a hand and found the little frilled lamp by the bedside. She switched it on.

Once the light clicked on, she saw her error.

The Queen of the Extras lay unmoving in Connie's bed. Frankie couldn't think why. Had Loretta hoped to help Frankie somehow, or had she come by to console, comfort, and reassure her? Frankie leaned closer.

The dark hair at the near side of the Queen's head shone with blood.

Somebody had struck her on the head and killed her. The Queen was dead.

"Oh, my Queen." Frankie switched off the light. She sat down on the side of the bed and buried her face in her hands. First Gilbert Howard, and now the Queen. Mother to all at Paradise Gardens. Almost a mother to Frankie herself.

Across the dark little room, Frankie heard a rustle. It was the sort of sound that a person might make who had been sitting out of sight on the floor and was now finding his or her feet. *Hers.* Frankie heard a soft footstep — a woman's step. She was sure of it.

There was no sense trying to hide. There was nowhere *to* hide. She reached over the Queen's body and switched the light on again.

There at the foot of the bed stood the Hollywood columnist, Blanche Carver.

"I knew Gilbert Howard's killer would return to the scene of the crime," Blanche Carver said. "But I never guessed that you'd kill my poor dear Loretta, too."

30

Frankie knelt in the pool of light by Connie's bed, where the Queen lay, her poor head resting on the bloodied pillow. "Dear Queen, dear Loretta, who will look after us now?"

From behind Frankie, near the bedroom door, Blanche spoke again. "I know who you are. In disguise! I heard a woman's voice in the dark, but I see a man when I turn on the light. We've met before, and more than once, *Francesca Ray.*"

With gentle fingers, Frankie touched the Queen's hair. "How long has she been lying here? How long have you known she was dead?"

"Not long. My poor Loretta." The columnist shook her head. "The police will be here soon to take you into custody. And then I'm going to print the hardest story I've ever had to write. The whole world will know what you did to the woman who welcomed and helped you."

Frankie faced Blanche. No wonder the columnist hadn't shown up at Camillo's, looking for gossip and scoops. She had been sitting beside the Queen's body, keeping vigil with her friend.

Frankie said, "I didn't do this. I would never hurt her."

"Lies. Every one of them takes you one step closer to trial, jail, and execution."

Frankie bent over the Queen again. She wanted to make sure that the dead woman's eyes were shut, not open like poor Gilbert Howard's had been. But the Queen's eyes were closed and she looked as if she were sleeping, which was how Frankie had always expected a dead person to look. In fact, the Queen, tucked up into Connie's bed with her head on the pillow, appeared to be simply resting her eyes after a day's hard work, if you didn't take into account the bloodstains on the pillowcase.

Frankie looked up at Blanche. The columnist held something in her right hand. A bag? A stick? It didn't matter.

"She's been hit on the head," Frankie said.

"Not exactly news to you, is it?"

Frankie grimaced but held back her retort. She said evenly, "The police were posted all around this villa after Gilbert Howard was found here. Why weren't they here to save her?"

"The police found evidence that Howie was murdered in his own bungalow, and the body merely transported to yours. They moved their investigation away from Paradise Gardens, next door to the Garden of Allah."

"If only they had left a policeman here." Frankie felt her throat grow thick with sorrow, but she wouldn't cry. How much better to recite poetry, as Billie had done over Gilbert Howard's body. For once, she couldn't recall a single verse of the Bible, nor a word of Shakespeare, except for *Alas*.

So she said that. "Alas, dear Queen."

"Alas, indeed, for Loretta." Blanche held up the item she'd been cradling against her breast. Frankie saw that it was the lamp from her own bedside table—like Connie's, minus its ruffled shade. The columnist's expression was fierce, as if she were going to strike out with it.

"Miss Carver, what are you doing with my lamp?"

"This was the murder weapon, wasn't it?"

"Was it?" Frankie stared. The columnist must be correct. Except for its twin still sitting on Connie's bedside table, this wrought-iron lamp was the only object in the room that might serve as a weapon. She leaned closer to look at the Queen's head wound in the light from Connie's lamp. She tipped back the frilly shade to examine the back of the Queen's head more closely.

"It looks like she was hit from behind."

"I'm remembering every word you say," Blanche said. "It's only fair to tell you. Each remark that you make will be printed in my paper and then, later on, revealed in court."

The columnist took a step closer to the side of the bed opposite Frankie.

Frankie clasped her hands in front of her, the way her father had taught her to stand during a church service. She said, "My Queen, on behalf of all of your kids at Paradise Gardens, thank you. I believe that all the good that you've done, all the help you've given, will come back to you, somehow, wherever you are now. Go in peace."

"It's practically a confession." Blanche held the lamp to her breast.

Frankie leaned over to kiss the Queen's cheek, almost as pale as the pillowcase beneath her head. The cheek was still warm. That meant that she had arrived only moments too late to stop whomever had done this terrible thing. If only she hadn't hung about, talking to Eugene, chasing after the blonde girl who was, all the time, hiding in Eugene's house.

Had Eugene attacked the Queen? But why would he? That thought sent the mystery spiralling even deeper than before. Because there was no getting around it. A second dead body in Villa 7B meant only one thing: the Queen had been killed because of Gilbert Howard. But by whom? Perhaps the Queen had found Gilbert Howard's blonde swimmer and communicated Frankie's suspicions to the girl herself.

Frankie leaned over the Queen's body and touched her hand. It was neutral to the touch, no colder than Frankie's own hand. Frankie started, put two fingers under the Queen's chin at the side of the neck, and looked sharply up at Blanche.

"She's not dead." Frankie was conscious of her own heart beating hard within her breast. "The Queen is alive."

"I felt for Loretta's pulse before you came." Blanche stood. She dropped the lamp onto the bed. A smear of blood stained her white jacket. "She had none."

"Her pulse is faint, but it's there."

"I must have missed it. Thank God," Blanche whispered. "Now, what should we do?"

"*What should we do?* Great heavens." Frankie took the gun out of her pocket. "We should call a doctor! Stop wasting time, Miss Carver."

Frankie yanked the door open, half expecting to receive a wrought-iron lamp on the back of her head, courtesy of the columnist. She sprinted into the brick patio area where she had lately danced the carioca with Eugene. She placed two fingers into the trigger loop, pointed King Samson's gun straight up in the air, peered into the darkness to see that the sky was empty of birds directly overhead, closed her eyes, and pulled the trigger.

Nothing happened—the trigger was stuck on something. She peered at the gun in the darkness, and saw a glint of light on the trigger, like a tiny star caught on a small new moon. Here it was after all: the engagement ring that Champ had given her that day in the snow. Her ring had hooked itself onto the trigger. With excruciating delicacy of movement, she wiggled it free and dropped the ring into her jacket pocket. She pointed the gun straight up and fired.

The gun went off with a sound like the end of the world. Frankie shouted for help. Then she aimed, checked again, and pulled the trigger.

The gun cracked again, but the Paradise Gardens kids were already running along pathways and out of bungalow doors toward her, some in bathrobes, some in bare feet. A nursery rhyme sounded in Frankie's head. *Leave your supper and leave your sleep. Come to your playfellows in the street.* She wished she were calling them to meet in a long conga line, to dance through the night.

Her chattering, friendly young neighbours gathered around Frankie. Eugene was among them—quieter, as always, than most—but the golden girl was nowhere to be seen. She spotted Tom's blue sweater in the crush of young people, took a handful of his sleeve, and pressed her face to his ear. Briefly, she filled him in on the Queen's situation.

"Got it," Tom said. "Thank goodness you found her. We'll get her to hospital, Frankie."

She jumped as if shot. "You know who I *am*?"

"*Frank Achilles*, of course. The Queen told me all about your disguise." Tom looked sharply at Frankie. "Did you think any one of us would turn you in, Frankie? The Queen trusts us."

Frankie exhaled. "I trust you, too. Let's get the Queen to hospital." But how they would carry the injured woman without harming her further, Frankie didn't know. She found that she didn't know anything at all, except that Eugene Ellery was the first through the door into Villa 7B. He carried one corner of the Queen's mattress. The mattress was too thin to behave like a proper stretcher, but with so many hands, the crowd of young people managed to keep the Queen something near to horizontal as they carried her out toward Sunset Boulevard. Tom picked up the corner of the chenille counterpane where it dragged on the bricks and tucked it safely out of the way. He handed off his spot at the side of the mattress to somebody else. "Frankie, we were all hoping you'd be halfway to Canada by now. The cops haven't come up with a single alternate suspect yet, which makes us wonder what they use for brains."

"I know," Frankie said, breathing hard. "They stopped me on the street a couple of times. They asked me to identify my own picture."

Somehow the sound of Tom's laugh made Frankie certain that the Queen would survive her attacker's blow. Tom said, "We'll take care of the Queen. Leave her to us. Make your escape before the police and the press find out you're disguised as a man, will you?"

He followed the rest out toward Sunset.

The press, of course, in the shape of Blanche Carver, already knew Frankie was disguised as Frank Achilles. But she couldn't do anything about Blanche Carver just then. She did, however, know at last where to find the golden swimmer. She plunged up the path and through Villa 7A's unlocked front door. Gun in hand, she burst inside Eugene's bathroom, but it was empty. She pounded through his house—tore the back of his cupboard open and checked under the bed, but found no golden swimmer anywhere. The blonde girl was gone again.

Frankie walked slowly out of doors. If Blanche Carver had called the police as she'd said, they would be here any moment now. If this were to be the end of the road for Frank Achilles — and for Frankie Ray — she had better savour her last experience of freedom in Hollywood.

She gazed up into the unfathomable California sky and told it, "I shouldn't have run in the first place. There was nothing to tie me to Gilbert Howard's murder except its location. I hardly knew him. I was never his lover, and the kids and the Queen of the Extras would have testified so. But I ran." What dreadful moments those had been, lightened only by the friendship and protection she had felt when Eugene Ellery took her and hid her. *The same way Eugene had sheltered the blonde swimmer.* "And now I'm the only suspect in a front-page murder investigation. But anyway, I won't run now."

Around her, the shrubs and hedges whispered. The stars stared down at her. She caught a glimpse of a pale face like a flash of moonlight at the door of Villa 7B.

Blanche Carver spoke from the bungalow's doorway. "You had a gun all the time."

Frankie put her hand in her pocket and left it there, resting on the gun. Yes, this gun had been with her that first night in Vancouver, when the adventure had begun. It had been with her the whole time, in fact, with the exception of the few hours during which somebody had used it to shoot Gilbert Howard. She almost laughed as she said, "Yes, I'm armed to the teeth."

"But you didn't use it? Why not, when you could have held me up and made your escape?"

Impatiently, Frankie shook her head. "Go ahead and print what I said: *I should never have run.* I should have shown better sense, but when you accused me of the murder, I was afraid."

Blanche took a few steps nearer Frankie. "You had a gun, but you were afraid?"

"I didn't have the gun when I found Gilbert Howard's body. But I would have been afraid even if I had."

A siren sounded not far off, and Frankie's shoulders tensed under her man's jacket. But the siren drifted away into the distance.

She asked, "Where are the policemen, Miss Carver? If you called them, shouldn't they be here by now?"

The columnist stopped, her white trouser suit glowing in the darkness. She opened her mouth as if to answer, but said nothing.

Understanding rose in Frankie like a great, round, illuminating moon. She said, "It's a mystery, isn't it, when you phone the police about a murder — even an attempted murder — and they don't show up. It's as if you hadn't even called in the first place. Perhaps you wanted the story all to yourself?"

Blanche Carver said nothing.

"But that's not it at all, is it, Miss Carver? Because an even stranger puzzle can be found in the geometry of the scene. The geometry that, according to you, had me hit the Queen with a lamp, escape, and then stupidly return to be caught by you, my accuser."

As if she hadn't heard a word Frankie had said, Blanche asked, "Do you think Loretta will be all right?"

"I don't know. How hard did you hit her?"

Frankie took out the gun again. She had a deep wish to say *an eye for an eye, a tooth for a tooth*. She wanted to rage against liars and bearers of false witness. She wanted to frighten the life out of the woman and then lead her at gunpoint to the police station.

Instead, she fired the gun twice more into the evening sky. Paradise Gardens was empty, and the night seemed undisturbed by the noise. Nobody came running. You'd think that the police next door in the Garden of Allah, at Gilbert Howard's bungalow, would hear and investigate a noise like that. But maybe they were slower on their feet than when you saw them in the movies.

"I wanted to empty the gun," Frankie explained. She slipped it back into her pocket. "Ammunition is really far too much of a temptation."

"I'll deny this if you tell anybody," Blanche Carver said, "but I thought Loretta was *you*. You had escaped the night before, and the police had finished with the scene and left. I was alone in your room, in the dark, trying to get a feel for the moment an aspiring actress becomes a murderess. I was trying to imagine how you killed my friend Gilbert Howard. Then I heard movement in the living room. The door opened. I thought you had returned to the scene of the crime. I knew you were armed and dangerous, so I took the lamp and I … I hit Loretta by accident," Blanche Carver said reasonably. "I wouldn't hurt a friend on purpose. And they couldn't … I mean, as a murderer, you couldn't be …"

Frankie finished her sentence for her. "They couldn't execute me twice for two murders, so I might as well take the blame." Would the world agree? If so, what a heartless world this was. She kicked a stone off the patio onto the grass in front of Villa 7B. "Two murders for the price of one. How thrifty. Well, Miss Carver, tell me this. You hurt the Queen. Hurt her badly. So I have to ask you, *did you kill Gilbert Howard?*"

Blanche said, "Don't be silly. He was my friend."

"Like Loretta — the Queen — was your friend?"

"I've known her all my life."

"I have a friend like that." Or she used to have, before their definitive quarrel. "Miss Carver, you need to decide what to do about me now. Call the police if you must. I can't stop you now that I've emptied my gun."

The columnist nodded. "You might have shot me, but you didn't. You could have run, but you chose to stay and see that Loretta got help." Blanche Carver pierced Frankie with her sharp newspaperwoman's gaze. "You know something? I don't think you killed Gilbert Howard at all. So I'd better give you a good long start, hadn't I?"

Blanche Carver walked past Frankie toward Sunset. Over her shoulder she said, "I'll keep your disguise to myself. There."

"If you're hoping I'll say thank you, Miss Carver, you're in for a long wait."

Blanche Carver's white form vanished round a corner. Frankie tried to feel angry with the woman, but she felt hungry instead—desperately so. Untimely so! That lobster dinner at Camillo's seemed a long time ago. Luckily, there was food in Villa 7B's kitchenette. From the kitchen cupboard she snatched the half-empty bag of bread that had provided her and Connie with such pleasant toast the morning before. She stepped out the back door and peered through the darkness into the branches of the famously productive orange tree, in hopes of finding some fruit to sweeten her plain bread supper. But she forgot all about oranges at the sound of a deep sigh. Turning, she spied the starlit figure of a woman kneeling in the grass in Eugene's backyard.

Almost at once she made out that the woman on the grass was not the golden swimmer. This woman's hair was dark, and she was bent over as if crying, as if she were a mourner. And she was kneeling over the spot where Frankie had helped Eugene uncover the 'anonymous' dead man. Frankie was certain there had never been two dead bodies in one day at Villa 7B. The backyard corpse and Gilbert Howard had been one and the same. While she and Connie had been extras in the movies, somebody had dug up Gilbert Howard's body and posed it on the sofa in Frankie's living room.

Frankie watched from the shadow beneath the orange tree as the weeping woman rose to her feet. Frankie saw first that she was barefoot, and second that she was Marietta Valdes. The actress picked up two objects that Frankie had not previously noticed: two buckets, one for each hand. She strode away, as all the world was doing tonight, toward Sunset Boulevard.

It occurred to Frankie that if Marietta Valdes had known where to kneel in Eugene's backyard to cry over Gilbert Howard's death, then it followed that she might very well know who had buried him there.

Frankie took three pieces of bread from the bag and dropped the rest against the base of the orange tree. Munching on bits of dry bread, she followed Marietta, staying out of the light and trying not to slap the soles of her brogues on the path between the bungalows.

She was back out on Sunset Boulevard, trailing Marietta at a conservative distance, before she realized that somebody was trailing *her*.

A line from the 'Rubaiyat of Omar Khayyam' came to mind. Her father, Sheridan D, had never approved of the poem. He thought it too sensual, and so Frankie had learned several bits of it by heart. She had been struck by the truth of one line among many: *The Moving Finger writes, and having writ, moves on.* You couldn't take back a lie once you'd spoken it.

Right now Frankie was sincerely glad that she had lied to Blanche Carver and left a single bullet in the gun.

31

A soft wind lifted and rattled the palm fronds as Marietta, followed by Frankie, who was trailed in her turn by a shadowy, unknown pursuer, walked swiftly along Sunset Boulevard.

Marietta certainly had tough feet. She covered ground with a speed remarkable for a barefoot woman carrying two buckets. What on earth was Marietta Valdes carrying in those buckets? Water? Why on earth would she be carrying a couple of gallons of water alone at night on Sunset Boulevard? At any rate, it was apparent that she was a walker. Connie's mother was a walker, too, Frankie recalled. Mrs Mooney was as round as a doughnut, but she could roll on forever once she started. And of course, Frankie's own mother had been very good at walking away.

The three of them, still keeping a neat distance one from the next, neared Monument Studios. Frankie became aware of a new sound, a distant hiss and pop. It sounded like the fireworks she and Connie used to buy with their pocket money every autumn. To match the two noises properly, you'd have to add the hiss of sparklers to the pop of the firecrackers.

Fire. Now Frankie remembered, for the Queen had told her the day before about King Samson's planned great conflagration, when he would burn the decade-old set for his epic *Ambition.* Earlier this very evening, Connie had been enthusing about going to the filming of the fire. She would have discovered the impossibility of entering the studio without a pass by now, Frankie supposed.

But Marietta must have a pass, or be named on a list, for the actress moved confidently across the street to the Monument Studio gates, past Dickie the guard's kiosk, and up to the small door set into the larger gates. The actress put down her buckets and pounded on the door.

Frankie stood behind a fat palm trunk to watch. High above, a puff of white smoke rose into the night, and Frankie wondered what would happen if the wind blew harder and swept the fire beyond the studio walls. No wonder Dickie's kiosk was empty. All hands, and no doubt a lot of firemen, would be on the far side of the studios, standing guard as the set of *Ambition* burned.

Between keeping an eye on Marietta hammering at the gate and on the rising clouds of smoke, Frankie completely missed the sound of footsteps coming up behind until they were right upon her. A hand touched her shoulder.

A voice said quietly, "Did you decide that you couldn't leave Hollywood without seeing the show, Frankie?"

Eugene. This was the first time she'd been so near him since she'd uncovered his lie about not finding the golden swimmer. And she had not forgotten that she was in this mess in the first place because he'd urged her to evade the law.

But he was still Eugene Ellery, the man with the calm and helpful grey eyes. And—perhaps because of her appreciation of his slight frame and elegant attire, and the way his jacket was always buttoned, with the tie perfectly tied in a Prince Albert knot—she still wanted to trust Eugene. It occurred to her that perhaps love was not a storm or a blessing or even a journey. It might simply be a choice you were driven by circumstances to make.

Frankie murmured calmly, "Oh! When you say 'watch the show', do you mean to watch the *Ambition* set burn down? I understand that the fire will be fearfully controlled."

"King Samson has fifty engineers on hand to help, I hear," Eugene said.

"So Connie told me." Frankie said, "Somebody told me that King Samson's got a team of firemen, too, and air pipes to make the flames climb higher while the cameramen film the blaze."

"No expense spared, the papers say."

"Naturally. It's King Samson." Frankie inclined her head. "Burning *Ambition*."

"What a well-turned phrase," Eugene said. "*And* you know how to dance the carioca. My, you're a clever young woman, Frankie."

She looked away from him, straight ahead at the angels guarding Monument Studios. She asked, "Do you love her?"

"Love who?" Eugene asked.

Before Frankie could answer, the gate to the studios was flung open from within. Marietta picked up her buckets and disappeared inside. The gate banged shut again, but Frankie made out the thin black upright line along the doorframe that told her the force of its closing had bounced it open again.

331

"Do you love the blonde girl?" she clarified.

"What blonde girl?" Eugene frowned.

Frankie walked away from him toward the studio gate. Over her shoulder she added, "The blonde girl who was naked in your bathroom."

She certainly hoped that would leave him speechless — stop him short, in fact, while she strode across the street and left him behind.

He caught up to her. She found herself a little closer to Eugene than she wanted to be at that particular time and place.

"No," he said. "I don't love the blonde girl. I guess I don't even like her very much." He drew breath. "Frankie, go home to your father. Be safe. Be yourself again."

With a fierce tug Frankie freed her arm from his grip, gave him a minister's Judgement-Day look, and strode through the gate into the studio lot. She knew he'd follow her. Or perhaps she hoped he'd follow her. But she didn't look back.

Once inside the studio gates, she looked to her left at the offices where Frank Achilles had so recently been given the star treatment. Only a couple of lights glowed in the office windows. Tonight, King Samson and all his employees would be at the fire. Here within the studio walls, the crackle of the fire sounded very close indeed, but she was certain it was well under control. There would be laws about that in Hollywood, or at least guidelines to be followed for the insurance companies.

The sounds the fire made, and the chemical smell it produced — an odour that she had no name for — excited her and hurried her steps along the same path she'd taken two days before, when the Queen had guided her and Connie among the sound stages to join the extras. Between the buildings she caught sight of the black-painted pillar topped with the head of the dog-faced Egyptian god Anubis. Its ears gleamed orange and gold from the flames that must soon catch up with it and burn it to the ground.

She rounded the corner of a sound stage and found herself in the open, gravelly area where she had met Bruno and the other extras. Was it only yesterday that they had gathered to smoke, drink coffee, and eat cheese and tomato sandwiches while waiting to be filmed? Tonight in the gloom, the litter of paper cups and cigarette butts shone like pearls against the ground. She remembered the extras' friendly banter, and the moment she had been chosen, against all the odds, for the role of pigeon girl. Despite all the darkness, unfairness, and danger the time between had brought, Frankie felt herself smile from ear to ear.

Eugene's steps rattled the gravel behind her. She snapped back to the present moment and hurried away from him, around the corner and onto the pigeon-girl set.

Beyond the statue of the horse with three feet on the ground stood the wall separating the pigeon-girl movie set from the old set of *Ambition*. A tongue of flames beyond this inner wall licked upward, and Frankie saw Marietta's two buckets resting on the gravel. Marietta herself appeared out of a gap in the wall, moving quickly in her swirling red dress. There was no sign on her angry, beautiful face that she'd been crying twenty minutes before. She looked like a goddess who'd never shed a tear in her life. Behind her, Luigi dragged a camera on wheels across the gravel. Marietta cursed him soundly over her shoulder, and the cameraman cursed back in Italian.

Eugene called, "Marietta! What lunatic scheme are you devising now?"

Marietta's eyes flashed as she turned from Luigi and his camera to face them. "Eugene! And Frank Achilles. Excellent. Please explain to this cameraman that a great film does not simply survive the plots and machinations of writers, cameramen, and engineers. Every inch of film must spring whole from the mind of a director, like Athena from the brow of Zeus."

"*Strega!*" the cameraman blazed at Marietta. "I know *everything* about directing. I agree, don't listen to the producer. And don't listen to the bloody actors. Above all, don't listen to the writers. But if you want a picture, you'd better damn well listen to your cameraman — me! — and also the one who let you in through the gate."

"You took my money, Luigi. You'll stay and shoot film as I say," Marietta told him coolly, "on *this* side of the wall, where I control the filming. Exactly as if I were the director of *The Emperor of New York.* Because that's what I'm going to be. Here, hold these matches."

Marietta tossed a box of matches to Luigi. Then she snatched up one of her buckets and swung it back.

Frankie cried, "Don't empty it!"

There was a frozen moment when the bucket hung horizontally as if defying gravity — and then its contents flew straight out in front of Marietta. The slosh of liquid spread across the façade of the columned building set, the one that had the look of a bank. She said, "That's liquid paraffin. Light it and film the results, Luigi. And don't overlook the visual ratio. The perfect rectangular shot! No burning obelisk can compete with a flaming colonnade."

Luigi looked doubtfully from the matchbox to the paraffin-glazed colonnade.

"How can you hope to control a fire without a team of engineers?" Frankie demanded.

"Damn the engineers." Marietta picked up the second bucket.

Frankie moved to stop her, but Eugene pushed Frankie aside and attempted to wrestle the second bucket away from her. Frankie heard the splash of spilled liquid. A shining string of dots shone like a small cluster of stars as some of the contents splashed across the arm and side of Eugene's jacket.

"Look out!" Frankie cried.

Eugene, still struggling with the actress for the second bucket, said, "Marietta, if you light this part of the set on fire without the engineers to control it, the fire may spread. The whole of Sunset Boulevard could go up in flames."

"Don't be a coward. Art is everything." Marietta won the struggle and slung the bucket's contents onto the set building so that the columns looked like a bit of Atlantis pulled up from the bottom of the sea. "Look behind you — see those big drums? Water. Water in case of fire. *I* had those set there for safety's sake. You see? I've thought it through."

Marietta might have been more convincing had she not, to Frankie's certain knowledge, been drinking quite a lot of champagne at Camillo's earlier that night. The two enormous cans of water were better than nothing, but they were no substitute for trained firefighters.

As if on cue, excited voices sounded from the far side of the old *Ambition* set. Out of Frankie's sight, firemen and engineers rattled off numbers, reports, and orders.

"Twenty-seven's on the line."

"Eighteen's a go."

"Nineteen's stuck. Give me a hand, will you?"

"Stand by with the hoses."

It was a comfort to know that, not far off, King Samson and all his brave firemen and engineers were standing by to handle the burning of *Ambition*.

Eugene gestured emphatically toward the columned building Marietta had drenched in paraffin. "What if you light this wall and it burns out of control? What if you kill somebody, Marietta?"

"Then I'll film it. Light the fire, Luigi, you lily-livered slave." Marietta snatched the matches from his hands.

Luigi roared, "*Ammaliatrice!* Go to hell and take your paraffin with you."

"That particular road runs both ways, Luigi, and don't you forget it." In a passion, Marietta flung out both arms. Her right hand, which held the matches, missed Frankie's left eye by a narrow margin.

"Ha!" Frankie cried and seized the matches from Marietta.

Marietta lunged and attempted to take them back, but Frankie slipped the matches safely into her pocket with the gun.

When Marietta drew back a fist, Eugene stepped between them and took hold of the actress by both wrists.

"You're both against me. You don't want me to become a director any more than King Samson does." Marietta grew calm in Eugene's grip. "But you'll see. I'll find myself some fire on the far side of this wall. I'll get my shots in there. Come on, Luigi. Unless you want to pay back all that money I gave you."

Marietta pulled free of Eugene and strode away through the gap in the firewall. Luigi followed her, grumbling and tugging his wheeled camera behind him. Frankie let out a long breath.

"Thank goodness." Eugene flung himself down on the plinth at the foot of the statue.

"Nobody could really like Marietta Valdes." Frankie eyed the columns and classical portico that topped them, all drenched in unlit liquid paraffin. "But I hope she does become Hollywood's first woman director. I do."

"I like Marietta fine. When she's not acting crazy," Eugene said. "Still, it would surprise me very much if she got the chance to direct." He added, "Except maybe a short film. I hear that a woman on Goldwyn's lot is directing short films."

Frankie shoved her hand into her pocket. She touched the gun, the ring, and the box of matches. She was very glad indeed that she'd taken the matches from Marietta, for the pigeon-girl set was at least safe.

A series of bangs sounded on the far side of the *Ambition* set firewall. The night breeze picked up, and something metallic popped loudly, out of sight. Standing side by side in the centre of the pigeon-girl set, Frankie and Eugene were perfectly placed to witness a long, slender arc of flame rise like a finger and top the firewall. The flame tip licked at the colonnaded bank façade Marietta had so recently drenched with flammable liquid. The actress's wish had come true. Along with the *Ambition* set, the pigeon-girl set was on fire.

Eugene leapt to his feet. Frankie gaped as the bottom of one of the columns caught with a liquid crackle. Flames sprouted across the set's façade like a magical golden vine. Eugene ran up to the burning façade, apparently forgetting that his jacket sleeve was wet with paraffin.

"That jacket's not safe." Frankie charged up beside him. "Take it off before it catches fire."

Eugene looked down at his jacket. "I'll keep it on."

And then, loud enough to be heard above the popping of the fire, the hissing of gas, and the faint bellows from the firefighters and engineers, Frankie heard a scream. It came from the far side of the firewall, and for a second she believed that the scream was part of the filming, acted out for the cameras on *Ambition's* burning set. But only for that brief moment.

She knew that scream. She had heard it brought out at intervals by grade-school tumbles in the schoolyard and, more often, by adolescent frustrations. She knew the author of the scream well enough to hear the genuine panic.

She said, "It's Connie. Connie's in the fire."

Eugene said, "Dear lord. Stay calm, Frankie. Samson's army of engineers can't be far off. I'll go find them."

Frankie didn't answer him. She didn't need an expert knowledge of fire to know that flames moved quickly once they'd taken hold. The opening in the firewall would take her to Connie. Head down, she tore toward it.

"Frankie, *wait.*"

"I can't."

"You must." He ran up behind her and took hold of her arm. "Listen. Take a moment to soak your jacket in Marietta's water drums. That way you can wrap the heavy cloth around your face if you run into smoke. Like this." He removed his suit jacket, and she tore her own jacket off and plunged it into the water drum with his. "I'm coming in with you," he added.

"Thank you, Eugene." Frankie hauled her jacket, dripping, out of the water. On second thought, she picked up one of the smaller buckets, swooshed it clean of paraffin, and filled it with water. She dumped it over Eugene's head and then her own, soaking their shirts and trousers. The stream blinded her for a moment as her hair, short as it was, plastered itself over her eyes. Frankie shoved it back with her father's second-best oath. She glanced down at herself. The water on her white men's shirt made the Xeno-Flex Combination show through, the lace trim around the neck marking it clearly and unmistakably as a woman's undergarment. But there was no time to worry about that. Anyway, Eugene already knew she was a woman.

She sped after him. He accelerated toward the gap in the firewall. Smoke poured through the opening in the wall now, so she held the wet sleeve of her coat to her face before passing through. Once inside, she peered around, looking for Eugene among the timbered, Egyptian-style wooden pieces standing almost obscured by smoke but as yet untouched by the fire.

She moved toward the sound of the fire, in the direction Connie's call had come from. Ahead of her she saw the reflection of flames on painted wood.

She put a hand to the firewall on her right. It was nearly hot enough to blister her palm. She stumbled over a pipe running across her path and knocked over a bucket of something she hoped to heaven was water. Connie was nowhere to be seen. Frankie called out Connie's name and then Eugene's, but heard no answer over the crack and sibilance of the fire. An urgent desire to run back the way she'd come overtook her. She hoped that the former Reverend Sheridan D Ray hadn't raised a coward.

She called out to Connie and soldiered on, moving deeper among the smoking panels and the reverse sides of building facades, glad of her tough men's brogues on the uneven terrain. How was it that men in paintings and poetry appeared so brave, striding into battle to protect country and hearth with their shoulders squared and jaws set? Perhaps their boldness was a disguise, like Frankie's brogues, haircut, and Xeno-Flex Combination. Maybe inside themselves, men felt like Frankie did now: scared to death.

She coughed to clear her throat and shouted Connie's name. On her right, the firewall split, and one side yawned toward her. She slipped through the V-shaped gap in the

Ambition set, ducking out of the way of falling sparks and bits of glowing wood. From atop a slender pillar, the dog-faced god Anubis stared down at her. A little farther off she made out the tail end of a sphinx, its curved hips lit by flames that consumed its face.

Running footsteps sounded behind her, and Frankie looked back through the gap in the firewall. A cry of wonder and relief escaped her, for on the other side Eugene was staggering by the opening. His arm supported Connie, and his bunched-up jacket half-covered Connie's face. Connie wore the white dress from Camillo's, now fringed in grubby grey. Eugene's shirt clung damply to his torso.

At the sight of that torso, revealed through wet shirting, Frankie was struck speechless. She gaped after Connie and Eugene, coughing into the wet sleeve of her jacket.

She struggled to grasp Eugene's secret.

Her delay proved an instant too long. Behind her, flames took hold of the pedestal at the base of the dog-faced statue. She heard the crack of breaking wood. She looked up at the falling shadow.

Darkness struck her and knocked her to the ground.

32

Frankie woke herself, coughing. Above her, the night sky was greyed with smoke. Around her, tattered, grimy bits of wall bore painted Egyptian symbols. From somewhere nearby she heard the crackle and scuttle of flames in the old wooden movie sets. The pillar that had held aloft the dog-faced god Anubis lay fallen across her legs. She could feel the pressure of it, but most of its weight rested on jumbled bits of set. She tried to push herself free but could not. She pushed at the pillar, but it wouldn't move. It was oily and slick, and she couldn't get purchase with her hands to move it or herself. She twisted one way and the other, and then both ways at once.

She slammed both palms hard against the pillar. The pain helped her focus on the geometrical problem she faced. She saw it as if it were drawn in chalk on a classroom blackboard. On the other side of the pillar, out of sight, her left leg was trapped and contorted by a smaller obstacle of some kind. If her geometry was correct, that obstacle lay across the farthest edge of the pillar that spanned and immobilized her legs and hips. Her left leg was the key. If she could get that one loose, the rest of her ought to follow. She wriggled and angled, an inch this way and an iota that.

She reminded herself that she was not alone on the burning set of *Ambition*. Firemen and engineers would be nearby, controlling the fire. Cameramen would be roaming about, seeking memorable shots. Somebody would surely find her.

As the flames approached, Frankie pulled her damp shirt across her nose and mouth and made three impossible wishes.

First, that she had never come to Hollywood.

Second, that for once in her life Connie would apologize for getting her into this situation.

Third, Frankie wished with all her heart that she had said a proper goodbye to her poor father, who would be devastated when he heard that she had perished in a movie-set fire. *Dad, they'll say I killed a movie star. They'll say I shot him. Don't believe a word of it. If only I could move, I'd get out of here and find out who really killed Gilbert Howard.*

She relived the shock she'd felt when she saw Eugene fleeing the fire with Connie. For it was then that Frankie had seen, through Eugene's soaked shirting, small but entirely female breasts.

Like Frankie, Eugene was a woman dressed as a man. Frankie was so mad at herself for not realizing the truth, and at Eugene for lying, that she regained a little more of her natural can-do spirit.

She struggled. She called. She rested.

And then she learned that when danger had you cornered and pinned down, you weren't alone after all. It was like when you were a little child and felt afraid. You'd call out in the darkness. One of your parents would come to you, sit down on the edge of your bed, and lay a hand on your shoulder. Your mother would say, *Close your eyes and go to sleep.* Your father would murmur, *That's my brave Frankie.* And the door would stand marginally open to brighten the night with a yellow slice of the adult world. What a surprise it was to find that, a thousand miles away, those gestures of comfort remained with her from so long ago, from even before memories began. Here in the middle of the smoke and danger, Frankie saw both her parents quite clearly, her mother on her left and her father on her right. She felt encouraged by their presence and tried again to wriggle herself free. And she prayed that they would stay — that they would not leave her alone with the fire.

Her struggles grew weaker.

She redoubled her attempts.

She rested again. The smoke was so thick that she was having trouble breathing, and she was well beyond speaking. But her mother urged her to hold on, and Sheridan D, with his great minister's voice, called for help.

33

Somewhere among the smoke and shadows of the burning *Ambition* set, a woman was laughing. The laughter sounded too harsh and cawing for Heaven, so Frankie guessed she was still alive. She had no idea how long she had been lying here, nor how late the night had grown.

One of her trapped legs was numb. Heat licked the left side of her face. She heard a rumbling, like a tumble of logs on the beach. A woman — the same woman who had been laughing? — swore. Without any more warning than that, Frankie's legs came free of the pillar that had trapped her. She rolled onto her side. Coughing, and weak with disbelief, she looked up into Marietta Valdes's inquisitive gaze.

The actress's face glowed in reflected light from the fire — the same fire that appeared to be eating the nearby sphinx whole. More dangerously still, the flames were chewing the end of the tumbled-down column of the dog-faced god.

Marietta, although dressed sturdily in a borrowed fireman's jacket and boots, couldn't have moved that pillar by herself. Even she, so capable and brilliant, must have had a man's help.

But whoever Frankie's other rescuer had been — firefighter? engineer? cameraman? — Marietta and Frankie were on their own now. Two women trapped in a fire! But she remembered that neither Marietta nor her other rescuer knew that Frankie was not really a man, and anyway the heaviest work was done.

Frankie was free. And now Marietta had an arm under Frankie's shoulder and was attempting to hoist her upright. Frankie coughed and lost her footing, pins and needles hot as fire in the leg that was asleep.

Marietta grunted, "Frank Achilles, old fellow, do you think you might try to help a little?"

Frankie did her best. The two of them stumbled over a dislodged chunk of rock on the uneven ground, and Marietta hauled them upright again, stumbling away from the fire, talking all the time. "A fire is wonderful theatre. Storytelling is transformation."

Frankie croaked, "It nearly transformed me, all right."

"Exactly. That's what fire does — causes a *metamorphosis* — and that's why it's so important to get the angles. As many as you can! And every angle of interception and direction has to be different. Every single angle must be so unrecognizable from the last that the audience senses itself riding helter-skelter into the unknown."

"Abso-tively."

They staggered alongside the smoky set wall, through a hole in a firewall, and burst out onto the pigeon-girl set. There, the fire Marietta had started with her buckets of paraffin oil had burned out.

"Well done, Frank Achilles." Marietta slapped her hands together. "Here we are. Safe as houses."

"Thank all the heavens for that—and thank you, Marietta." Frankie hefted her damp suit jacket. Her jacket pockets felt awfully light. Unweighted.

Somehow, she had lost the gun. She pictured the weapon lying amid the smoking rubble. In her imagination, it went up with a bang. But, in all the conflagration, what would one more explosion matter?

A small group of firemen emerged through the same opening in the wall. Black helmets shining, rubberized coats unbuttoned down the front, the men huddled together, lighting cigarettes and laughing in the darkness. Smoke drifted by, following the light wind.

To the right of the horse statue, three more firemen kicked at the last bits of the charred ruin of the colonnaded bank. On Frankie's left, Luigi the cameraman crouched at the foot of his wheeled camera, sorting through small, black tins of film. Straight ahead at the base of the statue sat two bedraggled figures. One was Connie, and the other was Eugene. Both were filthy. Connie's unladylike posture was at odds with the long white dress she'd worn to dinner. Now stained and torn, the formal gown appeared even more romantic than when it was new, in a *Wuthering Heights*, lost-on-the-moors sort of way. Eugene, jacket clutched tight, sat slumped at Connie's side on the plinth.

Frankie struggled to get her own damp jacket back around her before her female form became as obvious to everybody here as Eugene's had been to Frankie.

She said, "Thank you again, Marietta. It doesn't seem real now, but I almost died back there."

"All part of a good day's work." Marietta loped across the

gravel on her tough, bare, tomboy feet and slapped Luigi on the back.

"*Malatrice!*" Luigi growled.

Marietta said, "I told you, didn't I? By all that's holy, *I got the shot.*" She slashed her right arm in the air. "The flames traced a great arc over the sphinx's eye. As I predicted, the flame exactly bisected the pyramid's lit side and climbed up the obelisk like a golden monkey, to rest at the apex. I had to grab one of the studio cameras because you absconded—coward! So I filmed that perfect bit of footage myself."

Frankie stopped listening. She had more than film shots to think about. Now she knew for sure Connie was a treacherous friend, and she was fairly certain Eugene was a murderess.

Frankie approached the filthy pair.

She said coldly, "I see you got free, Connie. I'm happy, for your sake."

"I should hope so." Connie pulled her skirt straight. "But I must say I don't like your tone, Frankie."

"You almost got me and my tone killed," Frankie said. "However, I don't want to talk to you, Connie. I want to talk to your rescuer. Because I've been looking for her all day long."

"Who?" Connie asked.

"Me," Eugene answered. "She's been looking for me."

"Then she couldn't have been looking very hard." Connie glared at Frankie. "Any fool can find Eugene—the boy next door."

Several retorts occurred to Frankie, but she had no time for childish argument.

"I don't know your real name, *Eugene*," Frankie said. "But I do know that you've been lying to me from the start. You are not a man."

"How can you say that?" Connie protested. "Eugene bravely saved me from the fire. He was completely a man, and one to be admired and appreciated, so put that information in your stocking top."

Frankie gave Connie a withering glance. "You're not listening, Connie. *As* usual." She turned to Eugene. "You're not male—you are female. Dressed up, like me, to pass as a man."

"Eugene, you're a woman?" Connie demanded.

Eugene answered, "I'm tired, that's what I am."

Luigi rolled past with his camera and out of sight past the burned-out section of the set.

Frankie continued. "And that's not all, *Eugene*. You're *the* woman. You are the golden swimmer I saw with Gilbert Howard the night he died. The one he was kissing by the side of the pool."

Eugene buried her face in her hands.

Frankie asked, "How *could* you fall in love with a ladykiller like Gilbert Howard?"

"I'm not the first woman to cry over a man who betrayed her," Eugene said. "I'm not the first woman to mourn her own true love."

Connie stared. "Howie loved *you?* Of all the women in the world, he loved *you?*"

"Isn't it a funny old world?" Eugene said.

Frankie wondered how Eugene could joke at such a moment. "Gilbert Howard loved you, and you killed him."

In the pause that followed, Marietta's laugh rang out. Marietta ran lightly over the gravel toward them and threw herself down next to Eugene on the statue's base, bare feet splayed out in front of her. She said, "Frank, don't be an idiot. Eugene didn't kill Howie. She—Eugene—was with me last night."

"Will you swear to that, to the police?"

"Of course." Marietta squeezed Eugene's arm. "I'll swear in church if you need me to, Frank Achilles."

"In a court of law would do." Would a court of law believe Marietta? Probably.

But did Frankie believe her? She was not ready to say, either way. Frankie had a number of questions to ask Eugene, and no intention of accepting Marietta's unsupported word.

But before she could begin, Marietta did. "Well, Eugene, my old friend! Wipe your tears and celebrate the fact that we're all alive and I got the best shot in Samson's whole fire. And you, the red-headed hopeful," Marietta said to Connie. "What a night you're having! I'm only sorry Howie isn't here to see it."

Trust Marietta to send any conversation wheeling off Frankie's track and onto her own. An ethics question flashed through Frankie's mind: *How do you tell somebody who just saved your life to be silent, or preferably to go to Hades?*

She set the subject back on its course. "Eugene, can you prove you were with Marietta last night?"

Eugene stared down at the gravel between the knees of her men's trousers.

"Eugene was with me," Marietta insisted. "Will you get off that hobby horse, Frank Achilles? Yesterday you told my sister Billie that Leo Samson was guilty of killing Gilbert. Leo! A fellow who wouldn't slap a mosquito, let alone shoot a man. If you weren't so set on believing in women directors, I'd begin to doubt your judgment."

Since Marietta was doing all the talking, Frankie decided that the actress ought to at least do some of the answering as well. "Marietta, *can* you and Eugene prove you were together last night when Gilbert Howard was killed?"

"You're handsomer when you don't speak, Frank," Marietta said peevishly. Then, to Connie, she said "Well, you redhead, you're a pain in the whatsits, but you've got guts. How did you end up in the fire?"

Frankie glowered at this new change of subject. But honestly, she wanted to know the answer as well.

Connie leaned against one of the horse statue's legs and let out a long, tired-sounding sigh. "Ambition. Like the title of Samson's movie. Samson said he was going to use me in some of the shots in the fire, but he left a message with the doorman at Camillo's to say he'd cancelled my shot. The note didn't even explain *why* he'd cancelled. After all the build-up and publicity yesterday! Now I wonder whether he was ever really going to use me."

"Bless you for your innocent mind." Marietta smiled. "Sammy's not the first producer to try that nasty little trick with one of his actresses. I tried to explain it to you before, when we were having our lovely evening out at Camillo's Fine Bar and Grille. Sammy was throwing his weight around, using you, the phony starlet, to bring me into line and stop trying to direct films. He tried to frighten me with you — the beautiful new face."

Frankie was determined to move the subject of murder back onto its course. But she couldn't resist saying to Connie, "I told you so. Like at the audition in Vancouver — King Samson was using you then, too."

"It makes me so mad I could kick that grumpy so-and-so producer." Connie peered from one side of the set to the other as if reliving a moment of decision. "But I thought that maybe I could sneak myself onto the film. If I made an entrance out of the flames and got myself into the shot anyway, a film editor might take the film and use it in *The Emperor of New*

York. And then they'd have to use me in the film. Now the whole idea seems stupid."

"Speaking of film, I'd better see where Luigi is storing my reels." Marietta strode back towards the gap in the wall. Over her shoulder she called back, "And yes, redhead, yours was a stupid idea."

Connie isn't stupid. She's a complicated thinker. But Frankie didn't say it. She would not come to Connie's defence. Never again.

With a rustle of taffeta, Connie stood up. She walked around Eugene and squashed down next to Frankie. Frankie pulled back, and Connie frowned. "You're acting horrible, Frankie."

Frankie gazed at Connie's stricken, dirty face and felt nothing of the old friendship. "Leave me alone, Connie. Why don't you go home to Vancouver?"

That ought to do it. Yes, even in the flickering light, Frankie knew the colour was rising in her old friend's cheeks. Those eyebrows of hers rose at a dangerous angle, one that Frankie knew too well.

Connie said, "I'm never going back to Vancouver. And I might never speak to you again. So, Frankie, this is your last chance. *What do you want in a friend?*"

Frankie knew what Connie expected of her: to make light of the situation. To say in radio announcer tones, *Friends are good to the la-a-ast drop.* Or, *If you want to get ahead, get a friend with a hat.* Or, *A friend gets you twice as much for a nickel.* Frankie had played her part since she and Connie were children. But Frankie had never felt less like a child than she did at that moment.

Frankie said, "What do I want in a friend? I would like somebody who is grown-up enough to apologize for all the bad things she has done to me in the course of the time we have known each other."

"Is that right? Well, tough luck." Connie rubbed at her face with blackened fists. The blotches stood out strongly against her pale face. Then she stood and walked away through the gap that would take her out of the Monument lot and into the outside world.

The last Frankie saw of Connie was her torn and dirty white dress vanishing around the corner that led out to Sunset Boulevard. She looked down at her men's brogues and traced half circles in the gravel, first left and then right. She tried to feel sorry to see Connie go. She tried to remember what it felt like to be her best friend, without question or reservation. She could not.

"My, my," Eugene said. "Not so clever and kind anymore, Frankie?"

Frankie said, "You knew about my disguise. So why didn't you tell me about *yours*?"

"I'm not an actress like you are, Frankie."

"You're a pretty darned good one," Frankie said bitterly. "What should I call you now that I know you're not 'Eugene'?"

Eugene frowned. "What does it matter? Everybody calls me Eugene now."

"What is your real name?" Frankie asked again, more fiercely.

"Elaine. But call me Eugene. I prefer it. Gilbert named me that way."

"Why would he call you by a man's name?"

"He thought women who acted like men were fun."

"I'm not surprised."

"And I travelled here from Eugene, Oregon. So that's what Gilbert called me."

"Like you call a fellow from Texas 'Tex'?" Frankie nodded. "All right, Eugene. Answer my question. How long have you been masquerading as male?" But Eugene had already told her the answer to her question when he'd talked about Bruno's career as a child actor. *There are problems with pretending to be somebody else for any length of time. Day after day, it eats the soul.*

"The Queen first dressed me as a man a year ago, so I could come and go unnoticed from Gilbert's place in the Garden of Allah."

"She dressed you, too?" Frankie shook her head.

"So that people wouldn't know about Gilbert and me. Wouldn't know that we were together forever, even though he couldn't marry me." Eugene blinked. "*Wouldn't* marry me. Dressed like this, I kept my privacy from the newspapers and he kept his reputation as a ladies' man."

Frankie added, "And his freedom to be a ladies' man."

Don't fall in love in Paradise Gardens. That warning was inspiration enough to any girl to fall, and fall hard, for the first fellow she saw.

A long pause hung like a cloud of smoke in the night air. Even the Queen had deceived Frankie by not telling her straight out that Eugene was a woman. Eugene was right. Frankie didn't have a friend left in the world.

But Eugene did. She had Marietta. And, if she had Marietta for an ally, she also had the actress's sister, Billie Starr. The connection between these friends was obvious now — and should have been, since the first moment Frankie had found Marietta crying outside Eugene's villa. Marietta had provided Eugene with an alibi for Gilbert Howard's murder. How could Frankie believe it? Or disprove it?

On the far side of the set, the firemen were moving away. Marietta rose and saluted them as they left. She didn't look like a woman who had acted rashly, with no concern for anybody's peril. She looked like a woman in charge. She looked like she owned the place.

Eugene asked, "What are you scowling at, Frankie?"

"Be quiet while I think."

Frankie tried to imagine helping the police put Eugene behind bars. Impossible. Still, there were many things she'd never imagined doing that she'd done in the last couple of days. She'd climbed a roof, gone on the lam, survived a fire, and now she had accused Eugene, a person she liked more than most, of murder.

Where there was murder, there must be justice. It was the way of things, and without justice there was only chaos, like the Wild West and the French Revolution.

Frankie said to Eugene, "Marietta is lying to protect you."

Eugene dropped her head into her hands and began to cry.

Marietta cursed. "I know what you're after, Frank damnable Achilles. Leave Eugene alone. *I* did it. I killed Gilbert Howard."

34

In the silence that followed Marietta's confession, Frankie noticed that moonlight turned the actress's dress and lips grey, so that she appeared more than ever her screen self in the black-and-white world of the movies. And despite her skilled delivery of the line "I did it," Frankie was certain Marietta was acting.

Lying. Marietta had no motive to kill Gilbert Howard.

Was Marietta capable of murder? *Abso-tively.* Marietta was capable of anything in the pursuit of her career. Frankie had never met anybody so ambitious in her life. But capability was not enough.

Frankie said, "Marietta, it will be as obvious to the police as it is to me that you had no motive to kill Gilbert Howard. He was your only ally in your struggle to direct *The Emperor of New York.*"

Eugene scowled. "Yes. For once, try to control your need to be the centre of attention, Marietta."

"It's my *job*," Marietta said bitterly.

Frankie made a strangled noise in her throat that turned into a smoky cough. And she coughed again. She'd coughed so much since Marietta had dragged her out of the fire that by now her throat felt as rough as the gravel under her feet.

"Eugene knows every word I say is true," Marietta insisted. "I killed Gilbert Howard."

Eugene shook her head. "I killed him."

Frankie snapped a look from Eugene to Marietta. Then she raised her gaze to the heavens and wished she'd never met either of them. Of the three people sitting here, exhausted in the aftermath of the studio fire, one was lying about being the murderer. The second was lying about *not* being the murderer. And the third person — Frankie herself — was being sought by the police for the murder. For Pete's sake.

She said, "You're knitting a story out of pure deception, aren't you? Like screenwriters write movies. This story is a fake."

Eugene said, "Everything in Hollywood is phony."

"Hollywood," Marietta said, "is a law unto itself. It is also the axis of the spinning world."

"I'm sick of all the lies," Frankie said.

"Look who's talking," Marietta retorted. "You've told at least three since I dragged you out of the fire. And you call yourself a gentleman."

Frankie looked down at herself in her man's clothing. "I'm really not so much of a gentleman as I appear to be."

"That's all right," Marietta said. "I'm really not much of a lady."

Frankie nodded. "This particular lie ends right here. Marietta, I'm not Frank Achilles. I'm Frankie Ray, dressed up as a man, like Eugene here, in order to clear my name of Gilbert Howard's murder."

With vigour, and with a maximum of modesty in the circumstances, she wriggled the Xeno-Flex Combination down from around her middle, over her hips outside her trousers, and down to the ground. And what a relief that was. She took deep breaths of the smoky air while her rib cage expanded like a bellows. She desired nothing more than to stomp the Xeno-Flex into shreds. However, she reminded herself that the garment belonged to the Queen, now recovering in hospital after her attack, and she ought to return it undamaged.

"Frankie Ray?" Marietta stared. Then she laughed. "You really are the biggest liar here, then. Maybe you did kill Gilbert Howard after all."

Eugene let out a quiet groan. "Shut up, Marietta. I've put Frankie here in mortal danger, and we owe her at least the good manners not to joke about it."

Frankie said, "You owe me more than that. You owe me the truth. Tell me what happened that night. Eugene, exactly where were you when Gilbert Howard was shot?"

Eugene looked up at Frankie. "I was with you, Frankie. I was dancing the carioca with you. Don't you remember?"

Frankie did. She recalled everything about that first night at Paradise Gardens: the music turning on the Queen's gramophone, the velvet warmth of the air, the young women and men winding a conga line under the stars, and the cracking noise that had sounded like a gunshot. It really was a gunshot. She had danced with Eugene while Gilbert Howard was dying.

She said, "One of you, tell me what happened to Gilbert Howard."

Eugene looked at Marietta. Marietta looked at Frankie.

"I will tell you." Marietta got to her feet and stood in front of Frankie and Eugene. She said, "Picture the scene."

"I can't. I wasn't there. I was *dancing,*" Frankie said bitterly.

"Pretend it was a movie." Marietta smiled. "You watch movies all the time, Frankie. And I know how to make them, so I'll make this one for you."

"Please tell me, straight out, what happened."

Frankie might as well have begged night to turn to day. Marietta would do things her own way. She always had, and Frankie bet she always would.

Marietta began, "Here's the set-up for the action. It's a story of three girls from Eugene, Oregon, who came to Hollywood and met a famous movie star. Gilbert Howard helped one of them to a career in the movies—"

"That was Marietta," Eugene said.

"He sent one of them to hide in a brothel until a movie deal might be made for her—"

"That was Billie."

"And he fell in love with the third."

"That was me." Eugene swallowed hard. "I couldn't find Billie when she ran away to the brothel."

"Why a brothel?" Then Frankie answered her own question. "I see. It's the perfect place to make Leo, who loves her, feel as badly as possible for not making his parents help her in the movies. Why didn't Gilbert Howard help her instead of hiding her?"

"Howie was always unpredictable," Marietta said. "And he liked his little joke on King Samson, hiding his son Leo's true love in a brothel."

Eugene nodded. "I followed Billie's trail as far as the Garden of Allah. There I fell headlong in love with Gilbert Howard. And then I lived as a man so that I could visit Gilbert often without harming his Don Juan image."

"If only love had changed Howie that much," Marietta said.

"It did. He was happy with me."

"Was he? There were lots of other girls."

"Yes. He couldn't be happy if he had to leave other girls alone."

Marietta's expression softened. "He was crazy about you, Eugene, no matter how many girls he was with. Listen, Frankie, and I'll show you the scene. I'll be the camera."

Marietta tipped back her head as a light breeze picked up the smoke clouds and wafted them away over the studio walls. Frankie knew perfectly well how much Marietta was enjoying having an audience. She leaned toward Frankie and Eugene, eyes flashing.

"This story goes to the root of storytelling, back thousands of years, when *what's at stake* was formed out of an ancient idea of Hell ..." Marietta was wearing her director's face again, with its wild objectivity that made Frankie try like the furies to understand every word. "Even today, our lead actors must escape from Dante's condition: *alone in a dark forest.* I will tell you what happened that night."

At last. Frankie leaned forward as Marietta began to describe the events leading to the death of Gilbert Howard. When Marietta spoke, Frankie saw the scene as if from the front row of a cinema, a bag of sour lemon drops in her hand, and her eyes glued to the silver screen.

Fade in.

The scene: Gilbert Howard's well-furnished living room in the Garden of Allah. Outside the window, the night is dark but for the brilliantly lit swimming pool.

Our star performers, Marietta Valdes and Gilbert Howard, appear in the window. To the cinema audience, at first the scene between the two actors looks like love: the first clutch of romance.

In this way the camera proposes the cinematic question: Will the desirable Marietta Valdes give way to Gilbert Howard—a true Don Juan!—when she has always been so careful to keep him at arm's length?

But he, who has offered to help her become a film director against all the odds, now threatens to withdraw his support. Will Marietta submit to this man of perfect beauty and complete determination in order to further her career?

She will.

She will not.

Marietta resists; Gilbert Howard persists. He threatens her, mockingly, with the gun he found by the bushes at the edge of the property.

She doesn't laugh. She pushes past him toward the door.

He shoulders her away from the door and takes her in his arms. He believes he knows better than she what a woman really wants. And he is expert at pushing his luck.

She pushes back. They struggle, and she catches hold of the gun between them. His expression changes from amusement to anger.

We hear the first sound from the screen: a shot rings out.

Now the viewpoint character is revealed: the slim blonde woman attired in men's clothing. Eugene emerges from the shadows to see her lover dead on the floor. Her friend Marietta stands over him.

Fade to black.

Marietta sighed dramatically. "I was only going to use the gun to force Howie to let me go. In a way, he shot himself, although my finger was on the trigger."

Frankie said, "That's a pretty tidy way to describe a murder."

"Good point." Eugene rose to her feet. "And you got the timing terribly wrong in that scene, Marietta."

Frankie remembered that first night in Paradise Gardens, dancing the carioca with Eugene Ellery. She remembered the gunshot that sounded like backfire.

Eugene must have been remembering that moment, too. "I wasn't standing at the window when you shot Gilbert. I was dancing with Frankie. You ran over to my villa after Paradise Gardens had settled down for the night. You woke me up to tell me he was dead."

"What matters is the truth of the story, not the facts," Marietta said. "A director's reputation relies on logic in narrative, not accuracy."

"Shut up if you can't tell the truth, Marietta," Eugene said.

"All right, but only because I'm thinking," Marietta replied.

Eugene turned to Frankie. "These last few days, I decided I would never leave Hollywood, because I feel close to Gilbert here. But it's clear that I can't stay."

"Don't you dare talk like a martyr, Eugene," Marietta warned.

"I'm not a martyr. I'm a realist. It was my fault that you killed Gilbert, Marietta. If I'd been with him, he wouldn't have tried to seduce her, Frankie. Marietta would never have shot him except in self-defence. I loved Gilbert—"

"Gilbert Howard. A man who simply took what and whom he wanted," Marietta interjected.

"Yes. I accepted his weaknesses when I accepted his love. I should have protected Marietta from him."

"You should have protected every girl he seduced and then abandoned," Marietta said.

Eugene nodded. "Maybe. But instead I let him have his wandering way."

"You're still taking the blame for his behaviour," Marietta pointed out. "You should have grown up a little by now. In fact, for a satisfying narrative composition, you should have transformed *before* the showdown."

"Maybe this conversation is the showdown." Eugene scowled. "Anyway, I am stronger now. Gilbert's dead, and I have nothing to lose. That's why I'm going to take the blame for you, Marietta. I should have done it from the start."

"I've told you a hundred times to keep out of the whole—" Marietta began.

"But I'll have to leave Hollywood." Eugene looked ready to cry once more. "I had planned to visit Gilbert's grave every day. But Eugene Ellery will have to disappear. Eugene will take the blame for you, Marietta, and Eugene will clear Frankie's name as well."

Marietta shook her head. "You're a fool, Eugene. Even when you were Elaine, you were a very silly girl."

"Sure. How else did you and Billie talk me into coming to Hollywood when I didn't care a cent about the movies?" Eugene rose from her spot on the plinth. "I'm going to miss you, Marietta. And I'm truly sorry about getting you involved, Frankie. But this will pay for all."

Her pale, cropped hair shone white as snow against the shadowed walls and dark skies as she paced along the path leading through the sound stages to Sunset Boulevard.

Frankie rushed after Eugene and caught her by the shoulder. "Why, Eugene? *Why* did you dig up Gilbert Howard's body from your backyard and bring it into my house? *Why* did you have to leave him with me?"

Eugene paused. She pulled herself free. "Respect," she said. "Marietta wanted to bury Gilbert quietly so that everybody would think he'd simply disappeared because he was so unreliable. I thought it would be enough to keep him near me, under the grass behind my house. But Gilbert was a movie star. I couldn't leave him there. I loved him too much."

Frankie began to see. "And he loved fame with all his performer's heart."

"Gilbert would have hated to disappear without giving the world a chance to mourn him. When you and I were in the backyard, looking at his body lying namelessly in the dirt, you spoke to him with such respect, even though you didn't know who he was. You believed he was a poor old uncle." Eugene's eyes shone with tears. "I knew you were the right one to find Gilbert's body properly — to call the police and the newspapers and see that he was honoured. I'm sorry that it all went wrong, Frankie. I'll put it right now, as best I can."

Eugene turned again to leave. Frankie took two steps after the slender, retreating figure. Then she stopped. She had nothing more to say to her. So she watched Eugene — Elaine — Ellery walk away with a step so light it seemed as if her bones were hollow, like a bird's.

Frankie turned back to Marietta. "She shouldn't be alone."

"There's a lot that *shouldn't be* in this great big story of life. For example, I don't like the end to this particular scene, do you?"

Frankie followed Marietta's downward gaze. There on the plinth, ready to the actress's hand, lay King Samson's gun. The gun Frankie had dropped on the set of *Ambition*. The gun she'd believed to be lost in the fire.

It shone silver in the moonlight and contained, Frankie well knew, one remaining bullet.

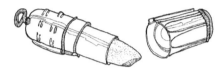

35

Almost home. Eugene leaned against Frankie's car and gazed up at the sign that read Paradise Gardens. *She felt exhausted after the night's exertions, transformations, and unhappy revelations. A reflective moment on her own was all she wanted in the world.*

No. She was putting off the moment when she would have to shed her pretence at being Eugene Ellery. In a way, it would be like losing a friend.

On the floor of Frankie's Model A, Eugene spotted a small dark shape. She leaned inside and picked up a woman's squashy tam, discarded and bereft. It would be just the thing to cover her head when she stopped being a man and became a young woman with very short, bobbed hair. She twirled the hat on the end of her finger, wondering what else she would lose when she parted with Eugene. But having lost Gilbert, nothing else mattered.

Without further delay, she passed through the gate into Paradise Gardens. It occurred to her that the murderous criminal mastermind

John Dillinger carried a ten-thousand-dollar reward—alive. A reasonable reward for Eugene, supposed killer of one movie star, ought to be around five thousand. But with such an international case, she bet that Gilbert Howard's accused killer would soon rank no lower than third on the Most Wanted list.

It was a pretty funny outcome for a girl who never wanted fame. She ambled along the path between the bungalows at Paradise Gardens, enjoying the swing of a man's walk for the last time. At home, Eugene slipped out of her suit and hung it on its wooden hanger in the closet—the closet where Eugene had created a hiding place for her women's clothing. The same closet where Frankie had hidden after first being accused of killing Gilbert. Eugene smoothed the collar of the grey suit as it hung empty, the way the Queen had smoothed it the first day she'd helped Elaine become Eugene.

"Confuse the senses," the Queen had said, handing Eugene a tube of Burma-Shave. And the Xeno-Flex Combination! After the first few days she'd given that torturously constricting garment back to the Queen and worn her jacket buttoned. She knew the Queen had passed the Xeno-Flex on to poor old Frankie.

How Marietta and the Queen had laughed the first day Elaine went to look for Billie Starr and fooled the ladies at the brothel, even though Billie had refused to answer her door. How Eugene had cried the second day, once she'd met Gilbert Howard and fallen in love for the first time in her life. Against all the odds, he'd admired her above all the others. Little Elaine O'Leary! It seemed impossible until she saw what pleasure he took in searching out the woman underneath the man's disguise. Gilbert loved that he was the only man who knew what Eugene really was.

For love of Gilbert Howard, Elaine had pretended to be Eugene Ellery, here in Villa 7A. Now, for love of Gilbert, she would leave this place forever. Faithful from first to last. Loyal to her true love and loyal to her lifelong friend, Marietta, who had shot Gilbert dead. Eugene knew such blind allegiances were her weakness, but they also served as a shield against grief.

She clicked the boards out from the back of the cupboard and peered into the dark space behind. She hadn't envied Frankie her night hiding inside it, but it had kept the girl safe.

She reached into the dark interior of the cupboard and gathered the armful of women's clothes she'd folded and hidden away the previous year, when she began dressing as a man. She ought to air them and iron them, but she didn't have that much time. She'd just iron her travelling dress.

Funny to think that since she'd become a man, she'd grown much better at ironing. It was those darned collars. Gilbert had taught her to iron her shirt collars first. So she ironed like a man, the way her lover had taught her. Eugene Ellery was faithful to the last in matters great and small.

Even on that horrible night when Marietta shook her awake to confess that she'd shot Gilbert and needed her help, Eugene hadn't lost her centre. She'd stayed calm while helping wrap her lover in his bed sheets and, with Marietta, dragging him behind Villa 7A and burying him in secret. Then she stood sentinel at his grave all night long, leaning on her shovel for support. But when dawn struck, she'd recognized her error in burying him without any marker, any mourners, any news reports of his tragic death. How he would have hated that particular anonymity. Gilbert Howard loved drama.

So she dug him up. Inch by exhausting inch, she'd dragged him in the sheet all by herself across the yard to Villa 7B. The steps at the back were the worst, but when she'd finally wrestled him onto the sofa and cleaned him up, he looked so well that she knew it had all been worthwhile. A pity about all the trouble it caused Frankie. Setting it up so that the true-hearted young

Canadian, Frankie, would find Gilbert and see that his passing was properly honoured had been an error, certainly. But there it was: Elaine — Eugene — had lost her own true love, and she wasn't thinking straight. Still, she'd done one thing right. Gilbert had been discovered the way he'd want to be, sitting up and ready to dominate the news reports.

She wiped a tear away and decided to leave Eugene Ellery's grey suit where it was for the police to find.

I must do three things quickly, *she told herself.* I must not become distracted.

First, I must write out a confession, telling how 'I' shot Gilbert Howard.

Next, I will sign it *Eugene Ellery, Howard's most loyal fan.*

And finally, Eugene Ellery will disappear forever.

Eugene looked into the mirror and said her true name aloud: "Elaine O'Leary." *Tonight her name sounded like a lie, but she would grow accustomed to it.*

Elaine.

Elaine O'Leary donned her travelling dress. She pulled on the squashy tam she'd taken from Frankie's car. She reckoned she'd have three weeks of hiding her hair under the tam before it grew back to a suitable feminine length. Her throat hurt, and she saw her reflection crumple and waver as tears rose in her eyes.

She mustn't cry. A weeping woman attracted help, and she must pass unnoticed. She was a woman wearing a hat, no different from a thousand others.

Soon, Eugene Ellery's face would be on the wall of every post office across the United States. Everywhere, four sharp tacks would puncture her picture, while across the bottom it would read:

Eugene Ellery. Wanted for the Murder of Gilbert Howard.

Their names would be joined forever. That would go a long way toward making this past year worthwhile.

The Extra

In the pocket of her travelling dress she found a coral lipstick. She uncapped it, applied the lipstick to her mouth, and blotted it with the back of her hand, the way women did. It was all coming back to her now.

36

Streaks of soot edged the movie-set walls. The last of the firemen had left the square. Frankie and Marietta sat alone together in the shadows. If the plinth underneath them had been real marble, it would have been too cold to bear. But as it was plywood painted to look like marble, the seat was tolerably comfortable.

Marietta moved the gun further to her right, out of Frankie's reach.

Frankie said, "So you really did kill Gilbert Howard."

"At last you believe me. It's about ruddy time."

"I believe that you killed him. But I don't believe you killed him in order to protect yourself from his unwanted advances."

"And you accuse *me* of not listening? You must remember what Eugene said. And what I told you."

"I was listening, like a good little moviegoer." Frankie shook her head. "And you directed the scene very well. But that wasn't a newsreel you showed me, Marietta—it was a movie story you made up."

Marietta rose from the statue plinth the way a queen would rise from her throne. She gazed down her nose at Frankie.

Frankie stood up and placed her hands on her hips. "You always knew what Gilbert Howard was—a womanizer. A seducer. And maybe worse than that. But he was your only important supporter in your struggle to become a director. You forgave Gilbert Howard for betraying your friend Eugene over and over again with other women, and you accepted him sending your sister Billie to a brothel—"

"Billie didn't sell herself!"

"Exactly so. Therefore, you lied to Eugene about why you shot Gilbert Howard."

"I'm a very good liar." Marietta inclined her head. "And let's be honest here: you're almost as good a liar as I am, Frankie. Passing yourself off as Frank Achilles."

"At least I have a good reason."

"I have a better reason."

"For killing a man?"

"Of course. You said it yourself—I'd make a great director." Marietta scowled.

"Yes. I believe you could do it."

"Not only me. Understand that I don't want to be the only woman director. I want to be the first of many women to direct a major motion picture. You're ambitious. You understand. I thought that Howie understood, too. But I was wrong."

Frankie stared. "Are you saying that Gilbert Howard turned against you? He'd stopped supporting your cause with King Samson?"

"I confronted Howie. I said he was a turncoat. A traitor. He told me I was gorgeous when I was being ridiculous. I couldn't direct a movie. All I could do was be beautiful, and that should be enough for me. It was certainly enough for him. *Excuse my little white lie*, Gilbert said." Marietta blinked her lovely eyes. "He laughed."

Frankie understood more than Marietta had perhaps intended to reveal. King Samson had called Marietta a virtuous woman. He had meant *difficult to seduce*. In other words, a pleasing challenge to a womanizer like Gilbert Howard.

Frankie said, "When you turned your nose up at Gilbert Howard's advances, he laughed at you. He'd only backed you to direct *The Emperor of New York* in order to make you grateful?"

"So that I would come to him."

"Make love with him."

"Yes. Gilbert Howard viewed me not as a talented director but as a challenge. As a notch on his romantic bedpost."

For a moment Frankie feared that Marietta would break out crying. She would do it beautifully, too, the tears streaming down her ivory cheek, shining in the night.

But Marietta didn't weep. She said, "When I first arrived, Howie showed me the gun he'd found in the bushes between the Garden of Allah and Paradise Gardens. He set it down on his sofa table between us. When he laughed at me, I picked up the gun. I meant to kill myself." She looked ironically at Frankie. "I know you don't believe me, but it's true. But then as I was steeling myself to do it I thought, the world has so many Don Juans, doesn't it?"

"And so few talented female directors." Frankie shook her head. The fact was, Marietta's reasoning was correct. Not moral—not even human—but correct.

But that didn't change a thing. The woman was a cold-blooded murderess. Justice had to be brought to the case.

Frankie had to go—leave the set, leave Monument Studios—now, before Marietta figured out what a threat Frankie was to her and her ambitions. Because Marietta could hardly direct a film from prison.

Frankie looked at the gun lying at the foot of the statue, pointing her way. Maybe she ought to make a grab for it. Now, while Marietta appeared to be lost in thought.

Marietta picked up the gun. "I wish you really were Frank Achilles. I could have used you on my side."

Frankie gazed at the gun. She wished she were Frank Achilles, too, because a man might have a chance of wresting the gun from Marietta. A man would probably have taken the chance the first moment he saw it.

Frankie said, "I still believe you'd be a wonderful director."

"Thank you. And what about you? You're an extra again."

"I was the pigeon girl," Frankie said. "You helped me get that role, remember?"

"I probably do remember," Marietta said, "but I can't think about that now."

She shifted the gun from one hand to the other.

"You can't shoot me. Not after saving me from the fire," Frankie said. "Not after making my dreams come true by helping me get a chance at my first speaking role as the sad manicurist."

"I have a mathematical question," Marietta said.

"I teach mathematics," Frankie told her. "Not past sixth grade, though."

"Answer me this, then. How many people would I have to save to make up for killing just one?"

"I don't know," Frankie said honestly.

Marietta wrapped both hands around the gun's grip. "I would have saved you a lot of trouble, wouldn't I? If I'd done what I'd intended and killed myself instead of Howie. If I'd remained true to what I know: that life, like filmmaking, is narrative, and storytelling requires your characters to struggle against the odds."

"You still can," Frankie said. "And I think you ought to."

"You would! Because you've struggled against the odds, Frankie. I wish I had followed my first instinct and shot myself instead of him."

Frankie's mouth felt dry, and she found it difficult to speak. "Gilbert Howard had no right to force himself on you, no matter what else your ambitions were telling you. You can explain about that when you turn yourself in to the police. I can find other girls to back up your story."

"I will never turn myself in. And I won't allow you to turn me in, either."

Marietta took a deep breath.

Frankie stayed absolutely still. Her thoughts were racing, and the loudest one was, *What a waste, if she shoots herself!* A waste of youth, life, and talent.

Frankie remembered Gilbert Howard's laugh, and the way he swung out his arms as if to embrace the whole world, whether it wanted to be embraced or not. All his talent and charm weren't enough to save him.

And maybe Marietta's talent and charm would prove equally useless.

No more reflection. It was time to take action. Frankie threw her full weight at Marietta. They fell onto the gravel together. She and Marietta struggled for control of the gun, while its muzzle slewed wildly back and forth across the set, now pointing at the smoky wall, now at the sound stage, now straight up at the statue of the horse and rider. Frankie hauled harder against Marietta's grip. At the same time,

Marietta seemed to grow stronger. Frankie remembered that this Oregon beauty had grown up playing with the boys. Between tomboy Marietta and Frankie the substitute schoolteacher, who would win out?

"Stop!" Frankie shouted into Marietta's ear, and the actress's grip faltered. Marietta pulled the gun free, and Frankie let it go. She scrambled backward, crab-like. "Wait a minute."

Marietta, gun in hand, pulled herself up to sit with her back against the statue's plinth. She pointed the gun at Frankie.

Frankie said, "Marietta, you killed him. You're going to have to …" What was her father's word? "You're going to have to make up for killing him."

"Atone?"

"That's the word."

Marietta looked into the gun barrel "What better atonement?"

"Shooting yourself is not atonement. It's the easy way out."

"I don't know the easy way to do anything." The gun wavered. "All I know is that I committed murder."

Frankie stepped closer. "What about Gilbert Howard's crimes? Years of them?"

"True. But is the world a better place now that Gilbert Howard is out of it?"

"No," Frankie admitted, but added, "Maybe it's better for all the women he would have bullied and seduced."

"He was a talented man, and that talent has certainly improved the world."

"The world of the movies, anyway." Was that enough? Frankie let out a strangled cry. How was a person supposed to judge anybody? Judicial robes, clerical robes, or no robes at all, the thing was impossible. With a suddenness that was almost frightening, Frankie lost her taste for justice.

She said, "You're going to have to give me King Samson's gun, Marietta."

Tentatively Frankie reached out a hand. When Marietta didn't step back, Frankie took hold of the muzzle and tugged at the gun in Marietta's grasp. She half expected it to go off, but this time Marietta let it go without a struggle. Pointing the gun carefully down at the gravel a few feet away, Frankie fiddled with the mechanism that opened the chamber in order to empty it of its one remaining bullet.

"I hate this gun." Frankie stopped fiddling with the chamber and got rid of that last bullet the natural way, by firing it into the rubble of the collapsed set.

Marietta jumped. "For heaven's sake, Frankie!"

"I really do despise this gun of King Samson's. But it's got one more job to do — for you, for me, and for Gilbert Howard." In her imagination, her father's voice added sternly, *To make amends for its misdeeds.*

Marietta frowned as Frankie tucked the empty gun into her pocket. "What are you going to do? I won't go to jail, Frankie. I won't."

"Be quiet, Marietta. Let me think what to do and how to do it. Because this gun of King Samson's has got to atone."

37

Frankie stood alone in the backyard of Villa 7B. She had hoped to have an orange for her breakfast, but the tree was bare of fruit. After the two most gruelling and dangerous days she had ever spent, she couldn't believe how disappointed she was that somebody had harvested every single orange. Furthermore, a mouse had found the half-empty bag of bread that Frankie had left under the orange tree the evening before, when she'd slaked her hunger before following Marietta into the fire. She brushed the morning dew off the bag and put a finger into the little hole in its side. How Connie's mother would shriek if she saw that a mouse had nibbled at it. And Champ's mother would about drop dead.

No, there was not an orange to be found in her own backyard, but at least the place was blessedly empty of police.

Frankie scrubbed away a yawn and wiggled her bare toes

in the spiky grass. One could buy an orange, or bread not nibbled by mice, *if* one had money, which she did not.

In fact, the problem of money for gasoline for Frankie's drive home to Vancouver was being addressed, although not by Frankie herself. Right now, Tom was somewhere nearby, a cup of cooling coffee in his hand, strolling from bungalow to bungalow. He was gathering coins for Frankie's trip home. Nobody at Paradise Gardens had much to give, Tom said, but everybody had something.

Tom and the kids were real troopers. She wished she didn't have to leave them.

She carried the bread insdie, past the rubbish bin on the back porch. There, peeking out of the top of the bin were Frank Achilles's suit and shirt, neatly rolled around the battered Xeno-Flex Combination. She had decided not to return any of it to the Queen. Hollywood was complicated enough without any more of the Queen's transformations.

Frankie had made one exception to the purge of manly wear. The sunglasses Billie had stolen, which had so neatly distinguished Frank Achilles from Frankie Ray, lay nestled in Frankie's skirt pocket. She was keeping them because she liked the way she looked in them. And because she wanted to remember that not everything about Hollywood was tainted by ambition and greed. In her other pocket she carried King Samson's gun, because she was certainly not going to leave it lying around the place for anybody else to find.

She decided she ought to say a polite goodbye to Connie. But Connie wasn't at the table in the living room or in the kitchenette. Frankie peered into the bedroom and then the bathroom, but she was nowhere to be found. So her former friend hadn't even bothered to wish Frankie a swift *bon voyage*. Well, that was just one more bridge Connie Mooney had burned behind her.

The Extra

Frankie set the loaf on the table and cut the nibbled corners off two pieces of bread to make toast. One slice fit into each side of the toaster. While they cooked, she attempted to imagine being back home in Vancouver, with her father calling for his tea and Champ whistling along the lane, swinging a milk bottle in one hand. No matter how hard she tried not to, she pictured Doris leaning in the kitchen door of the blue house in Vancouver, wanting a gossip. When she tried to imagine the vegetable truck trundling up the lane, she envisioned Tom on the back steps of her father's house, gesturing widely with his piece of toast so that he knocked the red geranium off the porch rail onto the grass below.

She flipped the toast slices over to the uncooked sides. When she snapped the toaster closed again, the diamond chip on her engagement ring, back on her ring finger, caught the light from the window. She set the pot of gem-red jam onto the table.

Steps outside on the pathway sounded like Connie's, moving at speed. Frankie remained unaffected. She opened the toaster and spread jam across each piece, not neglecting the edges. There was still no butter in Villa 7B, but there would be lots at home in Vancouver. She took a big bite of toast and closed her eyes so that she wouldn't see Connie come in.

At a nasty-sounding slap on the table, Frankie opened them again. A folded newspaper lay on the table next to the plate of toast. Frankie glanced down at the front page. There, above the fold, her own face stared back at her. Frankie shook her head in disbelief. The newspapers ought to have heard the news of her innocence by now, because Eugene had promised to deliver her written 'confession' to the police before she disappeared forever. Was every promise ever made in Hollywood to be broken? She made a little noise of despair.

Behind her, she heard the tap of an impatient foot. Frankie scraped more jam onto her toast. She would not turn around.

Connie said, "You are so stupid."

Frankie would have let her know that calling people *stupid* had no effect on their actual intellectual capabilities, but she doubted this information would do Connie any good, so she held her tongue.

"Frankie, look at the headline." Connie snatched up the paper, turned it over and dropped it back onto the table. Frankie stared down at *The Los Angeles Morning Gazette*, Blanche Carver's paper. Before Frankie could curse the columnist's duplicity, Connie read the headline out loud, her delivery as clear and crisp as ever.

Witch Hunt for Innocent Woman
Called Off

Innocent woman. Frankie felt a buzzing in her bloodstream. As the feeling rose, she wanted to rise with it, to dance barefoot around the room. She would like to tear out of the house, calling for all of the Queen's kids to come and celebrate with tea and toast and gem-red jam.

"Still giving me the silent treatment, I see," Connie said. "You know what? You're a completely different person since you came to Hollywood. It doesn't suit you, either. I should have left you behind in Vancouver, where you belong."

Entirely composed, Frankie bit neatly into the toast. She read the second, smaller headline, centred under the first.

The Extra

Maniac Fan Confesses
Killer Eugene Ellery Remains at Large

And Eugene Ellery would remain so, since he no longer existed. Only Elaine remained. Frankie sent her a heartfelt thanks for keeping her word after all.

But how interesting that Blanche cleared Frankie's name in the larger headline. One would have thought that *Maniac Fan Confesses* would have been the editor's choice for the top line, as a far bigger incentive to sales than a simple clearing of Frankie's name.

Connie said, "Yep, Hollywood's changed you, all right. You used to be kind and friendly, and now look at you. The silent menace."

Connie pulled three oranges out of her pocket and dropped them into the blue bowl sitting on the table.

At last Frankie broke her silence. "You stole all the oranges from the tree out back."

"It's my tree," Connie retorted.

"No, it's our tree," Frankie reminded her.

"Not anymore. You're driving our car back to Vancouver."

"My car."

"Your dad's car."

"And you stole it! Like the oranges."

Connie leaned across Frankie and seized the second piece of toast. She took too big a bite for manners. Connie said cheerfully through a mouthful of toast, "Yes, Hollywood, city of dreams, has turned you into a movie villainess. Theda Bara could play you, if she acted a little nastier."

Maybe Frankie had changed, for she met this supremely unfair accusation with a private accounting: *I saved the Queen, I saved Billie, and I saved you, Connie Mooney.*

What was more, she longed to explain that she was certain that Blanche Carver had placed 'Witch Hunt for Innocent Woman Called Off' as the top line under the *Los Angeles Morning Gazette* because Frankie had saved Blanche, too. The headline was the columnist's apology to Frankie. She considered revoking her silence long enough to explain the concept of regret to Connie, who wouldn't know an apology if it trotted up and whinnied for attention, but decided against it as too esoteric.

Frankie bit into the last burnt corner of her toast. She was about to rise when Connie dropped a folded blanket onto the table. "If you're leaving tomorrow, you can move your bed out here tonight." Connie said. "Your breathing keeps me awake, and I don't suppose you know how to stop."

Frankie turned and looked Connie in the eye. "Do you remember when we were thirteen and you talked me into forging a letter to excuse us from a Math test and then bragged about it?"

"No."

"No? That's very interesting. We were both caught and subjected to the most unfortunate scenes imaginable at home and at school. What about the time you cut my father's front door mat into twenty pieces and sold them as bits of flying carpet, and I got switched for it?"

"No."

"Well, Connie, these are no longer important incidents when compared with the events of the last forty-eight hours, but they are certainly representative. I can think of a hundred betrayals and a thousand burned bridges and not one single, solitary apology from you."

"You ought to write a book about it. Say, you'd never believe who's living in sin next door in Eugene's old place,

7A." Connie raised her eyebrows. "Billie and Leo. I guess it's practically married life compared to what she's used to."

Frankie would have smiled, had she been a little crueller. "They *are* getting married," she told Connie. It seemed like a good exit line. Far better than farewell. She wanted a cup of tea, though, before she snapped her suitcase closed for the road. "Billie's trying out for a part in *The Emperor of New York*. I had a screen test set up for this morning for a small but good part, and I'm going to give the chance to her. Billie knows what to say to the director so that he'll give her the chance instead of me."

Billie was to tell the director that she was the pigeon girl.

The pang she couldn't help feeling at giving away her own audition would subside over time. She hoped. After all, Frankie couldn't have her cake and eat it too. She couldn't win the part of the sad little manicurist *and* go home to marry Champ. Still, it was nice to know that if she had taken up acting as a permanent career, she might have known some small success. She wondered whether her children would listen with interest to her tales of Hollywood life, even if they were romanticized and exaggerated: *And there were real oranges, hanging right there for the picking, outside my back door.* But children are never much interested in their parents' lives, only in their own adventures. Frankie wondered how she would feel in twenty years when a daughter of hers and Champ's climbed out of a bedroom window and went off without a word to find her fortune.

Out in front, a flurry of pigeons landed in the centre of the patio, where later on the Paradise Gardens kids would get together and put on some music. Maybe Tom would light a fire in the oil barrel and the air would fill with the aroma of sausages. She smiled when she remembered the lights shaped like parrots, and decided she would buy some bird lights to string on her Christmas tree when she was married.

With a start, she saw that while she was dreaming, Connie had filled the kettle and made tea.

Frankie looked from the blue cup in front of her, to the toaster, to the stack of money in front of her on the table. This stack had quietly appeared when she was thinking about the birds.

It looked a lot like forty American dollars. A bolt of anger flashed through her.

She picked up the money in both hands and held it to her breast. "You stole my money, Connie! It was you all along."

"That cash wasn't safe under the sofa cushion." Connie dropped her eyes and fiddled with the knob on the toaster. She burst out, "And you're so *stingy* with it. Our first day on the movies, and you wouldn't bring a thin dime with us! I took it because I thought we might want to celebrate. Or buy something for this place. Butter for the toast, at least. Well, your money's all there."

"Is it?" That was something, anyway.

"Of course. You think I'm Bonnie and Clyde?" Connie fished in her pocket and brought out a few bits of change. "Well, almost all the money is here. I bought a pair of stockings and a Coke when I was driving around with King Samson."

On the top bill — a fiver — Frankie saw something shiny, right under the motto *In God We Trust*. It looked like a drop of water, round and flat.

"You're crying," Connie said.

Frankie touched the second drop of water that had fallen beside the first on the five-dollar bill.

Frankie rarely cried. She had always believed that was because, no matter what happened, nothing could be worse than losing her mother. And compared with what she'd been through over the last few days, she had nothing at all to cry about today. But as she sat at the breakfast table, eating toast with her former best friend, Frankie's eyes pricked and swelled behind her fingers, and tears streamed down her cheeks, wetting her palms and running along her chin and down her neck.

She buried her face in her hands and felt the tears run through her fingers.

Connie, the uncertainty plain in her voice, said, "Everything's all right now, Frankie."

"No, it's not. It's not all right, and it never will be again."

Outside there was a bustle of wings. Frankie looked up through her tears and saw the flock of pigeons take off and fly away above the roofs of Paradise Gardens. The bougainvillea waved as they passed. It was time for Frankie to leave, too. She ought to pack her things into the Model A and leave right away.

Still, she sat and wept. "Oh, Connie, I've been so awful. I took Champ's ring off after I promised I wouldn't, and I was going to hock it."

"Well, it's really not much of a ring," Connie pointed out.

"I ran out on my father and didn't even say goodbye. When my mother did that, he took to drink and got defrocked. And I left your mother to deal with my dad."

"My mother's a big, grown-up girl," Connie said. "And you know how your dad always lets you get away with murder, stealing the car all the time and everything."

Frankie sobbed harder. "I let Marietta get away with murder. I found out she shot Gilbert Howard, and I didn't turn her in to the police."

Connie blinked. But she said, "The only reason Marietta would shoot Howie would be to defend herself. So, I think that letting Marietta get away with it was a sweet thing to do. Seeing that nothing could bring Howie back."

"*Sweet?*" Rubbing at her eyes, Frankie shook her head. "It wasn't sweet. She killed him in cold blood, and I let her go, because—"

"Because you didn't want to send somebody you knew to fry in the electric chair?" Connie asked.

"No. That's not why."

"Anyway, you oughtn't to help those darned police, the way they treated you. But what if they figure it out for themselves? Will you lie for Marietta?"

"No. Yes." Frankie stared up at Connie, who would never be able to understand the real reason she had let Marietta go. "The thing is, what if I turned Marietta Valdes in for murder and they executed her? Connie, if that happened, then all those people would have been right. I would have *killed a movie star.*"

"Gosh." Connie sat down next to Frankie. "That's a pretty good reason, I guess. But that's not why you let her go."

"Yes, it is."

"Nope. I know you, Frankie Ray." Connie leaned in closely. "One thing about you, Frankie, you're fair-minded. And you pay your debts."

"So?"

"So, Marietta saved your life in the fire. And you saved her life from the electric chair."

"Maybe." Frankie wept some more. "I guess I've burned my bridges all over Hollywood."

Connie emitted a long sigh. She moved her chair closer and hugged an arm around Frankie's shoulder.

"Well, Frankie, if there's one thing I've learned in life, you can burn all the bridges you want, and they always grow back."

"Oh, gosh, Connie. I'm sorry," Frankie sobbed. "I'm so sorry."

"It's okay, Frankie." Connie patted Frankie's shoulder. She moved Frankie's money out of the way of her tears and poured another cup of tea.

38

Half-hidden by the bougainvillea that grew beside the front gate of Paradise Gardens, there was set into the stucco wall a metal mailbox with a flap. It was nearly lunchtime, and the mail was collected at two o'clock sharp. Frankie lifted the mailbox flap and felt in her dress pocket for the letters Connie had urged her to write home. Careful not to pull out King Samson's gun — which she was still carrying so it couldn't do any more harm — she pulled the letters out and looked at them. She had written them that morning, Connie had licked the stamps, and Frankie had sealed and addressed them.

The first letter contained her letter of resignation to the Vancouver School Board.

The second letter, written to Champ, ended her future as a woman married to a man with a perfect soft mouth she loved to kiss. This envelope also included her engagement ring, wrapped in tissue paper.

The Extra

The third and last letter was addressed to her father. It was a valedictory to evenings in Sheridan D's company, laughing with her father over Jack Benny on the radio; a goodbye to fond good-nights and promises of tea in the morning; and an unwritten but implicit farewell to the vegetable man with his rattling truck bearing beets and carrots to every housewife on Thirty-Sixth Avenue.

She let the mailbox flap drop and put the letters back in her pocket next to King Samson's gun. She would not post them after all. What was Hollywood compared to family, true love — whether it was Champ or another fellow — and neighbours like Hazel to help Frankie raise her children? Instead of letters, she would send herself home in the model A and claim her future in Vancouver. She had the whole drive northward to figure out whether she would end her engagement to Champ. One thing this trip had taught her: there are possibilities everywhere, and a woman could choose among them as she liked. She did not have to sit around, hoping to be chosen.

She was glad to be friends with Connie again, but that did not mean Connie should dictate Frankie's future, no matter how hard she sold a life in Hollywood to Frankie.

Frankie felt decisive, now, and completely in control of her own future. She determined that for lunch, she would make exactly three cheese sandwiches: one for Connie, one for herself, and an extra one in case Tom dropped by. There was not much cheese in the packet she'd bought at the corner store, but it would be enough to share among friends. Later tonight, there would be sausages on the fire and dancing around the dry fountain. And tomorrow, or perhaps the day after, she would say her farewells and drive her father's Model A home to Vancouver.

Frankie turned her back on the mailbox. She was halfway to the Paradise Gardens gate when she heard her name called in full, first and last.

"Francesca Ray."

"That's me," she said. *It is I,* the past and future schoolteacher inside her whispered. The detective movie star she had become over the last few days laughed silently, rocking on his heels.

She turned to look. Right in the middle of Sunset Boulevard, King Samson braked his car and climbed out, letting the engine idle. The big car stood shining in the sunlight, its engine muttering to itself while cars honked and drove around it.

King Samson walked through the traffic as if he were walking on water. A sports model nearly ran him down. "Goddamn it all." Samson turned and raised his fist. "You don't own the road."

"I guess I own as much of the road as you do, buddy. Move your car," the driver retorted.

With a rude gesture, King Samson angled his wide body between the Model A parked at the gates and the runabout in front of it. He walked up to Frankie at the mailbox and said, "Marietta Valdes says that you've got something I want."

"Hello to you too, Mr Samson." Frankie tipped her head a little to one side. She'd pinned her short blonde hair into pincurls and tied it up in a scarf. Tom said it suited her, so maybe she'd keep the platinum as long as Champ didn't object. It would remind her of her triumph as the pigeon girl. Billie Starr had gone ahead and taken Frankie's place at the audition for the sad manicurist. Frankie didn't have a doubt in the world that Billie would get the part. "What could little old me have for you?"

King Samson peered at her. "You look familiar."

"I drove you from Oregon to Los Angeles," Frankie said. "You did warn me that you don't have a memory for faces."

"I sure do remember those two girls who drove me to Hollywood. A redhead to die for, and a schoolteacher type." Samson scowled. "You don't look like her."

Frankie touched her pincurled, platinum hair. "Nothing is as it seems in Hollywood."

"You said it, sister," Samson agreed. "Now, down to brass tacks. Where's Frank Achilles?"

"Retired from the business, I hear," Frankie said evenly.

Samson scowled. "Frank Achilles has got a responsibility to Monument Studios and *The Emperor of New York*."

"He might be hard to find." Impossible to find, actually, since Frank Achilles—embodied as he was by his clothing—remained curled up in the garbage bin by the back door of Villa 7B. All of him except his sunglasses. Frankie slipped her hand into the dress pocket that didn't have her three letters or the gun in it and rubbed her thumb across the lens.

"None of your impudence. Get me Frank Achilles." King Samson turned red around the ears. Frankie took a step back, but with the wall behind her and the big man in front of her, there was nowhere far to go.

She smelled the coconut pomade in his hair. She raised her right hand, hesitated, and then placed it flat against his lapel. "You'll never find him. Frank Achilles is gone forever."

"But I'm cooked without him," Samson said.

Frankie looked King Samson in the eye. Poor old King Samson. He had only his hard heart, money, and power to get him through each day. She, on the other hand, had some very good friends who could use her help. She patted Samson's lapel and bowed to the inevitable.

"Well, maybe I can track him down, so long as we can work something out. I've got a few things to trade." She would have to be careful not to let Marietta's secret out. Very careful indeed.

She reached into her right-hand skirt pocket. With a glance around to see that nobody was close enough to see her, she pulled out King Samson's gun. It felt by now as familiar in her hand as her teacher's blue correction pencil used to feel. She looked down at it. He looked down at it, too. She said, "This gun …"

"Yes?" He stepped toward her.

"It's yours?" She peered up at him. "Is it the one your wife gave you?"

"Of course it is," he said. "Look at the crown engraved on the grip. It's one of a kind. It's mine. Give it to me."

Frankie nodded. "I will. With great pleasure, believe me. But first, I'm afraid you're going to have to make a choice, Mr Samson."

Samson growled, "Exactly who do you think you are, anyway?"

"I'm nobody," Frankie said quickly. "Just a Vancouver girl, and you're a self-made man. I've not accomplished very much in my life so far. But even so, I'm afraid that you really need to decide something: Do you want to know about this gun, or don't you? Do you want to know where it's gone, and what it's done?"

King Samson stared from her to the gun. Frankie watched as his face transformed from anger to frustration to understanding. Gilbert Howard himself, with all his acting genius, couldn't have made his feelings clearer.

"No," King Samson said. And again, more heavily. "No."

Frankie nodded. "That's how I feel, too. Because it's already done enough damage. Here. Take it."

King Samson took the gun from her. "What do you want?"

"I want you to put it on your mantelpiece, locked up behind glass or something."

Samson gave a sharp nod and slipped the gun into his pocket. Frankie said, "About time. Now, down to work."

"What does that mean?" King Samson raised a thick, well-groomed eyebrow. "Blackmail?"

Frankie almost laughed aloud, because she actually had considered blackmail. Considered and rejected it. There was enough dirty work going on around Hollywood without her adding her two cents' worth.

"Mr Samson, you told me that you are looking for Frank Achilles. I know for a fact that Frank didn't sign a contract with you," Frankie said. "Why do you want him, anyway?"

"*I* don't want him. He's unreliable." Samson said. "But Marietta wants Frank Achilles. She showed me the footage that she took of the fire, and it's better than anything else we got last night. Damn her. So I'm going to let her direct a scene. *One.* One scene only. And she insists on using Frank Achilles."

Frankie rolled her eyes. Trust Marietta Valdes to get it all wrong. Frankie had wanted help for the Paradise Gardens extras, not a part for her own discarded alter ego. With a sigh, Frankie began pulling the pin curls out of her platinum hair. She slipped the bobby pins into her pocket as she spoke. "I guess you'll be going back to your wife now, Mr Samson?"

"Sure, I'd go back to my wife," he said, baring his teeth. "*If* she hadn't moved in with her golf pro six months back. Listen! Give me Frank Achilles's agent's number. I don't need to waste any more time with you."

"No, I guess not." She combed her fingers through her short hair. It was time to lay her cards on the table. "But you do need me to keep another secret for you if you want Frank Achilles. And this one I do want to negotiate."

"You?" King Samson stared. "Exactly what has Frank Achilles got to do with you?"

Frankie pulled the sunglasses out of her pocket and put them on. "That's what," she said. "Let's talk."

"*You're* Frank Achilles?" King Samson stared, then dragged the palms of his hands across his face. "I hate this business."

Out on the street, the cars complained, passing Samson's abandoned sedan.

"It must be very difficult to be you," Frankie agreed. "Come on. Park your car properly, and let me make you a cheese sandwich."

Frankie held the door open for King Samson. He hurried past her, late for his early afternoon casting meeting at Monument Studios before a three o'clock shoot. In one hand he carried a second cheese sandwich Frankie had cut for him, and in the other the list of demands that Frankie insisted upon. It was a short list, but it had punch.

She shut the door behind him, rinsed King Samson's plate, and set it on the drain board.

She had negotiated well in a tight spot. Now she made a particular effort not to think of any further demands, because that would be taking advantage. And she would keep her part of the bargain right now, before the long drive home. She was perfectly happy to do so. She could hardly wait for this afternoon's shoot.

Frankie smoothed down her platinum hair with Eugene's Burma-Shave and wished her former next-door neighbour well, wherever she was. She stepped into Frank Achilles's pants one leg at a time. Leaving the Xeno-Flex in the bin with three letters, she buttoned up her men's jacket and set her sunglasses on her nose.

She strolled out into the patio area by the fountain and called all the extras at Paradise Gardens to gather round to hear what she'd negotiated for them. They massed around her and listened with noisy pleasure for the good news she had to tell them.

A cheer rose into the hot Hollywood sky.

Frankie was not at all sorry that there would be one last gasp for Frank Achilles before he disappeared forever out of Hollywood. King Samson was not the only one who ought to pay for unwittingly providing Marietta with the gun that had killed Gilbert Howard. Frankie, too, felt the need to atone, and that was why she had agreed to be Frank Achilles one more time for the camera. She would play Marietta's sweetheart at the beginning of the movie, not to be seen again until the end. Two scenes for Frank Achilles. It was the least she could do to help out poor old King Samson.

"Follow me, kids," Frankie said.

She led the way among the bungalows toward Sunset Boulevard. As she passed the orange tree in front of Villa 9A, Frankie plucked an orange from its twig as if it were opportunity itself, juicy with promise under the thick skin necessary for happy survival here in Hollywoodland.

She pressed the orange against her lips—a kiss for good luck—and then tossed it up into the air. Connie caught it. She chucked the orange to Tom, who threw it over his shoulder to somebody farther back in the crowd. Frankie didn't look back to see who caught it—somebody caught it, she was sure, and somebody threw it again, even though over the noise of the kids chattering and laughing she couldn't hear the slap of palms against the fruit. This wasn't a moment for looking back. This was a day for marching onward. This was a day she'd never forget, no matter how long she lived her life in Vancouver.

Tromp, tromp, tromp went the footsteps of the little army of extras, with the quick counter-beat of Tom's steps as he scurried to catch up to Frankie and Connie at the front of the troop. He hooked one arm through Connie's, his other through Frankie's, and for no reason but high spirits, the three of them laughed fit to bust.

But they didn't stop. They'd never stop.

The script was in her man's jacket pocket, and Frankie rehearsed Frank Achilles's first lines in *The Emperor of New York* in her head. *Don't leave, my darling. Never let me down.*

Never let true friends down. Right off the bat, she had made Samson agree that the Paradise Gardens extras would have lots more work. And she hadn't forgotten the Forgotten Man — she'd sent word to the doorman at Camillo's to meet the crowd of them there so that he'd have a little part, too.

Frankie's second demand was screen credit for everybody. Gosh, how King Samson hated that one.

Her third and penultimate demand of King Samson regarded Billie Starr. *Make sure that your daughter-in-law is welcomed into the family. Talk to Blanche and make her listen, too.* Billie would have Frankie's part as the sad little manicurist. And Leo would have Billie.

So far, success.

But it wasn't success that mattered most. Most important were these uncertain moments before you succeeded — when you still could lose, but you wouldn't. Frankie's final demand was that Marietta Valdes direct the first and last scenes of *The Emperor of New York*. And she would bet her nearly forty dollars that Marietta would end up directing more scenes than two by the time filming was done. The world would have its first famous and respected woman director, and more of them would follow. That was Marietta's atonement: to help other women direct motion pictures. Unbidden, the thought occurred to her that if only Frankie stayed in Hollywood, then maybe, just maybe, one of those woman directors would someday be Francesca Ray herself.

Frankie laughed out loud in her Frank Achilles voice. She hadn't wanted to be Frank anymore, but she adored taking big manly strides and laughing from her diaphragm. Good old Frank Achilles. He was not long for this world, but while he still existed, she decided to enjoy the fact that her alter ego was a very popular man.

The day expanded like a hero's chest and shone like a heroine's smile. It was as warm as the final kiss, the fade out, and *The End*. Let the credits roll with a roar of timpani or trumpet! For up there on the screen, an actress would read her own name among those unfurling white on black or black on white. When she saw her name she would know — posterity would know — that she was *here*. In Hollywood. And Frankie's name, with all the others, would live forever on that bit of clattering celluloid. One film before she went home. This one film.

Tom gave a hopping skip that knocked both of them sideways. They might have fallen, but Connie, laughing, held them upright. Frankie put her hands in her jacket pocket and found three envelopes tucked in there. Connie must have put them there. Frankie pulled them out and stared at the three letters she thought she'd left in the garbage bin back at Villa 7B. Three letters saying that she was not coming home. That she was staying in Hollywood. Three letters she had decided not to post.

Or had she? At what point was a decision made? Did thought or deed constitute resolution?

It was a few minutes yet to two o'clock, when the mailman would empty the box. Frankie turned and ran back against the tide of excited extras to the mail slot in the wall outside Paradise Gardens.

She rested the envelopes in the iron mouth of the postal slot and noted how white they looked against the black iron, and how blue the ink appeared against the white.

She dropped Champ's envelope into the mailbox. It made a whispering sound as it fell. And as of that moment, she was no longer an engaged woman.

The draught from the passing cars rippled her suit jacket and the cuffs of her trousers. She removed the second letter and let it fall in with the first. The Vancouver School Board would hardly shed a tear at losing her.

She held onto the third letter a little longer than the first two. It was addressed to her father, and contained an invitation to visit her and see Hollywood with his own Vancouverite eyes. She would never tell him how cross she'd always been with him that her mother had run away. And her father would never recount how tough it was to be left alone with a toddler, trying to keep his little girl on the straight and narrow. But she knew he missed her like she missed him.

The third envelope followed the first two down the rabbit hole. She felt a sudden chill and wished that she had not been so swift to post them. She might be able to get them back. She could squeeze her hand partway into the slot and catch the corner of at least one of them between her fingers and pull it back out.

She shoved her hands deeply into her pockets. It was illegal to interfere with the mail once posted. She now saw that this was a very good law.

Frankie hesitated, gazing along Sunset Boulevard at the Paradise Gardens extras walking ahead of her. She was their leader, and it would not do to let them get too far ahead of her. Still, this moment of import deserved some kind of recognition.

She raised two fingers to touch her forehead below her platinum hairline. Frankie snapped a Girl Guide salute at the mailbox, and ran off to join the rest of the extras marching toward Monument Studios.

Acknowledgements

Thanks to all at Pulp Literature Press for the meticulous work and genius ideas that produced this edition of *The Extra.*

To JM Landels, Amanda Bidnall, Mark Halden, Roger Anastasiou, Robin McGillveray, Sandra Vander Schaaf, Kate Landels, Daniel Cowper, Karen Cowper, Susan Pieters, Mary Rykov, and JTF King, thanks a million for your keen eyes, wonderful judgement, and support.

My thanks to Maureen Docharty for her friendship, for her encouragement, and for Frankie's house on Thirty-Sixth Avenue.

And my gratitude to Velma Docharty, who gave me, along with so much else, the spirit and Vancouver stories from Frankie's remarkable age.

About the Author

Mel Anastasiou writes mysteries starring sleuths who are often fish out of water and gifted amateur 'tecs. She is a founding editor with Pulp Literature Press, and she authors their in-house thirty-day writing guides.

Mel can be found every day writing, editing, walking for miles to look at inspired Victorian architecture, and eating scones with clotted cream and jam—hence the walking.

Look for Mel's **Fairmount Manor Mysteries** starring Mrs Stella Ryman, and the **Hertfordshire Pub Mysteries** featuring Spencer Stevens and the Seven Swans Public House. As well, she is working on the further adventures of Frankie Ray and Connie Mooney in the next **Monument Studios Mystery**.

You can follow Mel on her Amazon author page, on Twitter @MelAnastasiou, and at melanastasiou.wordpress.com.

Also by Mel Anastasiou from Pulp Literature Press

Fiction
Stella Ryman and the Fairmount Manor Mysteries
The Labours of Mrs Stella Ryman
Stella Ryman and the Search for Thelma Hu

Artwork and Writing Guides
Colouring Paradise
The Writer's Boon Companion: Thirty Days Towards an
Extraordinary Volume
The Writer's Friend and Confidante: Thirty Days of Narrative
Achievement